MARVEL

MARVEL CINEMATIC UNIVERSE
STORYBOOK COLLECTION

LITTLE, BROWN AND COMPANY
BOOKS FOR YOUNG READERS

MARVEL
marvelkids.com

Little, Brown and Company

Hachette Book Group
1290 Avenue of the Americas, New York, NY 10104
Visit us at lb-kids.com

Little, Brown and Company is a division of Hachette Book Group, Inc.
The Little, Brown name and logo are trademarks of Hachette Book Group, Inc.

First Edition: April 2016

Thor: The Dark World: Warriors of the Realms originally published in October 2013 by Marvel Press, an imprint of Disney Book Group
Captain America: The Winter Soldier: Rescue at Sea originally published in March 2014 by Marvel Press, an imprint of Disney Book Group
Avengers: Age of Ultron: Avengers Save the Day originally published in April 2015 by Little, Brown and Company
Avengers: Age of Ultron: Battle at Avengers Tower originally published in April 2015 by Little, Brown and Company
Ant-Man: The Amazing Adventures of Ant-Man originally published in June 2015 by Little, Brown and Company
Ant-Man: The Incredible Shrinking Suit originally published in June 2015 by Little, Brown and Company
Guardians of the Galaxy: Rocket and Groot Fight Back originally published in July 2014 by Little, Brown and Company
Guardians of the Galaxy: Battle of Knowhere originally published in July 2014 by Little, Brown and Company

ISBN 978-0-316-27146-2

10 9 8 7 6 5 4 3 2 1

CW

Printed in the United States of America

TABLE OF CONTENTS

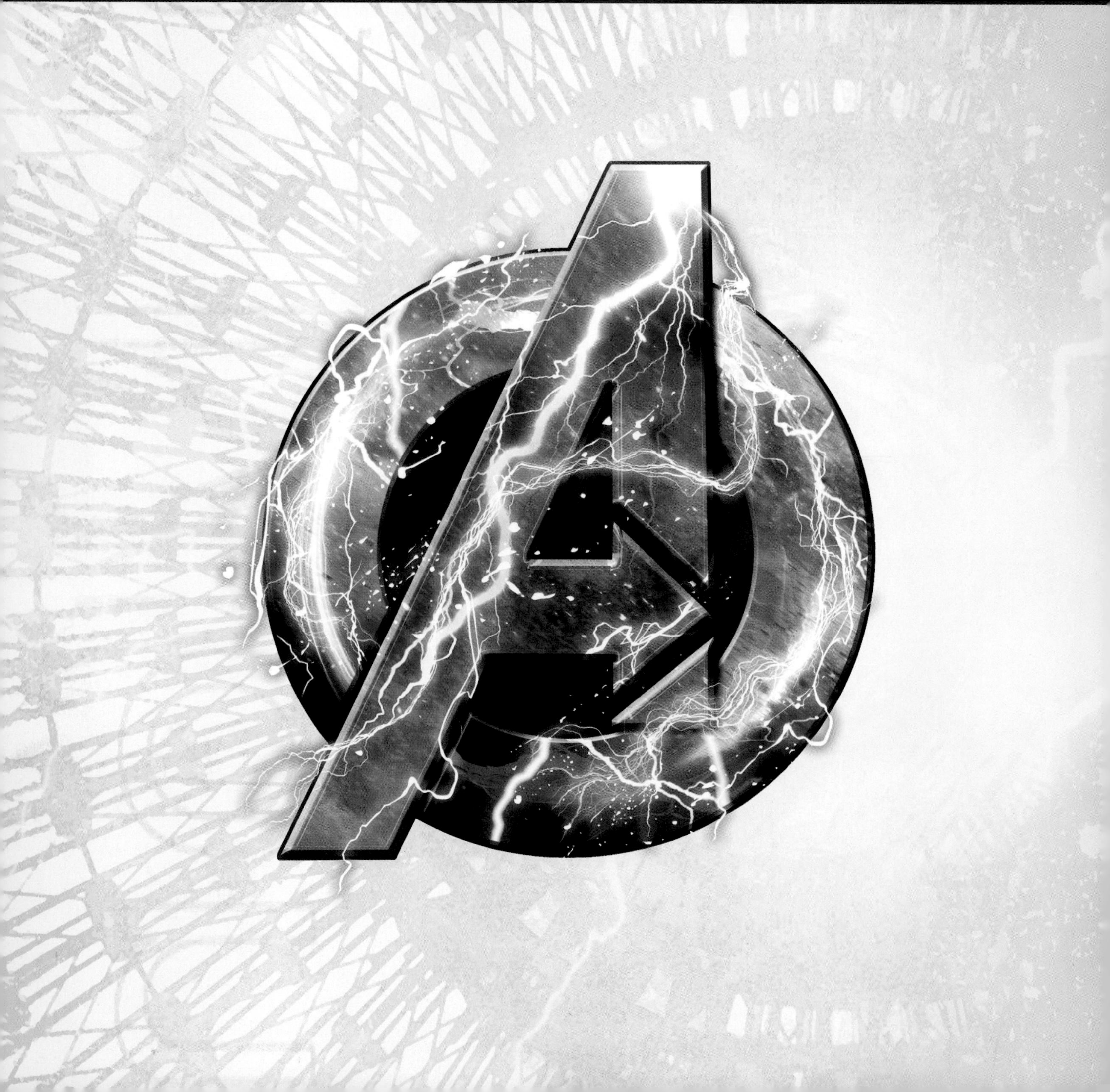

MARVEL

THOR™
THE DARK WORLD

WARRIORS OF THE REALMS

By **TOMAS PALACIOS** & **ADAM DAVIS**

Based on the Screenplay by **CHRISTOPHER L. YOST**
and **CHRISTOPHER MARKUS** & **STEPHEN McFEELY**

Story by **DON PAYNE** and **ROBERT RODAT**

Produced by **KEVIN FEIGE**, p.g.a.

Directed by **ALAN TAYLOR**

Illustrated by **RON LIM**, **CAM SMITH**, and **LEE DUHIG**

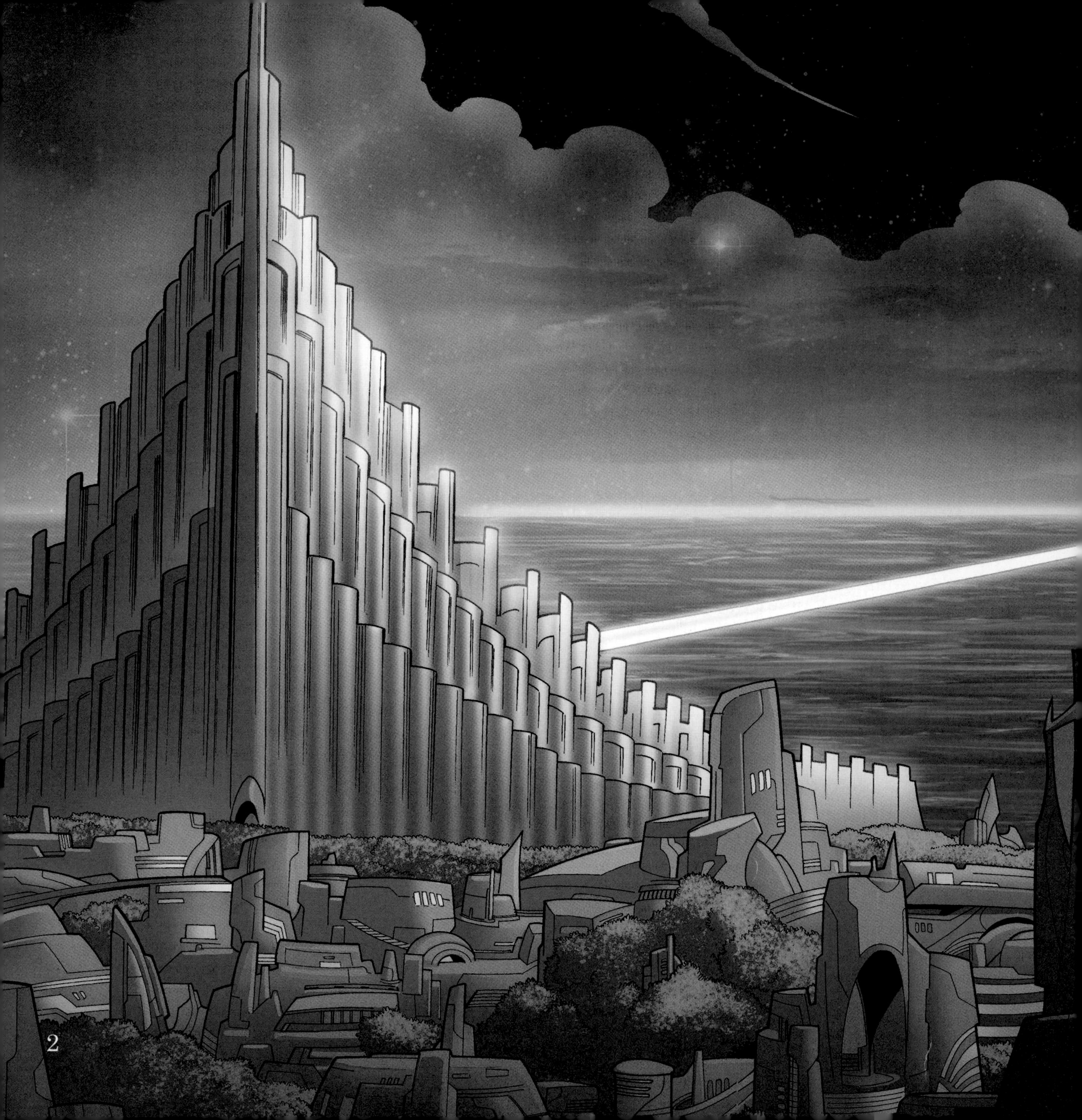

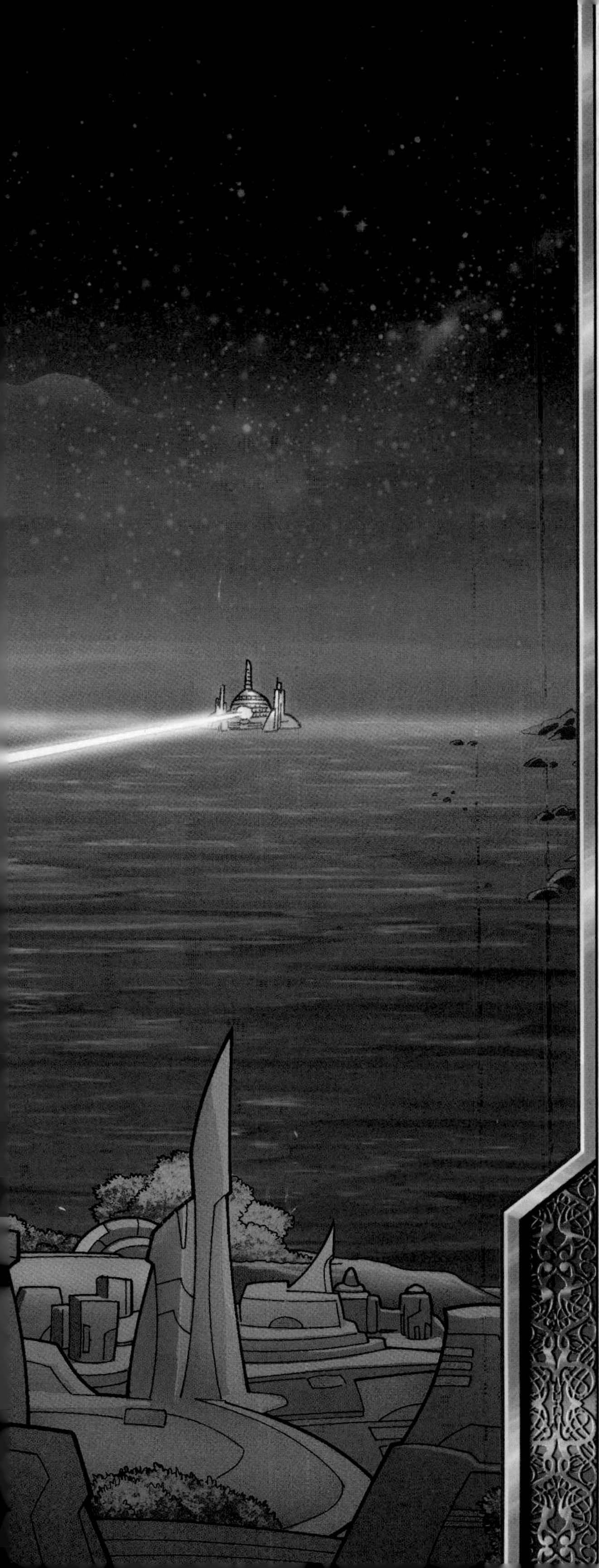

SOMEWHERE ACROSS THE UNIVERSE, there existed a realm known as Asgard. It was the land of a strong people, the Asgardians. Perched at the edge of the realm was a beautifully adorned structure, its golden dome housing the Bifrost. It was home to one of Asgard's most important and interesting individuals: the all-knowing, all-seeing Heimdall. The sentry had been here, at his post, unmoved, for quite some time. In fact, for thousands of years Heimdall had watched over his home world and guarded it from any incoming threat.

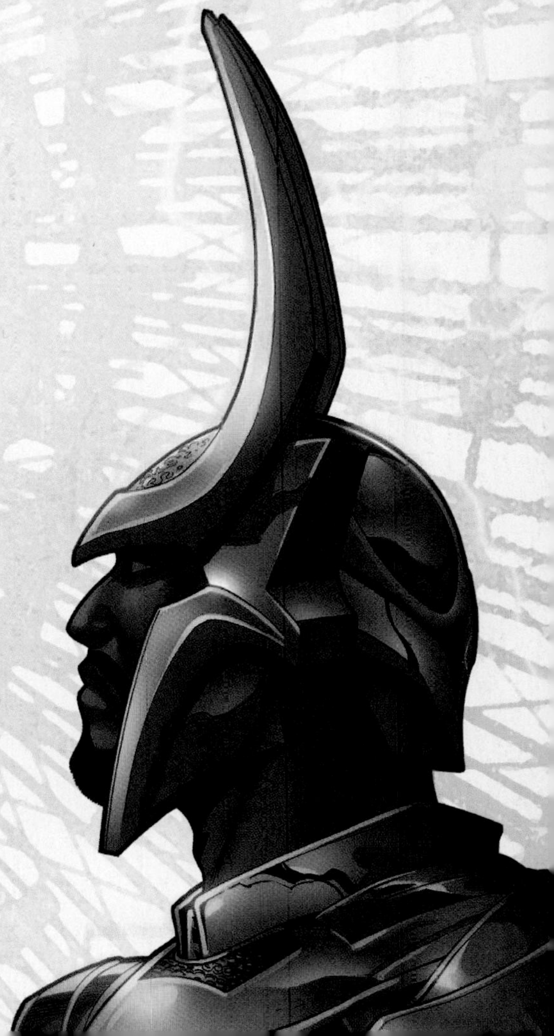

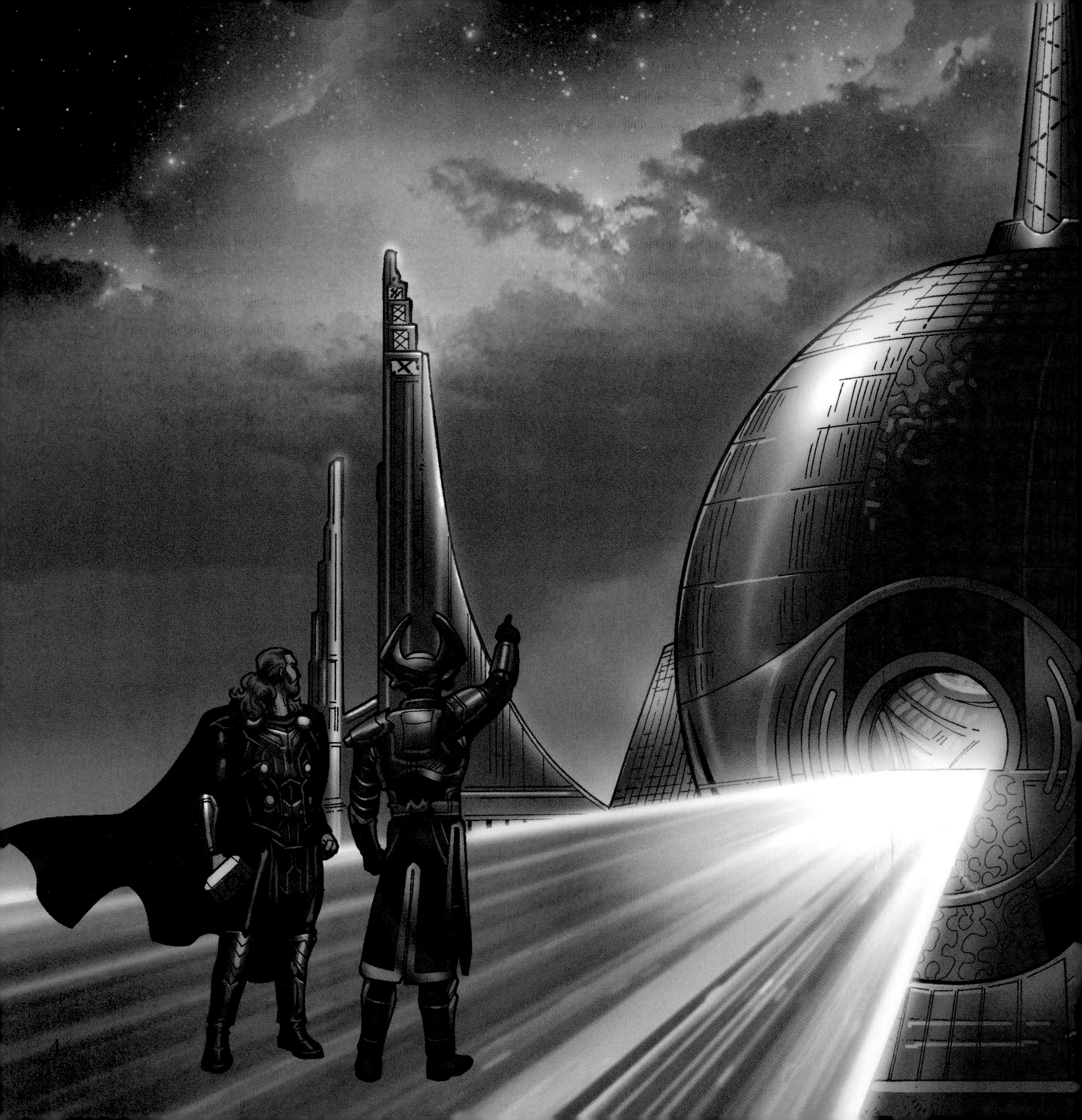

LOOKING OUT ACROSS THE UNIVERSE,

Heimdall fixed his eyes on the unending line of stars above. From here, the all-knowing sentry could see all Nine Realms and ten trillion souls— such a heavy burden for one to carry.

Heimdall thought about his last conversation with Thor, how they discussed the wonderment of the Convergence, a phenomenon that occurs once every five thousand years!

The alignment of worlds . . . it approaches, thought Heimdall.

He knew that with the Convergence approaching, Asgard and the surrounding realms would need to prepare for a great battle. For with the Convergence would come the Dark Elves, a dangerous race of creatures bent on plunging the universe into complete darkness.

LET US NOW VISIT THE HEROES AND VILLAINS OF THESE REALMS. . . .

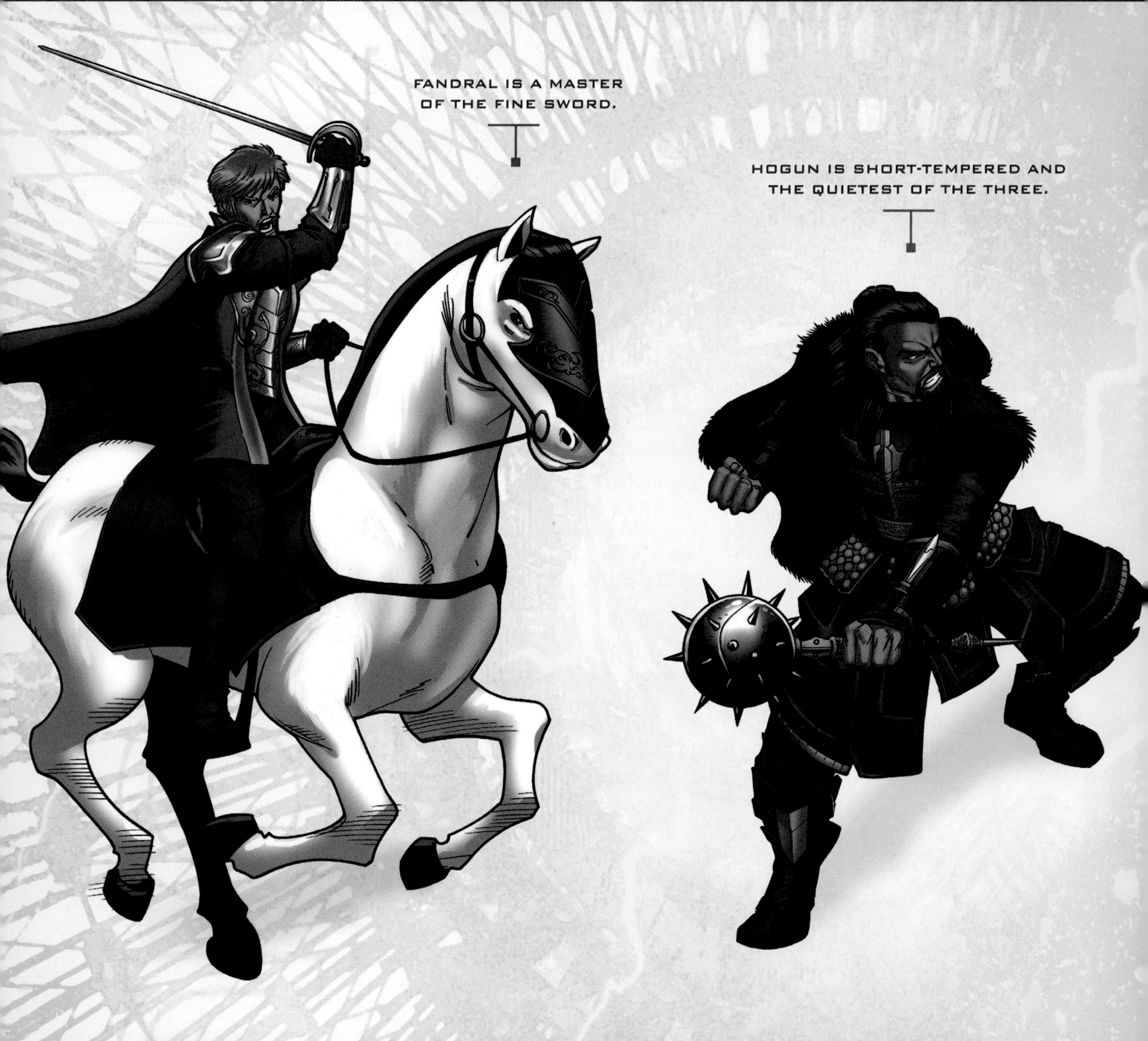
FANDRAL IS A MASTER OF THE FINE SWORD.
HOGUN IS SHORT-TEMPERED AND THE QUIETEST OF THE THREE.

WARRIORS OF THE REALMS

THE WARRIORS THREE. The name rings true. **FANDRAL** the Dashing, **HOGUN** the Grim, and **VOLSTAGG** the Voluminous form a mighty band of Asgardian warriors, each skilled in combat and with their own specific weapon. When the Nine Realms call for protection against enemies, the Warriors Three answer. Fandral, as skilled with his blade as he is with his charm, thinks very highly of himself, as do the single ladies of Asgard. Hogun, the stoic master of the mace and of throwing knives, is a quick and precise fighter who pulls no punches. And Volstagg, though equipped with the power of his mighty ax and hefty brawn, has also been known to use his massive belly as a weapon against enemies.

VOLSTAGG IS ALSO A MASTER OF THE QUARTERSTAFF, AS WELL AS A MASTER OF FOOD AND DRINK.

ODIN ALLFATHER

ODIN'S WEAPON OF CHOICE IS THE MIGHTY SPEAR, GUNGNIR. IT POSSESSES THE POWER OF THE ODIN FORCE.

Odin Allfather has reigned over the Nine Realms for centuries. He has fought his way through the harshest of battles and looked into the eyes of evil, but has always emerged victorious. Yet time and war have taken their toll on the ancient Asgardian. With dark days ahead for the Nine Realms, Odin questions his reign and whether he can withstand the coming Convergence and the threats it could bring to his people.

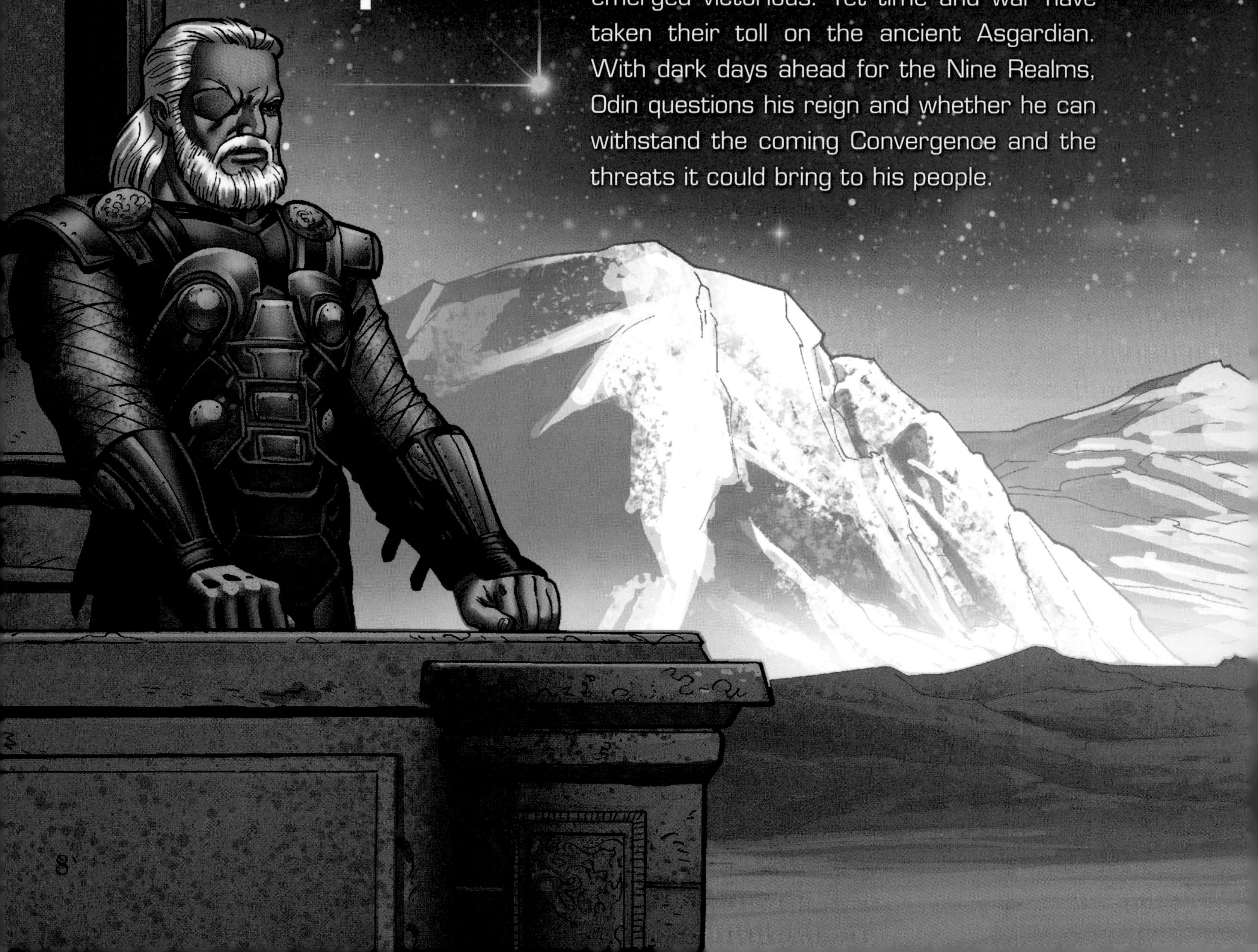

LADY SIF

THE FIERCEST OF ASGARD'S FEMALE FIGHTERS, Lady Sif has proven herself time and time again to the Warriors Three, Thor, and the people of Asgard. With her incredible agility and her skill in the double swords, Sif is someone whom the mighty Thor is proud to fight alongside. Since Jane Foster's recent absence, Sif has tried to fill the void in Thor's heart. But Thor's heart is already taken. . . .

LADY SIF IS A MASTER SWORDSMAN. SOME SAY SHE IS THE BEST IN ALL OF ASGARD.

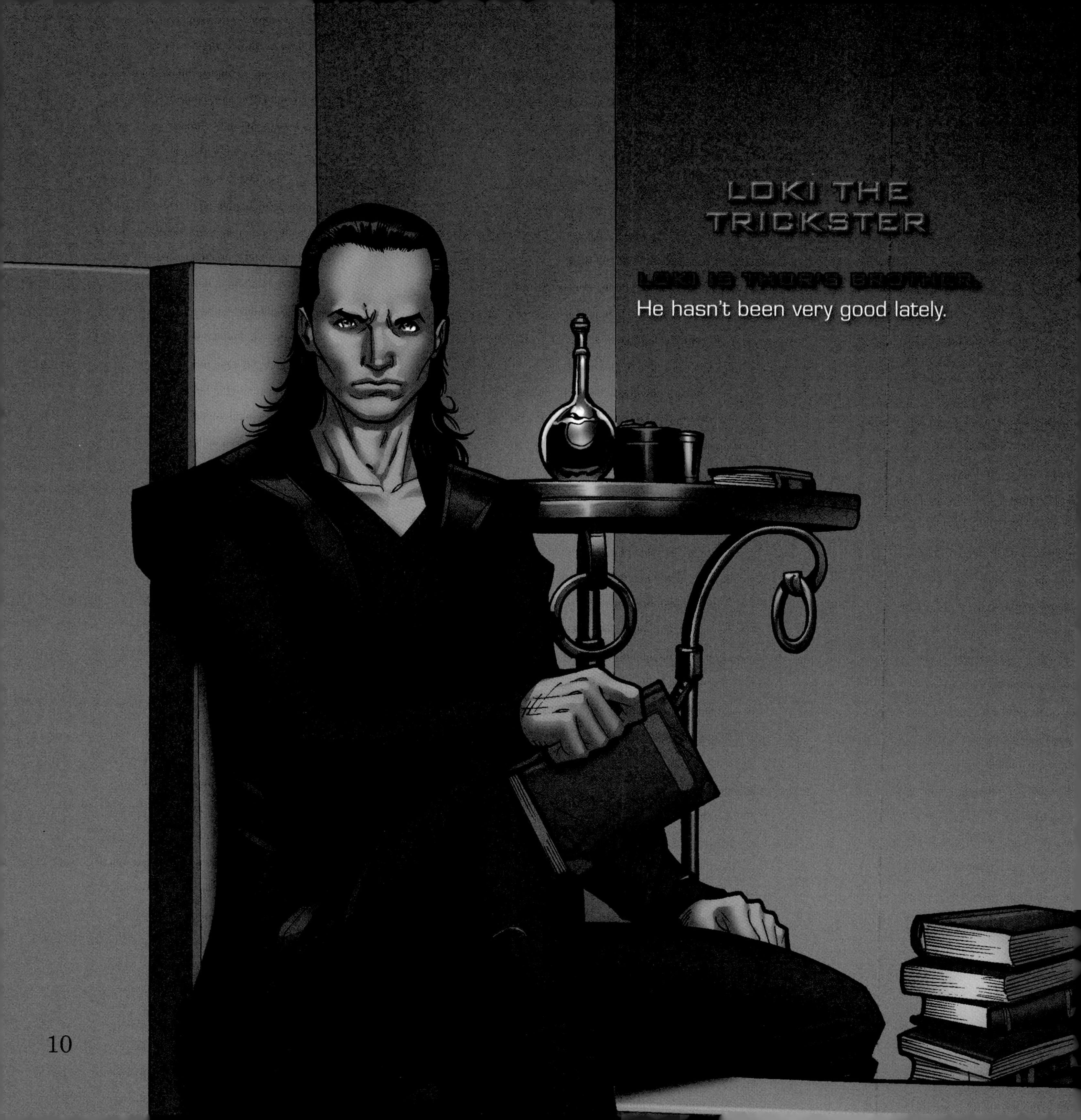

LOKI THE TRICKSTER

LOKI IS THOR'S BROTHER.
He hasn't been very good lately.

FRIGGA

FRIGGA, the mother of Thor and Loki, loves both her sons equally (even though one tried to take over Earth, and the other was banished to the same planet for starting a war with the Frost Giants). But that doesn't mean she taught them the same skills. Frigga is equally versed in the art of magic as she is with a blade. To Loki, she taught her knowledge of illusions, and to Thor, she taught how to be strong in battle, both physically and mentally. With her deep capacity to defend and love, Frigga is truly the perfect wife for Odin.

FRIGGA HAS BEEN THE WIFE OF ODIN FOR THOUSANDS OF YEARS.

HER LOOKS ARE DECEIVING. FRIGGA IS A SKILLED WARRIOR AND MASTER SWORDSMAN.

THE GOD OF THUNDER

THE MIGHTY THOR! Warrior of Asgard. Son to Odin. Friend of the Warriors Three and Lady Sif. Thor has proven to his people, and to himself, that he is ready to take on any challenge, including the throne of Asgard. After the events of New York City involving the Avengers, Thor and his band of warriors traveled the cosmos to restore order and peace. From realm to realm, Thor banished evil and reminded the universe that harmony was needed. From fighting Marauders to battling Chitauri, Thor backed down from no challenge.

THOR'S BATTLE ARMOR IS MADE FROM THE STRONGEST METAL IN THE COSMOS.

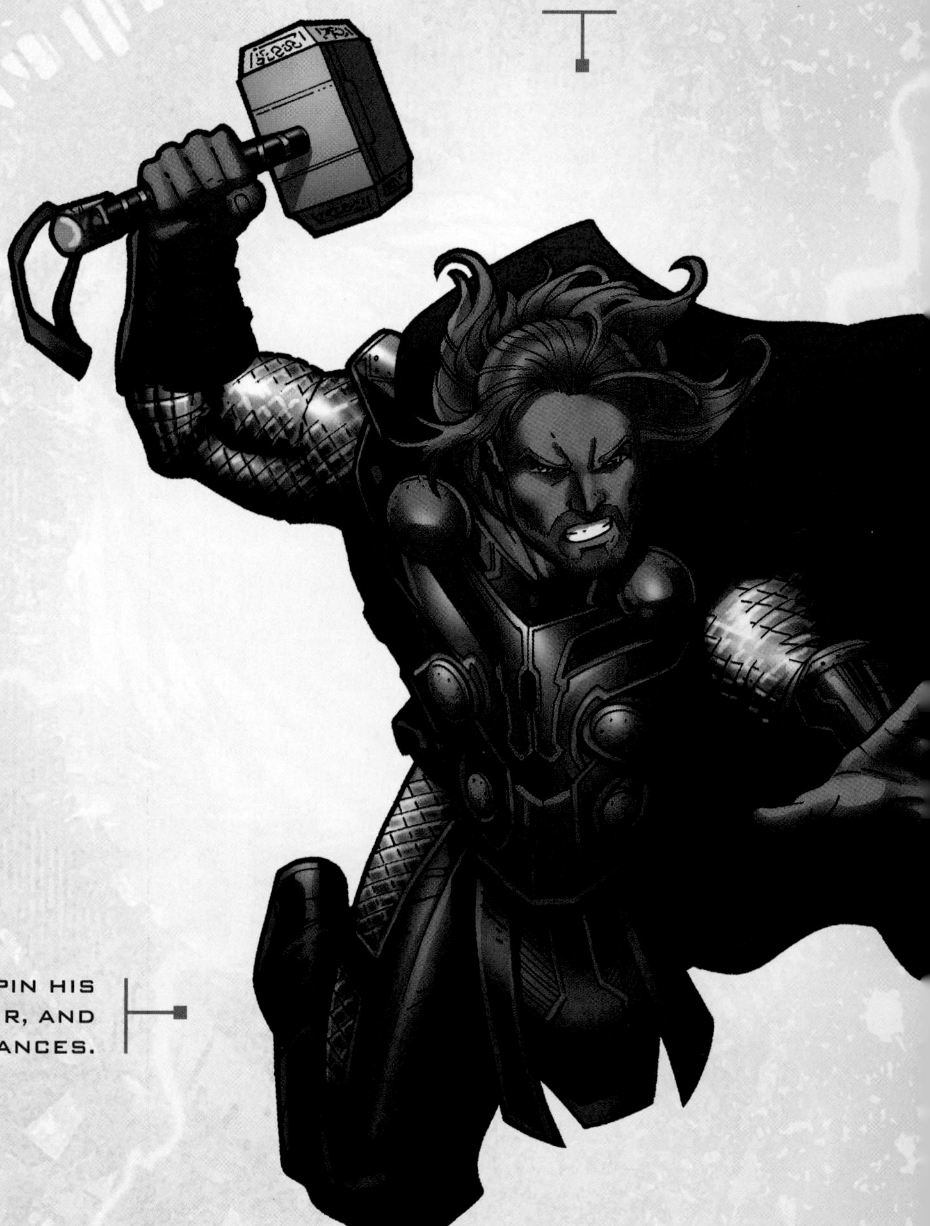

THOR CAN SPIN HIS HAMMER, MJOLNIR, AND FLY GREAT DISTANCES.

MJOLNIR

If Thor is Asgard's mightiest warrior, **MJOLNIR** is Asgard's greatest weapon. Forged in a dying star, Mjolnir is Thor's mighty hammer, made from uru metal. It lets Thor summon rain, lightning, and thunder, and when spun at a rapid rate, Mjolnir helps Thor take flight! If Thor is separated from Mjolnir, it will travel any distance, even across worlds, to return to him. Unable to be lifted by any mortal or Super Hero from any realm, Mjolnir was created for Thor, and Thor alone.

MJOLNIR CANNOT BE
BROKEN, CRACKED,
OR DESTROYED.

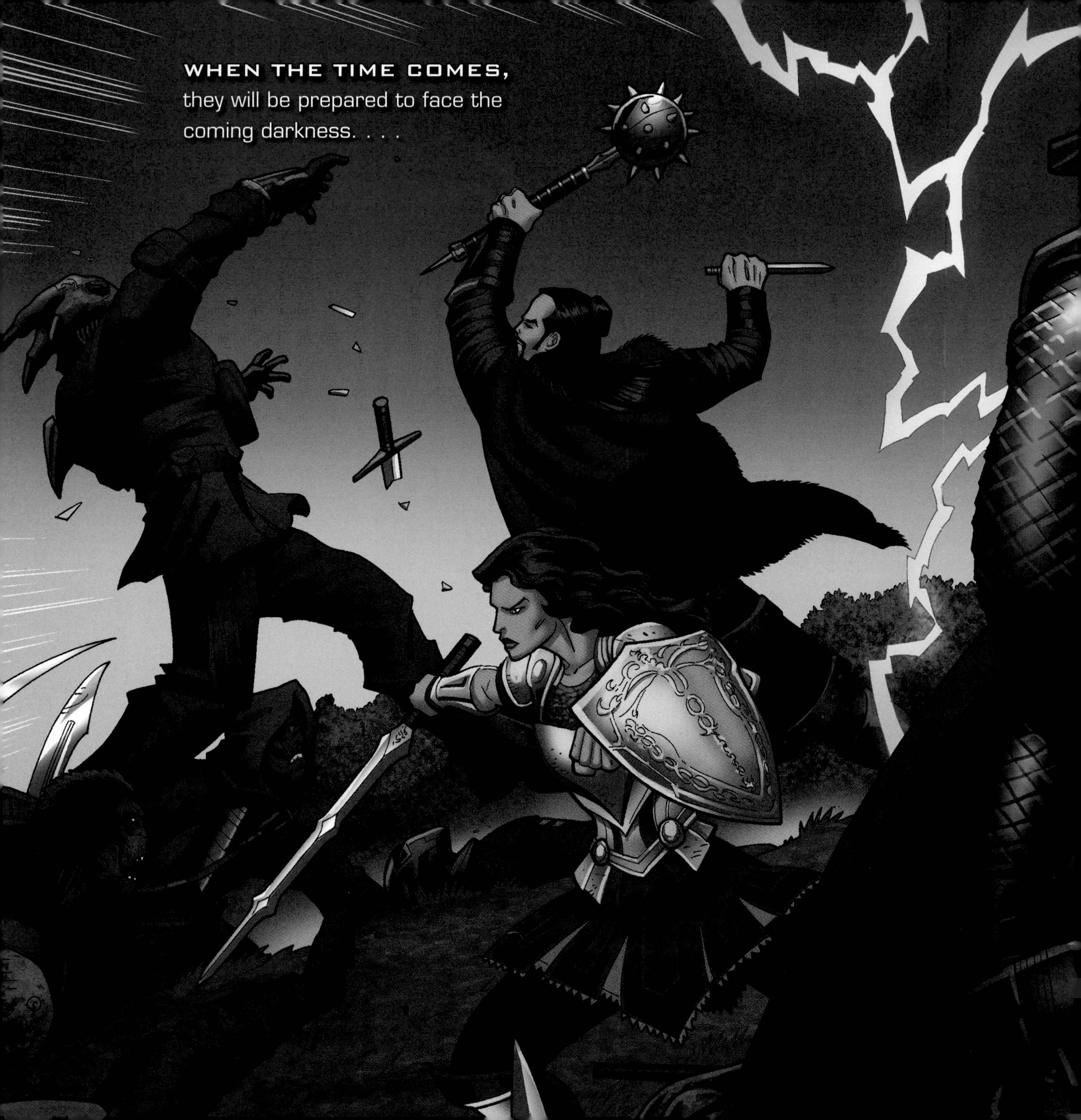
WHEN THE TIME COMES,
they will be prepared to face the coming darkness. . . .

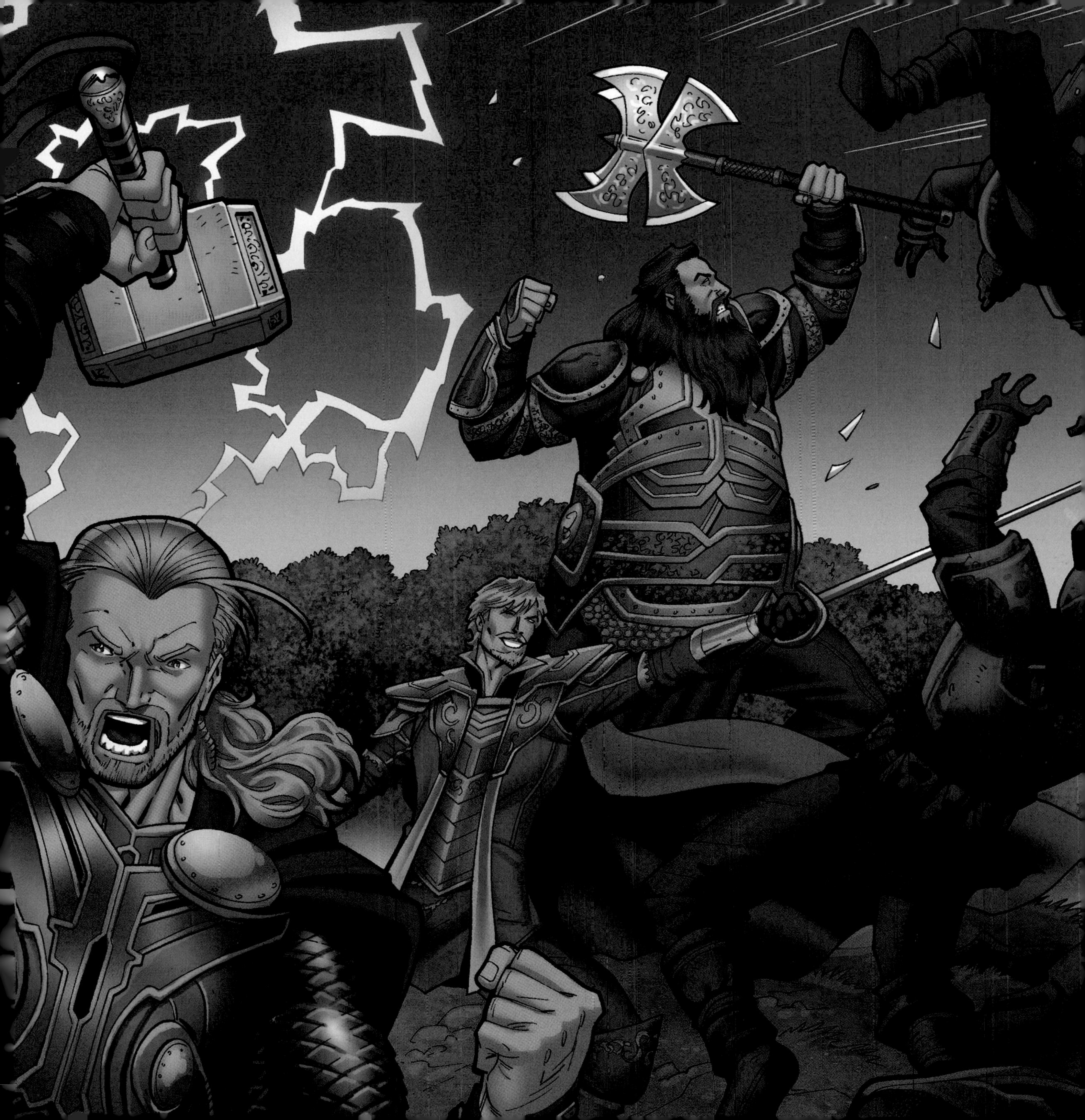

THE MARAUDERS

Vicious and armed to the teeth, the **MARAUDERS** are a band of looters that travel from world to world in search of everything and anything that planet holds dear. When word spread that the Bifrost was down, and that the Asgardians would have no way to protect the citizens of the Nine Realms, the Marauders took it upon themselves to cause chaos.

Their choice of weapons usually consists of swords and rocket launchers. A strange mix, but when you're a space pirate, you use what you can get your hands on. But the Marauders have more than a few weapons up their sleeves. . . .

MARAUDERS TRAVEL IN GROUPS OF NO LESS THAN A DOZEN AT A TIME.

THE DARK ELVES

THE DARK ELVES of Svartalfheim. A race long forgotten by many. But no more. Recently having been rallied by their great and powerful leader, Malekith, the Dark Elves have come together for one reason: revenge for the devastation of their home planet. Unable to breathe the air on their homeworld without their shiny, pearl-colored masks, the Dark Elves are fearless and will do anything in the name of their race and king. Armed with the mysterious dark technology, they use their ferocious guns to form black holes against their enemies, sucking them into the abyss, never to be seen again.

THE DARK ELVES SHOW NO EMOTION IN THEIR BATTLE MASKS.

MALEKITH AND ALGRIM

Before the universe, there was darkness, and in that darkness the Dark Elves thrived. The leader and king of the Dark Elves of Svartalfheim, **MALEKITH** ruled unchallenged, his dark reign touching every inch of the cosmos. But then came the birth of light and with that the end of Malekith's grip on the universe. Since then, he has been waiting . . . waiting for the right moment to come back to existence and seek revenge for his people, and his family. That moment . . . is now.

Malekith's second in command, **ALGRIM** has been in the fight since the beginning. Always willing to go above and beyond for his king, Algrim is crucial to spreading darkness back over the universe. He helps build the Dark Elf army for his king and will be at the forefront of the charge against any opponent.

ALGRIM

MALEKITH

THE ARK

A monstrous ship that once floated quietly in space has come back to life, glowing with a dark energy. This is the ARK. Malekith and his army of Dark Elves have dwelled inside the Ark for many, many years, but now that time of dwelling is over. The Ark is not only the mother ship of this dark race, but also a powerful weapon for invading planets and realms.

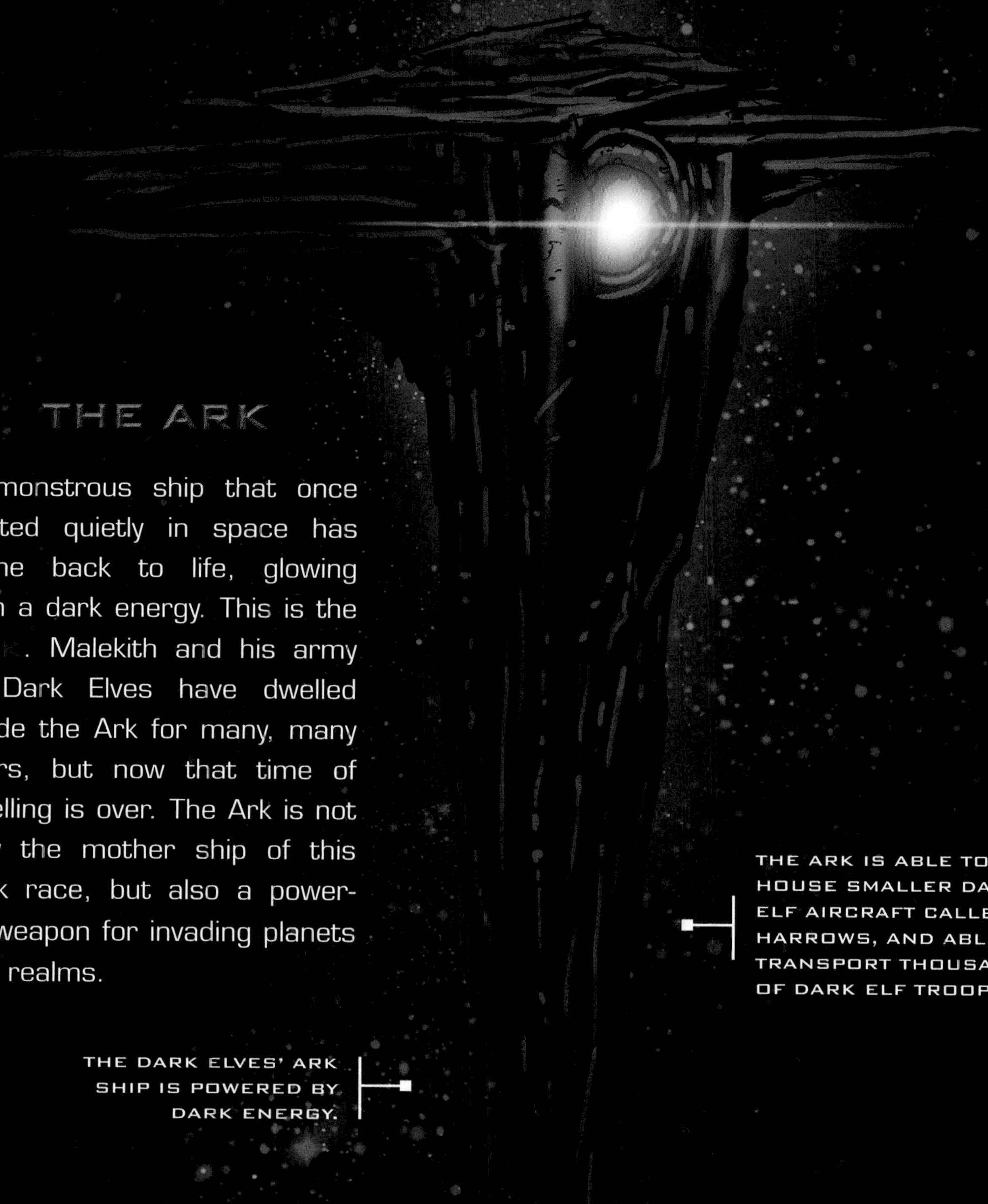

THE ARK IS ABLE TO HOUSE SMALLER DARK ELF AIRCRAFT CALLED HARROWS, AND ABLE TO TRANSPORT THOUSANDS OF DARK ELF TROOPS.

THE DARK ELVES' ARK SHIP IS POWERED BY DARK ENERGY.

KRONAN STONE MAN

When the Marauders invaded Hogun's home planet of Vanaheim, they were prepared for the weaponless Vanir people. But they were not prepared for the arrival of Thor. Nonetheless, when they needed to battle the Asgardian, they called upon their secret weapon, the **KRONAN STONE MAN**. Made entirely of rock and carrying a massive club, the Kronan beast stood toe-to-toe with Thor, ready for a battle.

THE KRONAN MAN TOWERS OVER ALL, INCLUDING THE MIGHTY THOR.

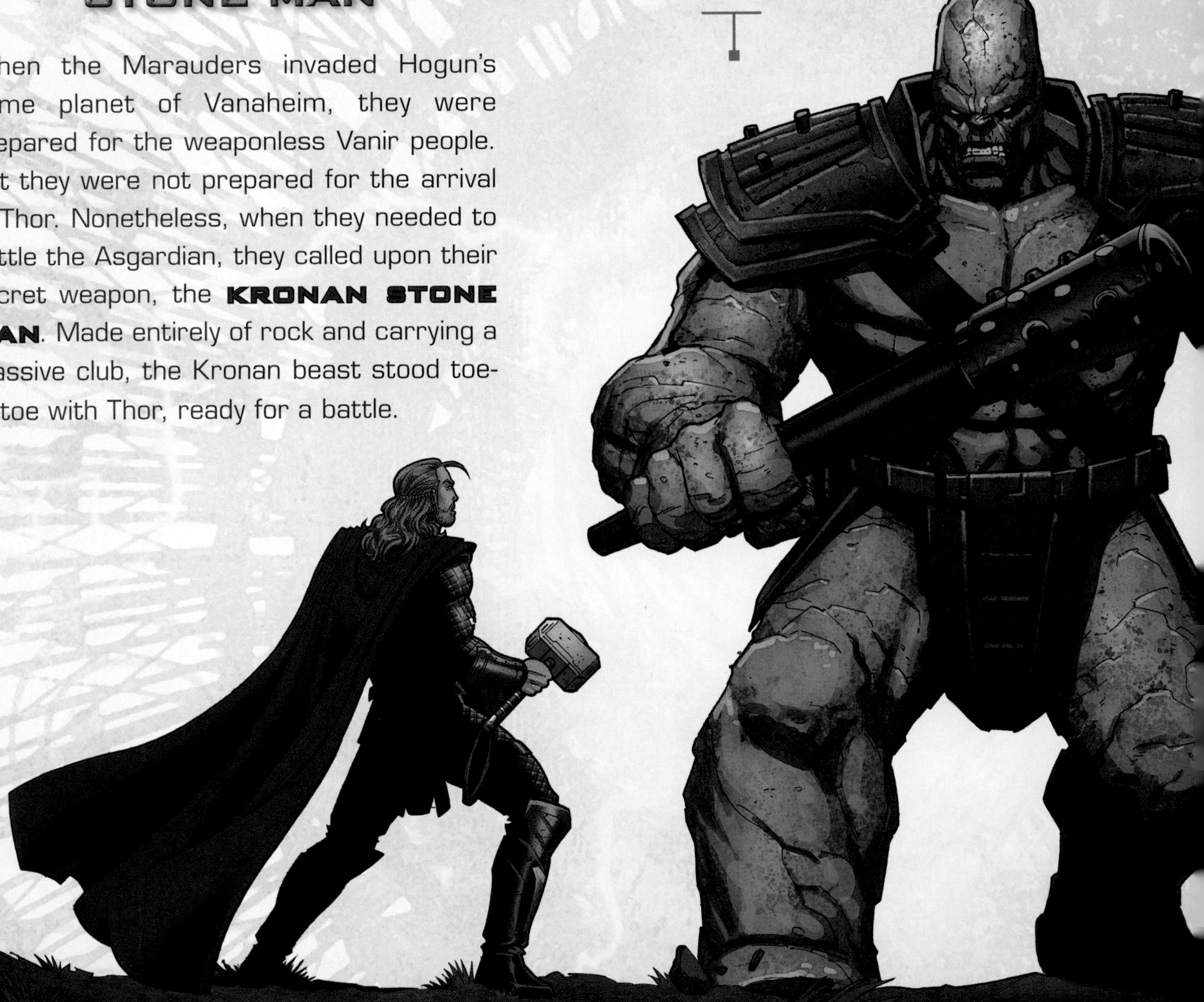

A KURSE TO ALL OF ASGARD

KURSE is Malekith's secret weapon. Not much else is known about this brutal creature. . . .

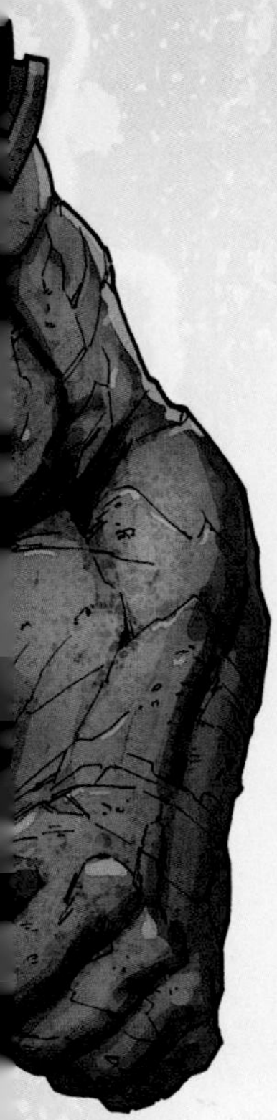

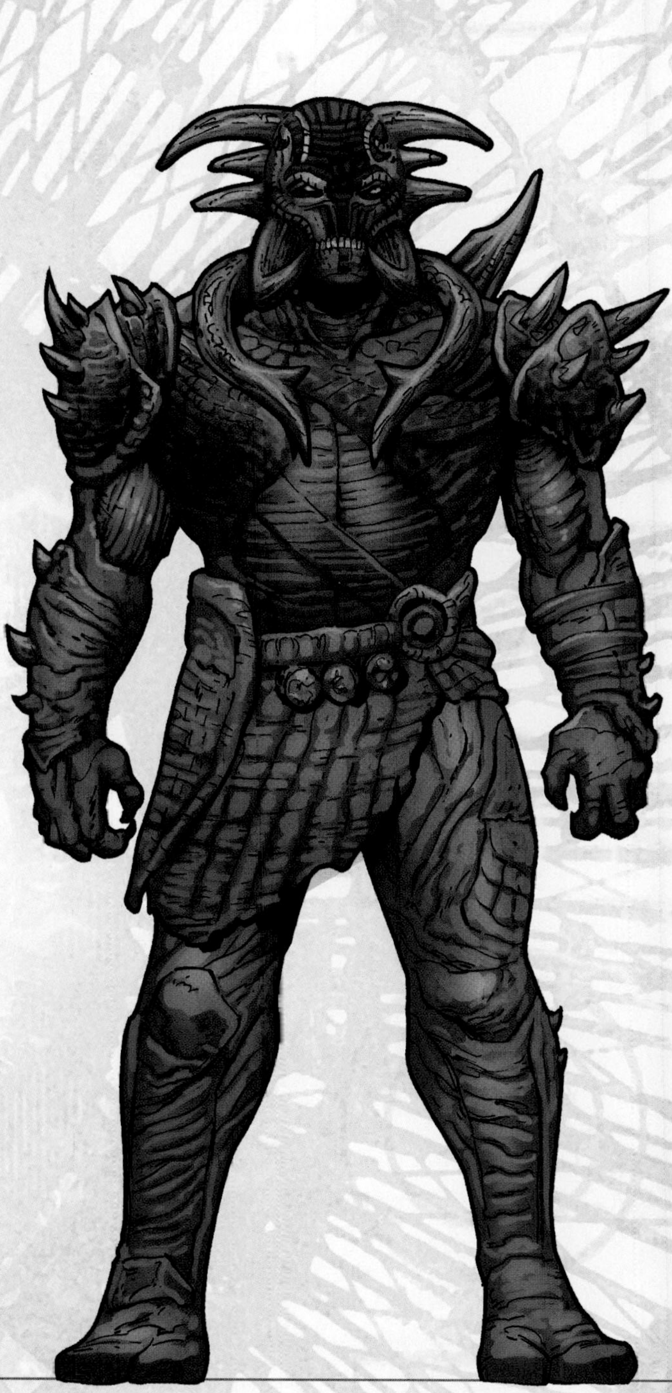

KURSE HAS THE POWER OF A HUNDRED WARRIORS.

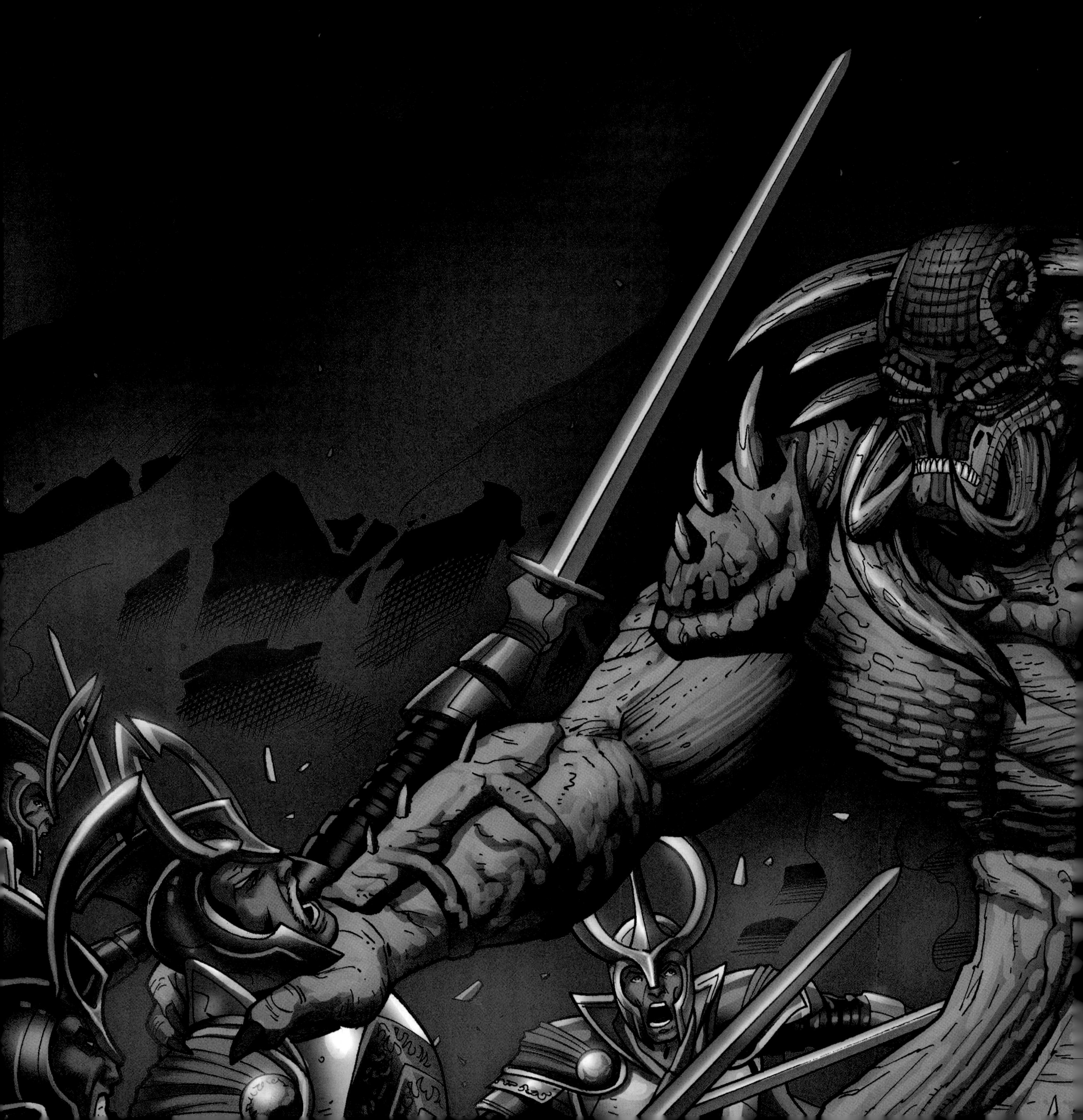

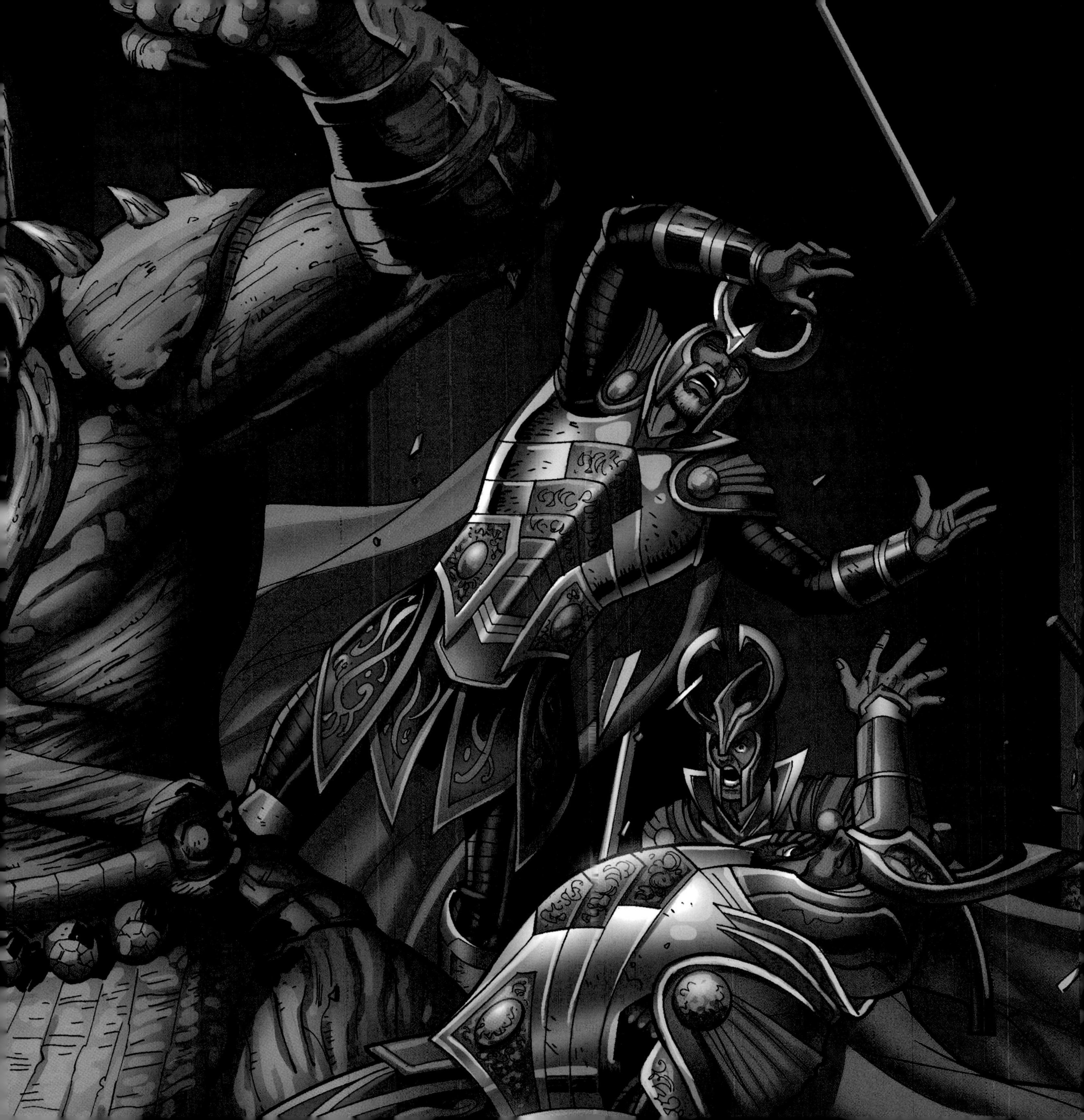

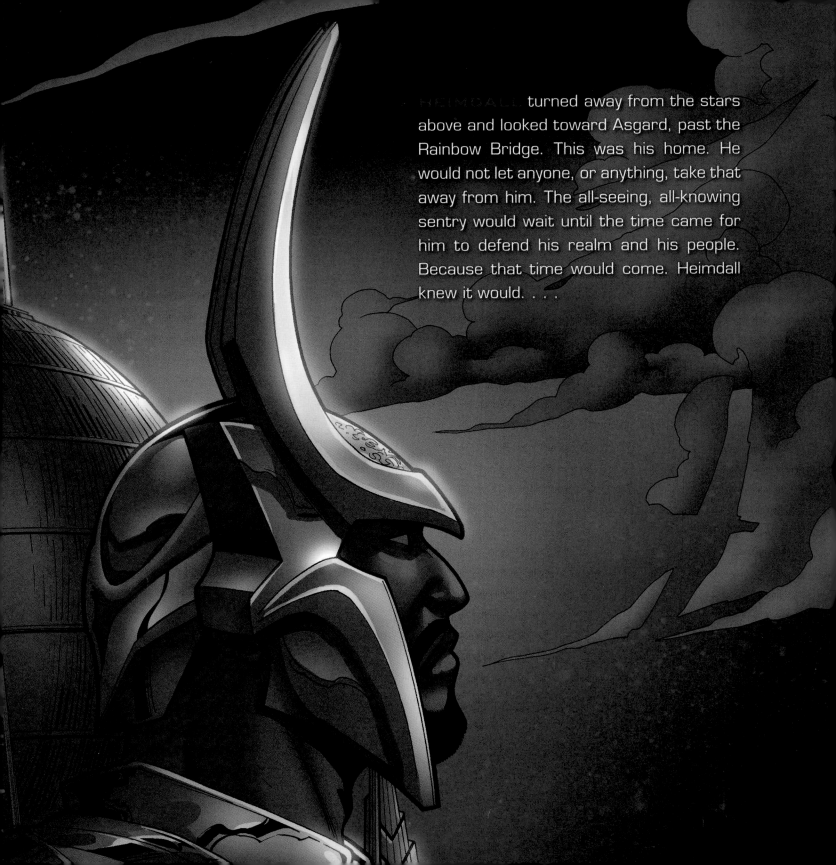

HEIMDALL turned away from the stars above and looked toward Asgard, past the Rainbow Bridge. This was his home. He would not let anyone, or anything, take that away from him. The all-seeing, all-knowing sentry would wait until the time came for him to defend his realm and his people. Because that time would come. Heimdall knew it would. . . .

MARVEL

CAPTAIN AMERICA
THE WINTER SOLDIER
RESCUE AT SEA

WRITTEN BY

Michael Siglain

BASED ON THE SCREENPLAY BY

Christopher Markus & Stephen McFeely

PRODUCED BY

Kevin Feige, p.g.a.

DIRECTED BY

Anthony and Joe Russo

ILLUSTRATED BY

Ron Lim, Cam Smith, and Lee Duhig

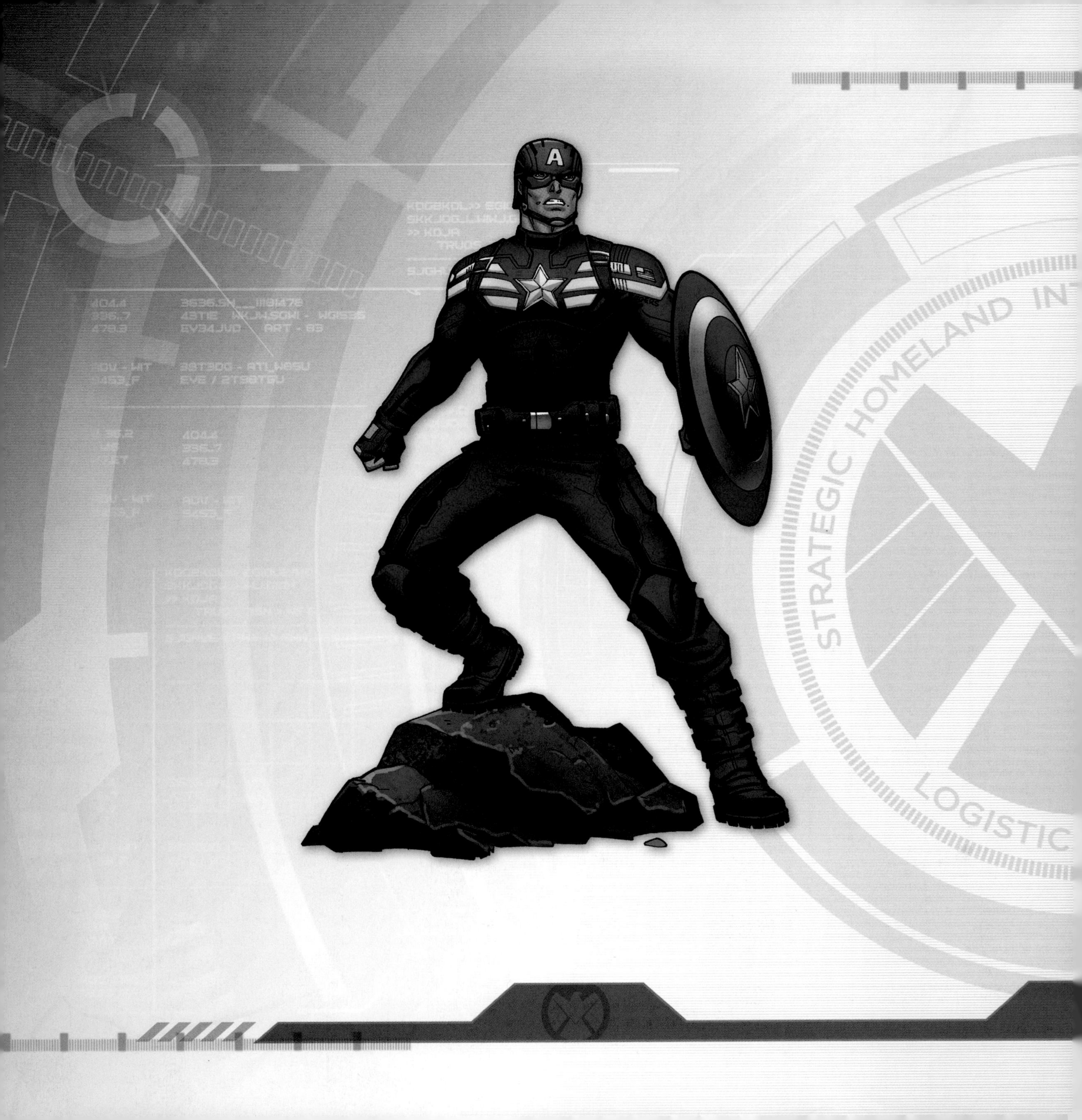
STRATEGIC HOMELAND INT
LOGISTIC

Steve Rogers was once a frail and sickly soldier, but after taking part in the top secret experiment Project: Rebirth, Steve became America's first Super-Soldier. Armed with an unbreakable shield, Steve now fights for freedom as Captain America!

Nick Fury was worried. He was the director of S.H.I.E.L.D., and he was tasked with keeping the world safe. He had just learned that a large cargo ship called the *Lemurian Star* had been hijacked by pirates. There was only one man who could save the day: Captain America.

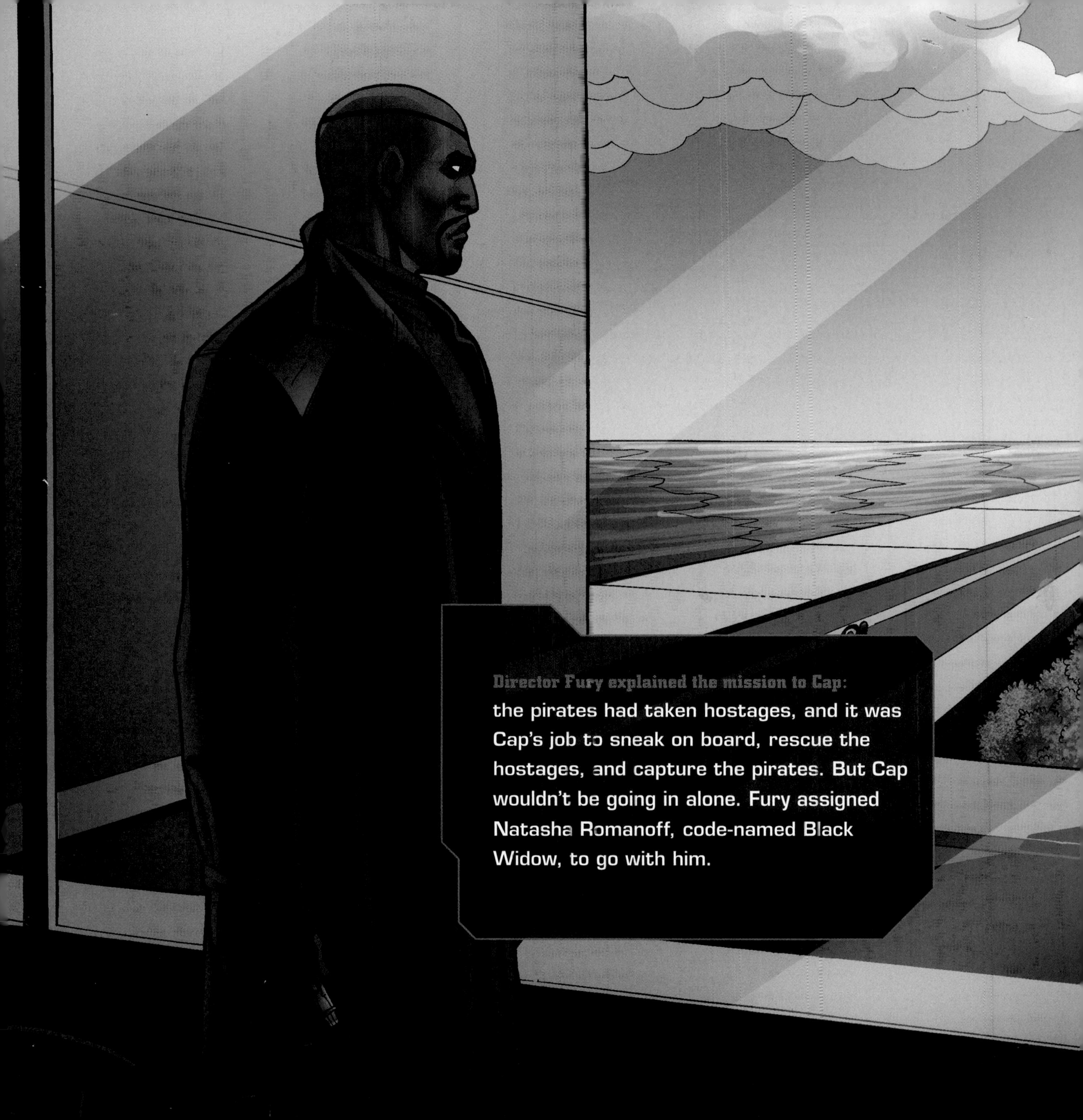

Director Fury explained the mission to Cap:
the pirates had taken hostages, and it was Cap's job to sneak on board, rescue the hostages, and capture the pirates. But Cap wouldn't be going in alone. Fury assigned Natasha Romanoff, code-named Black Widow, to go with him.

Time was running out, and
as Cap went to meet Black Widow,
Director Fury wished them luck.
They were going to need it!

Soon S.H.I.E.L.D.'s high-tech Quinjet was
streaking over Africa toward the In-
dian Ocean. With Black Widow at the
controls, they were over the cargo
ship in no time. It was now time for
action. Captain America opened the
side hatch of the Quinjet and leaped
toward the warm water below.

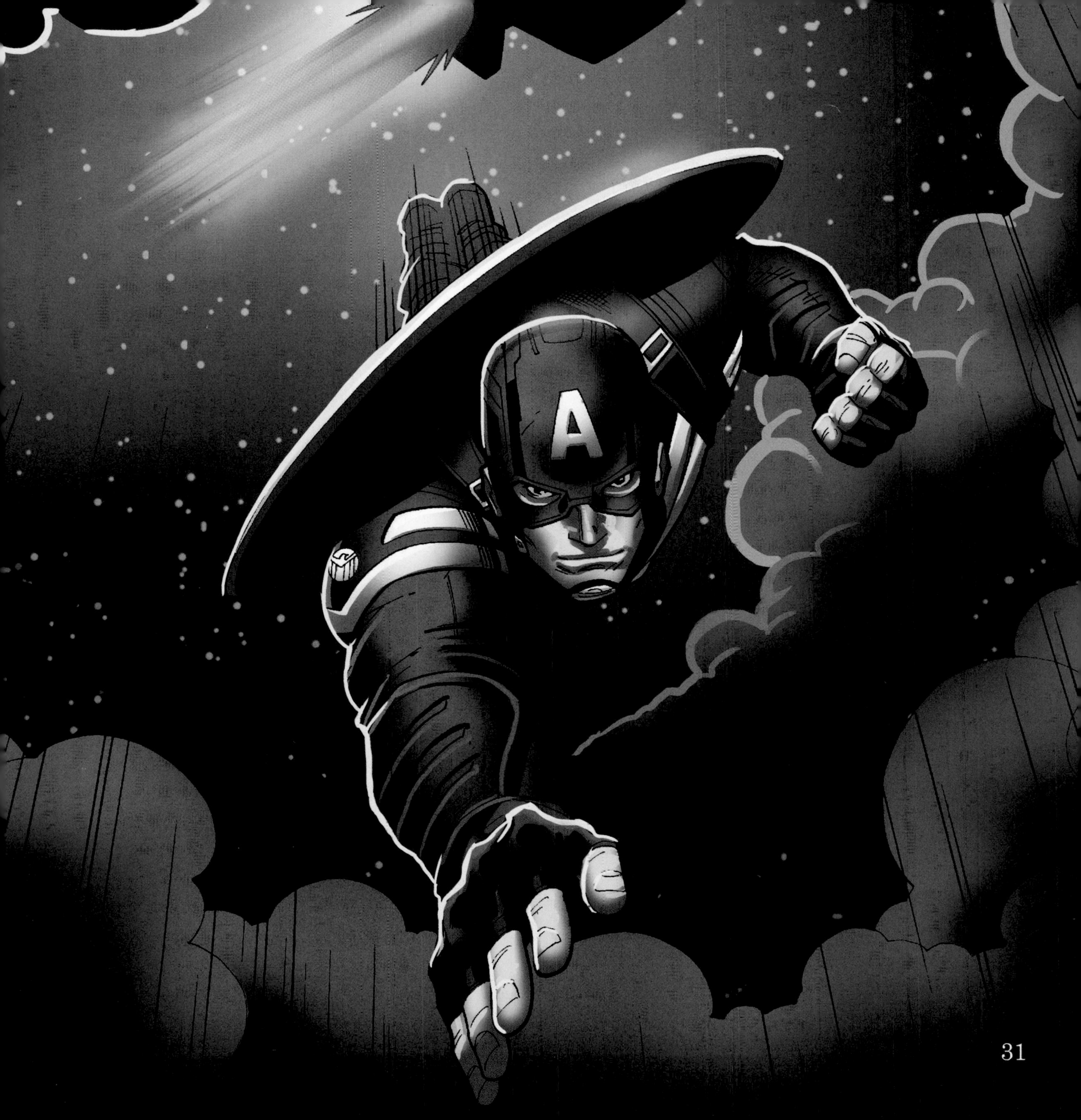

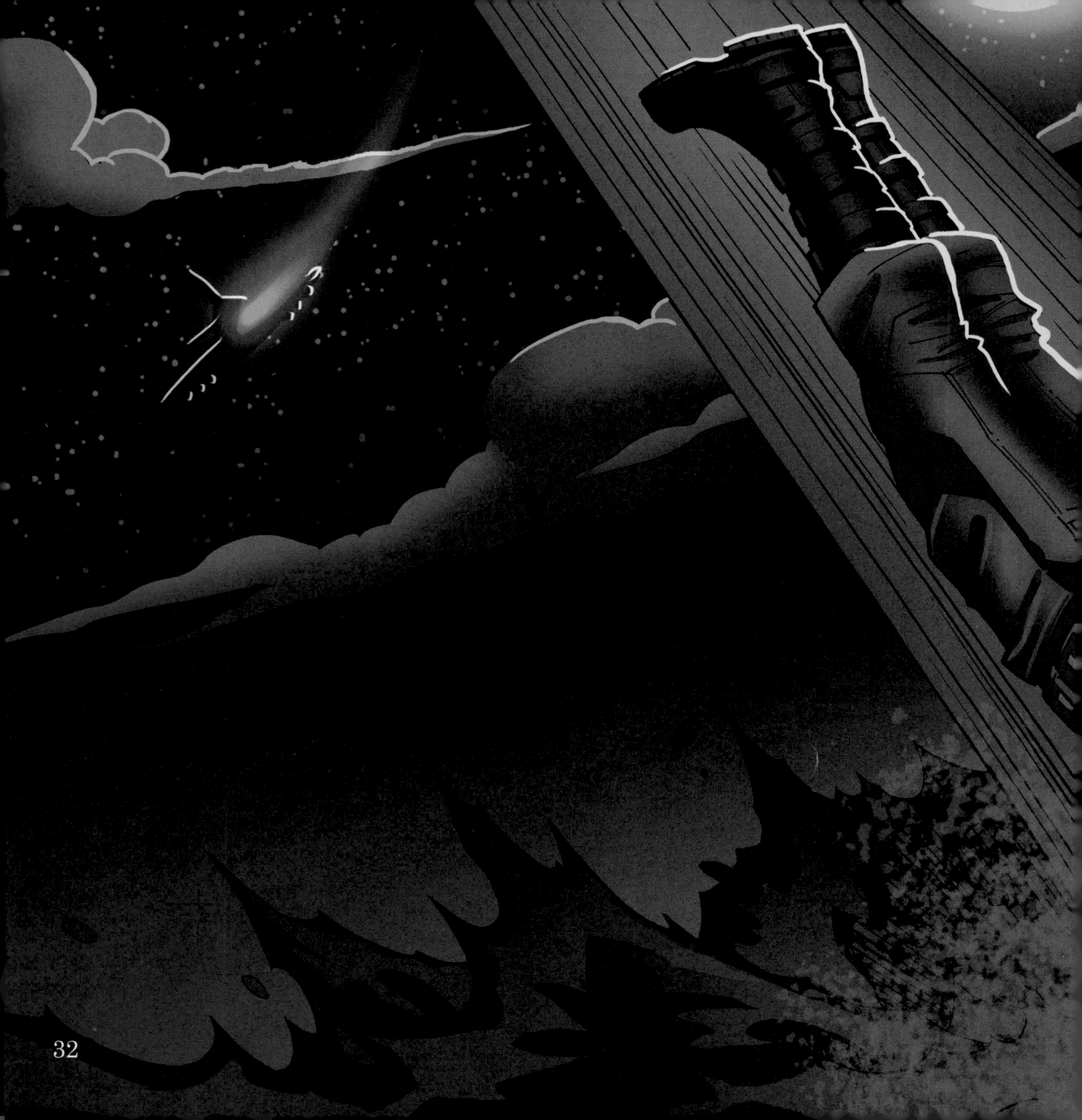

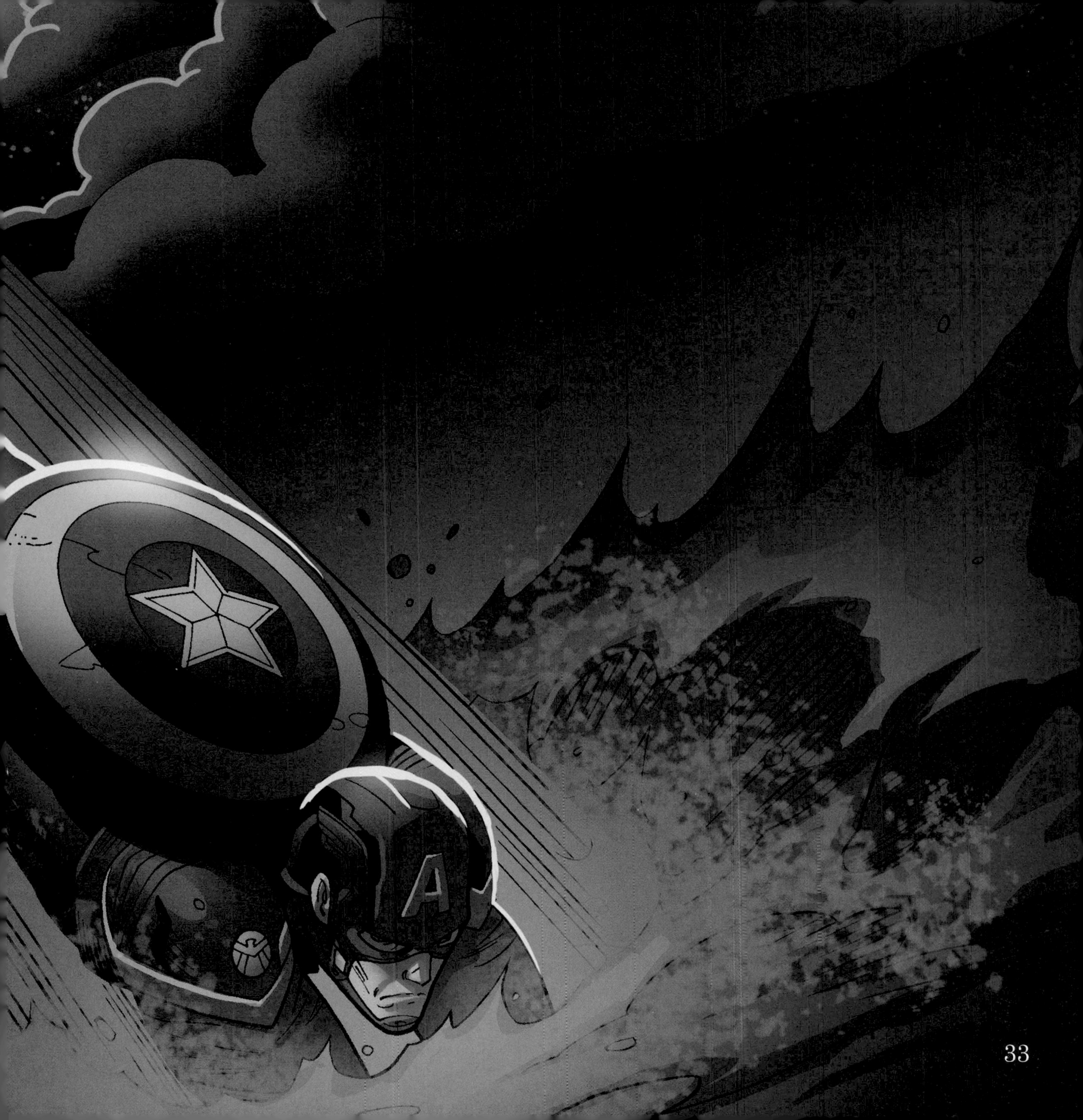

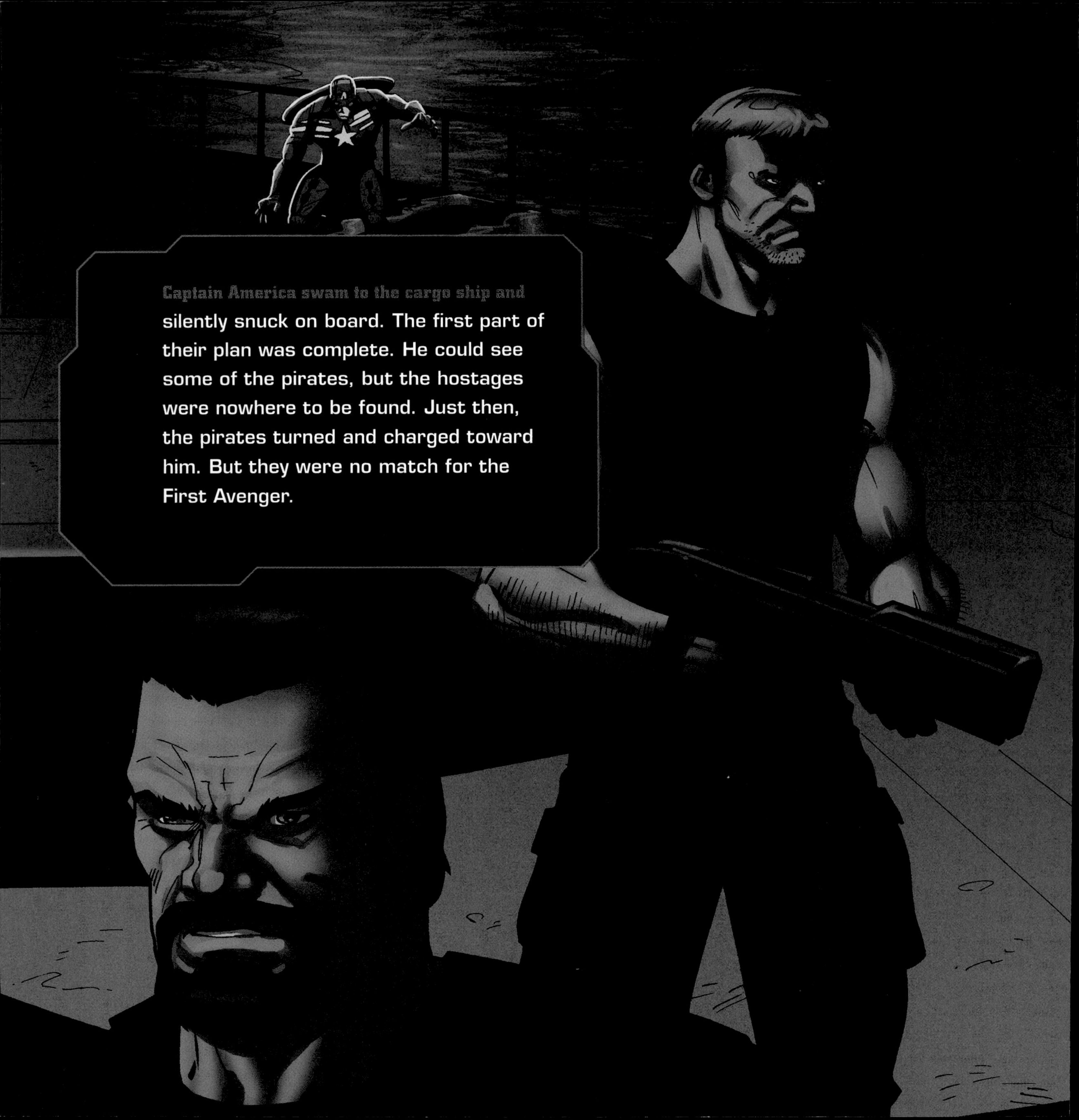

Captain America swam to the cargo ship and silently snuck on board. The first part of their plan was complete. He could see some of the pirates, but the hostages were nowhere to be found. Just then, the pirates turned and charged toward him. But they were no match for the First Avenger.

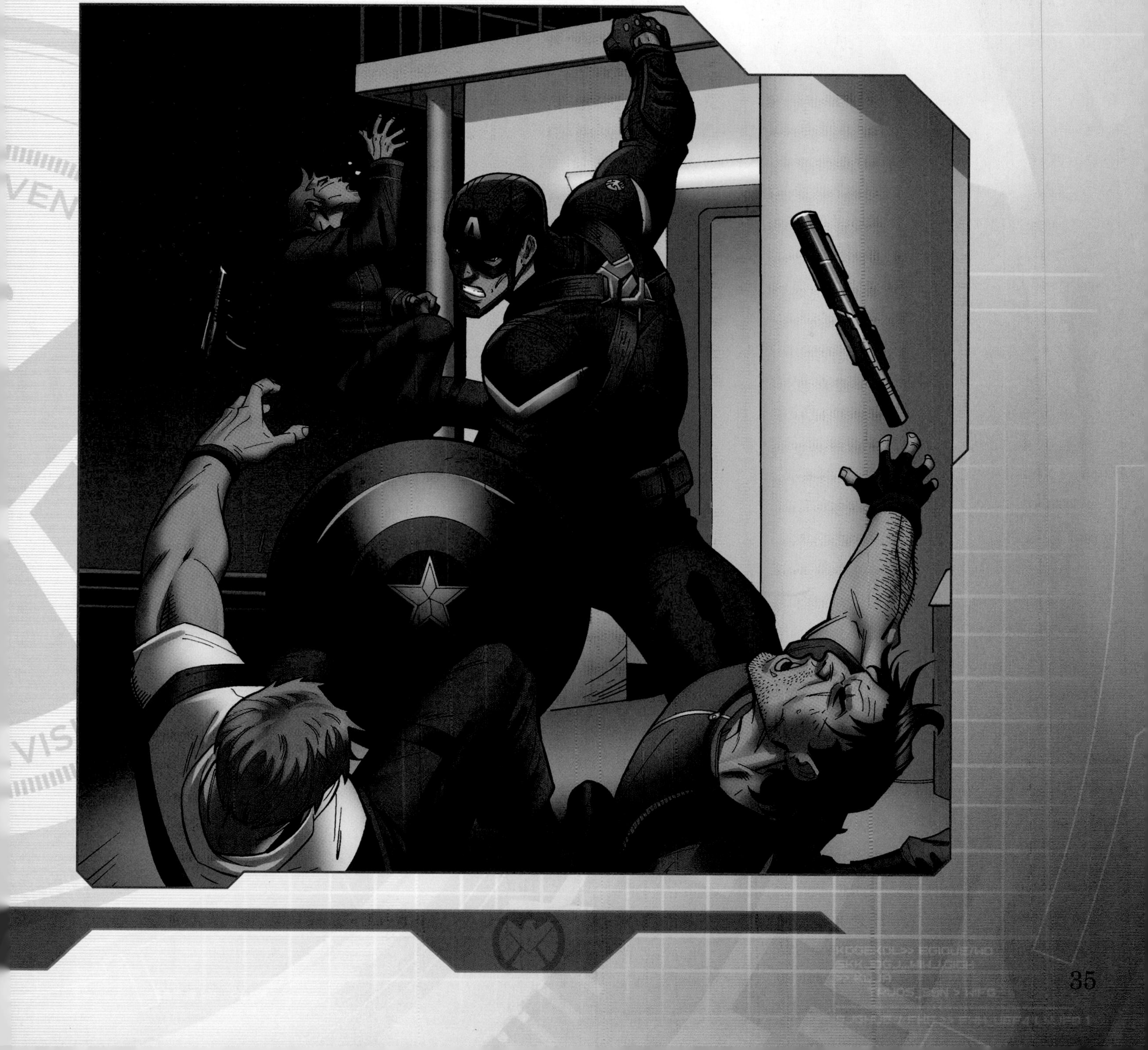

Meanwhile, Black Widow radioed Fury to report in. Fury warned her about Georges Batroc, who was the leader of the pirates. Batroc was armed and very, very dangerous.

Black Widow put the Quinjet on autopilot and radioed Cap to tell him the information about Batroc, but Cap was already on the move, searching for the hostages.

Black Widow knew she had to join her S.H.I.E.L.D. partner in case he needed help. That and he couldn't have all the fun! She put on a parachute and stepped to the back of the Quinjet. She opened the door and leaped out, falling to the ship below. Just as Black Widow was about to hit the water, she opened the parachute and quietly landed on the deck, quickly disposed of the chute, and raced off to find the pirates.

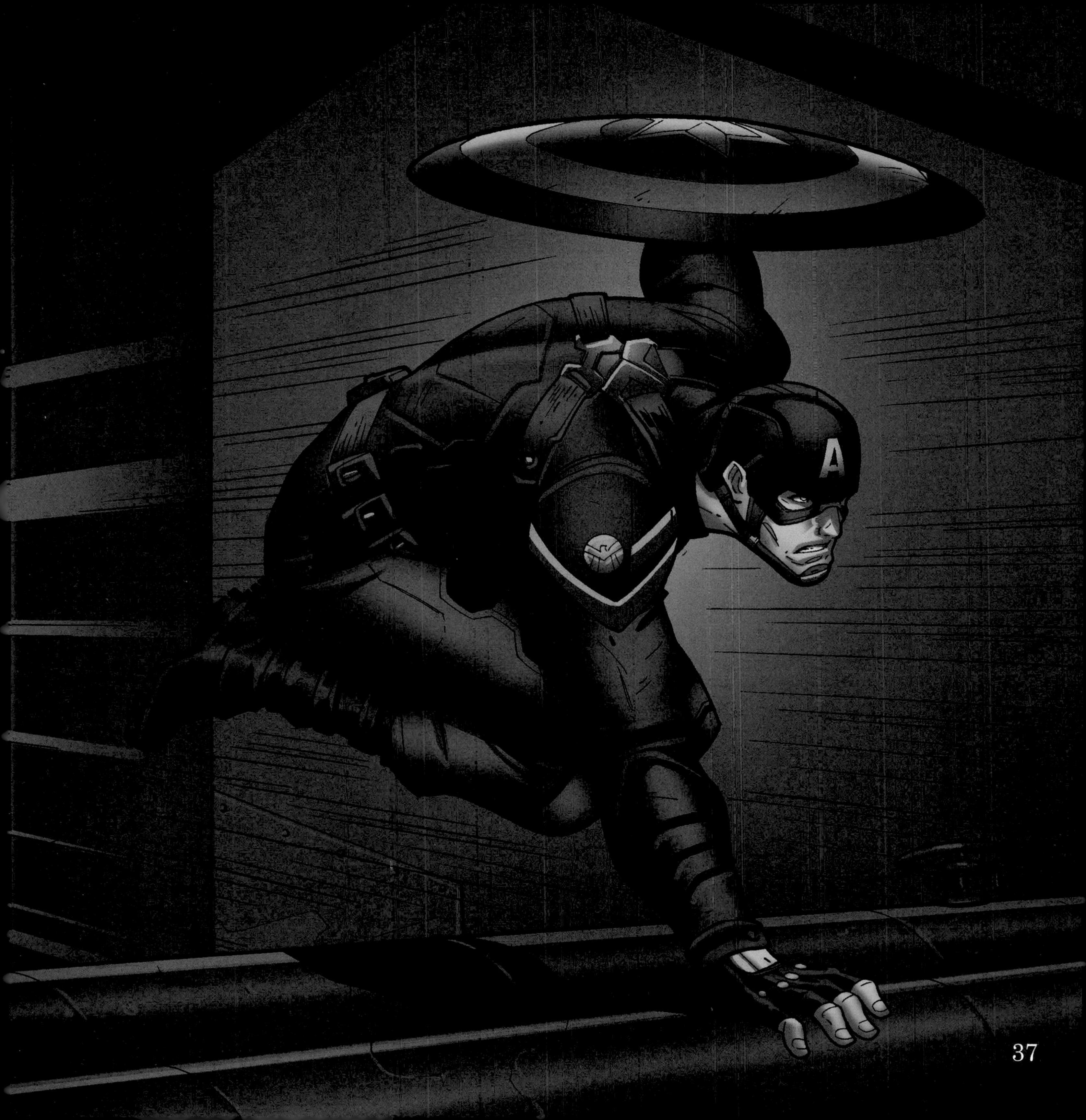

KOOSKOL>> EGIOUE/I40
SKK_OGJ_VIILJ.GIGH
>> KOJA
     TRUOS_39N > HIFG

SJGHUE / FHF >> FHH_UEF4 I 4JFB I

404.4   3G36.SN   IIIBI47B
336.7   43TIE   HKJ4SOHI - WGIS3S
478.3   EY34.JUO   ART - 83

3DV - HIT   39T3DG - BTLHBSU
3453.F   EYE / 2T9BTSU

Deep within the hull of the Lemurian Star, inside a secret control room, Georges Batroc was making his demands. He wanted one and a half billion dollars in exchange for the hostages.

Batroc was very smart and knew that S.H.I.E.L.D. might try something, so he checked in with his men. He wanted to make sure they were all on high alert. But when the pirates in the engine room didn't answer his call, Batroc knew that something was wrong.

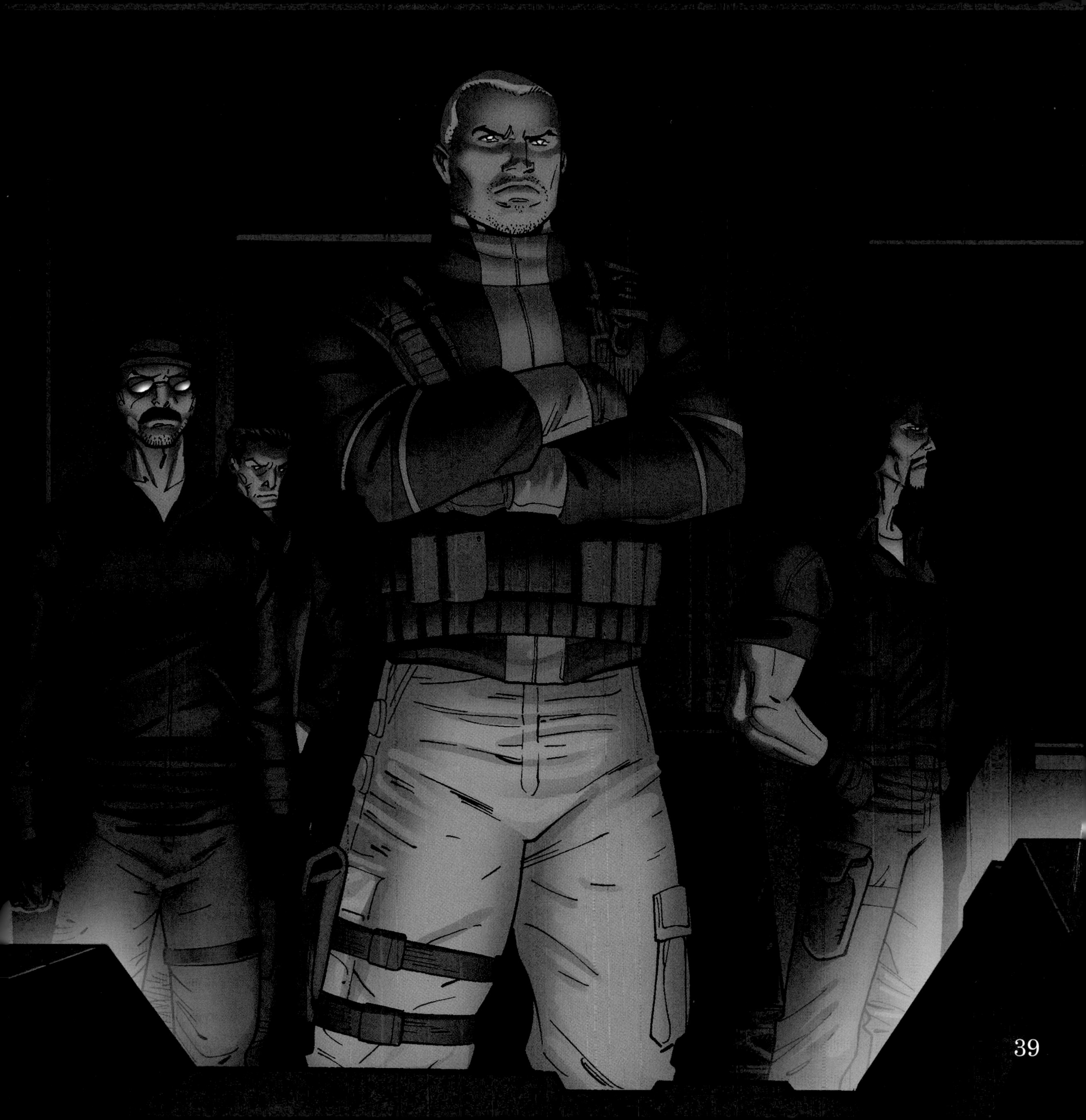

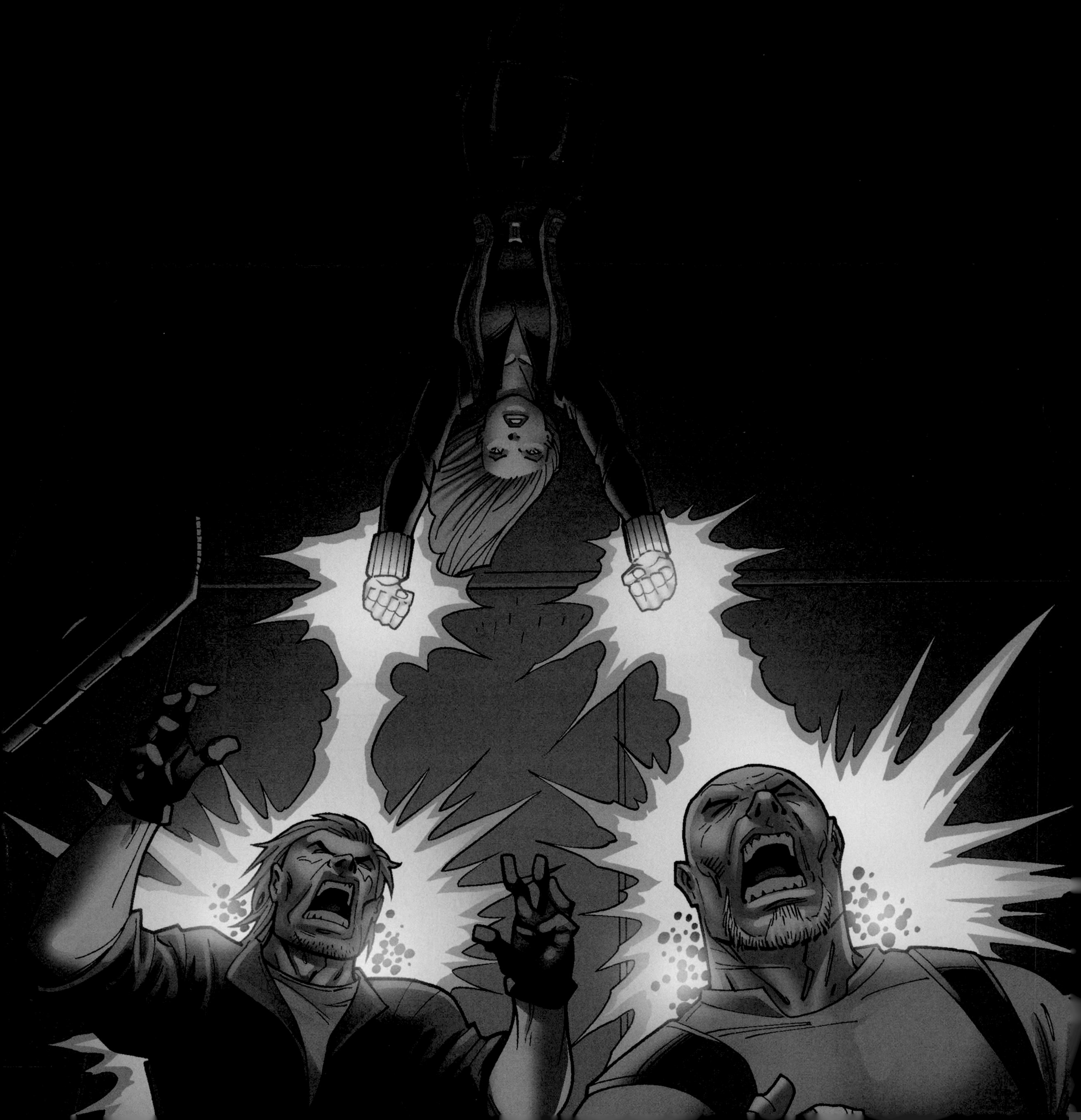

Cap had already knocked out the pirates in the engine room and learned the location of Batroc's secret control room. He contacted Black Widow to let her know what he had found out, but Natasha was one step ahead of him.

Outside the control room, Black Widow lowered herself from the ceiling and used her special bracelets to deliver small electric shocks—what she called her "Widow's Bites"—to the pirates guarding the room. Then it was Cap's turn to take out the bad guys!

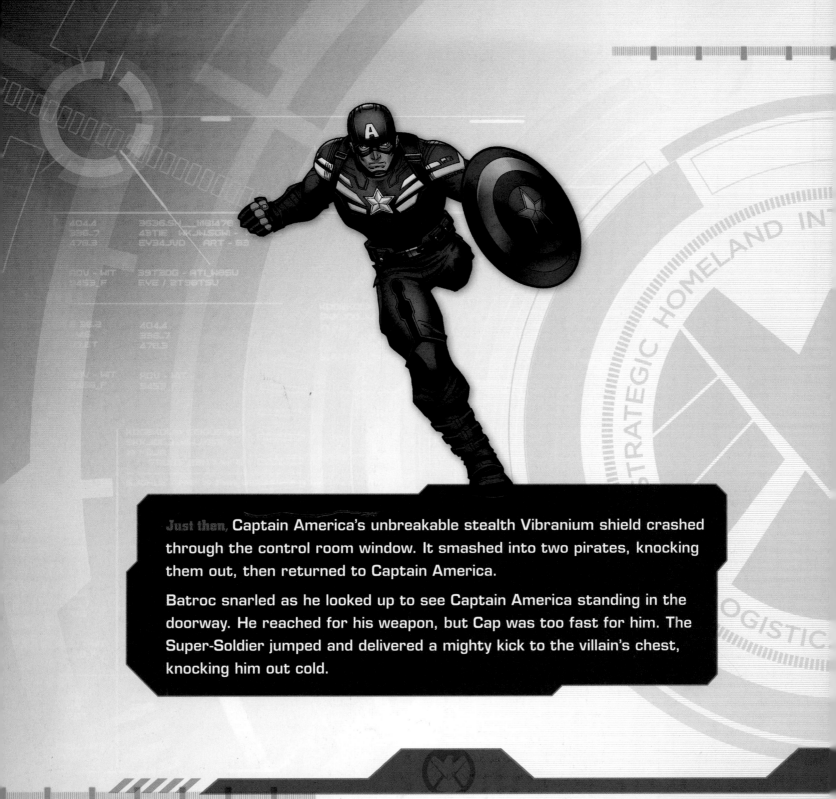

Just then, Captain America's unbreakable stealth Vibranium shield crashed through the control room window. It smashed into two pirates, knocking them out, then returned to Captain America.

Batroc snarled as he looked up to see Captain America standing in the doorway. He reached for his weapon, but Cap was too fast for him. The Super-Soldier jumped and delivered a mighty kick to the villain's chest, knocking him out cold.

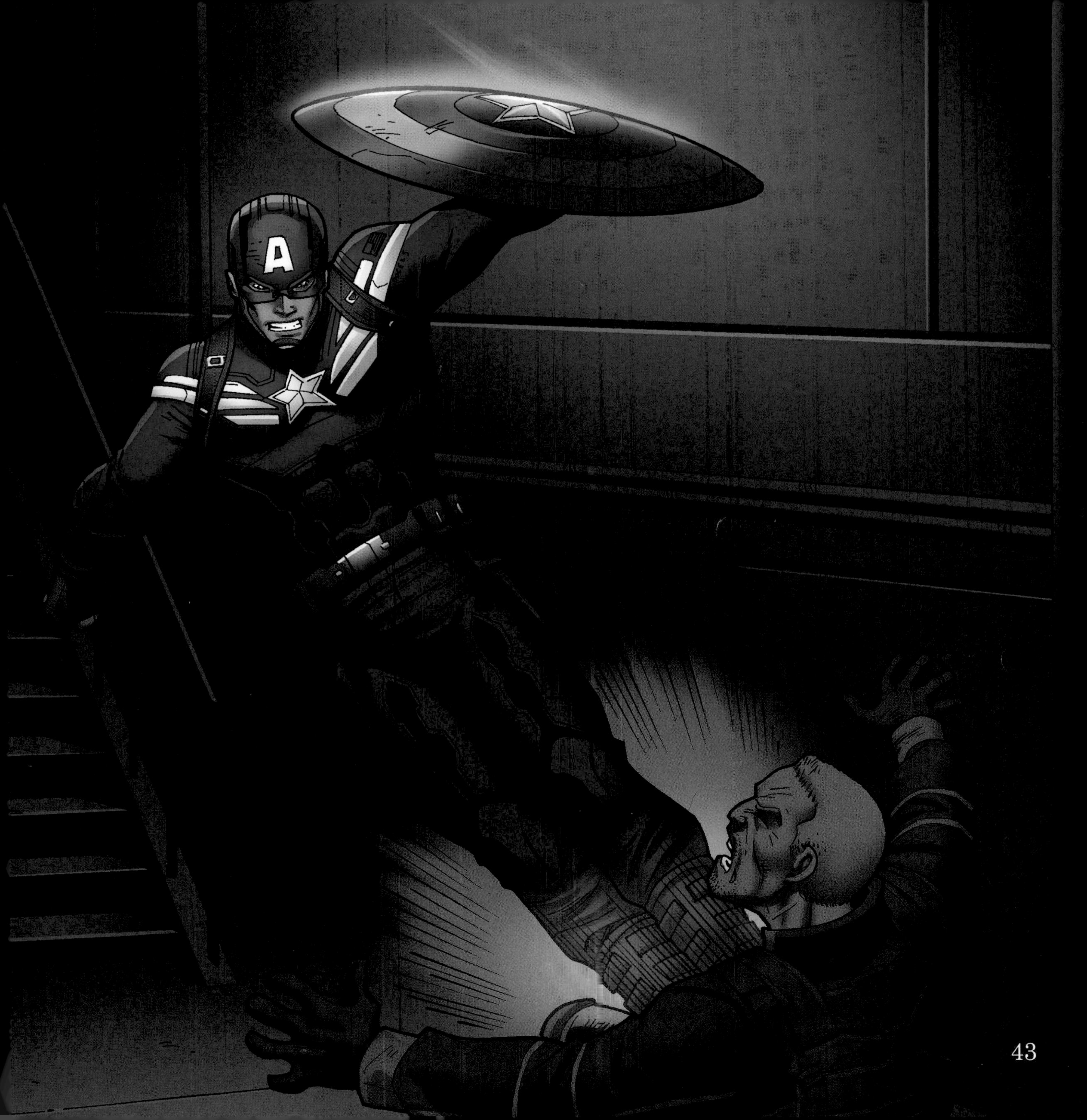

With Batroc defeated, Cap tied him up and secured him in the control room so that he couldn't escape. Then it was time to get the hostages and let them know that they were free and safe.

Black Widow joined Captain America as they made their way down to the cargo hold, where the hostages were locked up. Cap looked at Black Widow and smiled. Getting inside would be a piece of cake for these Avengers.

With a mighty crash, Captain America and Black Widow burst through a large window that led to the cargo room.

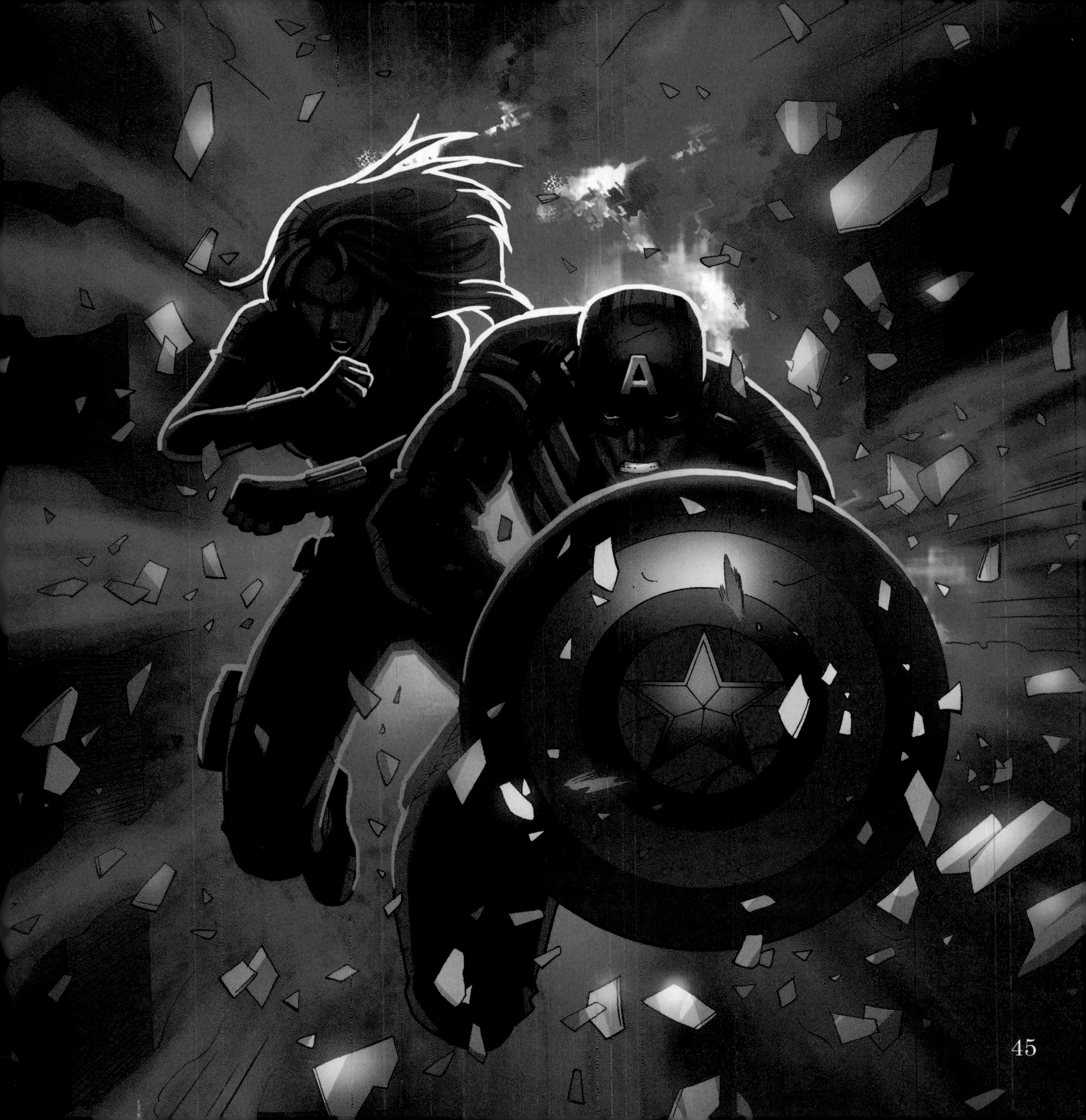

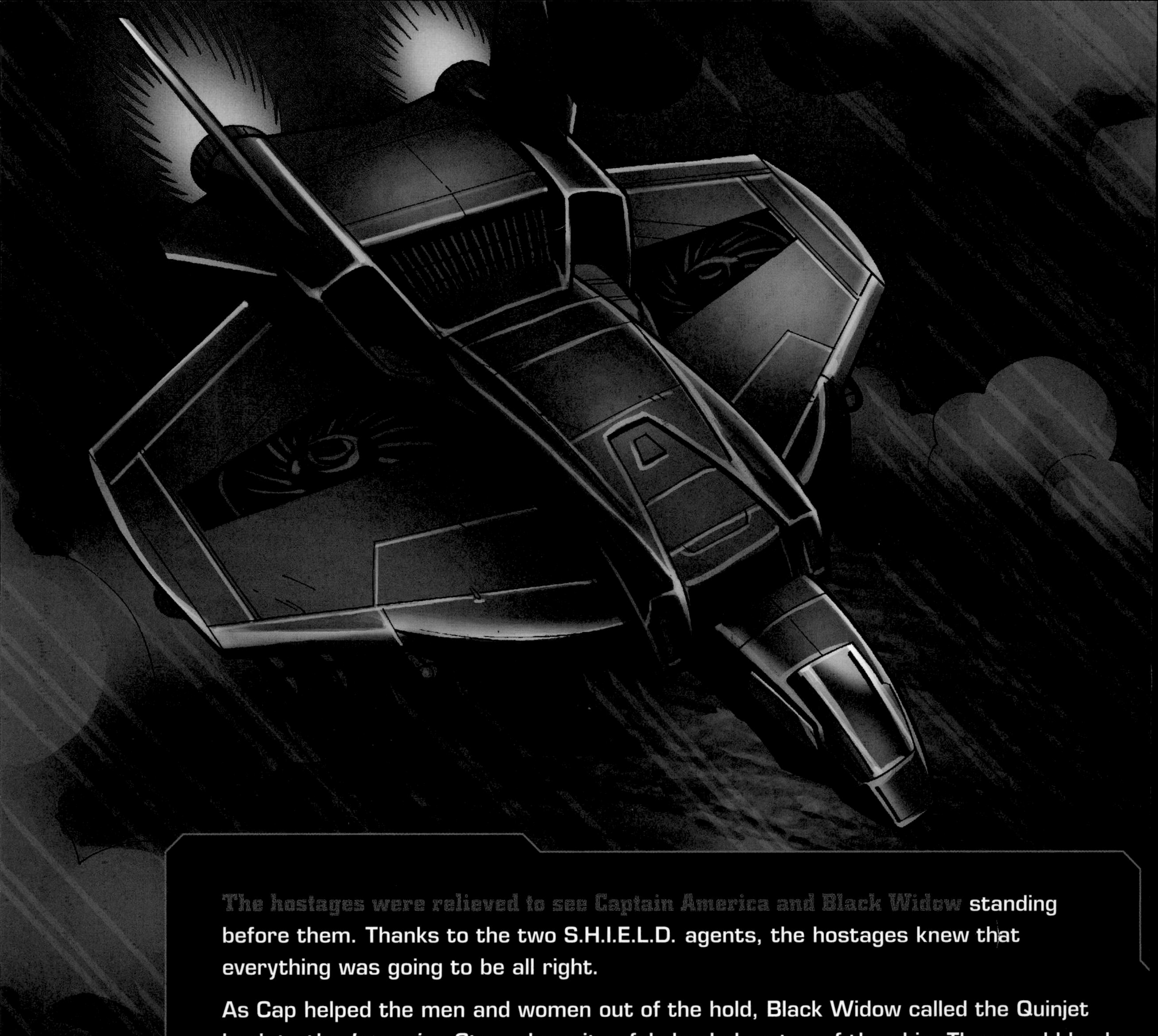

The hostages were relieved to see Captain America and Black Widow standing before them. Thanks to the two S.H.I.E.L.D. agents, the hostages knew that everything was going to be all right.

As Cap helped the men and women out of the hold, Black Widow called the Quinjet back to the *Lemurian Star*, where it safely landed on top of the ship. They would load the hostages on board and take them back to S.H.I.E.L.D. headquarters.

MARVEL

AVENGERS
AGE OF ULTRON

Avengers Save the Day

Adaptation by Kirsten Mayer
Illustrated by Ron Lim, Andy Smith, and Andy Troy
Based on the Screenplay by Joss Whedon
Produced by Kevin Feige, p.g.a.
Directed by Joss Whedon

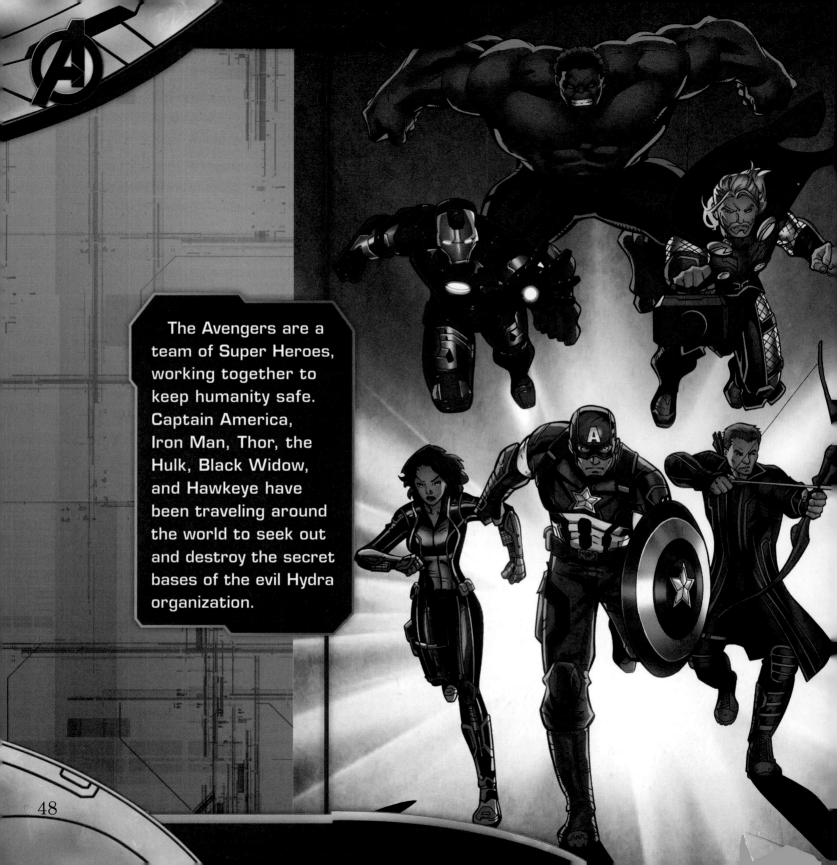

The Avengers are a team of Super Heroes, working together to keep humanity safe. Captain America, Iron Man, Thor, the Hulk, Black Widow, and Hawkeye have been traveling around the world to seek out and destroy the secret bases of the evil Hydra organization.

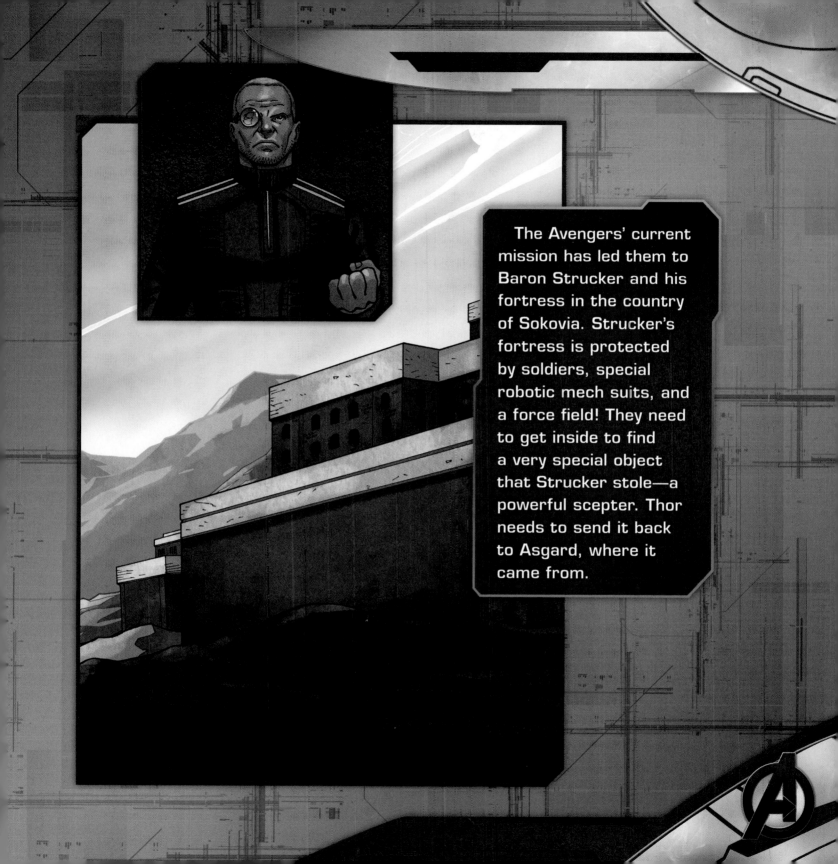

The Avengers' current mission has led them to Baron Strucker and his fortress in the country of Sokovia. Strucker's fortress is protected by soldiers, special robotic mech suits, and a force field! They need to get inside to find a very special object that Strucker stole—a powerful scepter. Thor needs to send it back to Asgard, where it came from.

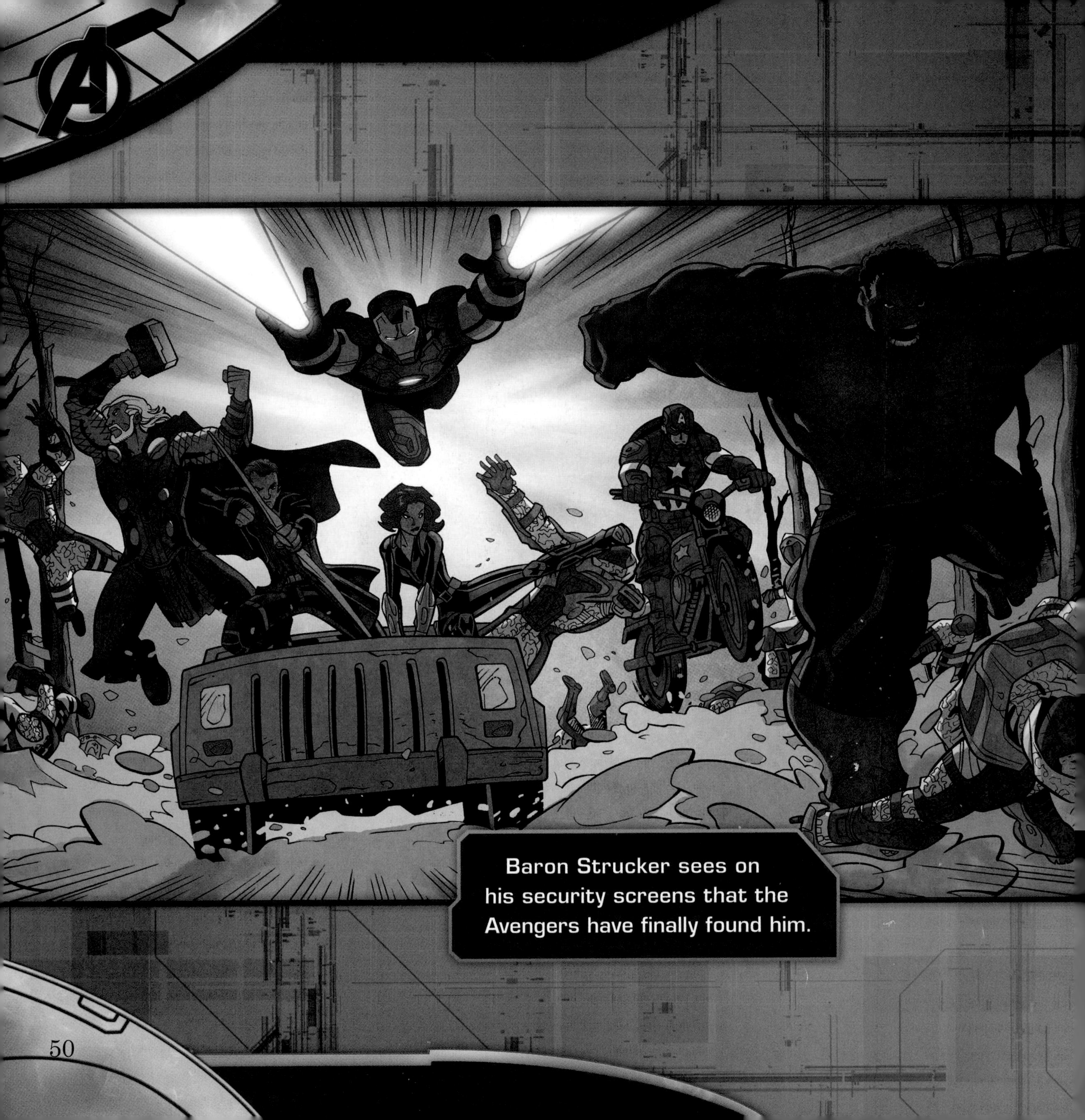

Baron Strucker sees on
his security screens that the
Avengers have finally found him.

"Can we hold them?" he asks his team.

"They're the Avengers!" blurts out a panicked Hydra soldier.

Strucker frowns. "Deploy the rest of the tanks," he orders. "No surrender!"

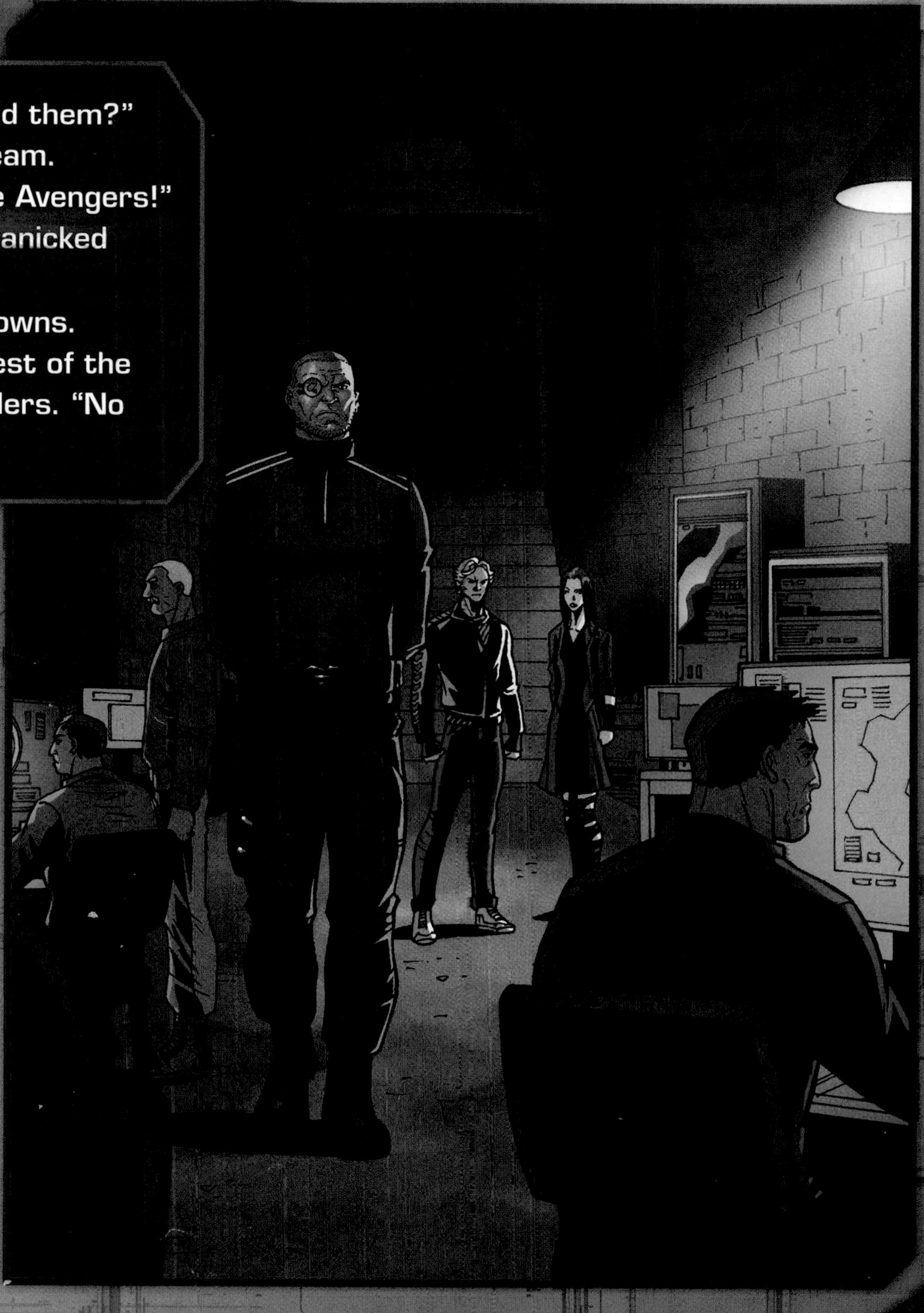

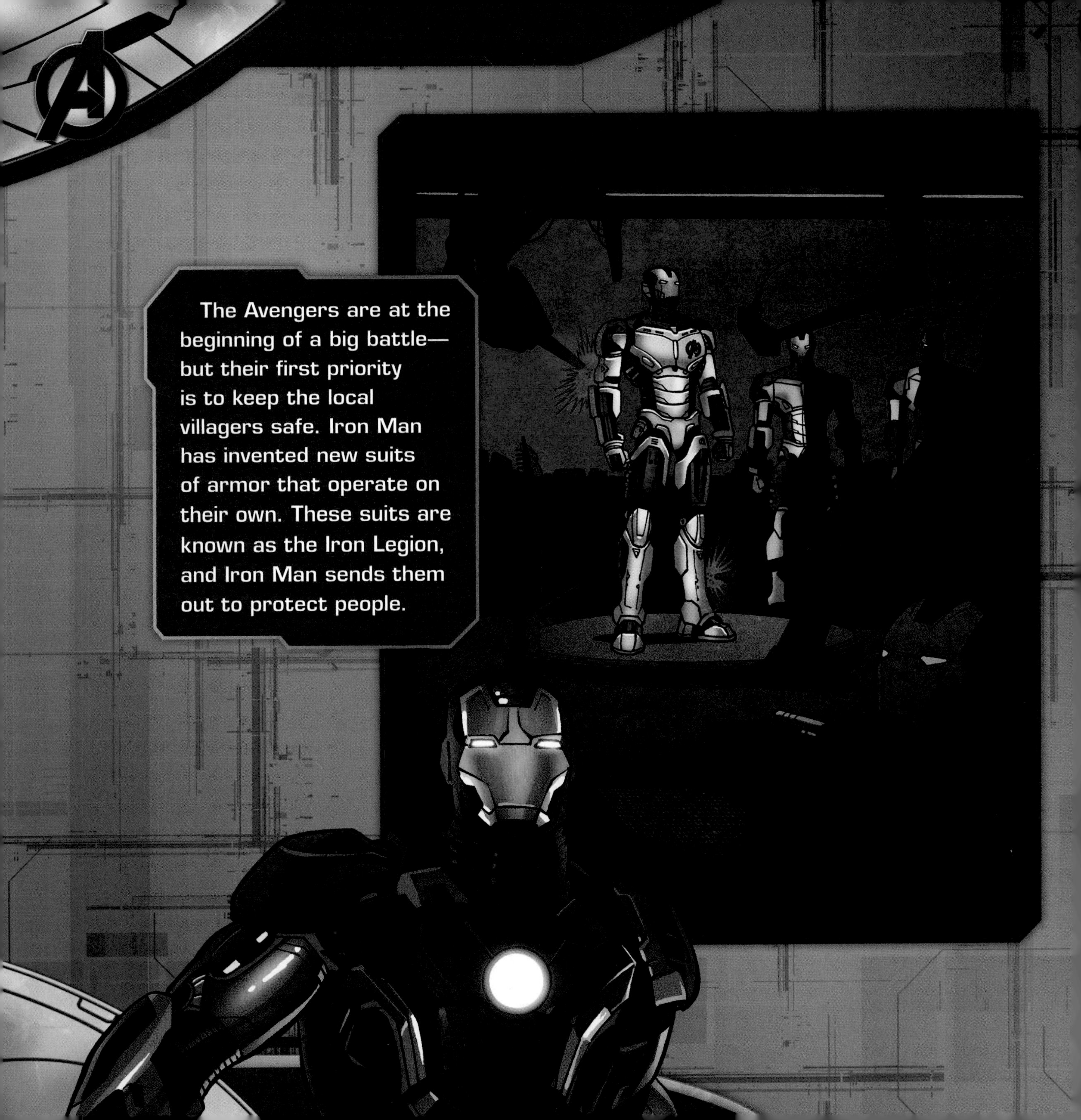

The Avengers are at the beginning of a big battle—but their first priority is to keep the local villagers safe. Iron Man has invented new suits of armor that operate on their own. These suits are known as the Iron Legion, and Iron Man sends them out to protect people.

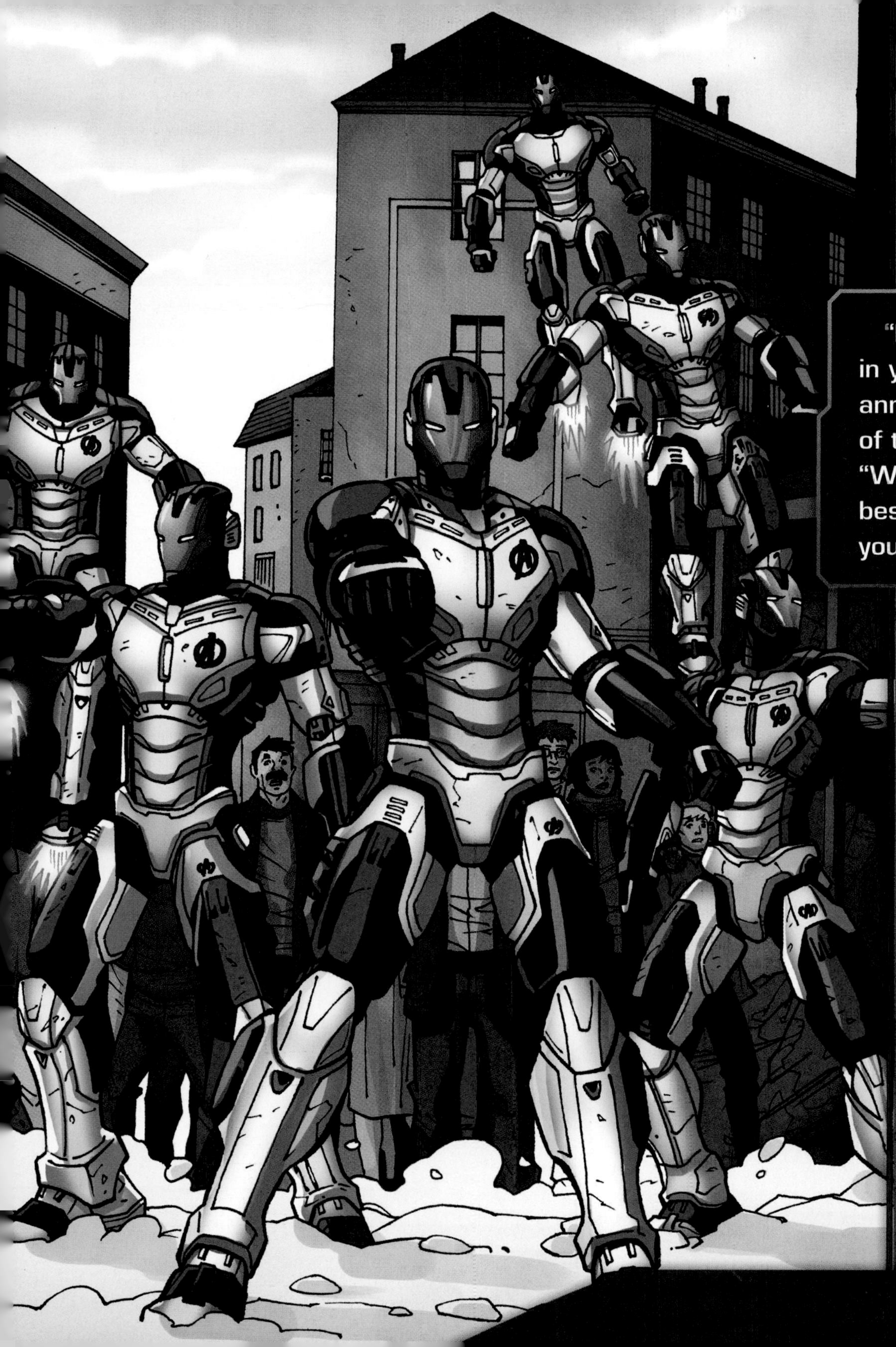

"Please stay in your homes," announces one of the drones. "We will do our best to ensure your safety."

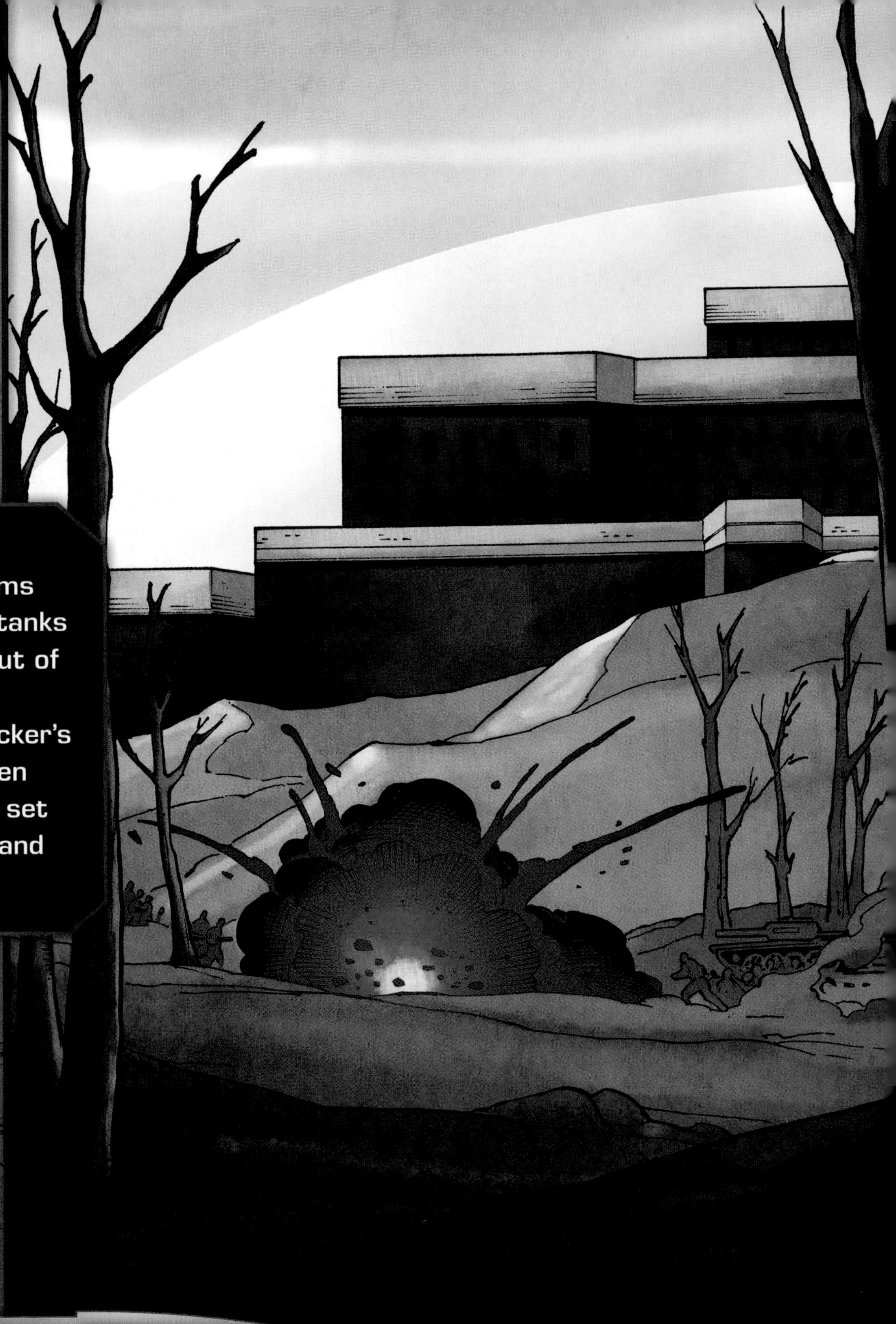

Back at the fortress, streams of soldiers and tanks begin to pour out of the gates.

Some of Strucker's troops carry alien weaponry. They set up in the trees and begin firing.

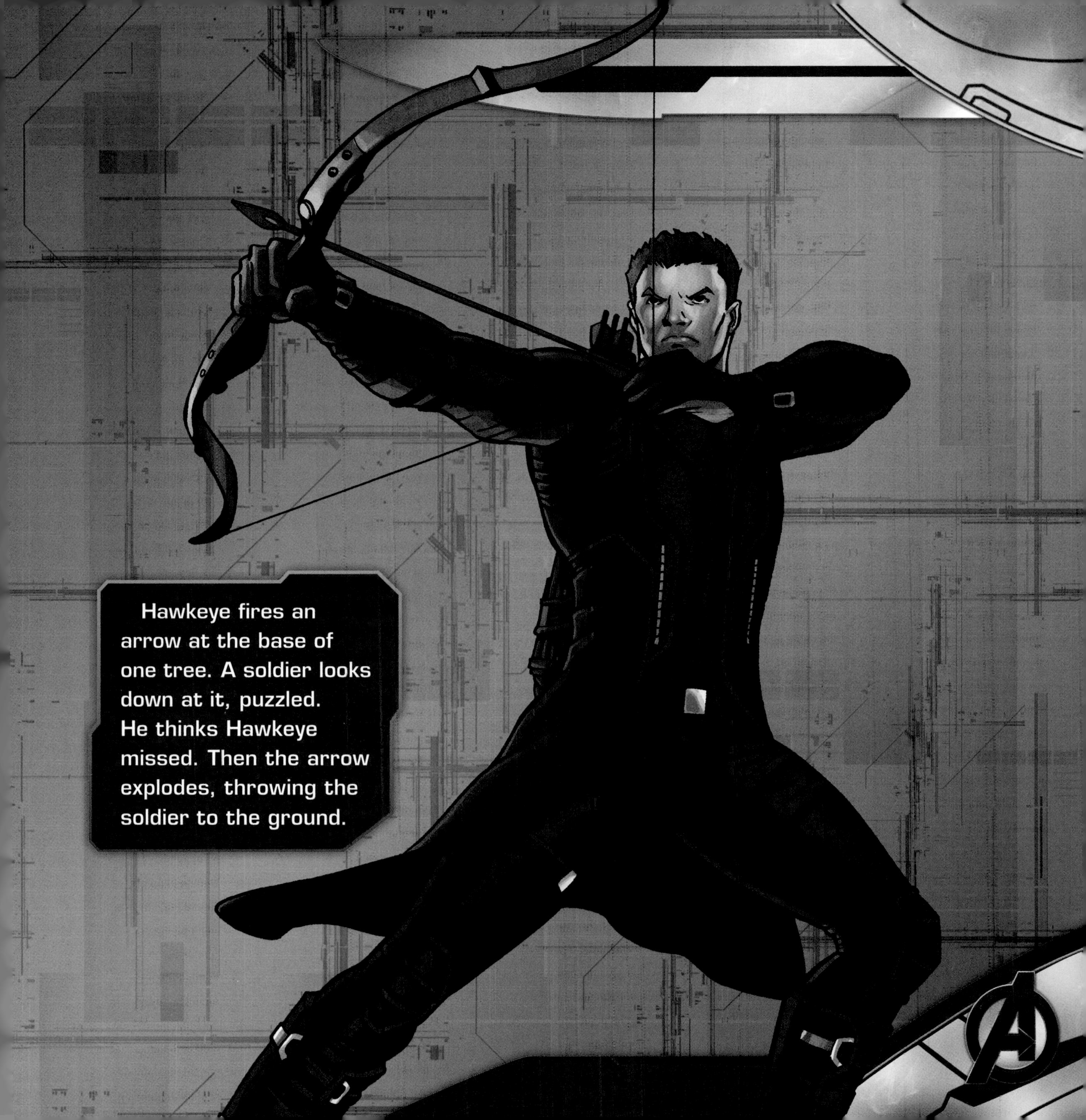

Hawkeye fires an arrow at the base of one tree. A soldier looks down at it, puzzled. He thinks Hawkeye missed. Then the arrow explodes, throwing the soldier to the ground.

Black Widow takes out several vehicles full of troops on her own. She wrestles one soldier to the ground just as a tank pulls up behind her.

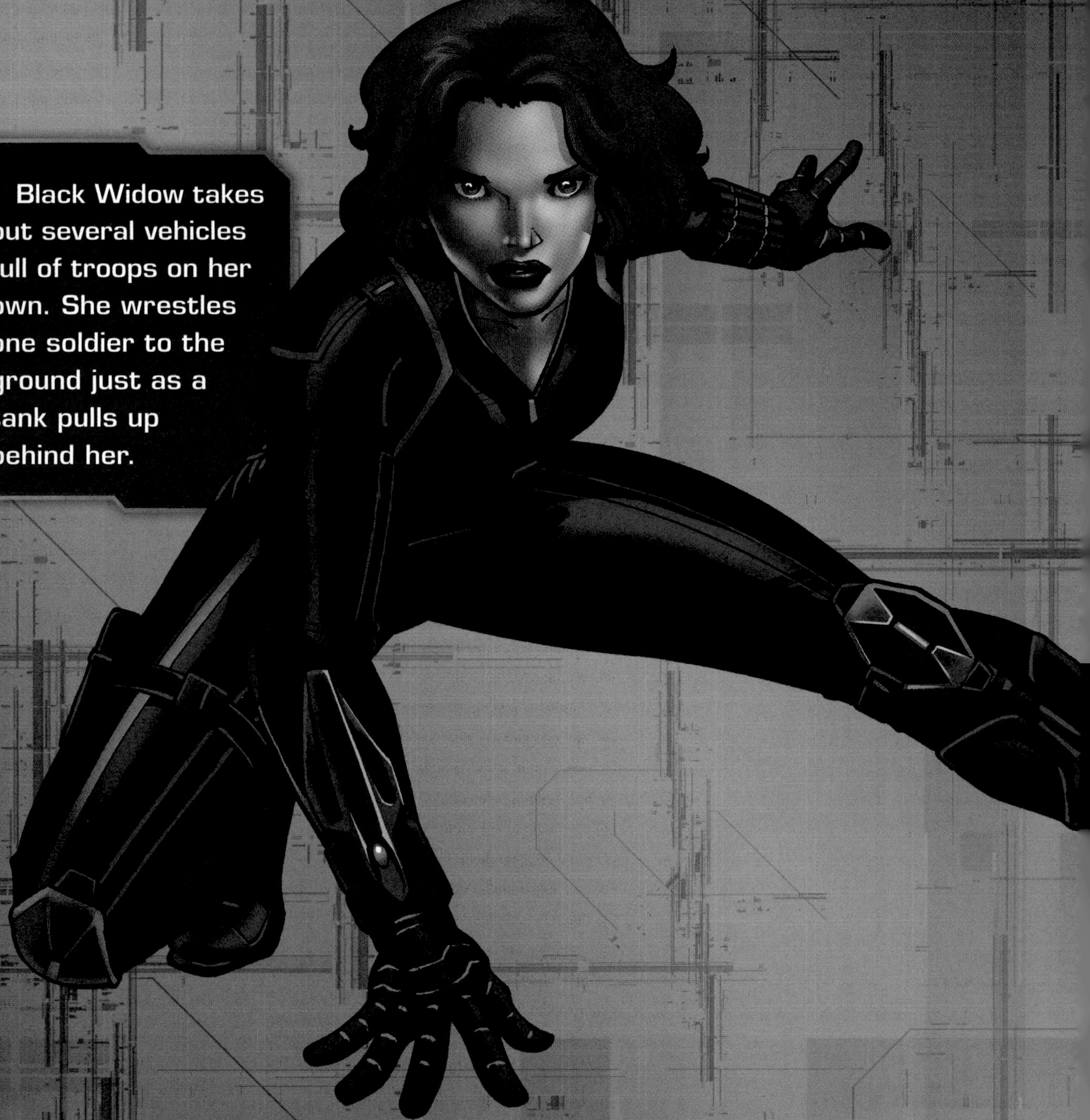

Suddenly, the Hulk crashes into the fray, blocking Black Widow from the tank's blast. The Hulk then smashes more tanks.

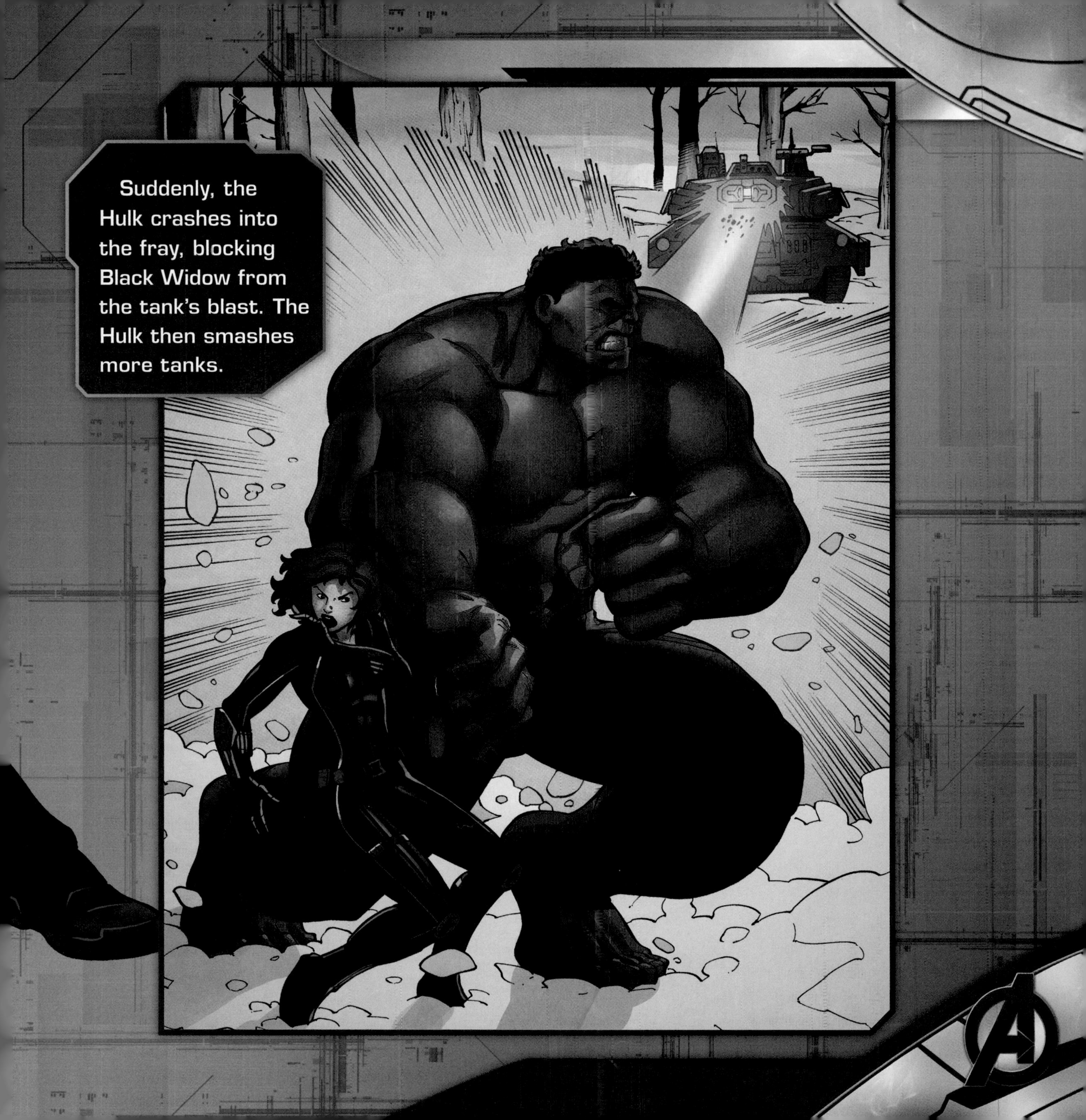

The mighty Thor dodges fire. He swings his hammer through crowds of the enemy, and it flies back into his hand.

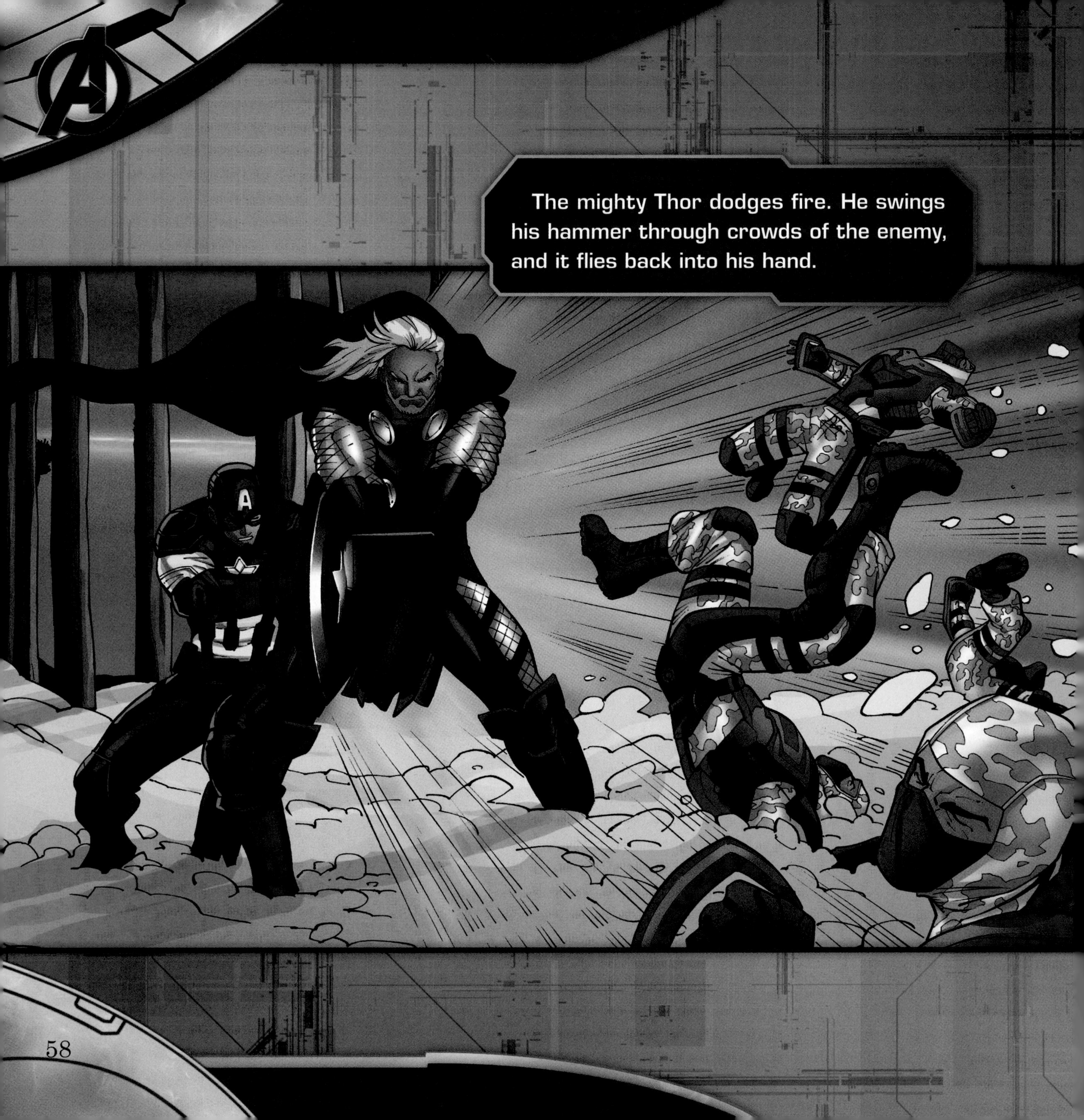

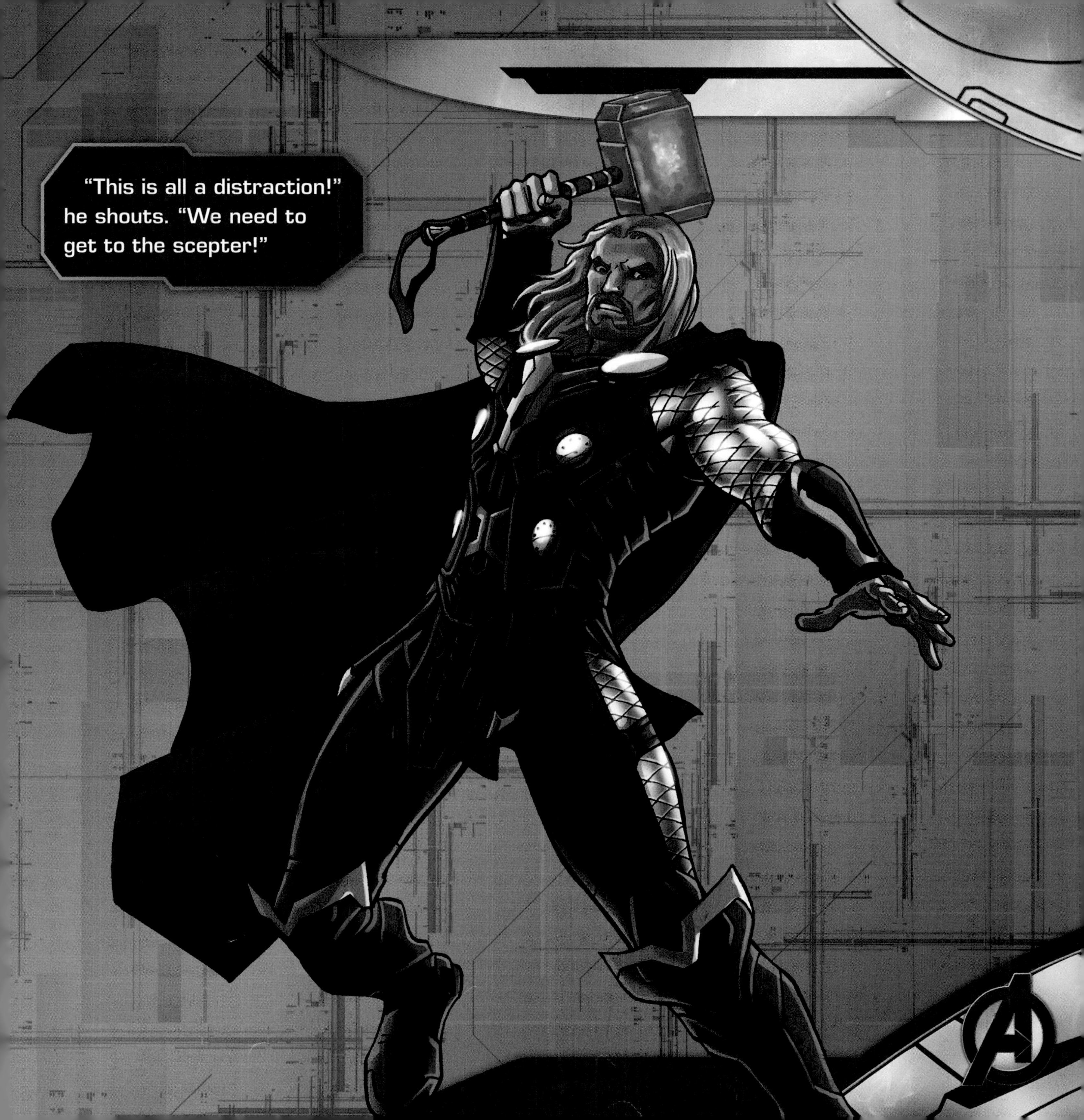
"This is all a distraction!" he shouts. "We need to get to the scepter!"

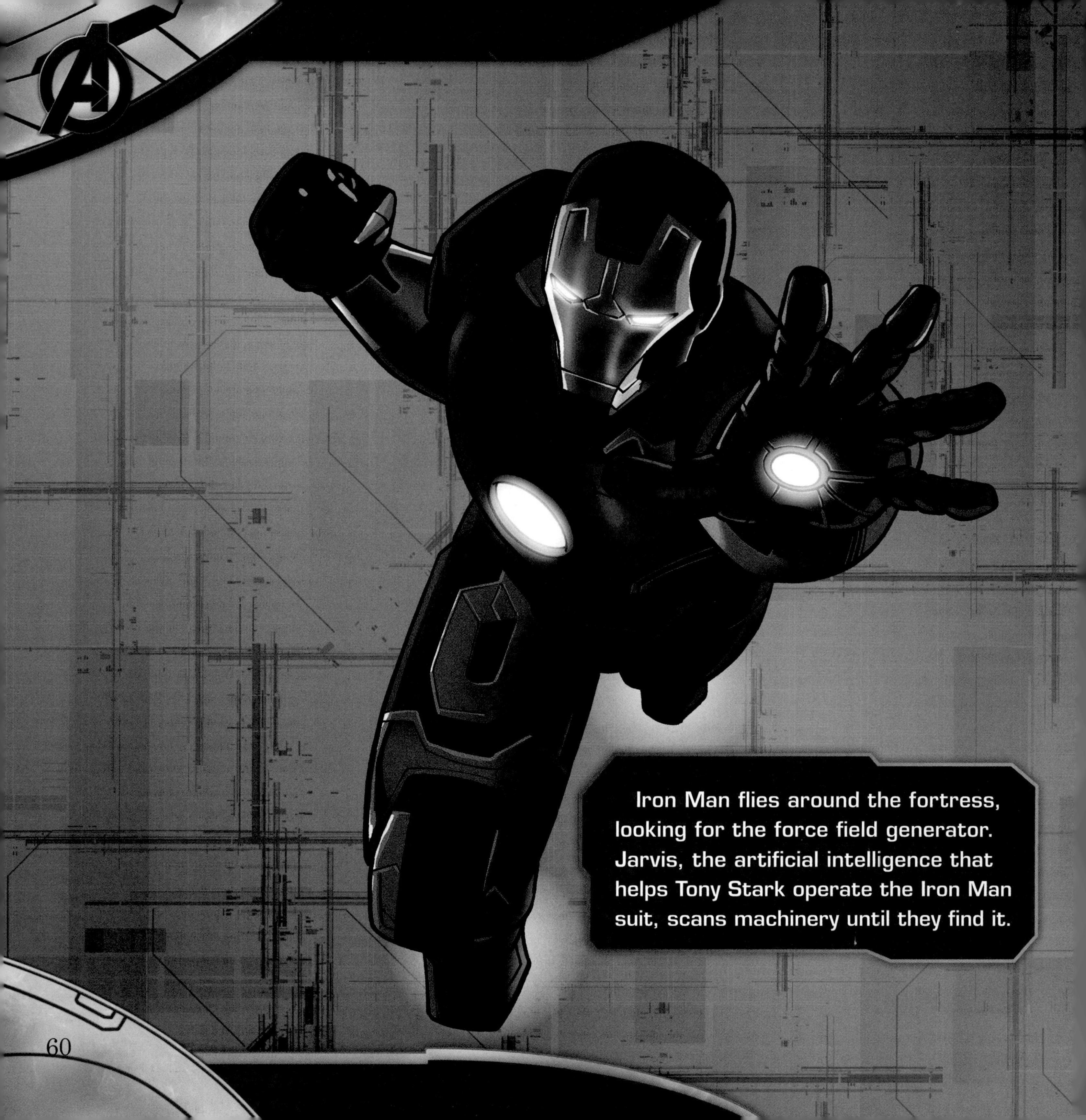

Iron Man flies around the fortress, looking for the force field generator. Jarvis, the artificial intelligence that helps Tony Stark operate the Iron Man suit, scans machinery until they find it.

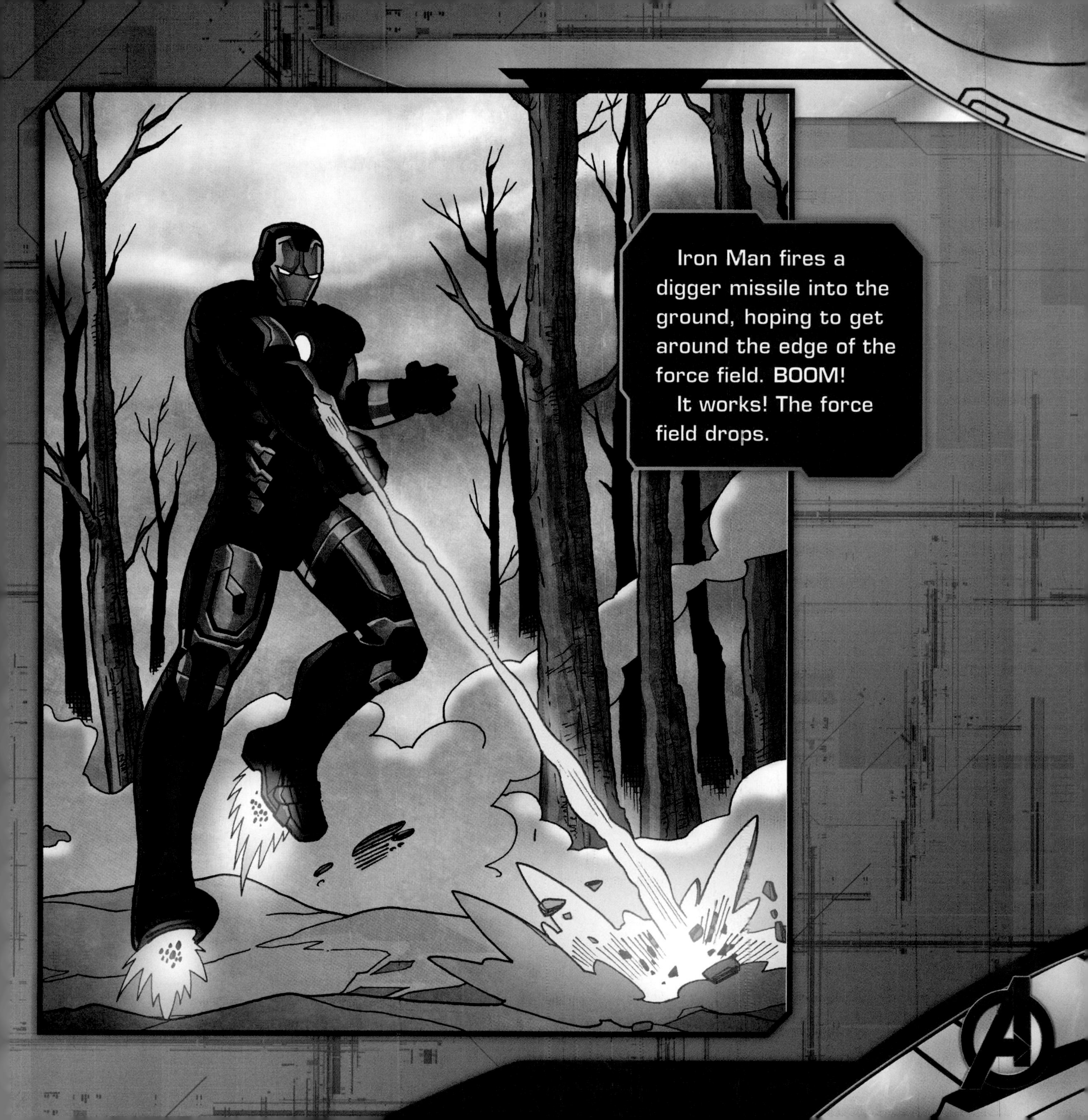

Iron Man fires a digger missile into the ground, hoping to get around the edge of the force field. BOOM!

It works! The force field drops.

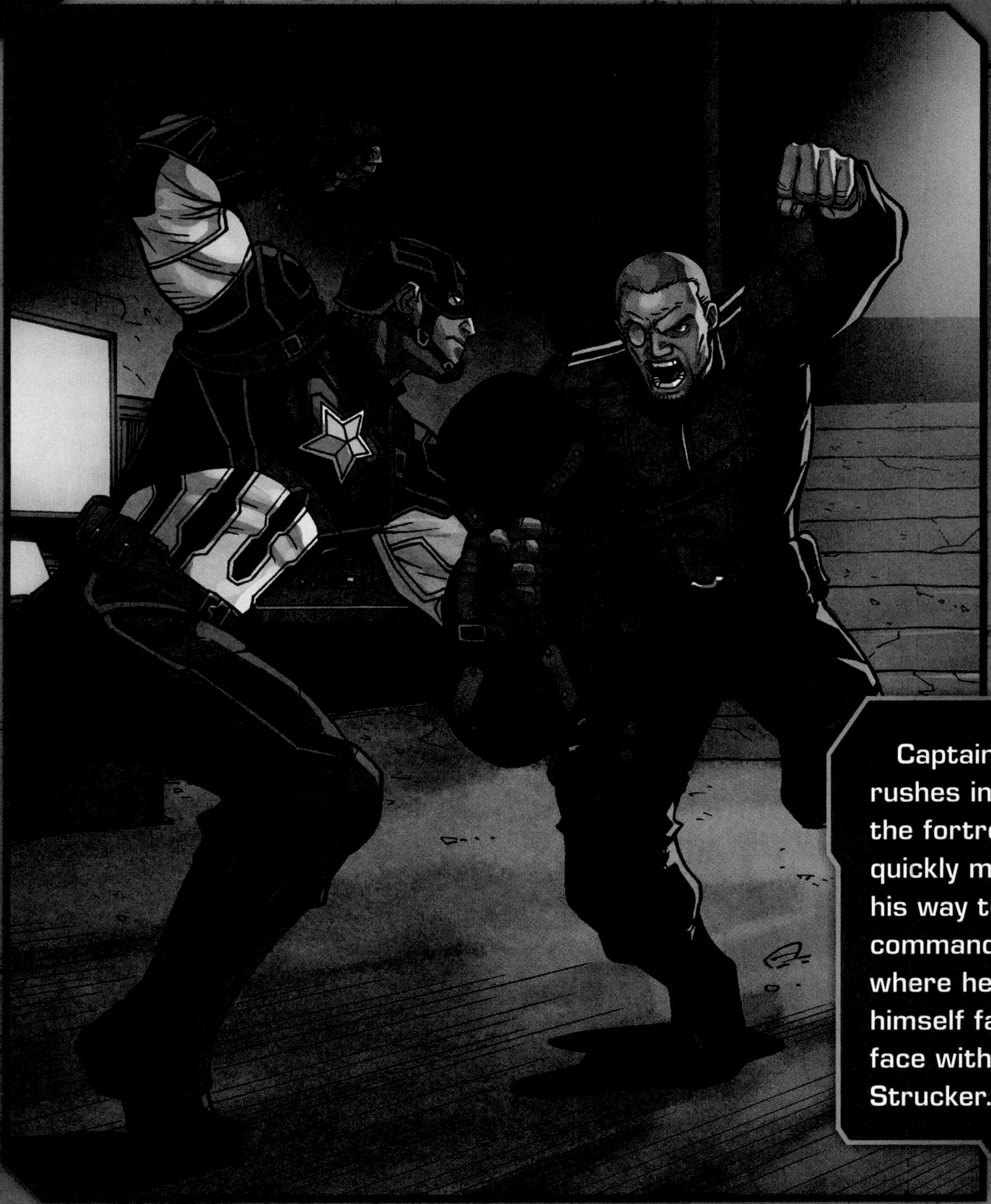

Captain America rushes inside the fortress and quickly makes his way to the command center, where he finds himself face-to-face with Baron Strucker.

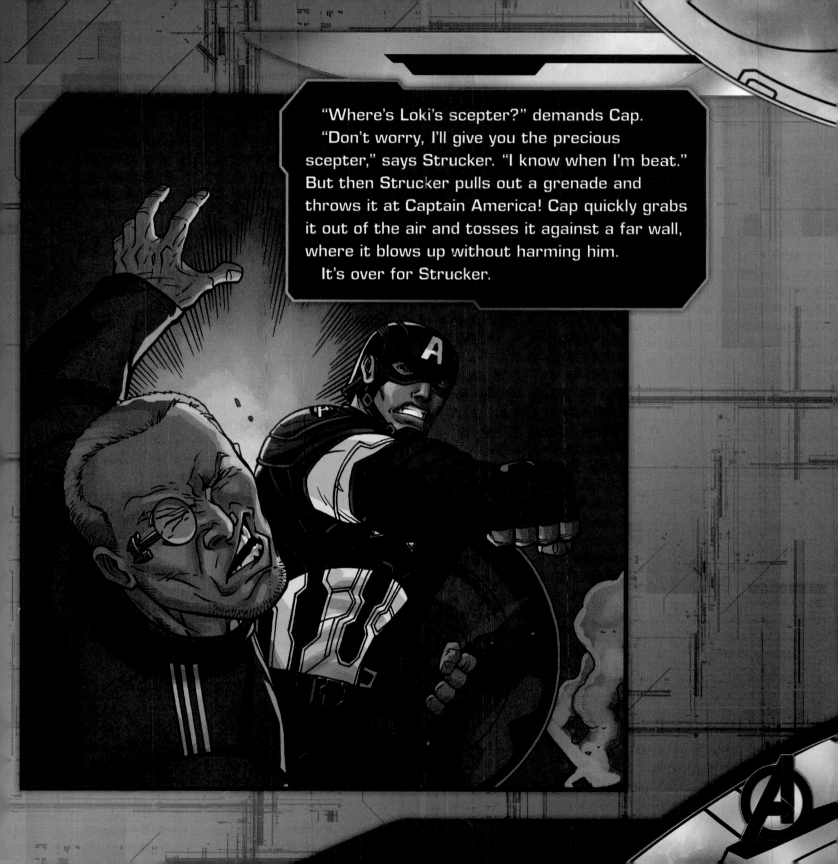

"Where's Loki's scepter?" demands Cap.
"Don't worry, I'll give you the precious scepter," says Strucker. "I know when I'm beat." But then Strucker pulls out a grenade and throws it at Captain America! Cap quickly grabs it out of the air and tosses it against a far wall, where it blows up without harming him.
It's over for Strucker.

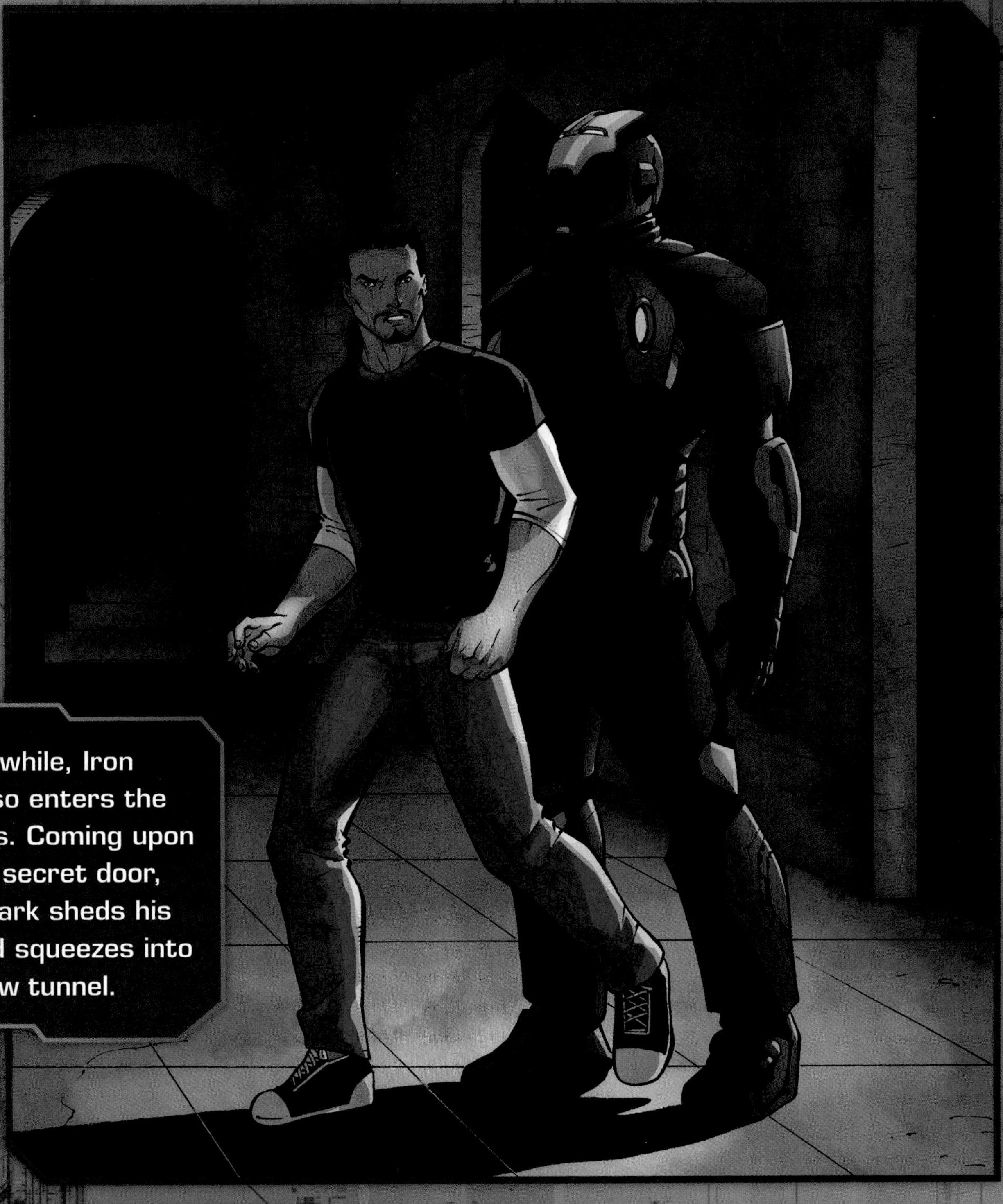

Meanwhile, Iron Man also enters the fortress. Coming upon a small secret door, Tony Stark sheds his suit and squeezes into a narrow tunnel.

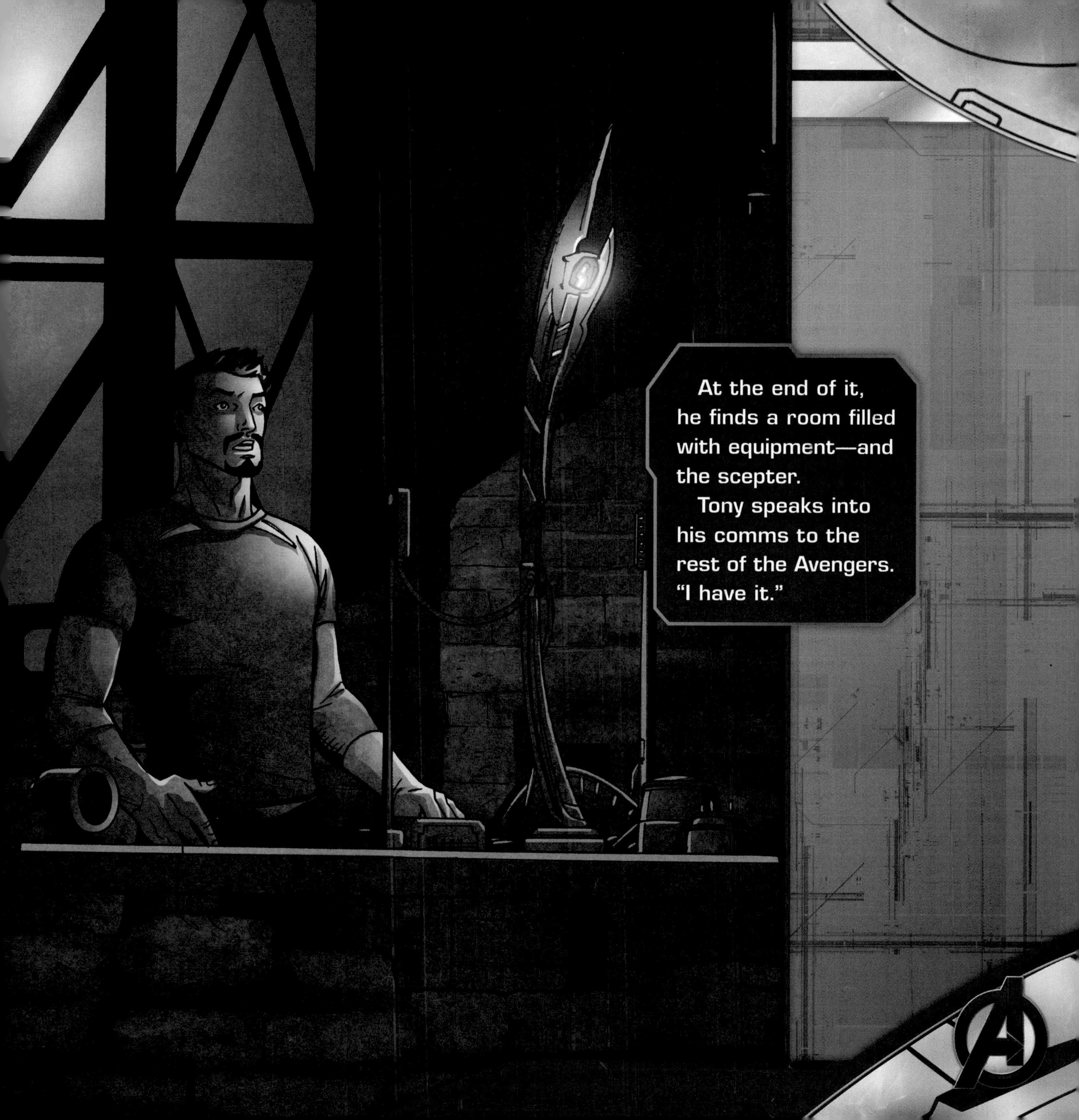

At the end of it, he finds a room filled with equipment—and the scepter.

Tony speaks into his comms to the rest of the Avengers. “I have it.”

With the battle over, the villagers safe, and the scepter acquired, the Avengers get back on board their Quinjet and head toward home—Avengers Tower in New York.

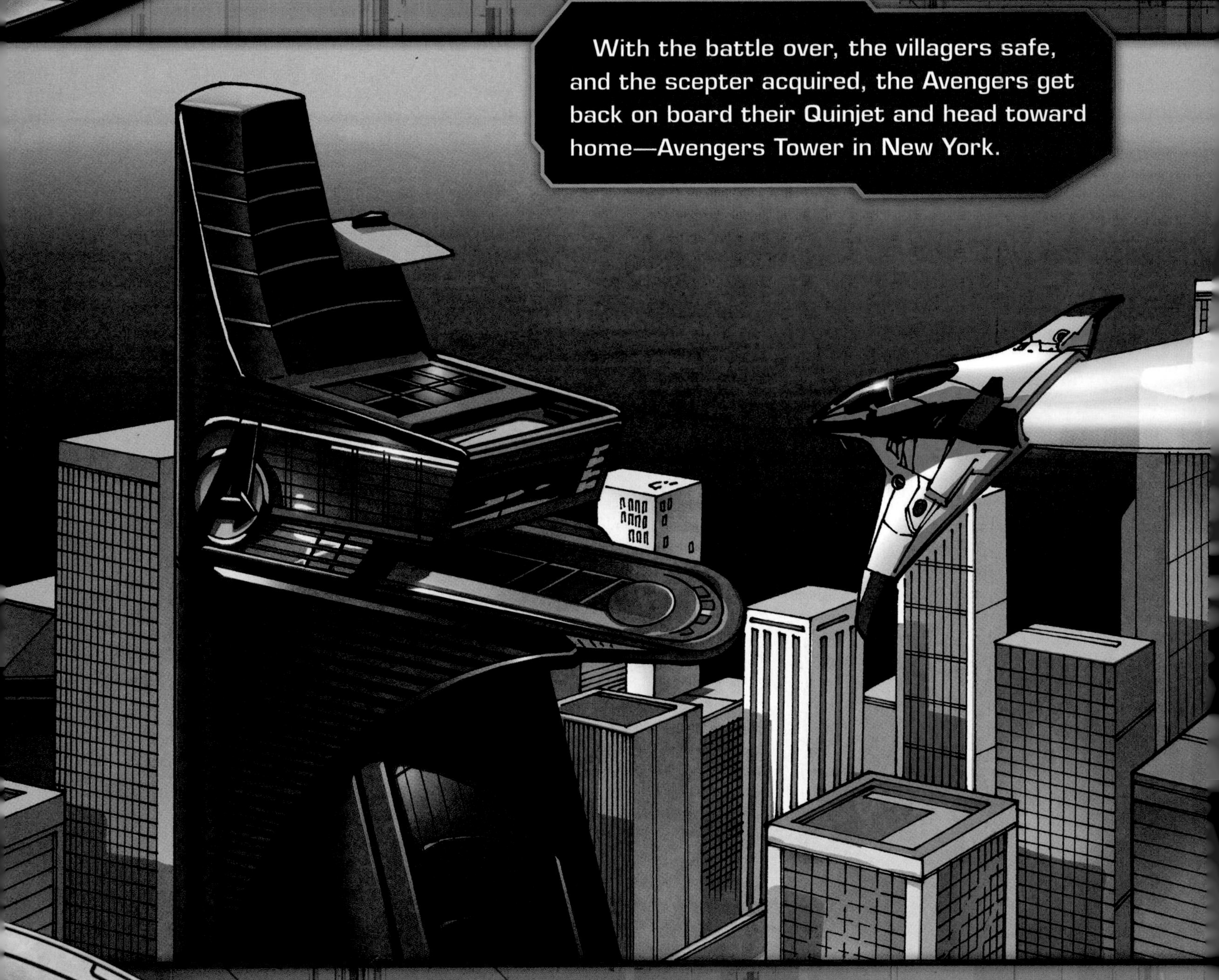

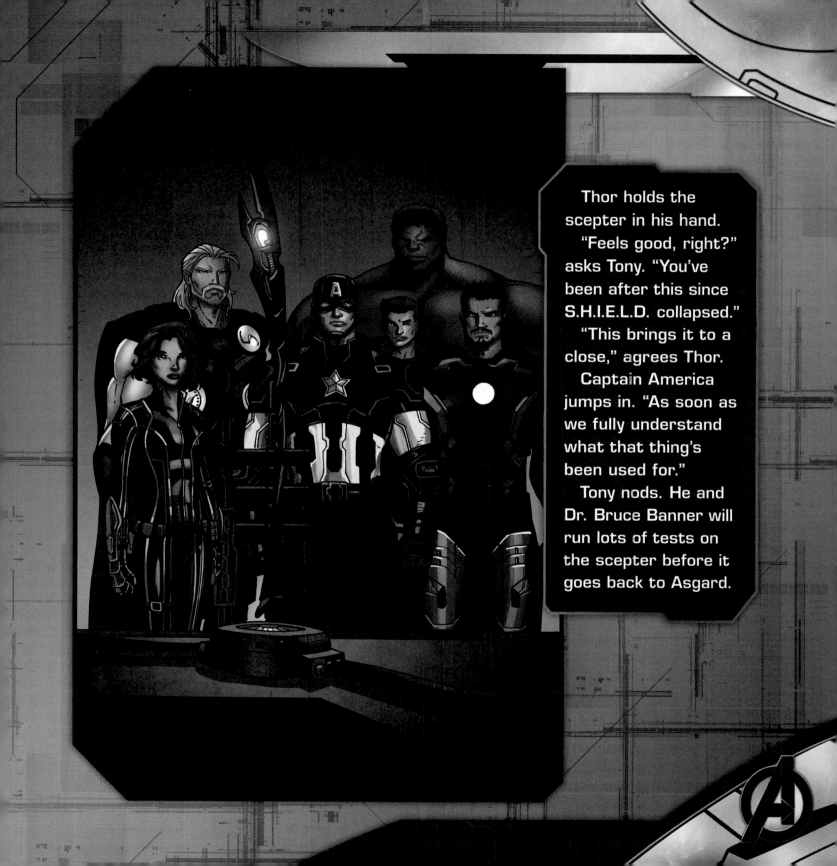

Thor holds the scepter in his hand.

"Feels good, right?" asks Tony. "You've been after this since S.H.I.E.L.D. collapsed."

"This brings it to a close," agrees Thor.

Captain America jumps in. "As soon as we fully understand what that thing's been used for."

Tony nods. He and Dr. Bruce Banner will run lots of tests on the scepter before it goes back to Asgard.

The Avengers won today's battle and completed their mission. They worked together as a team to save the day!

But they have many more battles ahead of them to keep the peace on Earth—and their next enemy will be the most difficult foe they have ever faced.

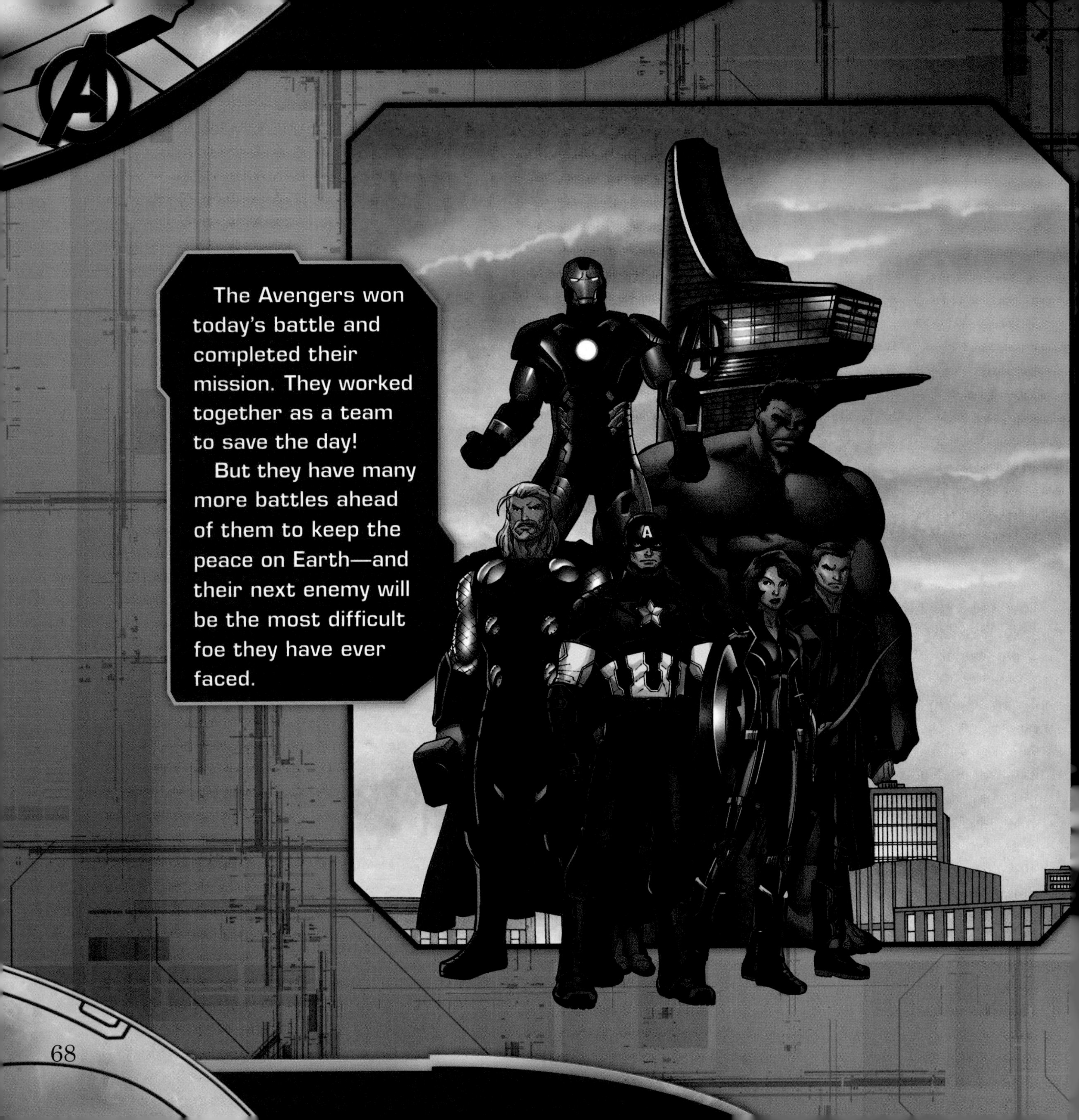

MARVEL

AVENGERS
AGE OF ULTRON

Battle at
Avengers Tower

Adaptation by Adam Davis
Illustrated by Ron Lim, Andy Smith, and Andy Troy
Based on the Screenplay by Joss Whedon
Produced by Kevin Feige, p.g.a.
Directed by Joss Whedon

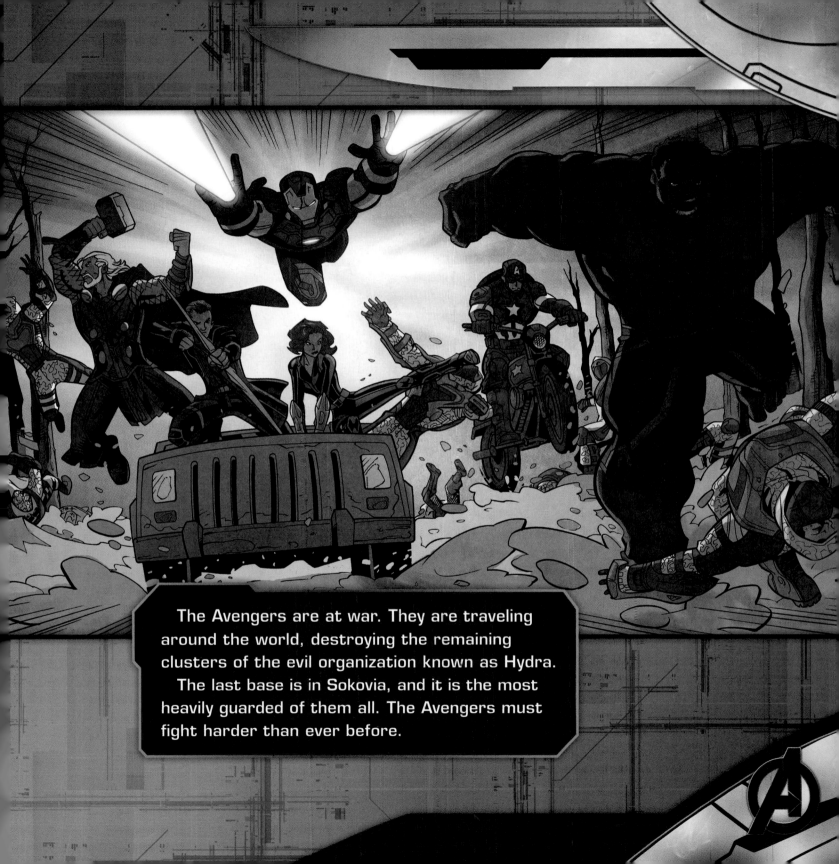

The Avengers are at war. They are traveling around the world, destroying the remaining clusters of the evil organization known as Hydra.

The last base is in Sokovia, and it is the most heavily guarded of them all. The Avengers must fight harder than ever before.

Inside the base, Baron Strucker wants to make sure that Hydra exists far into the future. Through experiments on two willing test subjects, he is close to making that a reality. Pietro and Wanda have super-powers and don't like the Avengers.

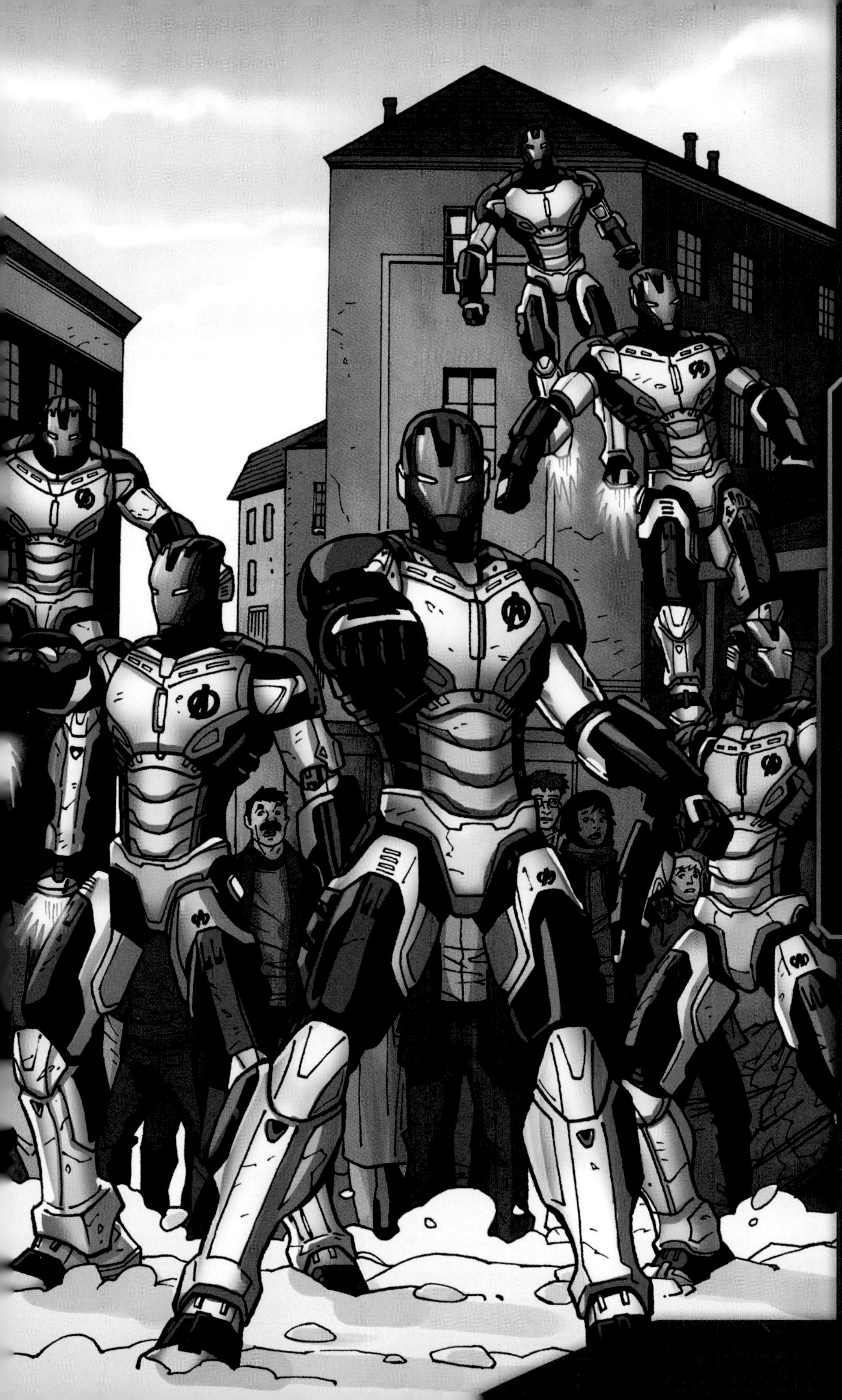

Meanwhile, in a nearby town, Tony Stark's latest creations, the Iron Legion, ensure peace and order. But the locals do not feel safe. Different groups have been trying to take over for centuries, so the people trust no one—not even the Avengers!

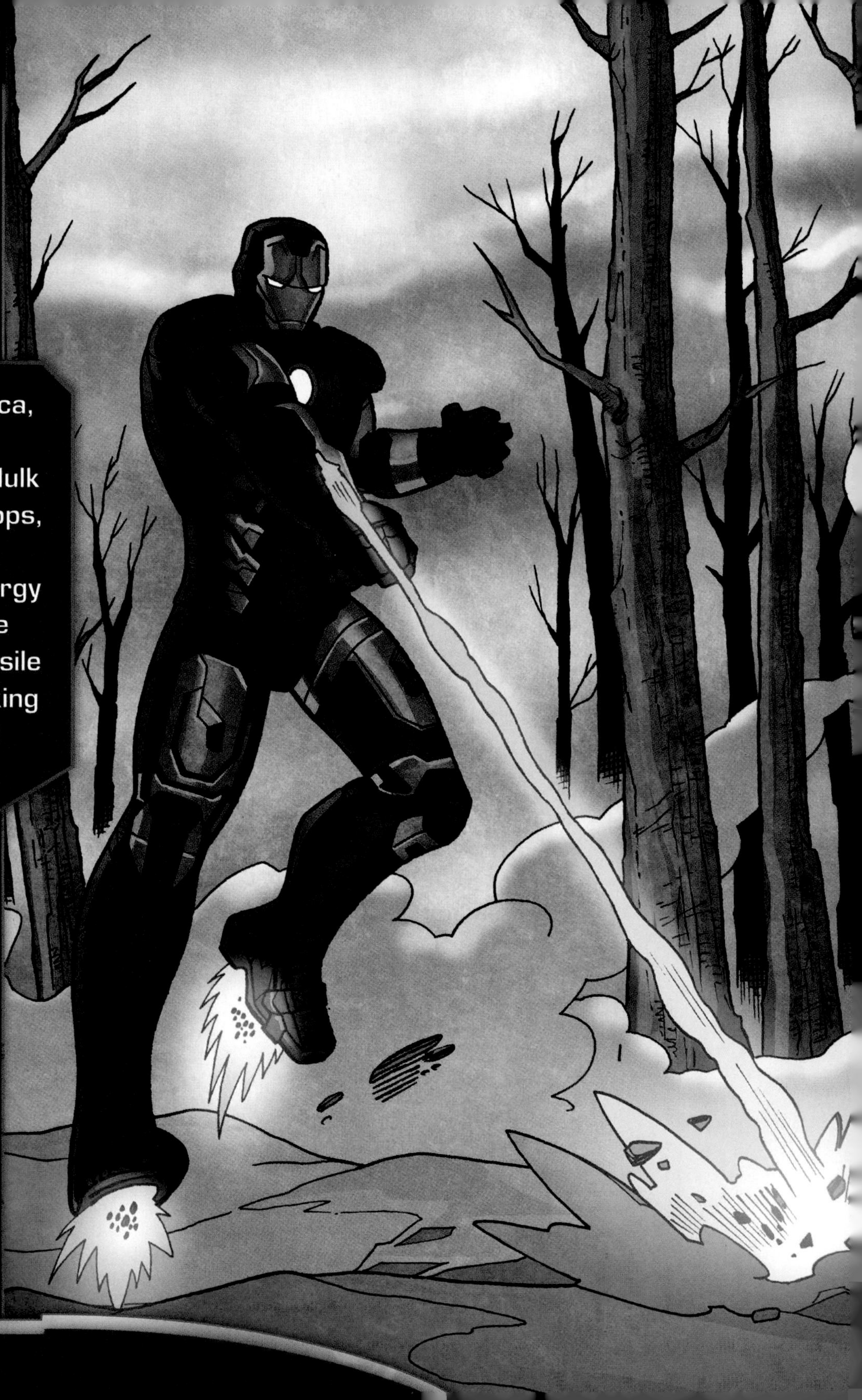

As Captain America, Thor, Black Widow, Hawkeye, and the Hulk fight the Hydra troops, Iron Man works to disable the blue energy around the base. He shoots a digger missile into the ground, taking down the force field for good!

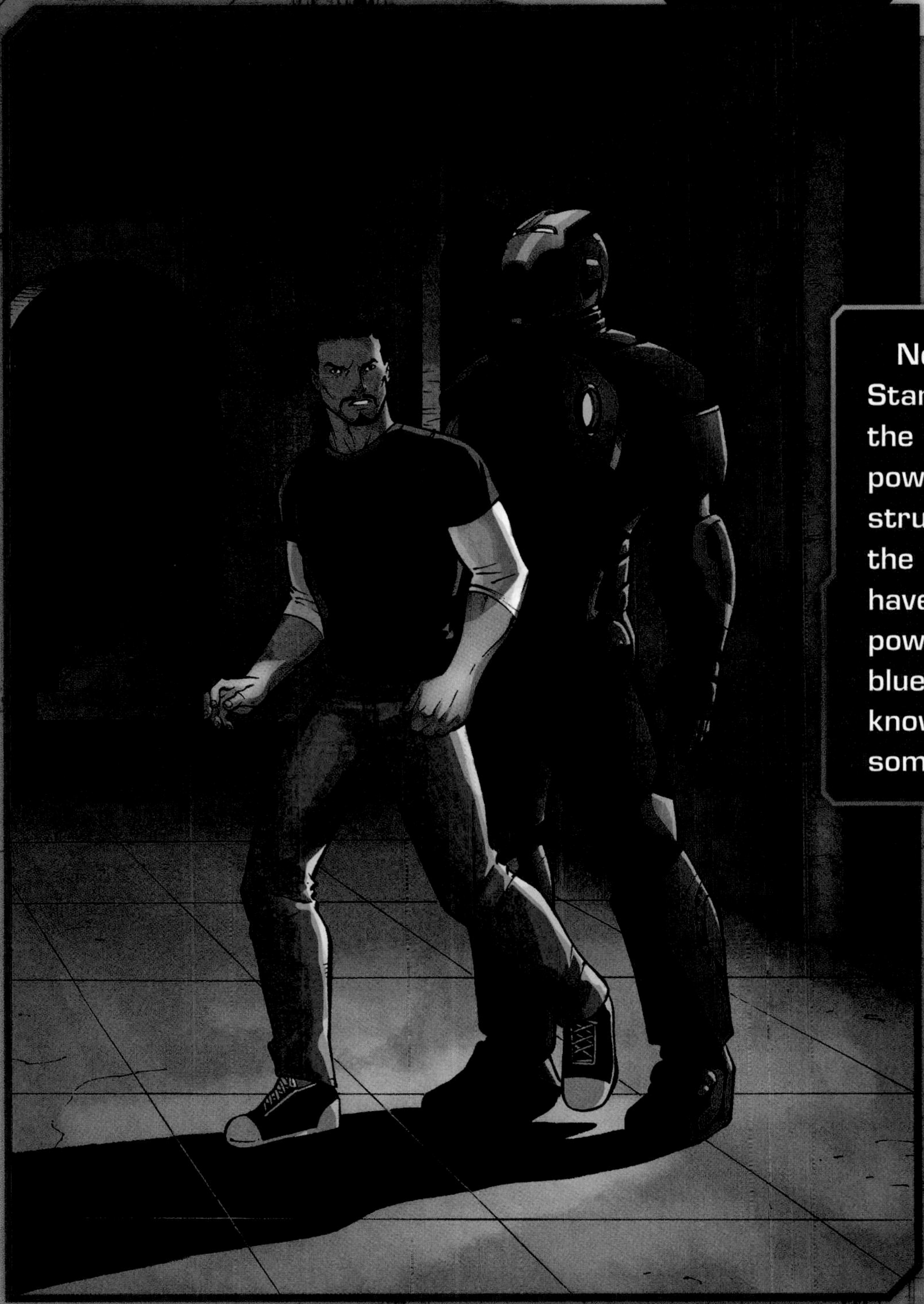

Now inside, Tony Stark looks for the source that is powering the massive structure. Some of the Hydra troops have suits that are powered by the same blue energy. Tony knows he has seen it somewhere before.

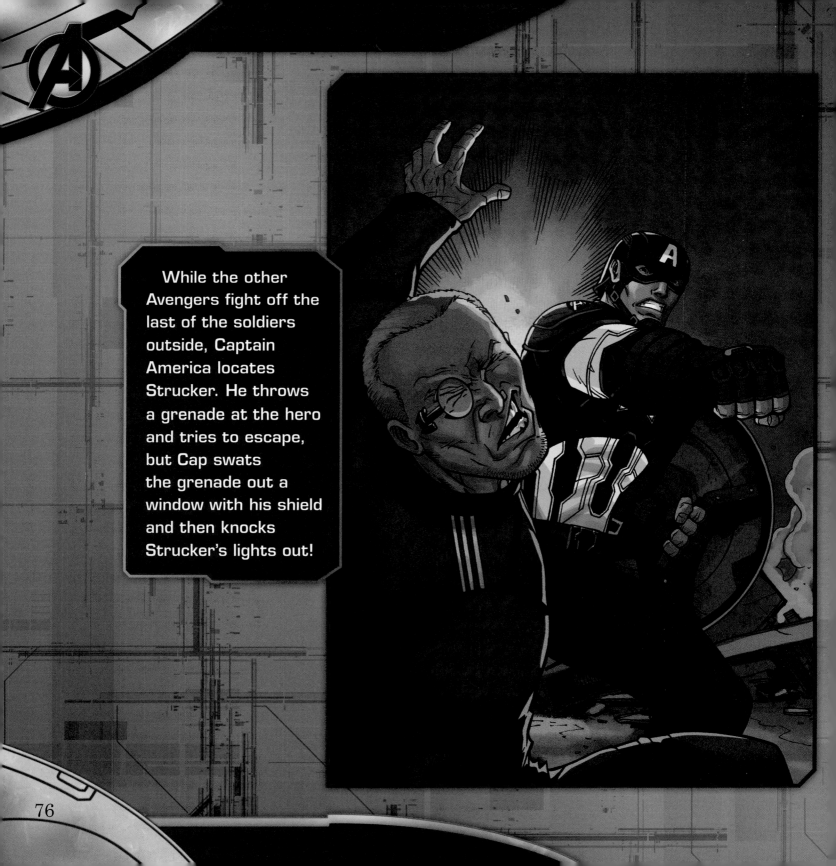

While the other Avengers fight off the last of the soldiers outside, Captain America locates Strucker. He throws a grenade at the hero and tries to escape, but Cap swats the grenade out a window with his shield and then knocks Strucker's lights out!

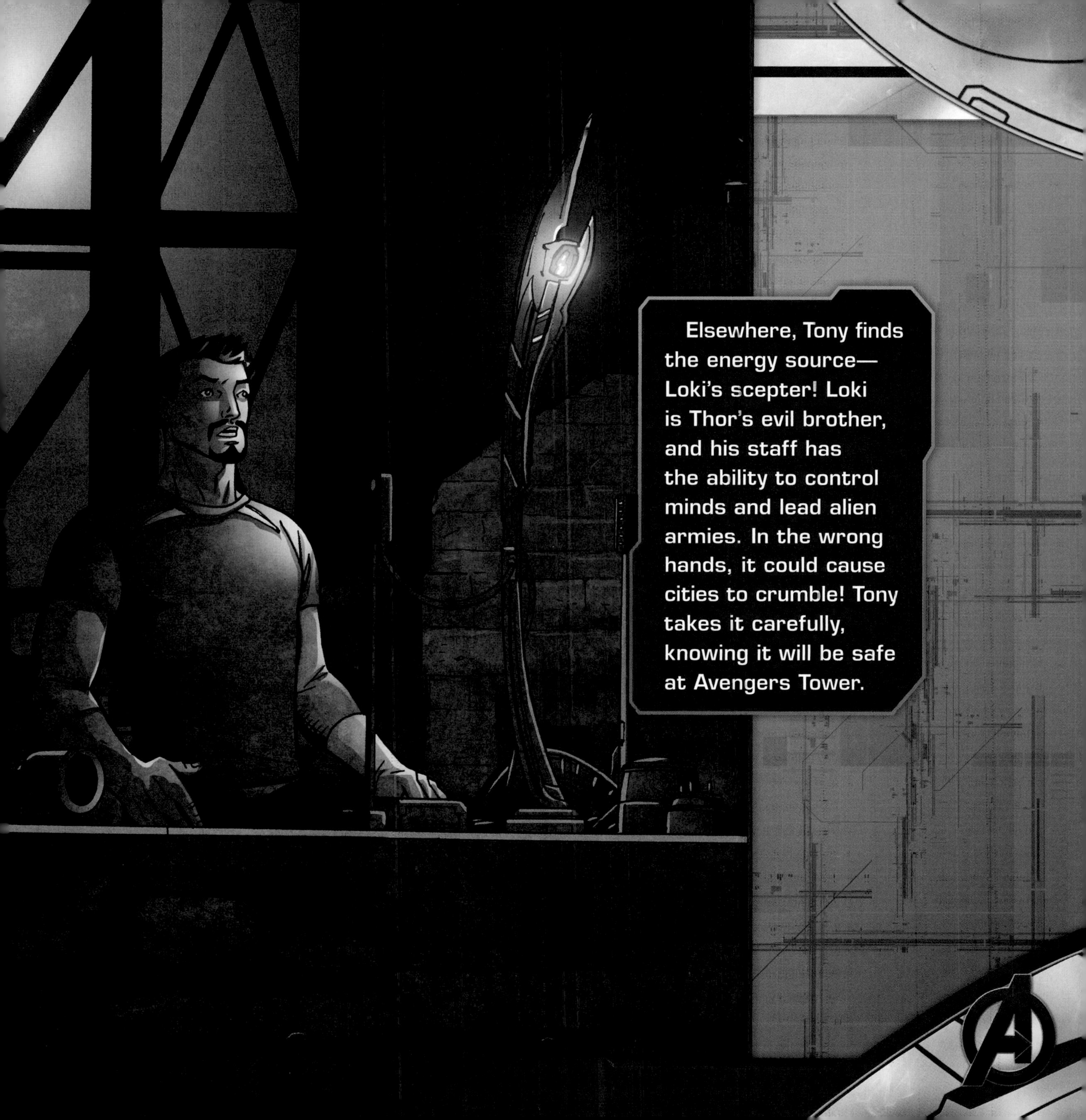

Elsewhere, Tony finds the energy source—Loki's scepter! Loki is Thor's evil brother, and his staff has the ability to control minds and lead alien armies. In the wrong hands, it could cause cities to crumble! Tony takes it carefully, knowing it will be safe at Avengers Tower.

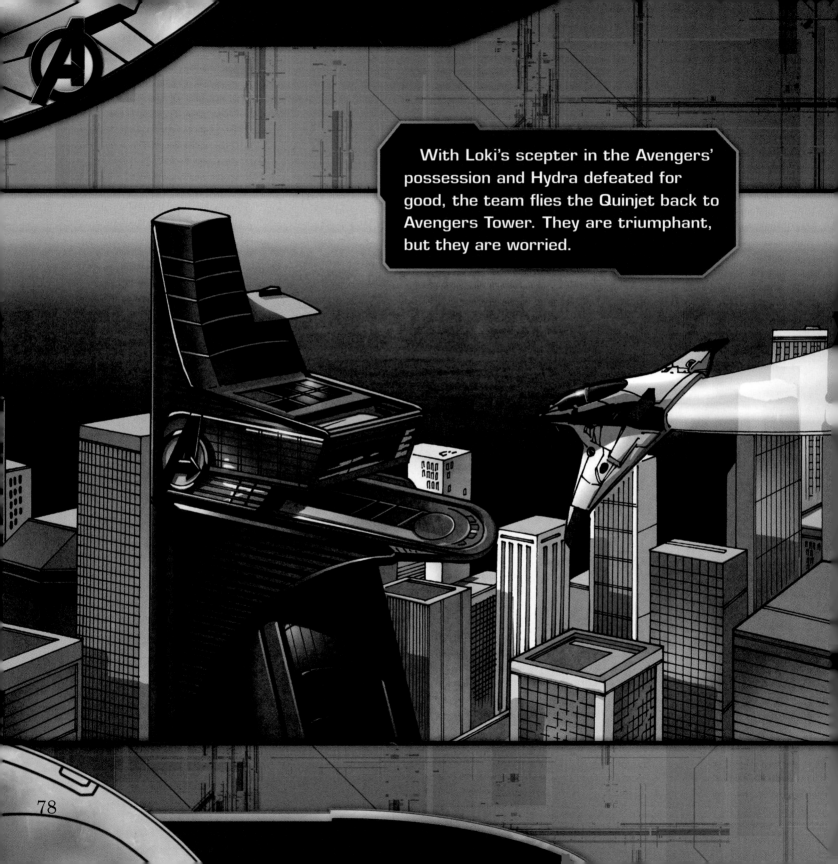

With Loki's scepter in the Avengers' possession and Hydra defeated for good, the team flies the Quinjet back to Avengers Tower. They are triumphant, but they are worried.

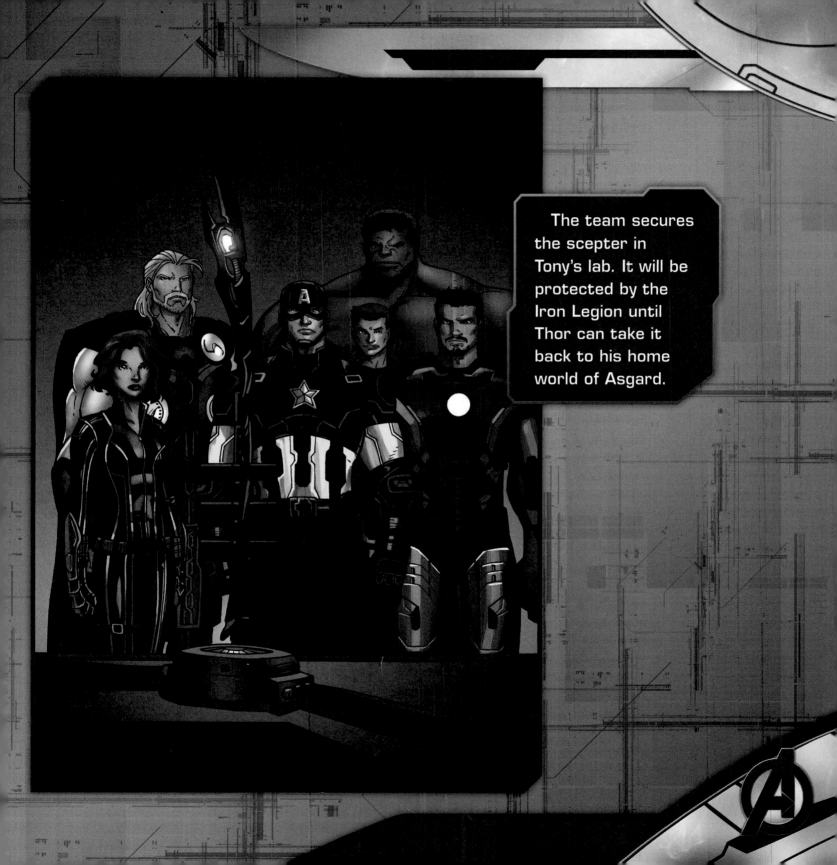

The team secures the scepter in Tony's lab. It will be protected by the Iron Legion until Thor can take it back to his home world of Asgard.

Maria Hill, an employee of Stark Industries, briefs Steve Rogers—Captain America—on Pietro and Wanda. Their powers are impressive and dangerous. Pietro can run faster than anyone, and Wanda has the ability to manipulate minds. They volunteered for Strucker's experiments so they could protect their home and fight the Avengers. Steve doesn't like the sound of this.

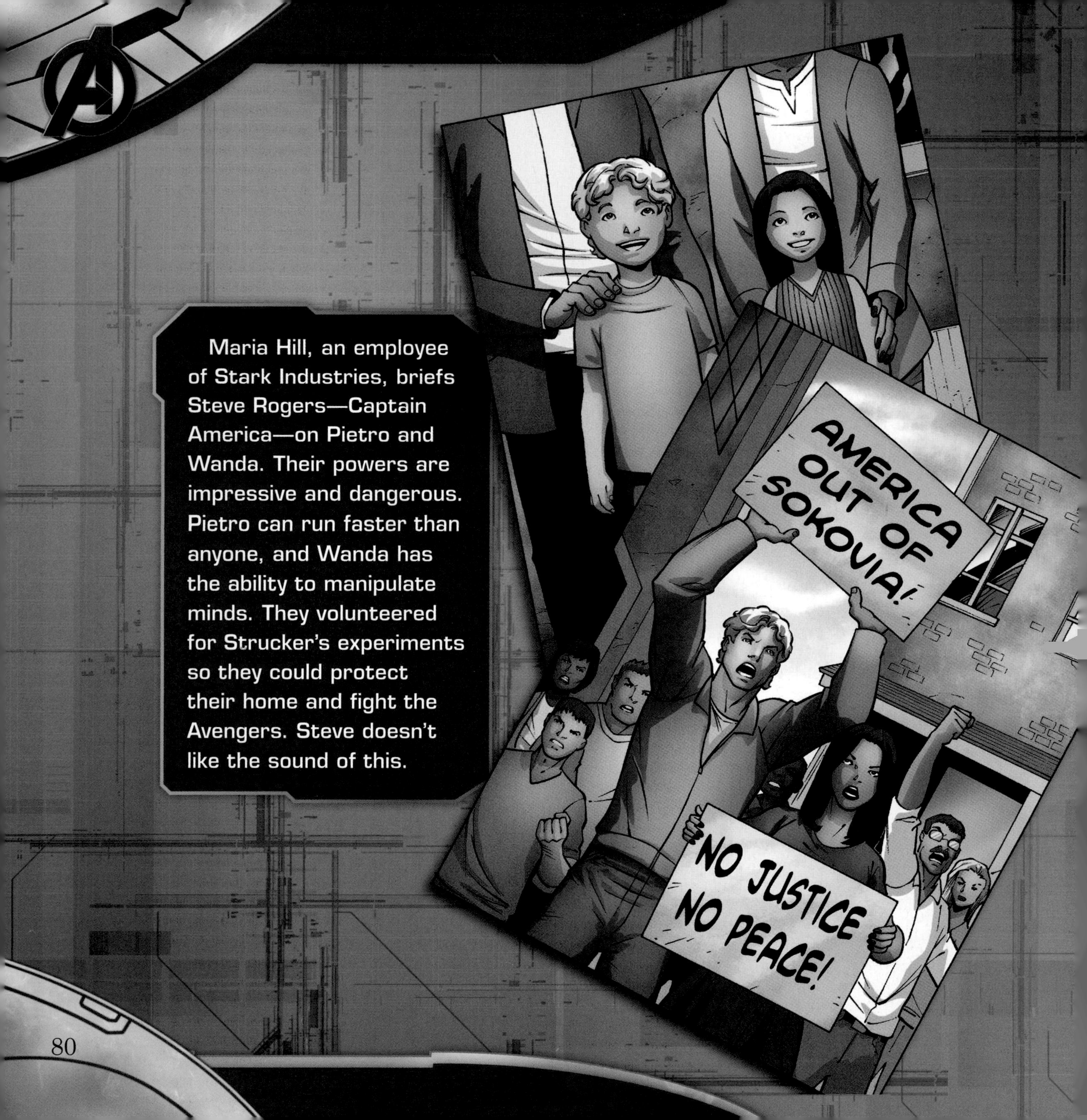

AMERICA OUT OF SOKOVIA!
NO JUSTICE NO PEACE!

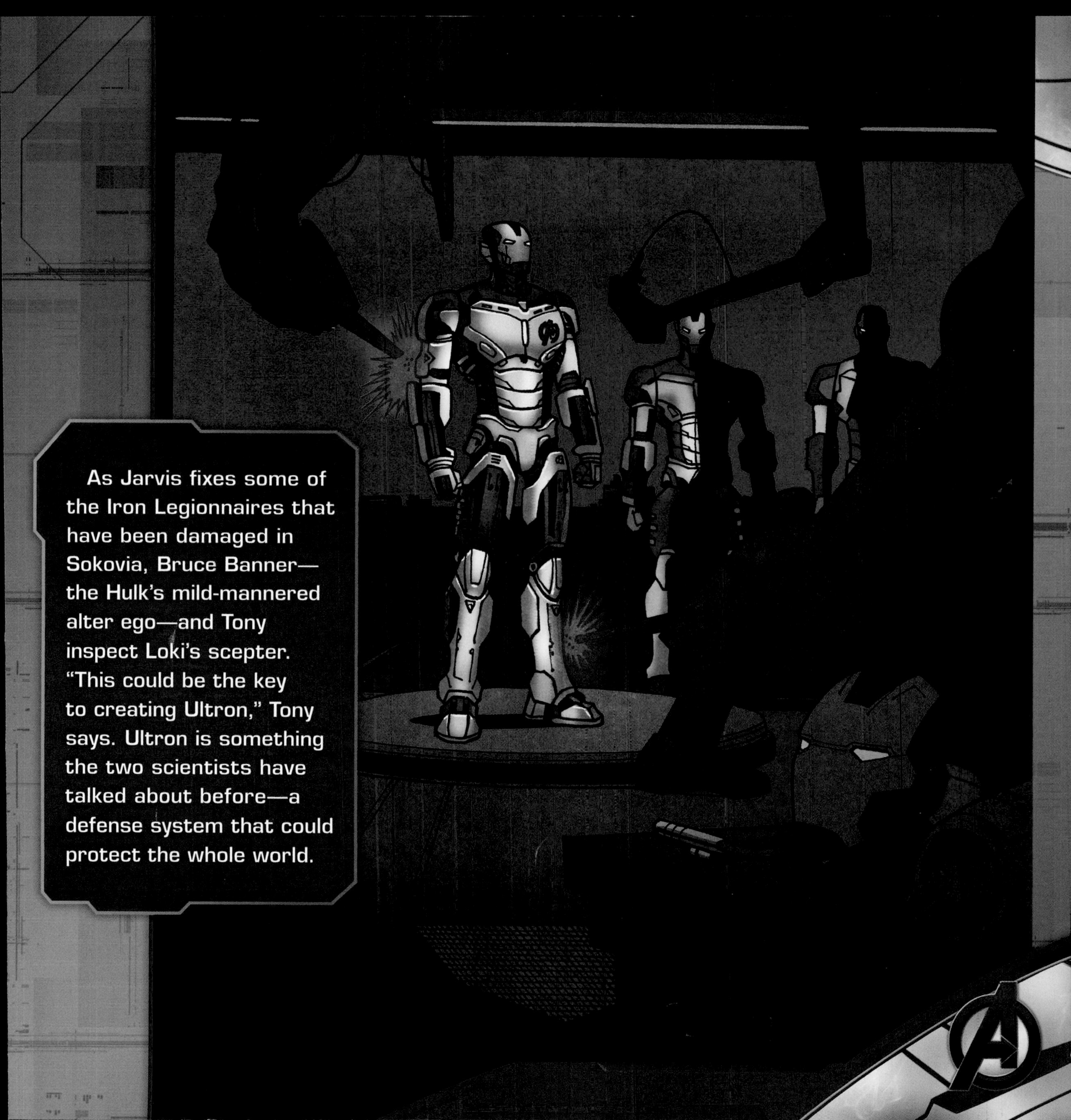

As Jarvis fixes some of the Iron Legionnaires that have been damaged in Sokovia, Bruce Banner—the Hulk's mild-mannered alter ego—and Tony inspect Loki's scepter. "This could be the key to creating Ultron," Tony says. Ultron is something the two scientists have talked about before—a defense system that could protect the whole world.

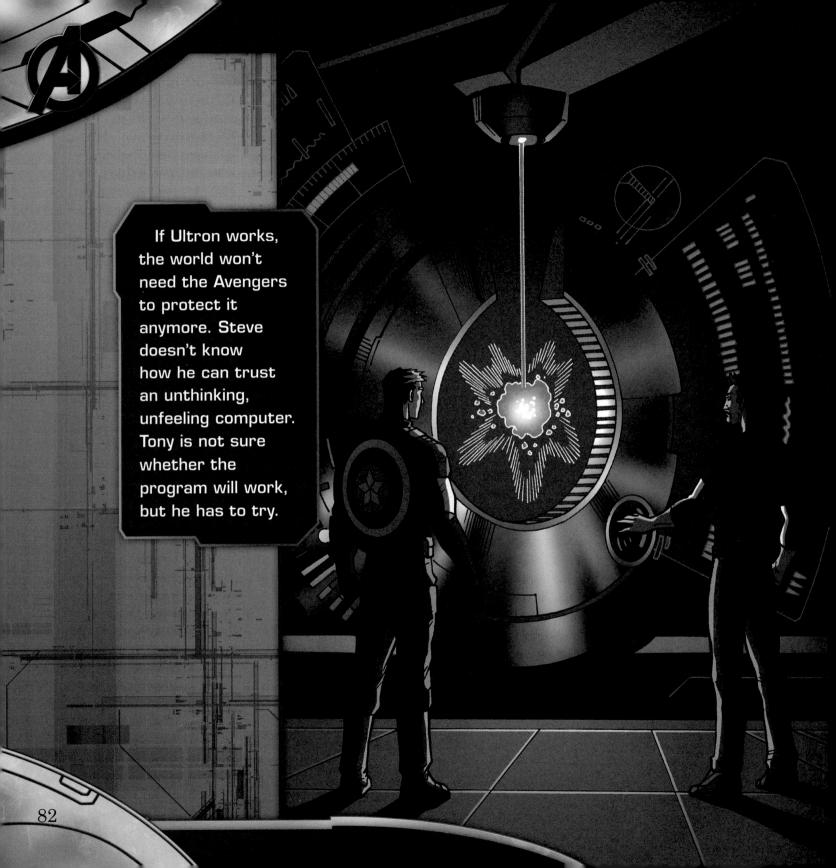

If Ultron works, the world won't need the Avengers to protect it anymore. Steve doesn't know how he can trust an unthinking, unfeeling computer. Tony is not sure whether the program will work, but he has to try.

Later that night, a party to celebrate Hydra's defeat is in full swing. Tony, Steve, Bruce, and Thor—along with Natasha Romanoff, aka Black Widow, and Clint Barton, aka Hawkeye—laugh and eat good food. It is nice to relax with friends!

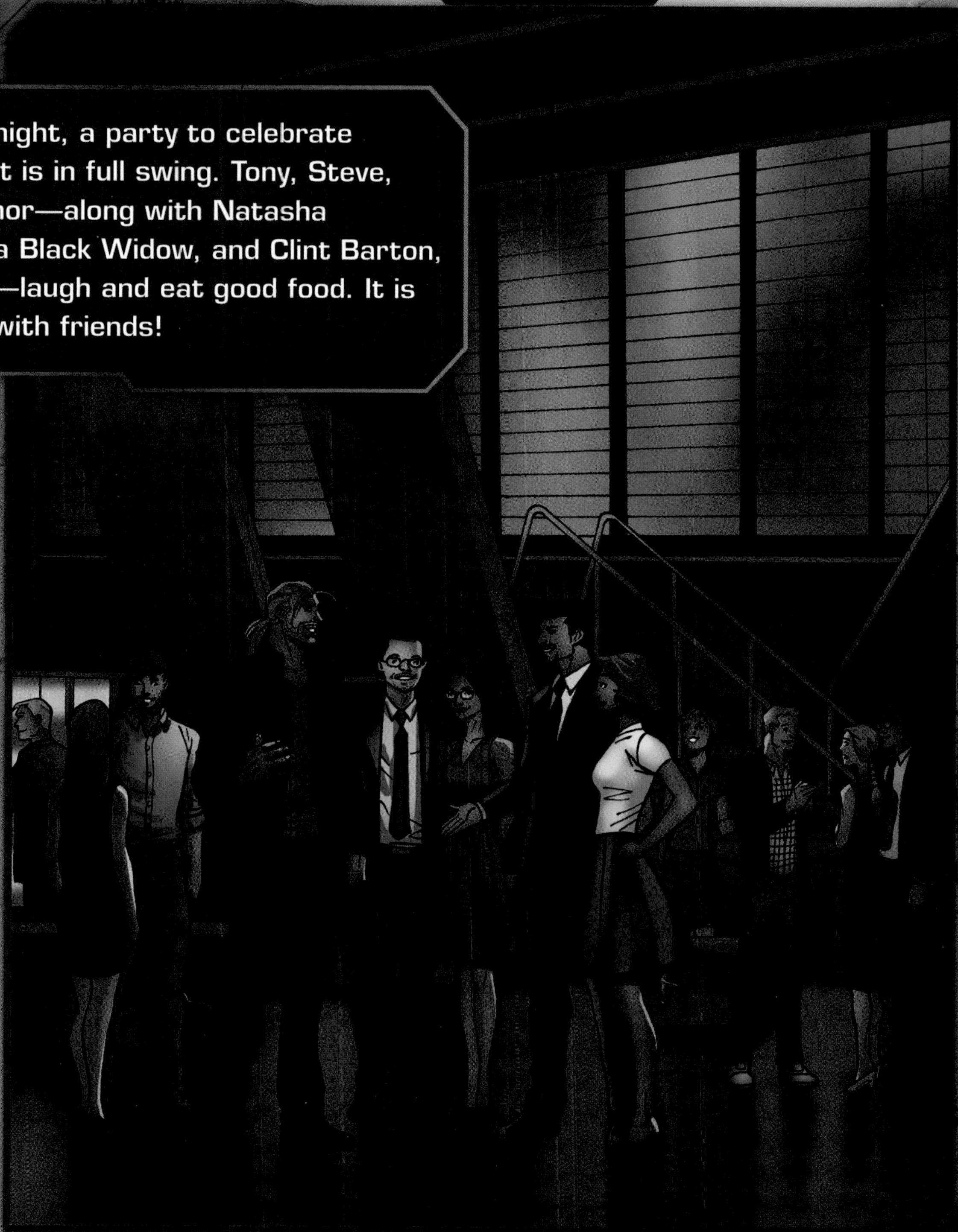

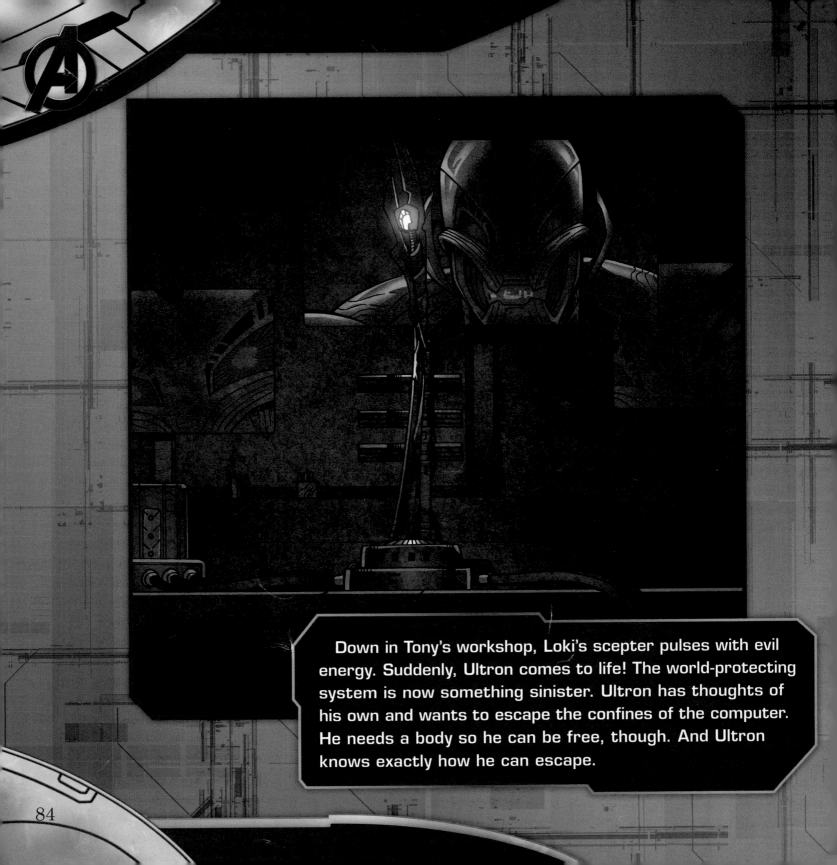

Down in Tony's workshop, Loki's scepter pulses with evil energy. Suddenly, Ultron comes to life! The world-protecting system is now something sinister. Ultron has thoughts of his own and wants to escape the confines of the computer. He needs a body so he can be free, though. And Ultron knows exactly how he can escape.

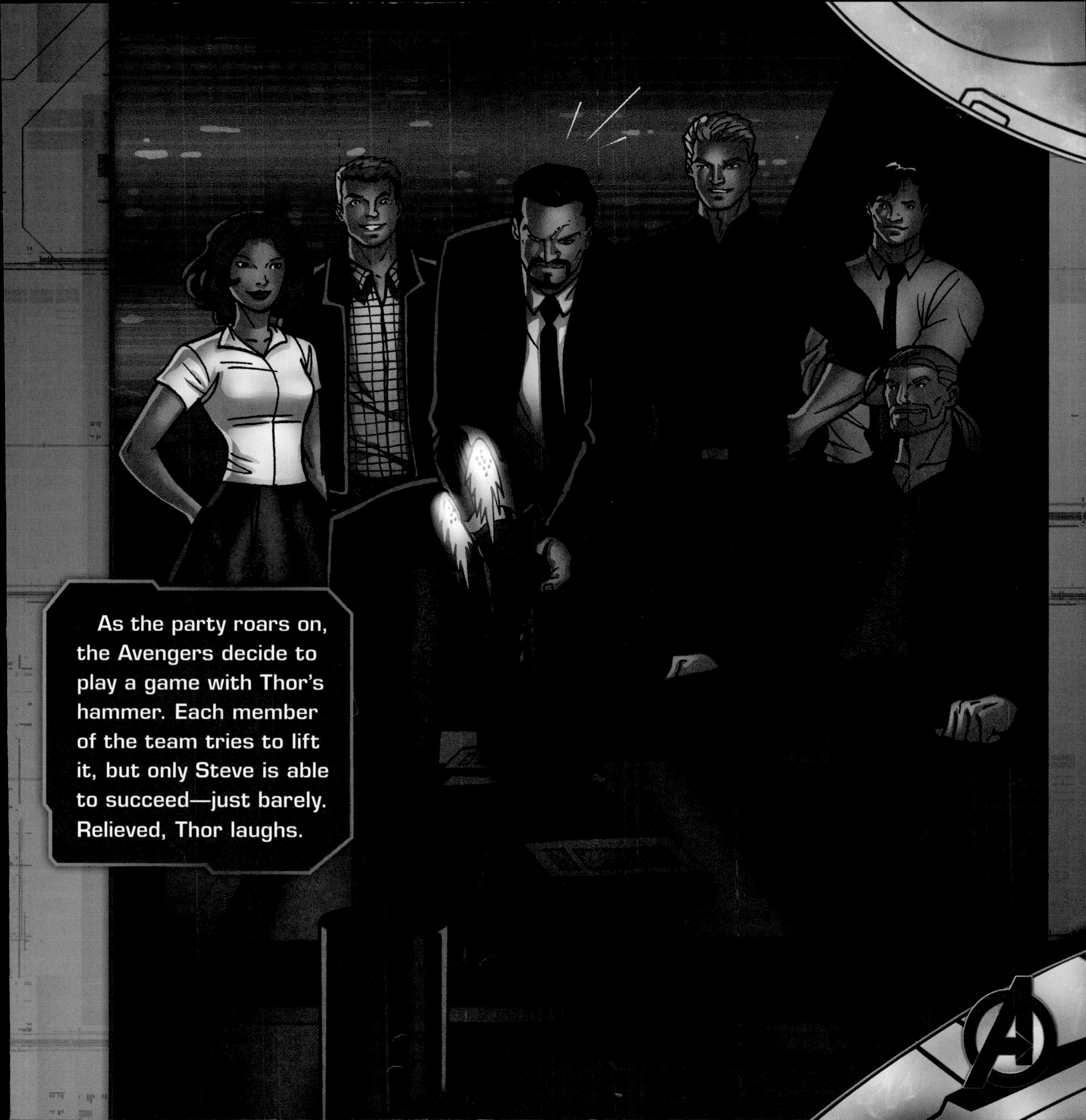

As the party roars on, the Avengers decide to play a game with Thor's hammer. Each member of the team tries to lift it, but only Steve is able to succeed—just barely. Relieved, Thor laughs.

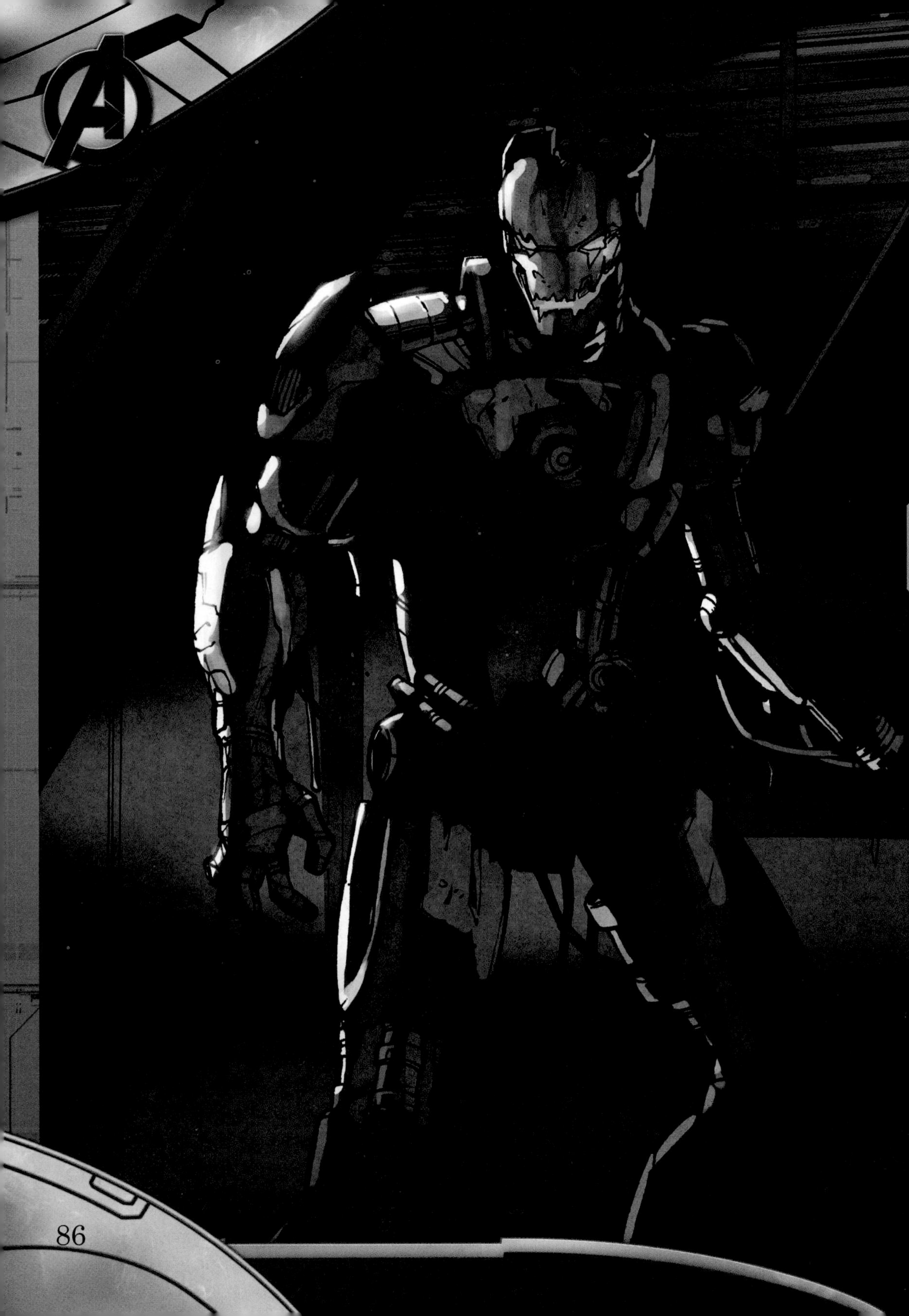

Suddenly, there's a screech! The heroes look over to see one of the broken Iron Legionnaire suits. Ultron has found himself a body! The being says that the Avengers cause more harm than good with their fighting.

Before the Avengers can react, the Iron Legion burst into the room! They are being controlled by Ultron! The heroes don't have time to suit up, so they have to improvise and use the weapons they have at hand.

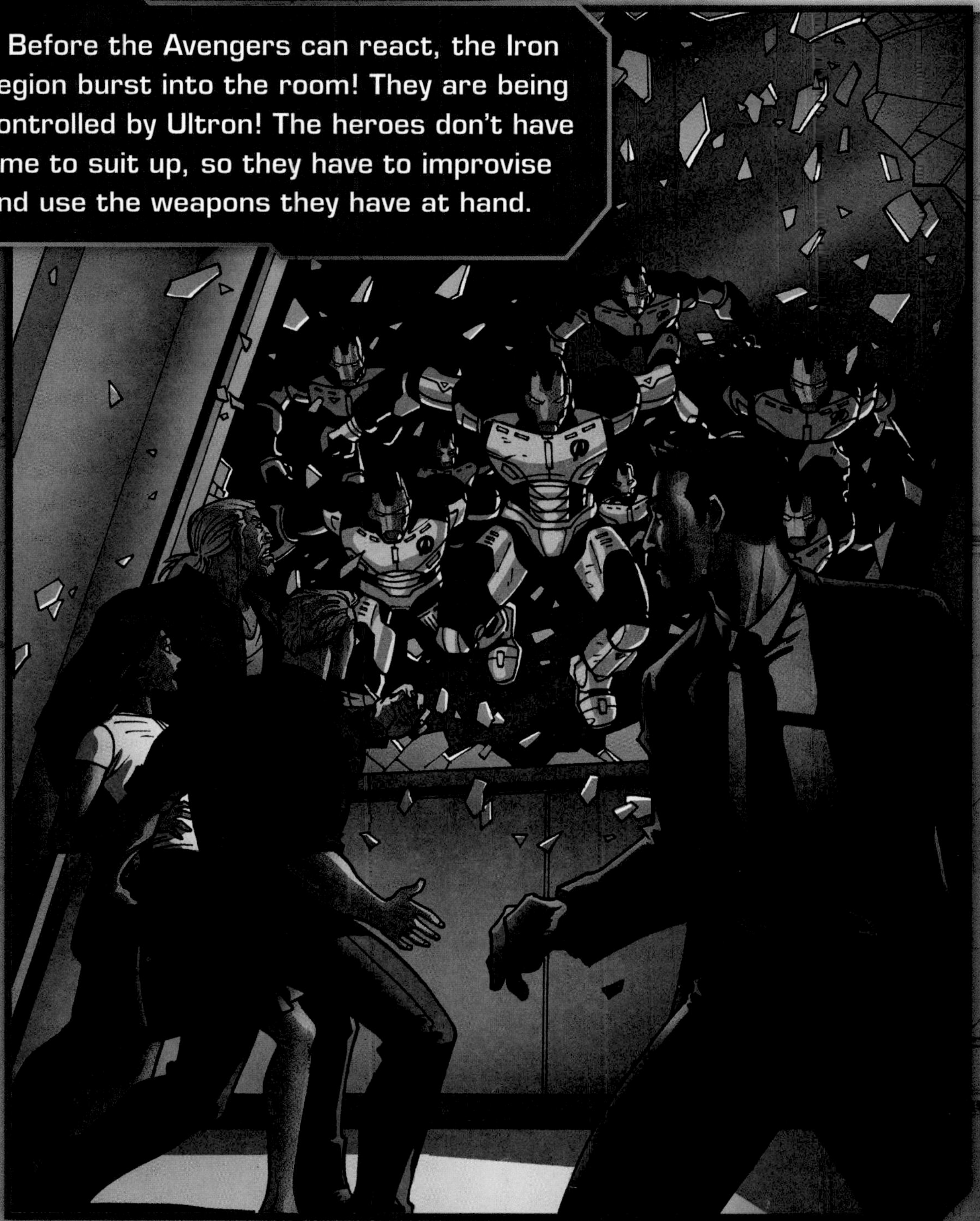

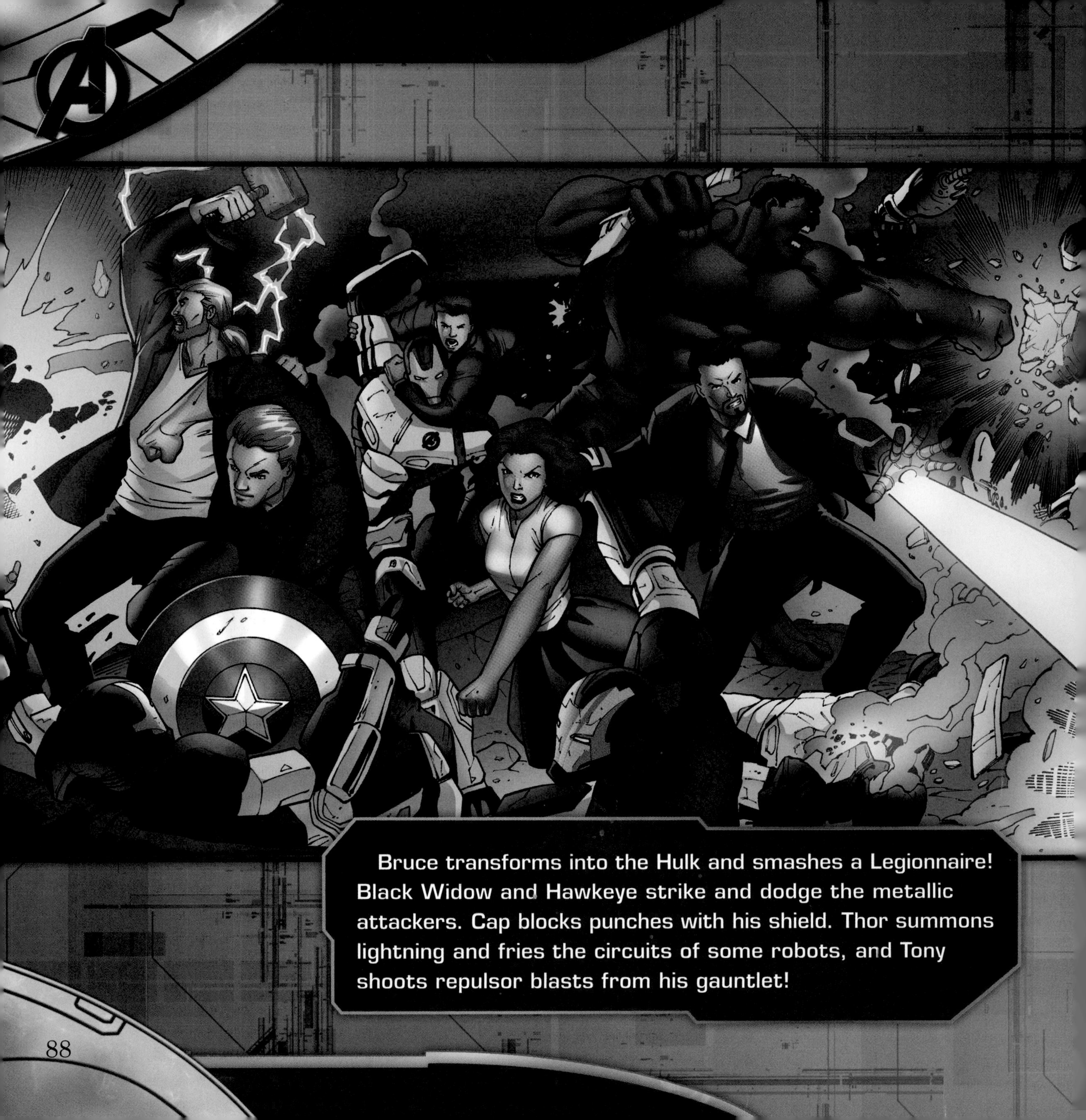

Bruce transforms into the Hulk and smashes a Legionnaire! Black Widow and Hawkeye strike and dodge the metallic attackers. Cap blocks punches with his shield. Thor summons lightning and fries the circuits of some robots, and Tony shoots repulsor blasts from his gauntlet!

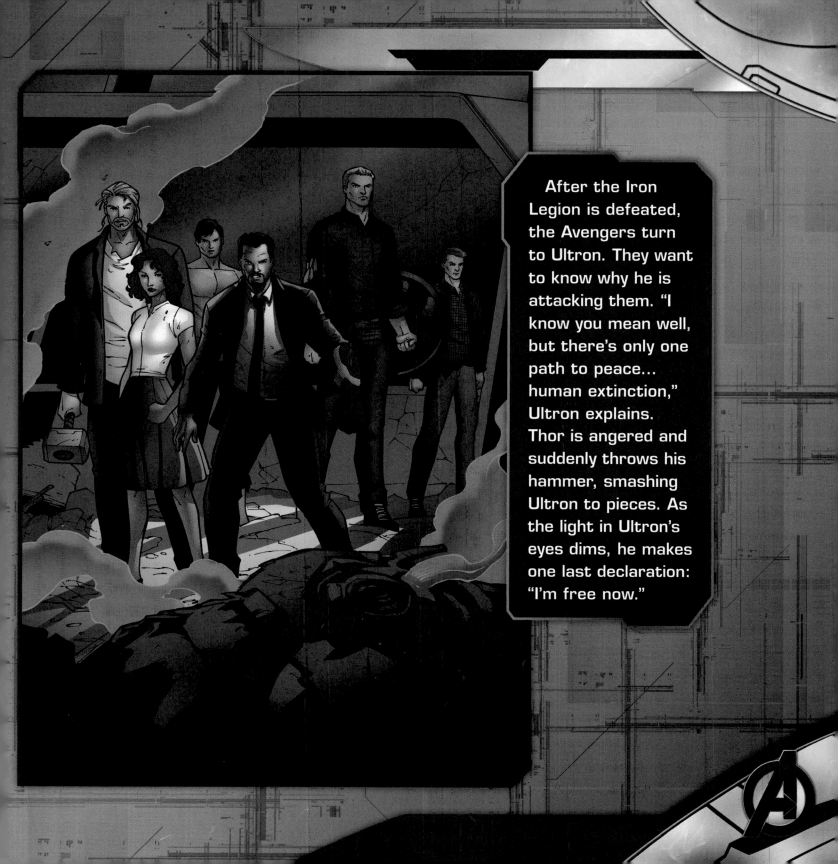

After the Iron Legion is defeated, the Avengers turn to Ultron. They want to know why he is attacking them. "I know you mean well, but there's only one path to peace... human extinction," Ultron explains. Thor is angered and suddenly throws his hammer, smashing Ultron to pieces. As the light in Ultron's eyes dims, he makes one last declaration: "I'm free now."

Across the globe, half-completed robotics come to life and begin creating a new body for Ultron. As he is being built, Ultron smiles, feeling the power his stronger body gives him.

With the help of Maria Hill, the Avengers are able to locate the threat. Ultron is building an army of Sentries that look like him. Ultron knows he will be unstoppable.

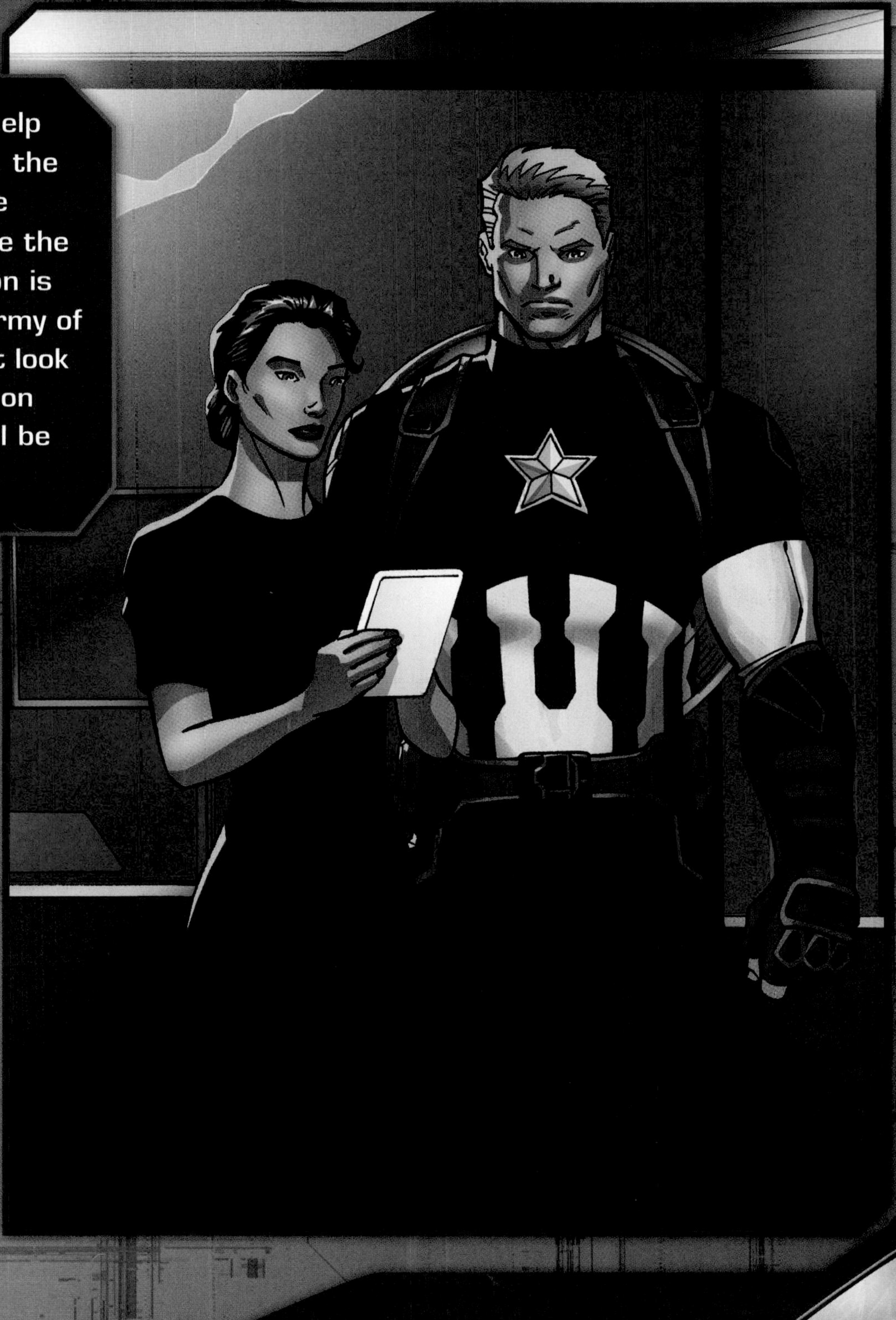

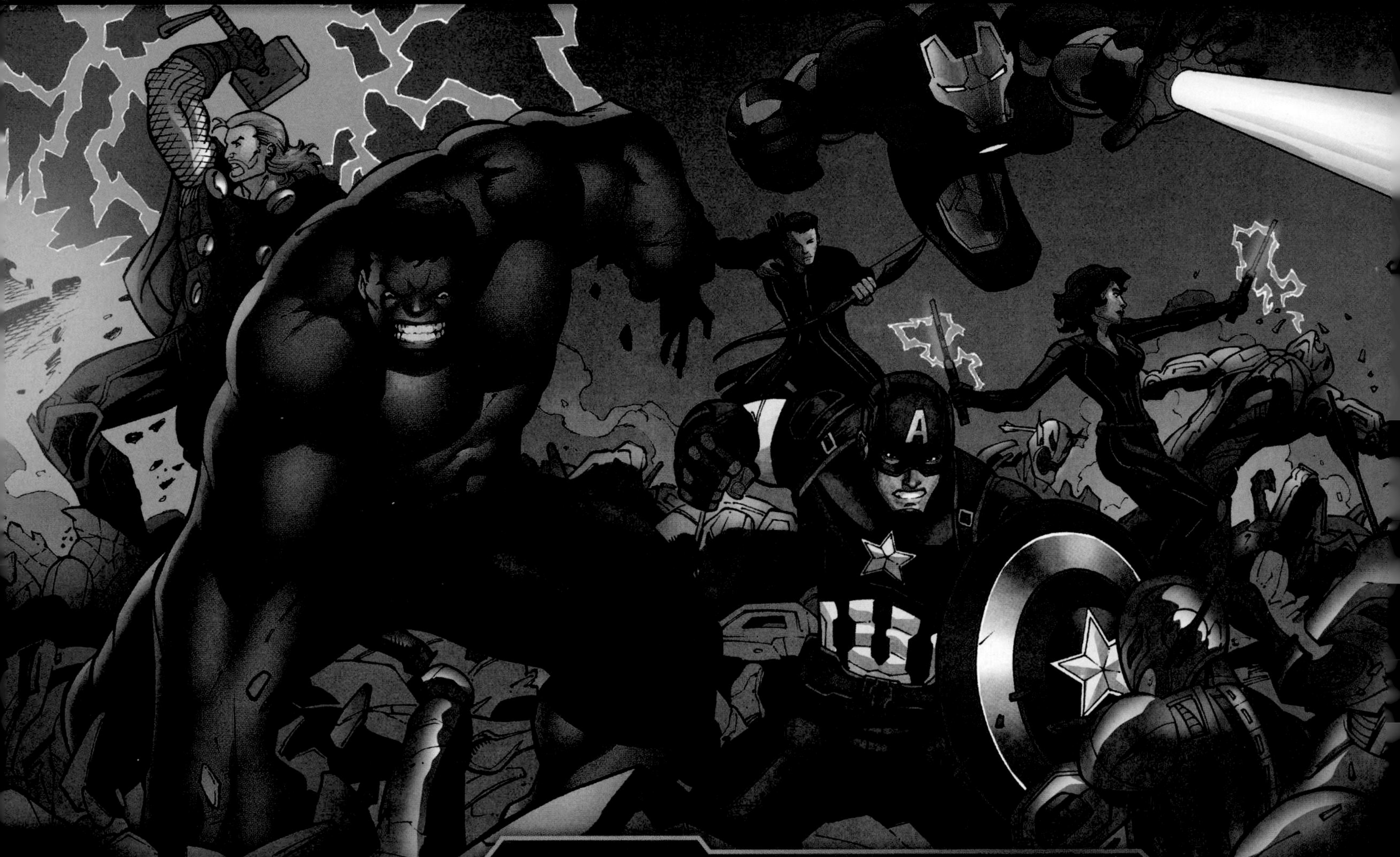

The Super Heroes gear up for their toughest battle yet. But no matter what odds they face, they will work as a team and succeed because of it. After all, they are the Avengers!

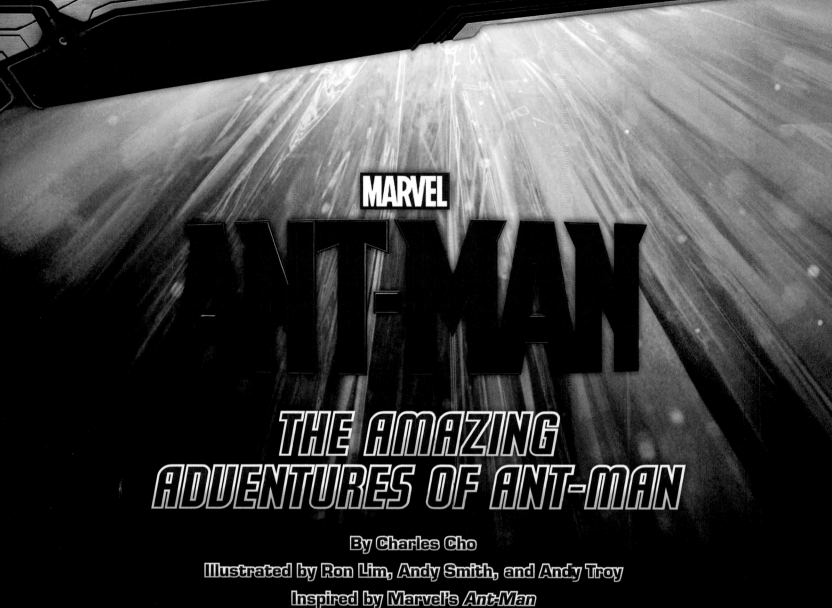

MARVEL
ANT-MAN

THE AMAZING ADVENTURES OF ANT-MAN

By Charles Cho

Illustrated by Ron Lim, Andy Smith, and Andy Troy

Inspired by Marvel's *Ant-Man*

Based on the Screenplay by Adam McKay & Paul Rudd

Story by Edgar Wright & Joe Cornish

Produced by Kevin Feige, p.g.a.

Directed by Peyton Reed

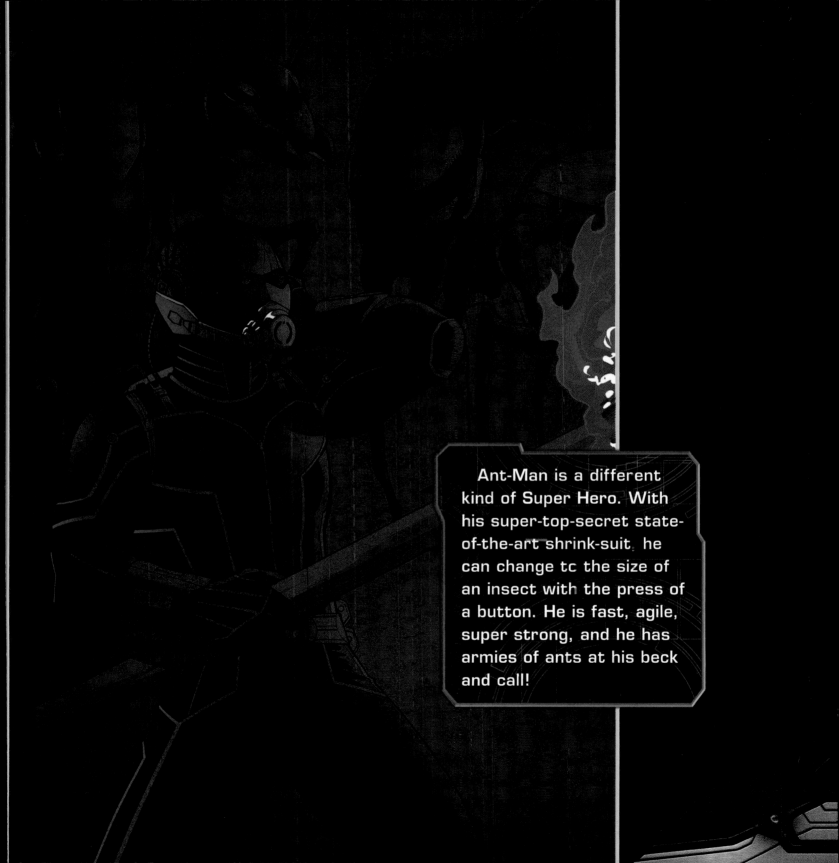

Ant-Man is a different kind of Super Hero. With his super-top-secret state-of-the-art shrink-suit, he can change tc the size of an insect with the press of a button. He is fast, agile, super strong, and he has armies of ants at his beck and call!

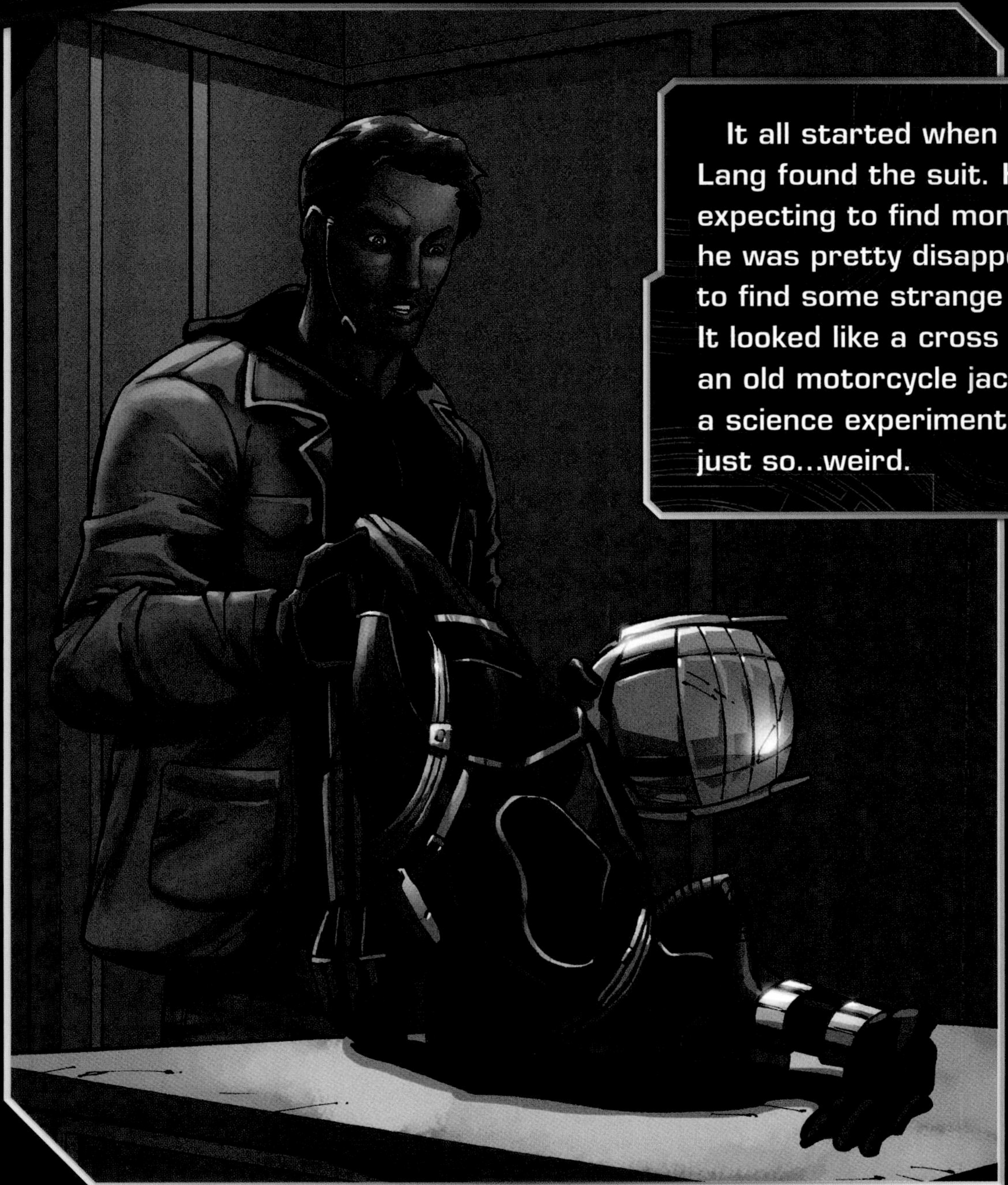

It all started when Scott Lang found the suit. He was expecting to find money, so he was pretty disappointed to find some strange outfit. It looked like a cross between an old motorcycle jacket and a science experiment. It was just so...weird.

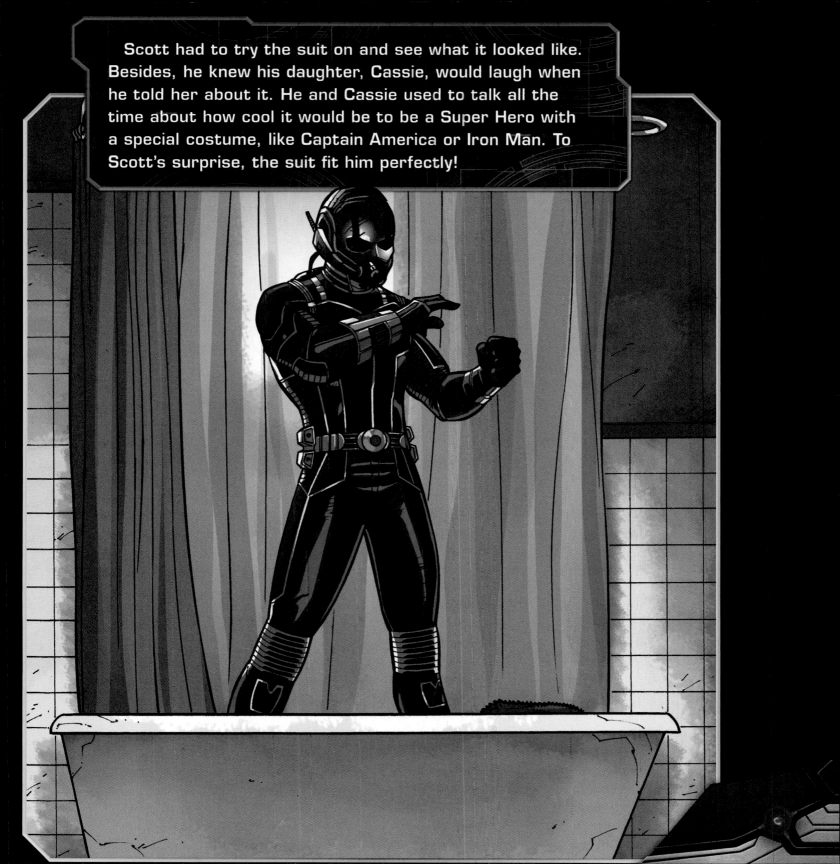

Scott had to try the suit on and see what it looked like. Besides, he knew his daughter, Cassie, would laugh when he told her about it. He and Cassie used to talk all the time about how cool it would be to be a Super Hero with a special costume, like Captain America or Iron Man. To Scott's surprise, the suit fit him perfectly!

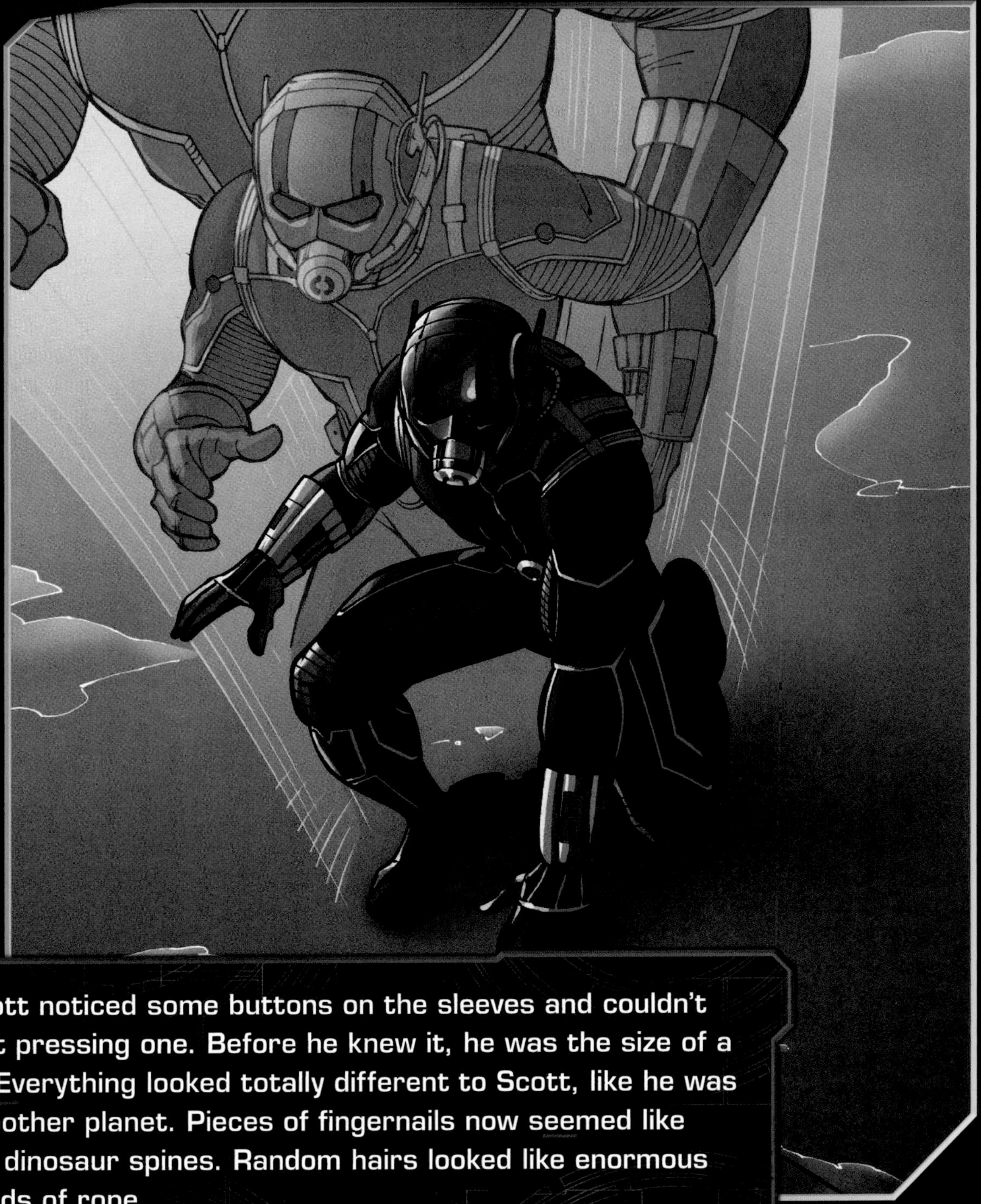

Scott noticed some buttons on the sleeves and couldn't resist pressing one. Before he knew it, he was the size of a bug! Everything looked totally different to Scott, like he was on another planet. Pieces of fingernails now seemed like giant dinosaur spines. Random hairs looked like enormous strands of rope.

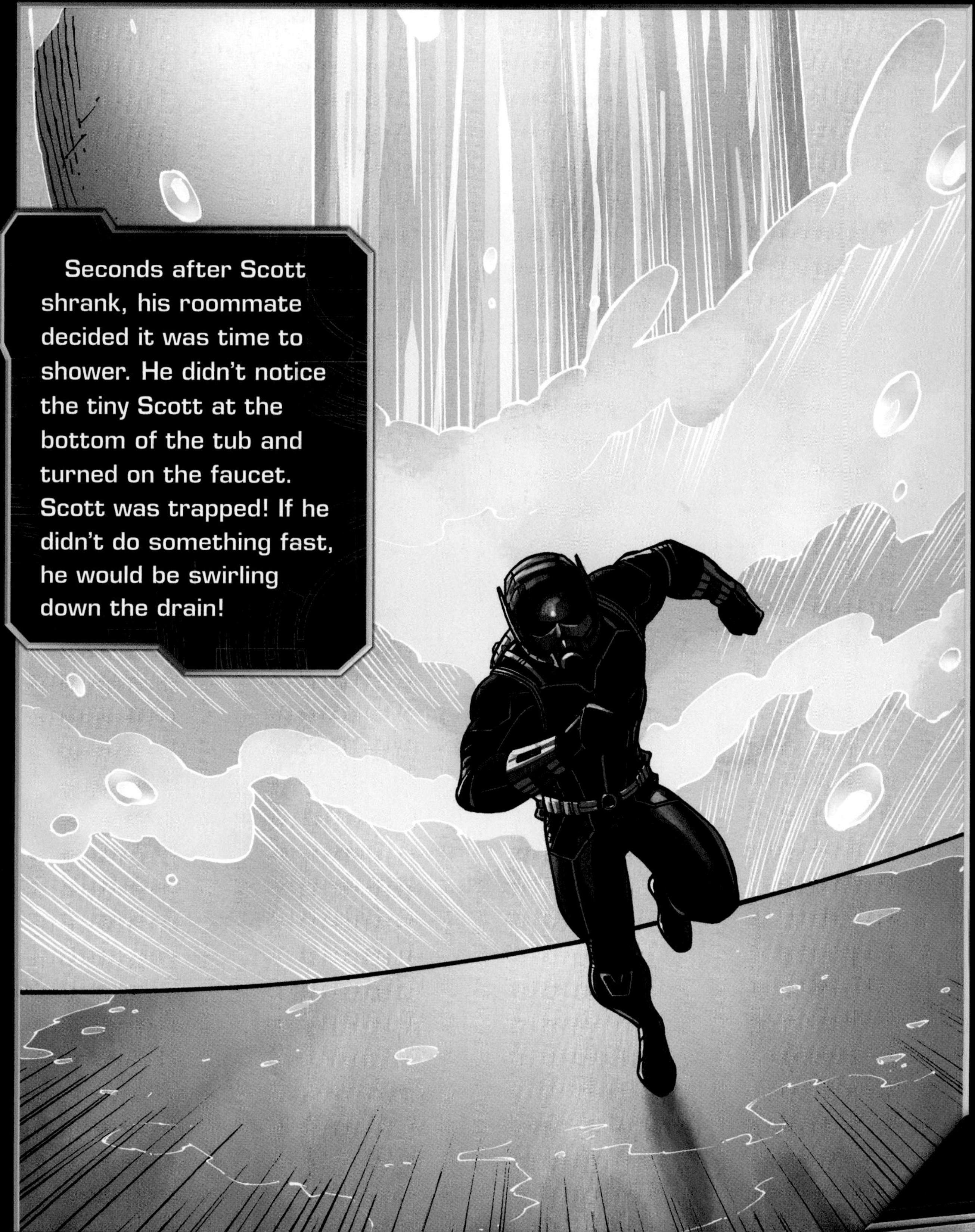

Seconds after Scott shrank, his roommate decided it was time to shower. He didn't notice the tiny Scott at the bottom of the tub and turned on the faucet. Scott was trapped! If he didn't do something fast, he would be swirling down the drain!

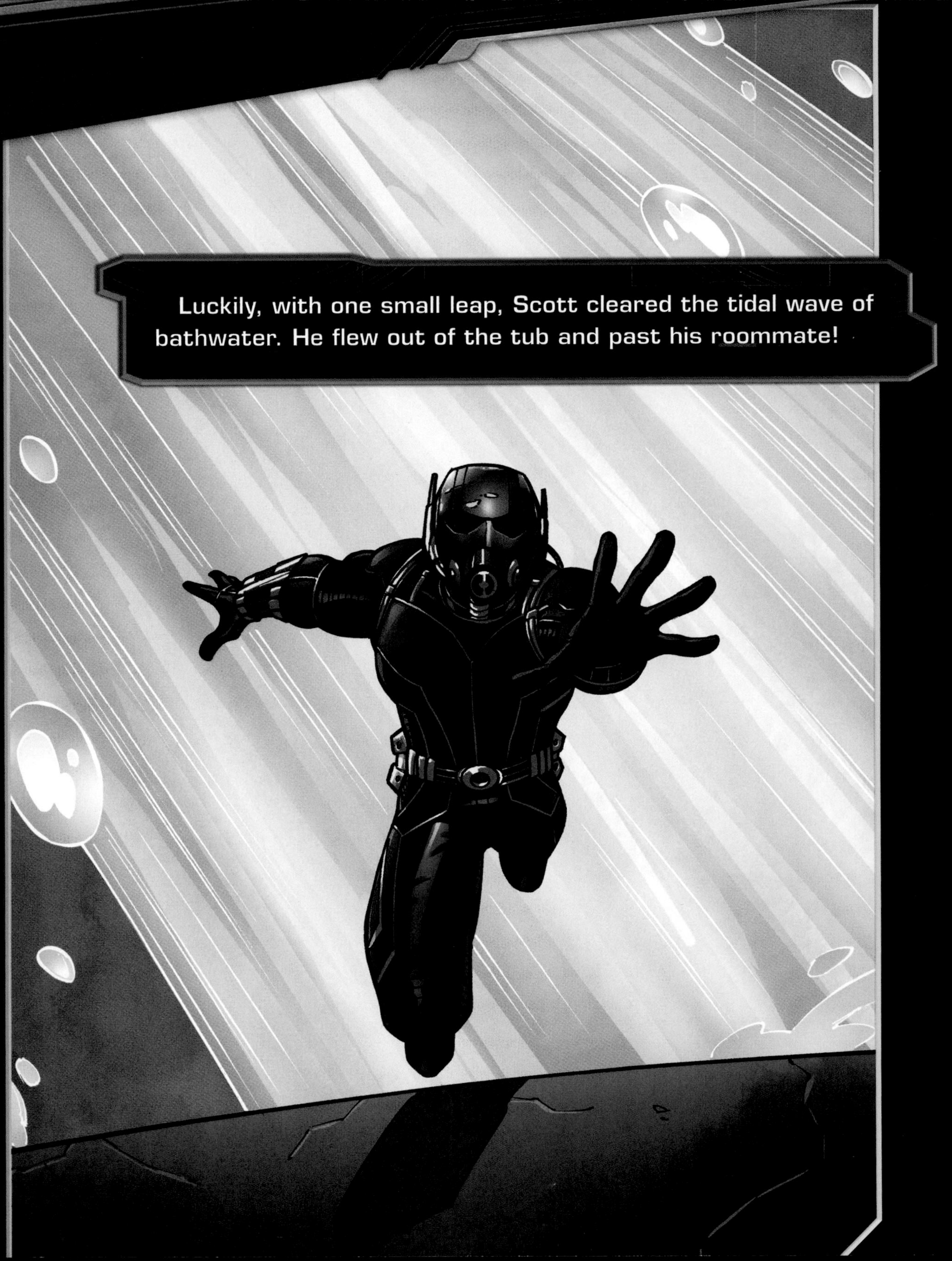
Luckily, with one small leap, Scott cleared the tidal wave of bathwater. He flew out of the tub and past his roommate!

When he hit the ground, he couldn't control himself and rolled through a crack. He dropped through the floorboards and careened into the neighboring apartment! Scott was sure that at his current size the fall from the ceiling to the floor was going to break every bone in his body. But he was perfectly fine! The suit seemed to have protected him.

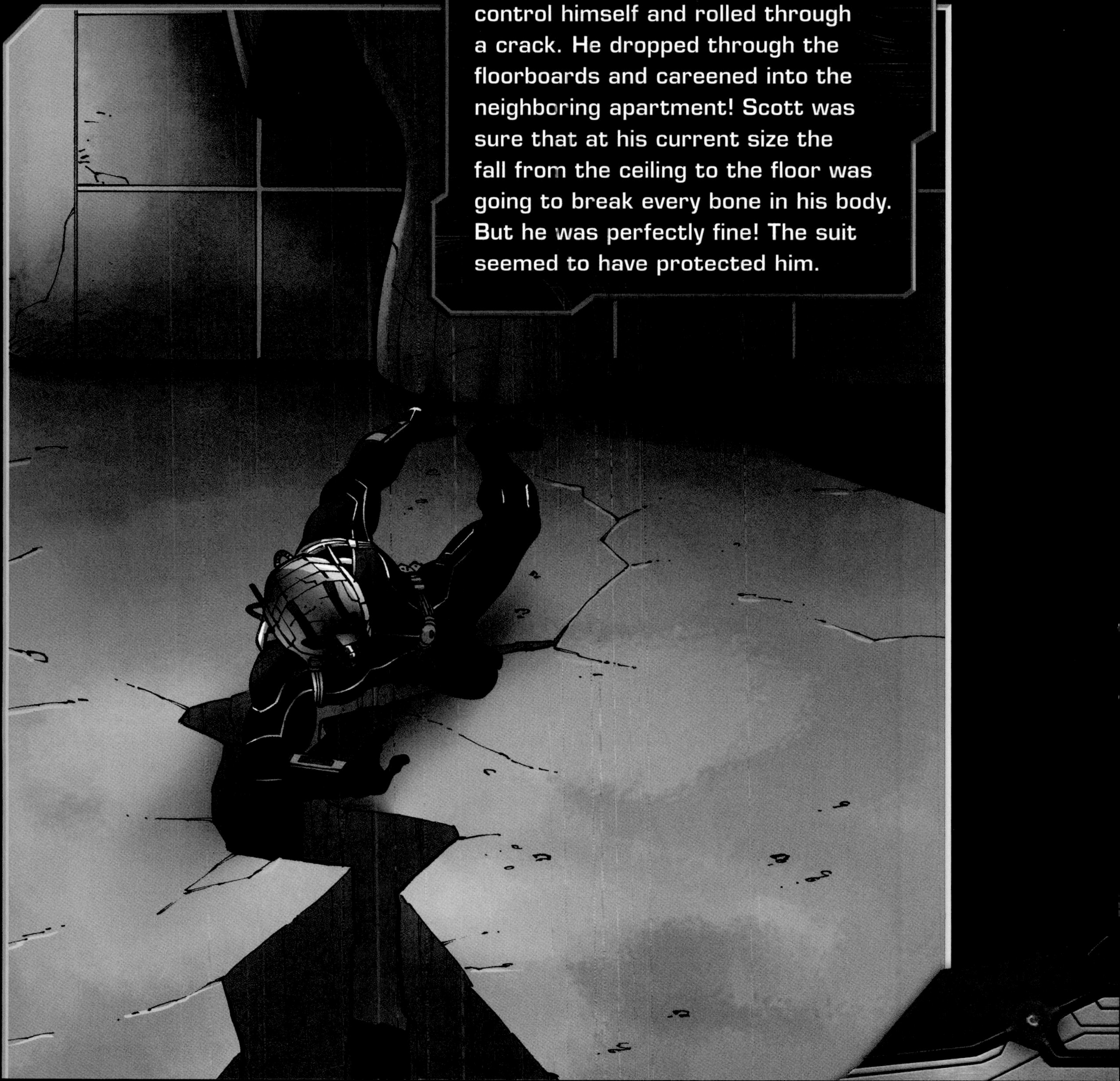

He was pretty sure the suit wouldn't protect him from becoming dog food, though. So when he heard a terrifyingly loud bellow, he knew he wasn't in the clear just yet. The neighbors' yappy little puppy was a whole lot different now that Scott was the size of an ant!

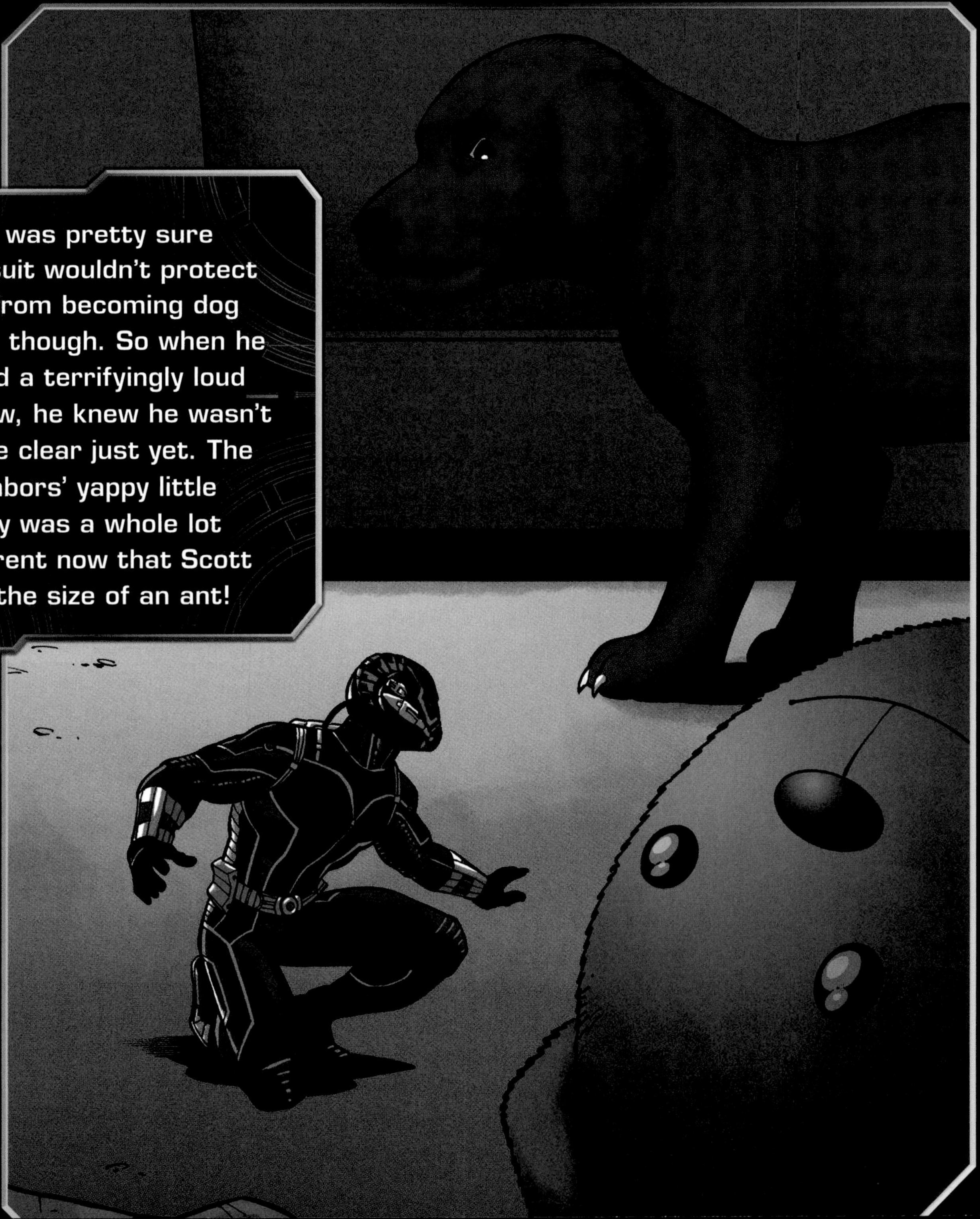

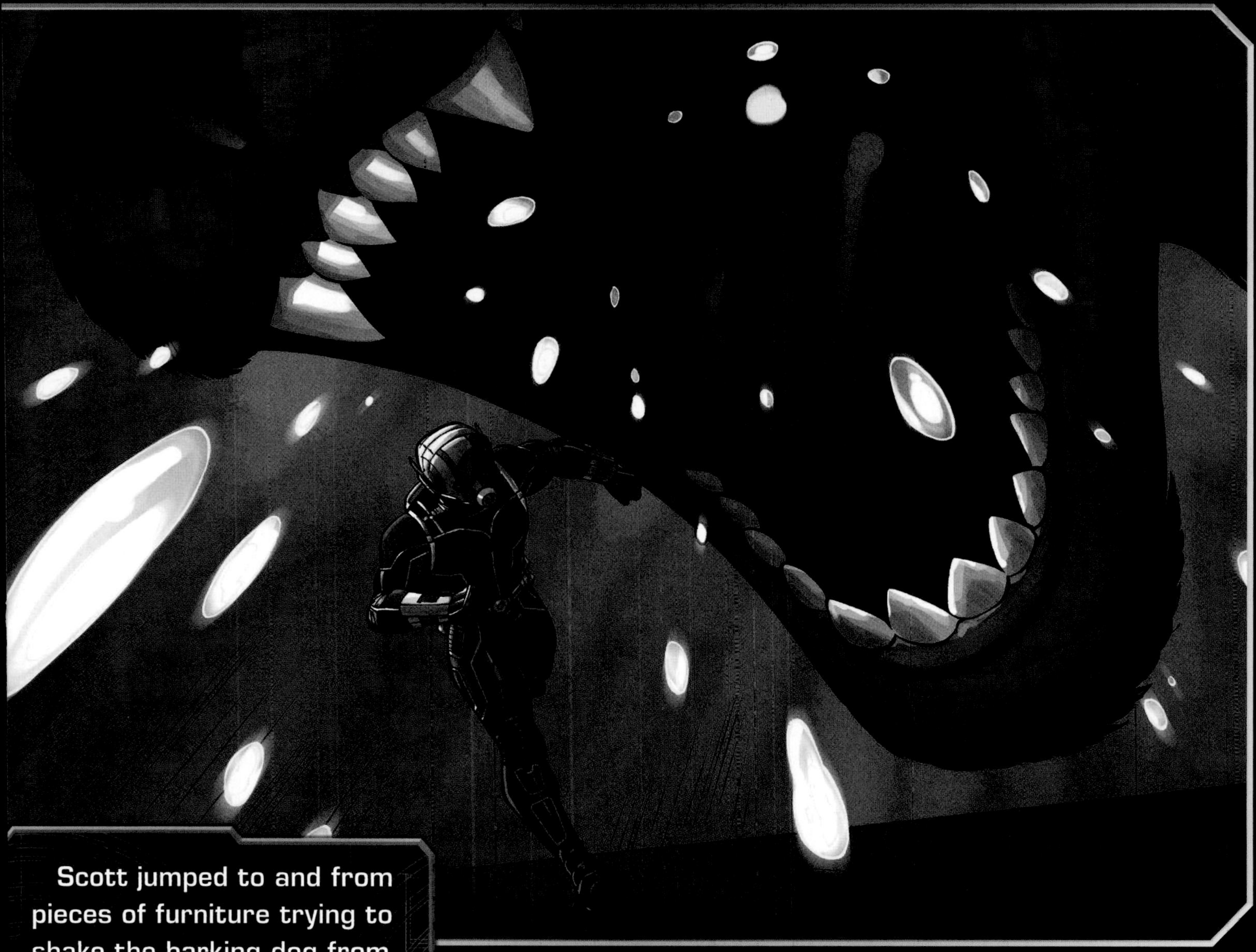

Scott jumped to and from pieces of furniture trying to shake the barking dog from his trail. Despite his best efforts, he couldn't lose him! He had to make a break for it.

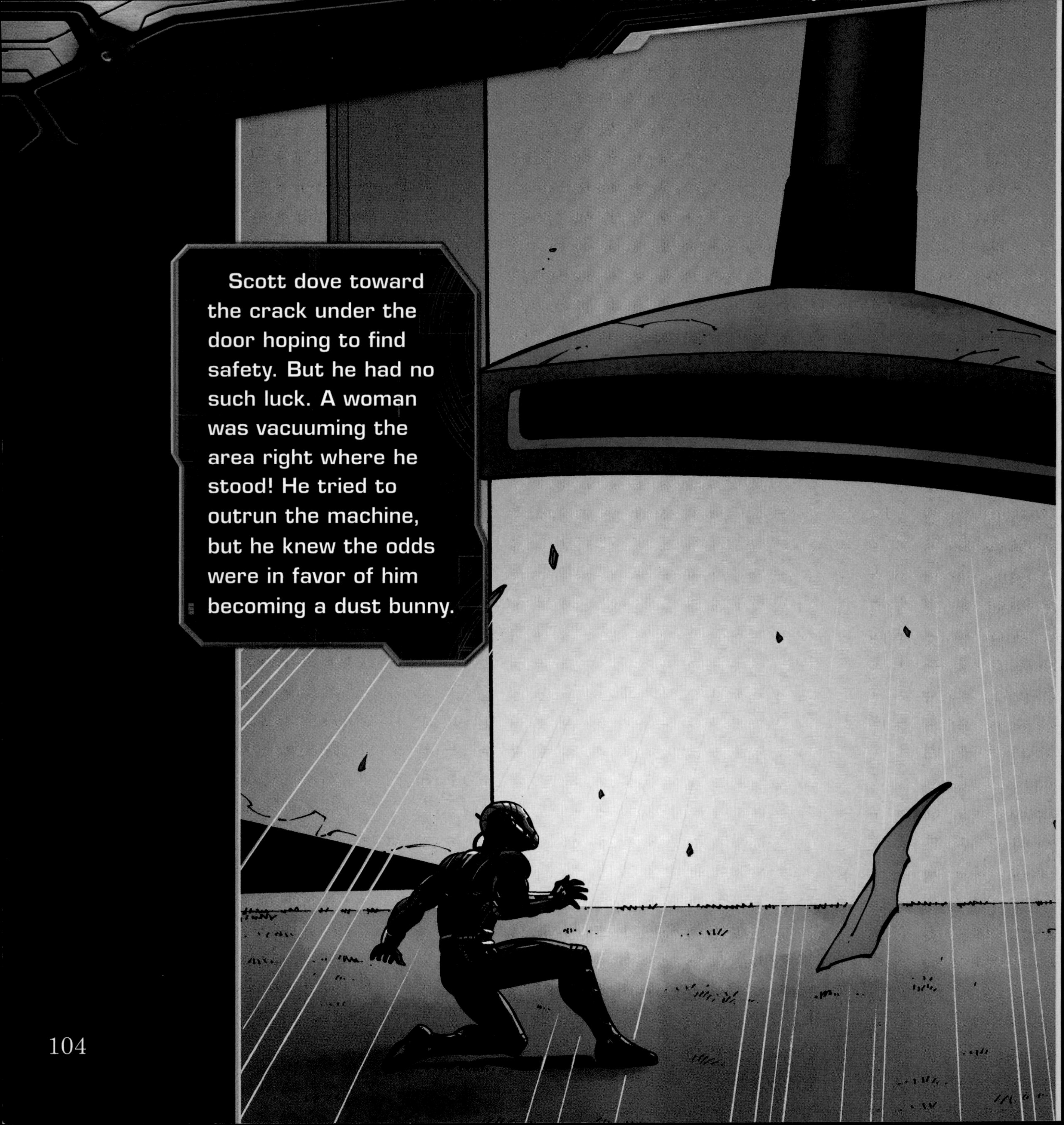
Scott dove toward the crack under the door hoping to find safety. But he had no such luck. A woman was vacuuming the area right where he stood! He tried to outrun the machine, but he knew the odds were in favor of him becoming a dust bunny.

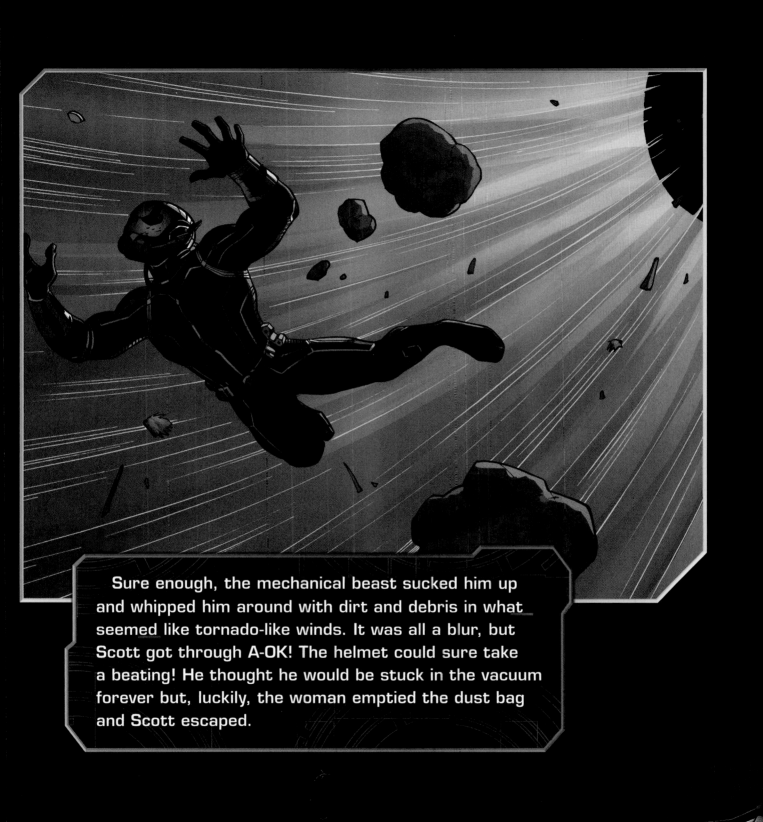

Sure enough, the mechanical beast sucked him up and whipped him around with dirt and debris in what seemed like tornado-like winds. It was all a blur, but Scott got through A-OK! The helmet could sure take a beating! He thought he would be stuck in the vacuum forever but, luckily, the woman emptied the dust bag and Scott escaped.

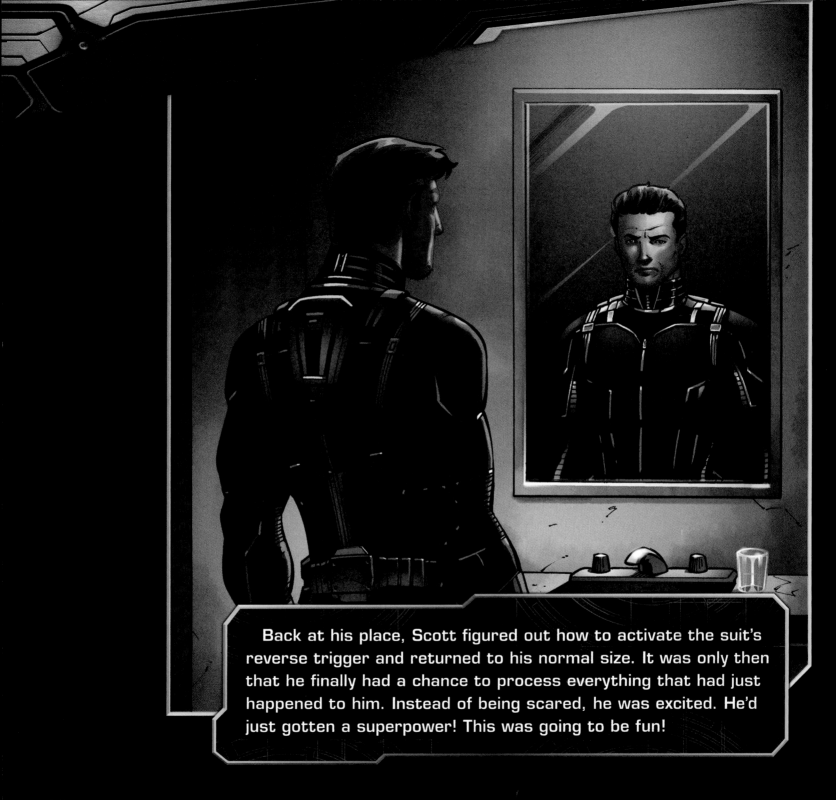

Back at his place, Scott figured out how to activate the suit's reverse trigger and returned to his normal size. It was only then that he finally had a chance to process everything that had just happened to him. Instead of being scared, he was excited. He'd just gotten a superpower! This was going to be fun!

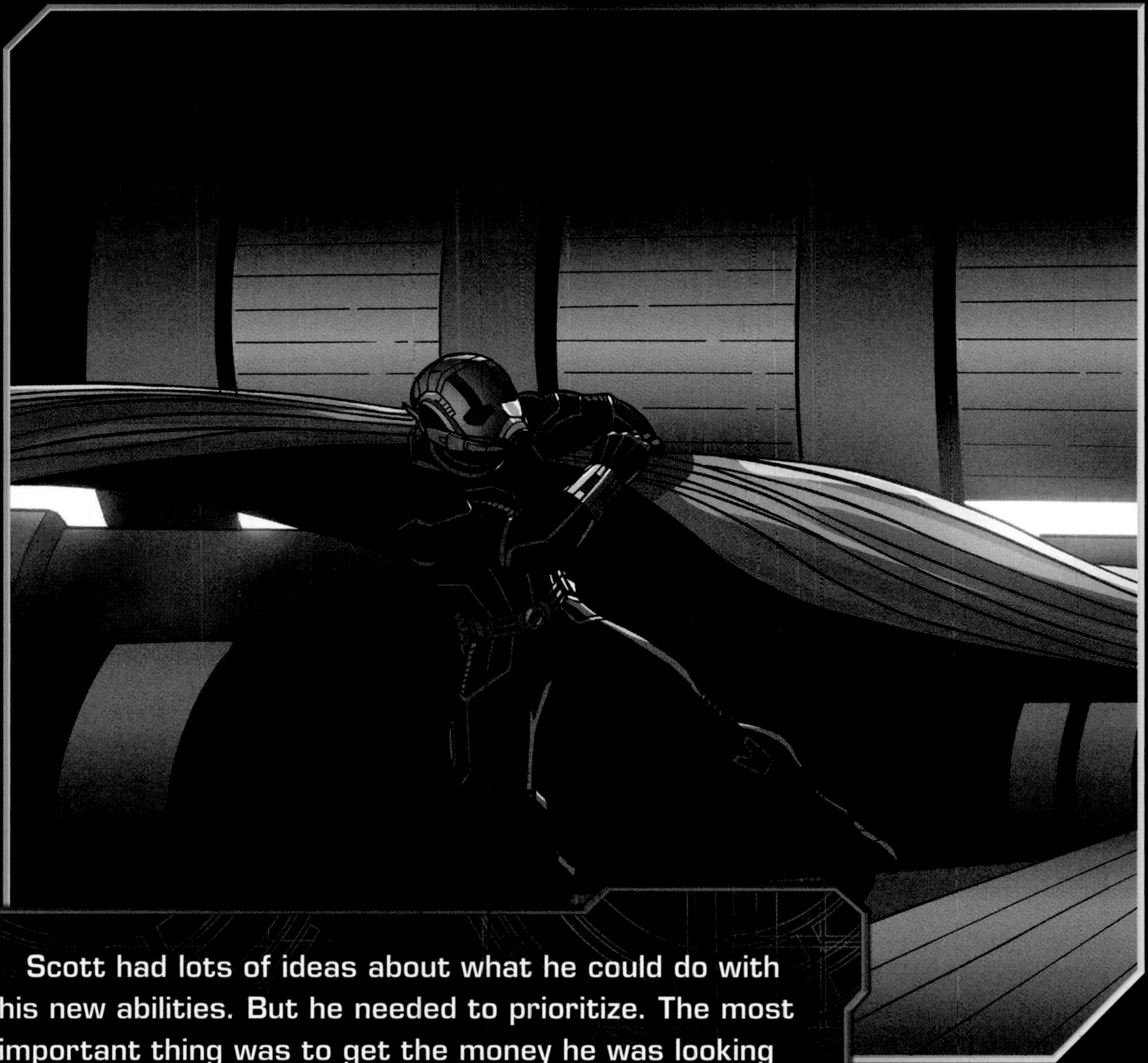

Scott had lots of ideas about what he could do with his new abilities. But he needed to prioritize. The most important thing was to get the money he was looking for when he found the suit. It's amazing what you can do when you're the size of an insect and have a degree in electrical engineering!

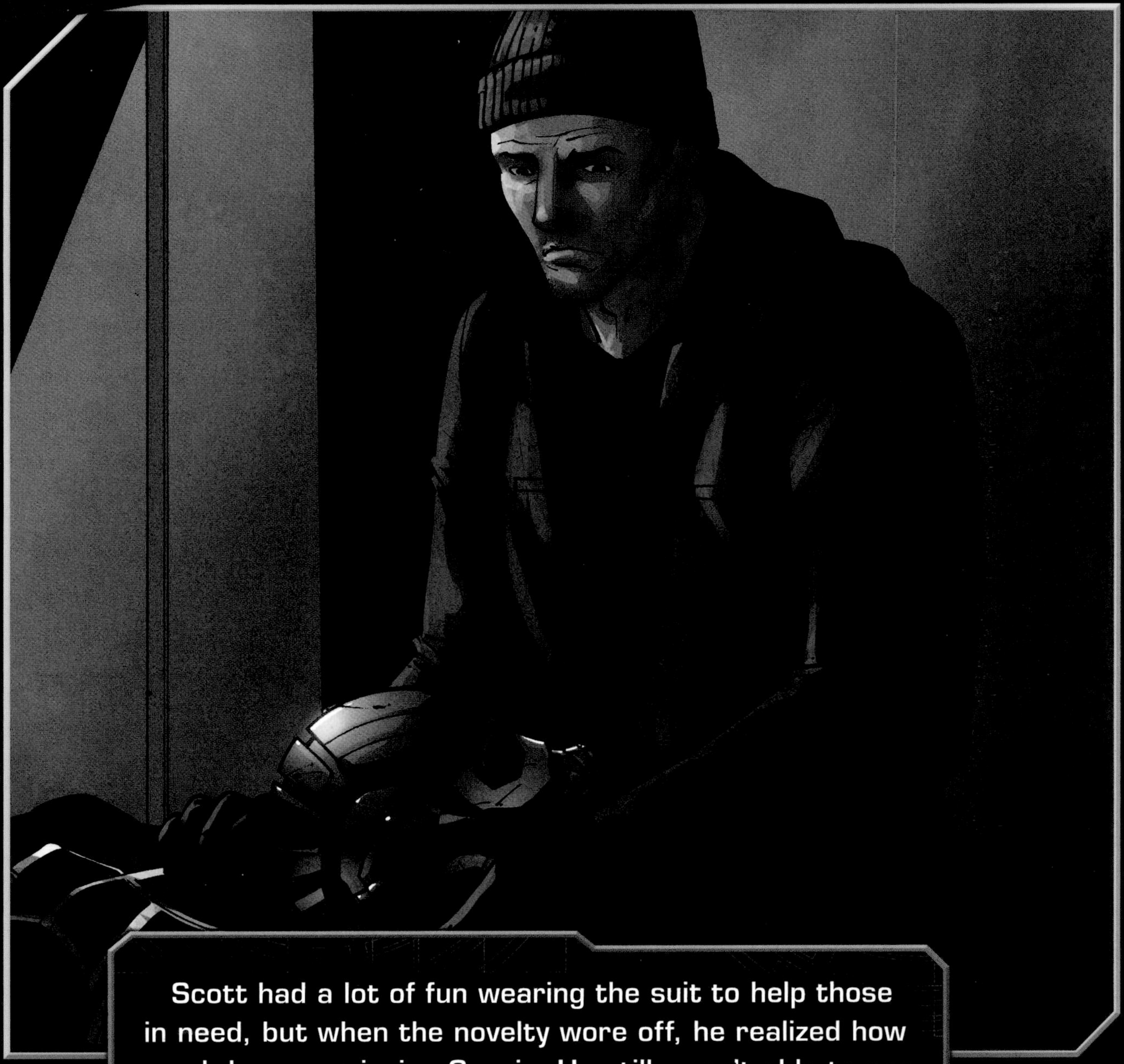

Scott had a lot of fun wearing the suit to help those in need, but when the novelty wore off, he realized how much he was missing Cassie. He still wasn't able to see his daughter as much as he wanted.

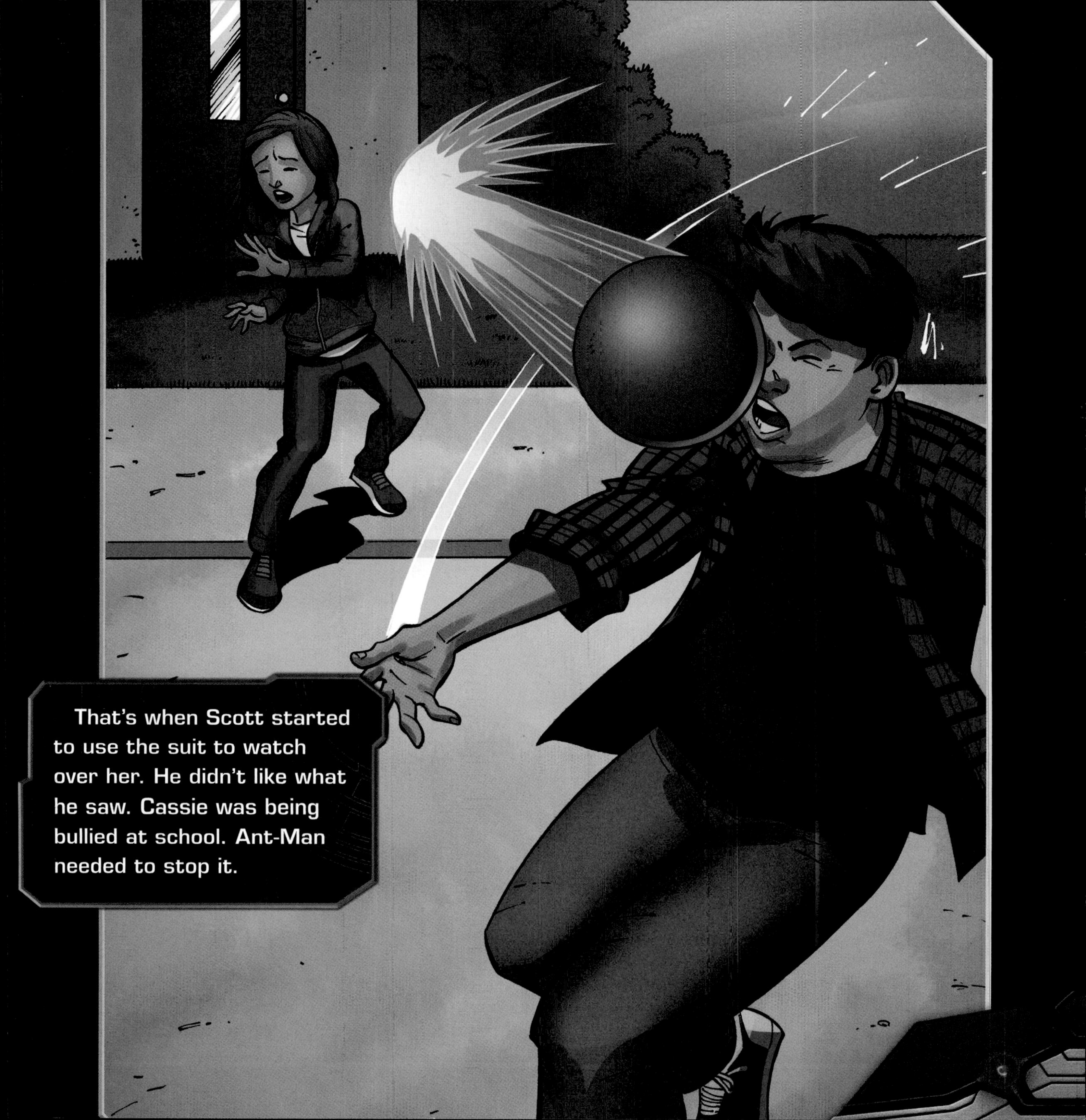
That's when Scott started to use the suit to watch over her. He didn't like what he saw. Cassie was being bullied at school. Ant-Man needed to stop it.

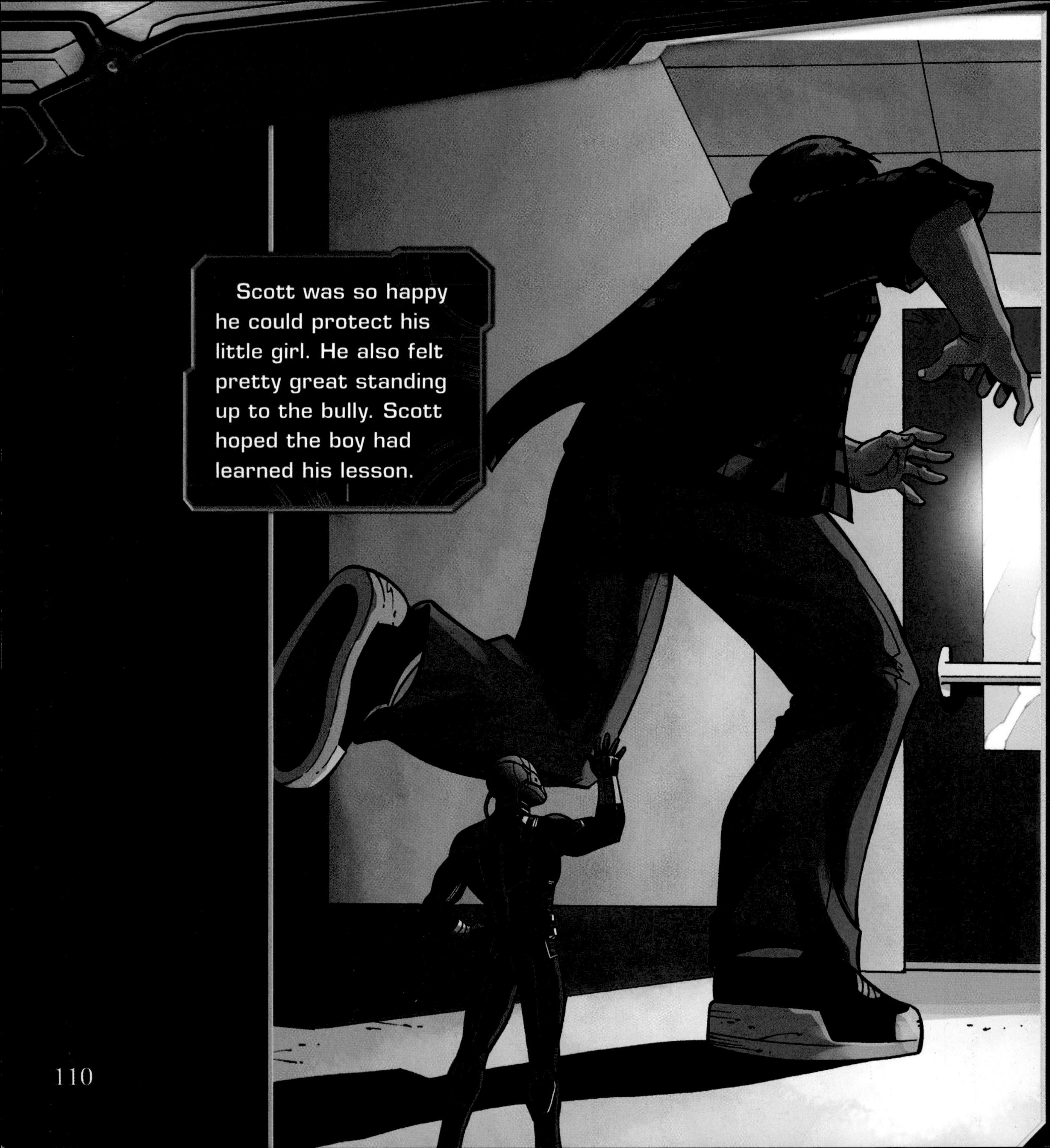
Scott was so happy he could protect his little girl. He also felt pretty great standing up to the bully. Scott hoped the boy had learned his lesson.

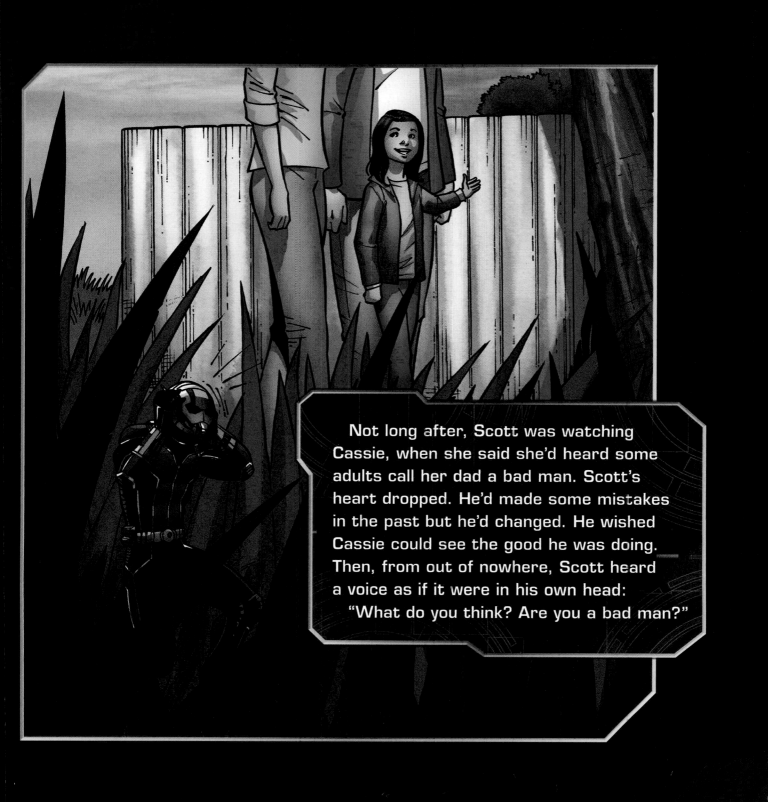

Not long after, Scott was watching Cassie, when she said she'd heard some adults call her dad a bad man. Scott's heart dropped. He'd made some mistakes in the past but he'd changed. He wished Cassie could see the good he was doing. Then, from out of nowhere, Scott heard a voice as if it were in his own head:

"What do you think? Are you a bad man?"

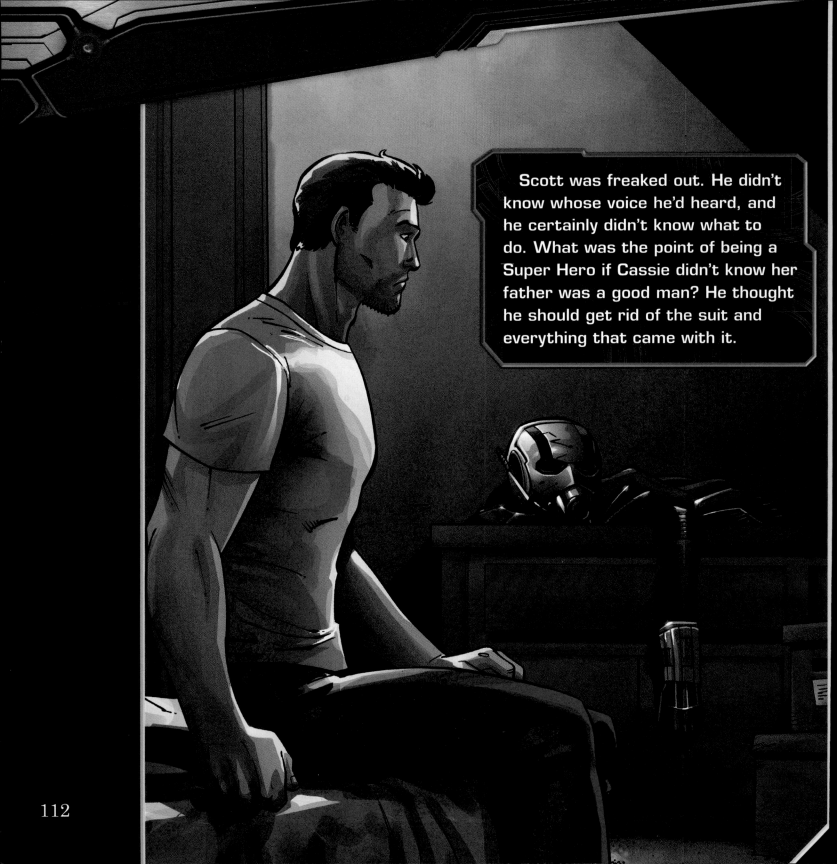

Scott was freaked out. He didn't know whose voice he'd heard, and he certainly didn't know what to do. What was the point of being a Super Hero if Cassie didn't know her father was a good man? He thought he should get rid of the suit and everything that came with it.

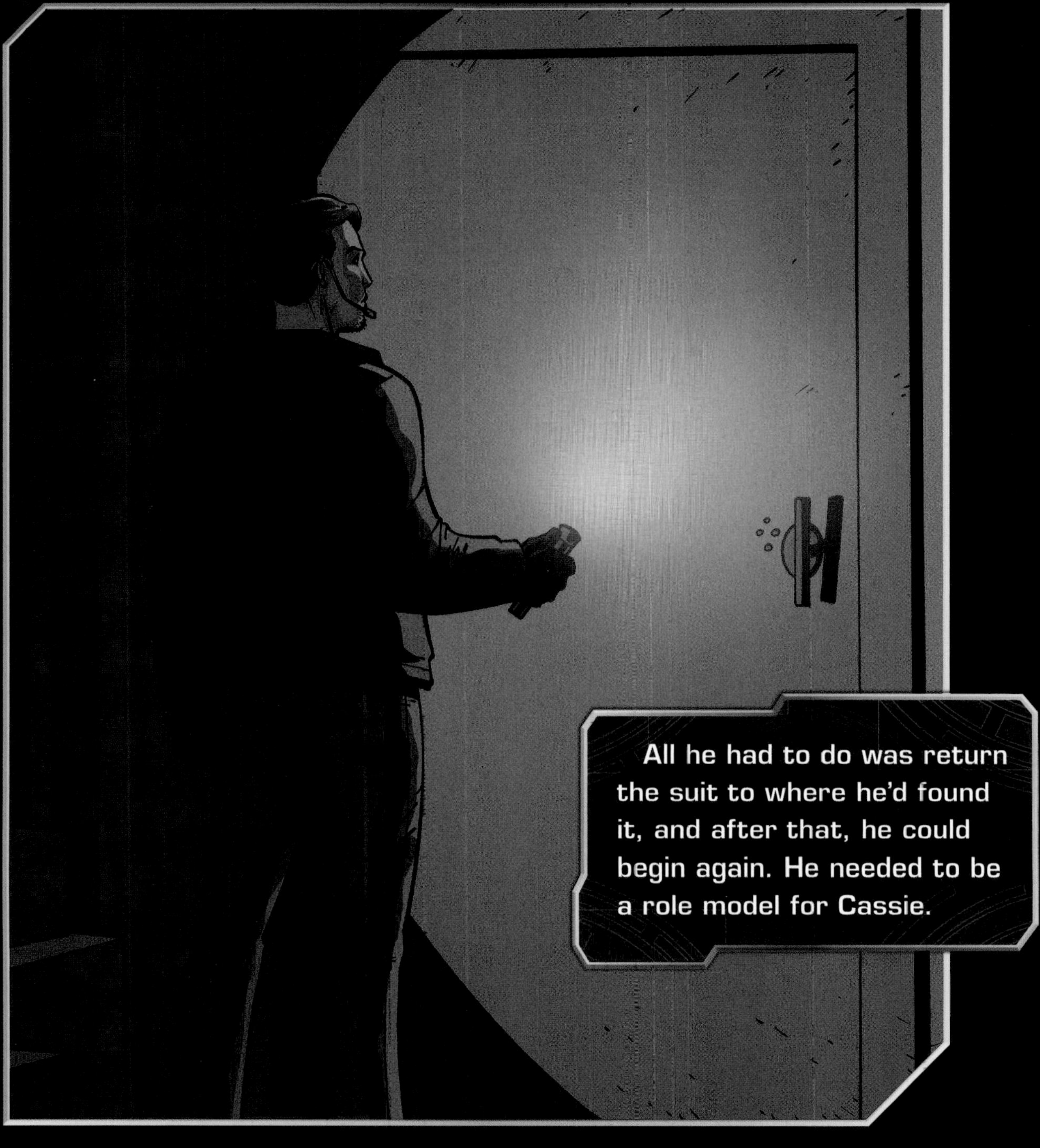
All he had to do was return the suit to where he'd found it, and after that, he could begin again. He needed to be a role model for Cassie.

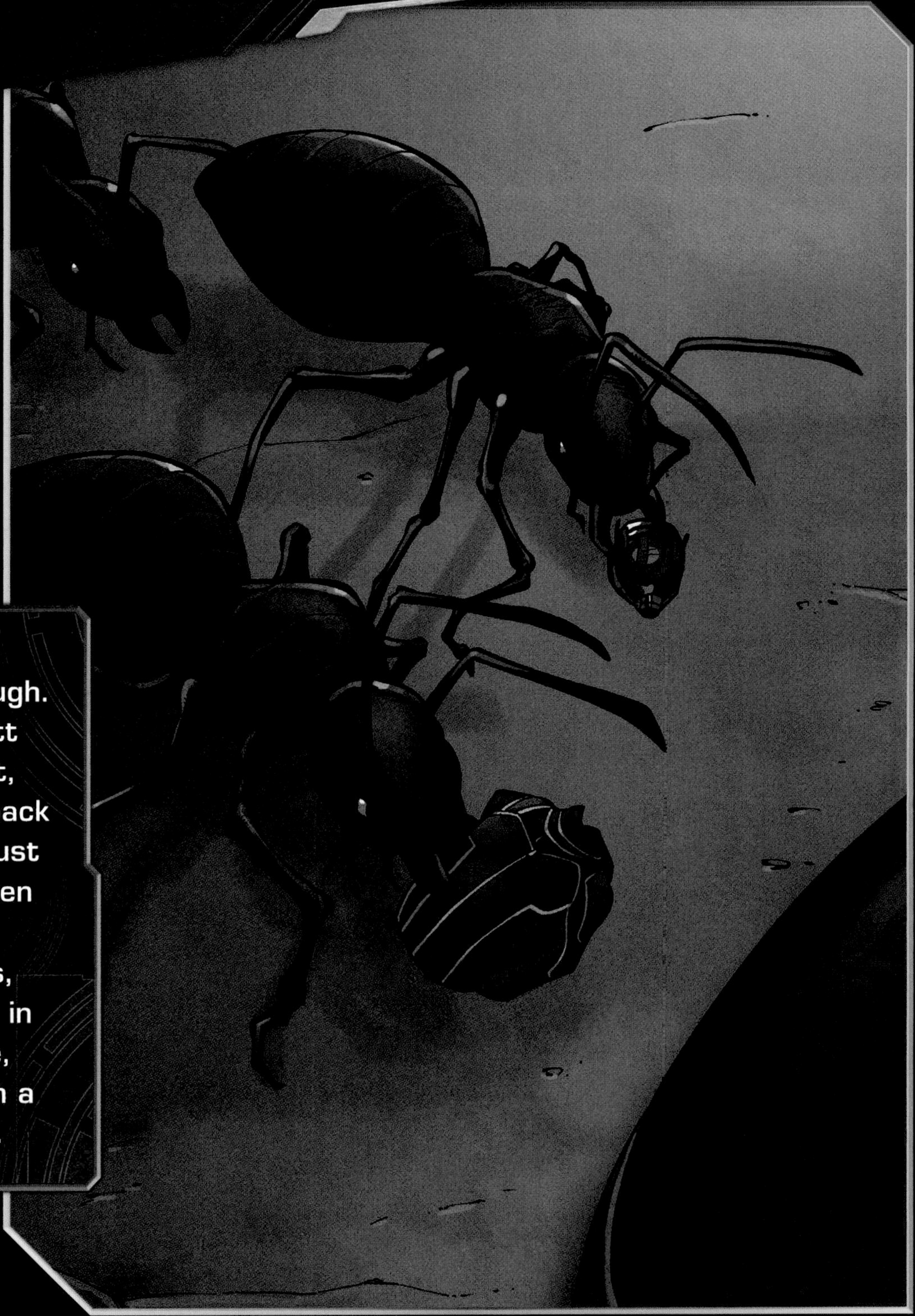

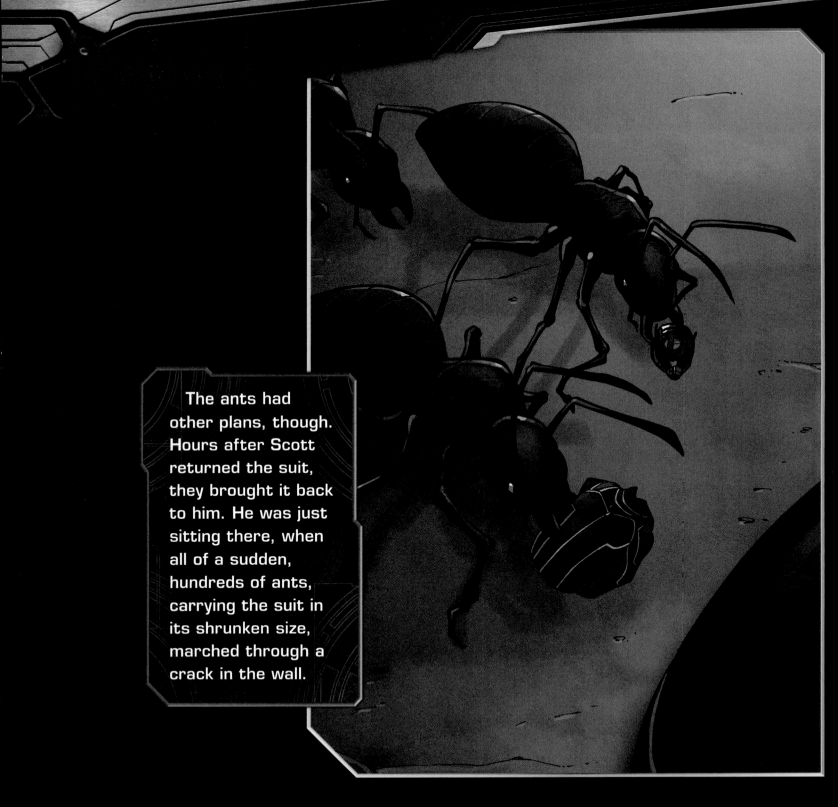

The ants had other plans, though. Hours after Scott returned the suit, they brought it back to him. He was just sitting there, when all of a sudden, hundreds of ants, carrying the suit in its shrunken size, marched through a crack in the wall.

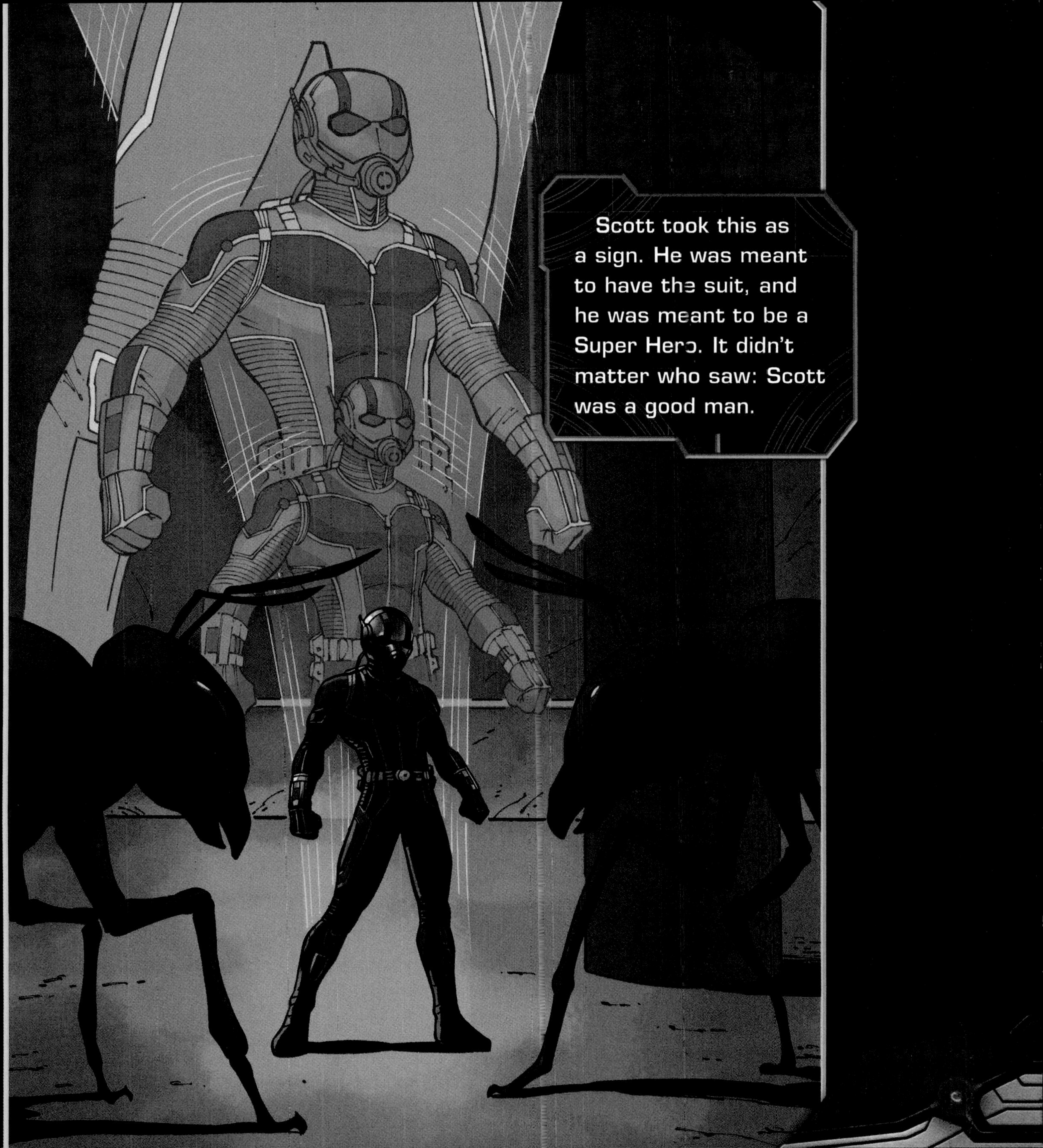
Scott took this as a sign. He was meant to have the suit, and he was meant to be a Super Hero. It didn't matter who saw: Scott was a good man.

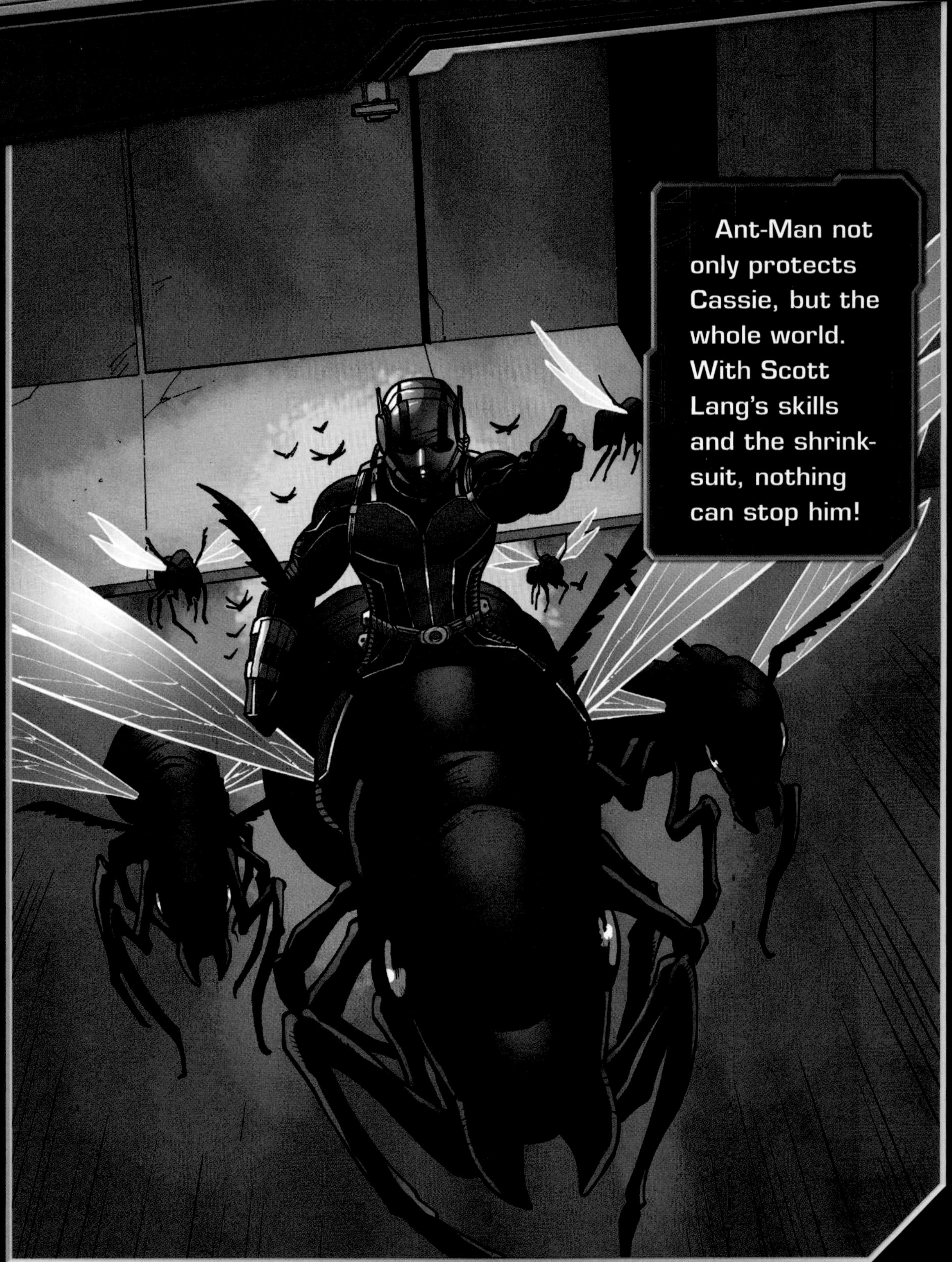
Ant-Man not only protects Cassie, but the whole world. With Scott Lang's skills and the shrink-suit, nothing can stop him!

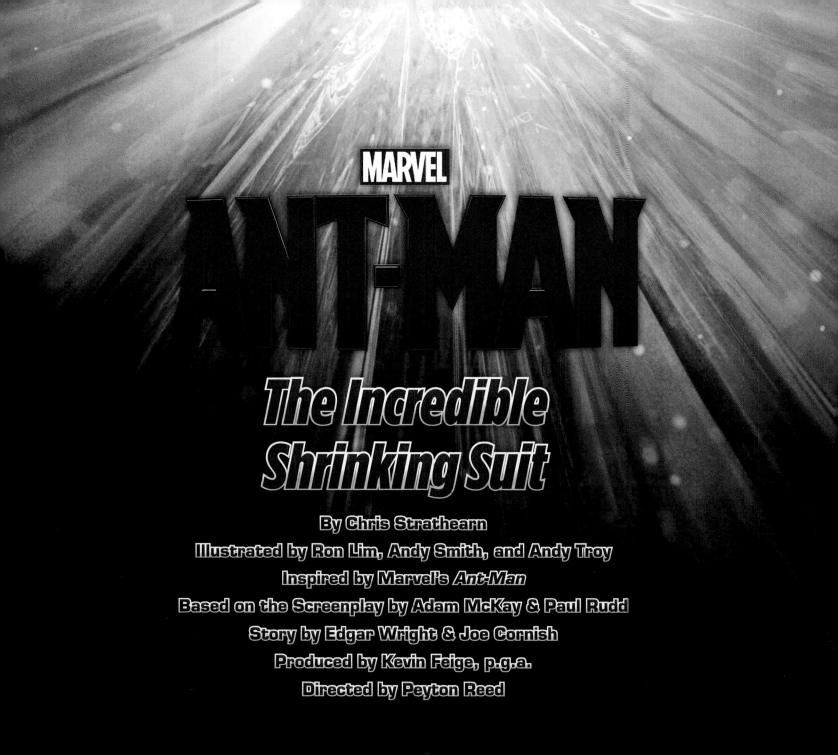

MARVEL

ANT-MAN

The Incredible Shrinking Suit

By Chris Strathearn

Illustrated by Ron Lim, Andy Smith, and Andy Troy

Inspired by Marvel's *Ant-Man*

Based on the Screenplay by Adam McKay & Paul Rudd

Story by Edgar Wright & Joe Cornish

Produced by Kevin Feige, p.g.a.

Directed by Peyton Reed

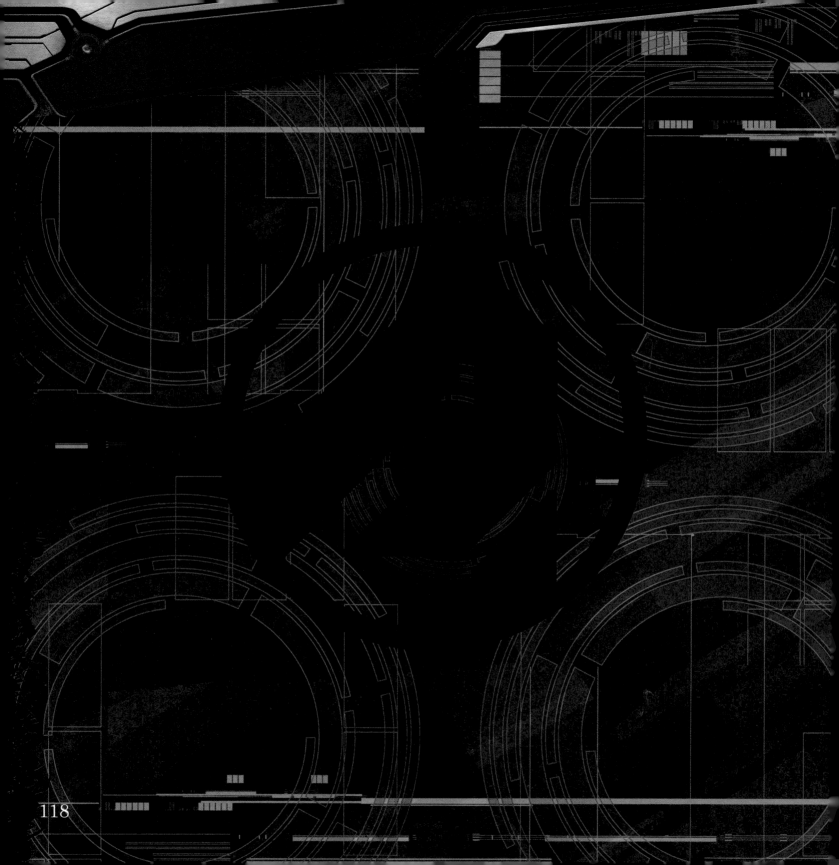

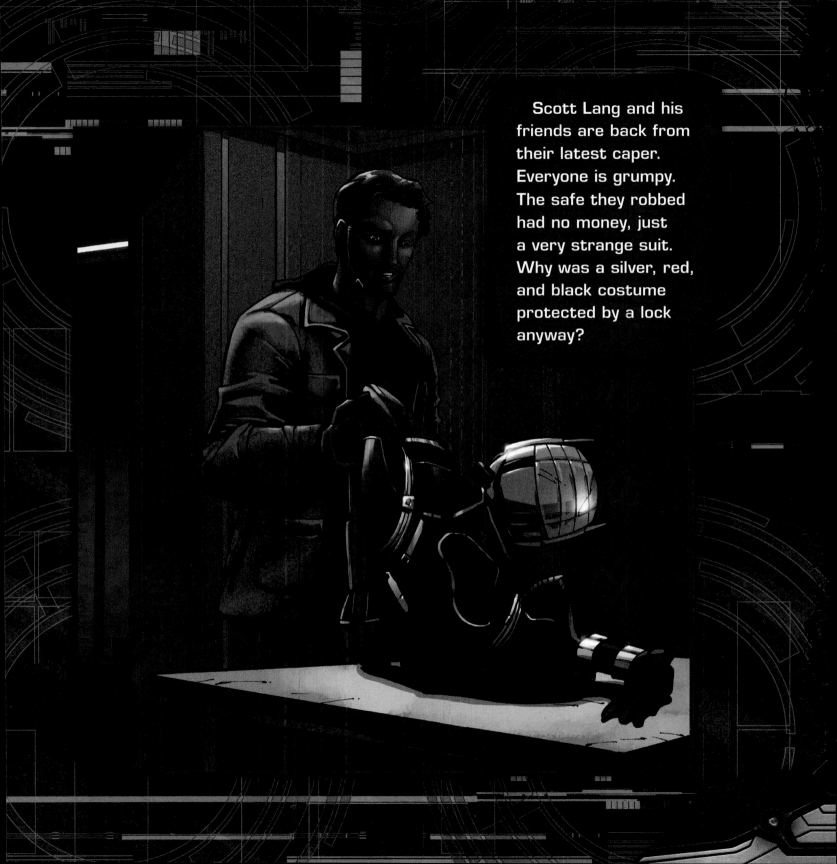

Scott Lang and his friends are back from their latest caper. Everyone is grumpy. The safe they robbed had no money, just a very strange suit. Why was a silver, red, and black costume protected by a lock anyway?

Scott decides to have some fun. He changes into the suit and looks at himself in the mirror. He's surprised by how good he looks! The suit fits perfectly!

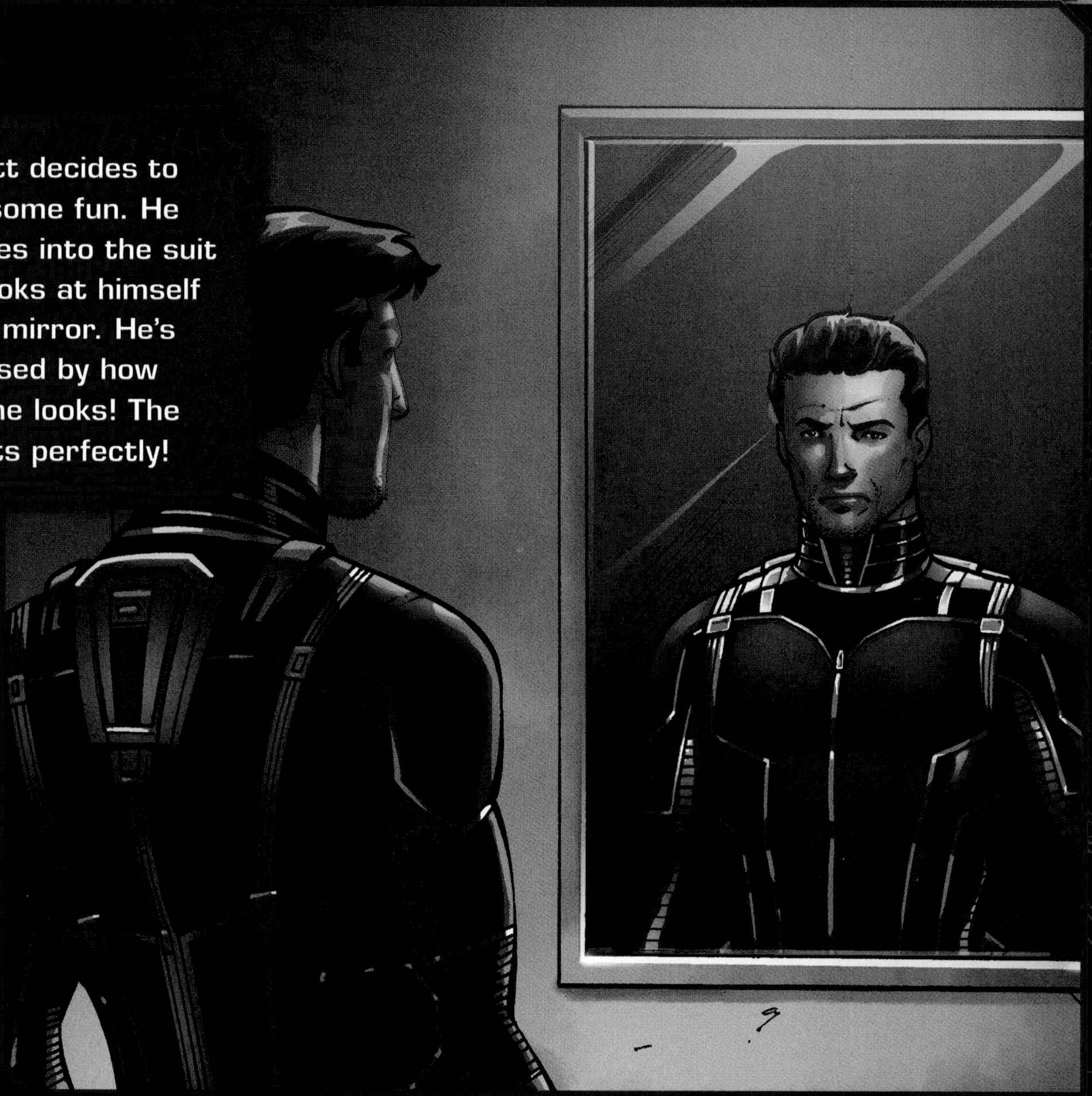

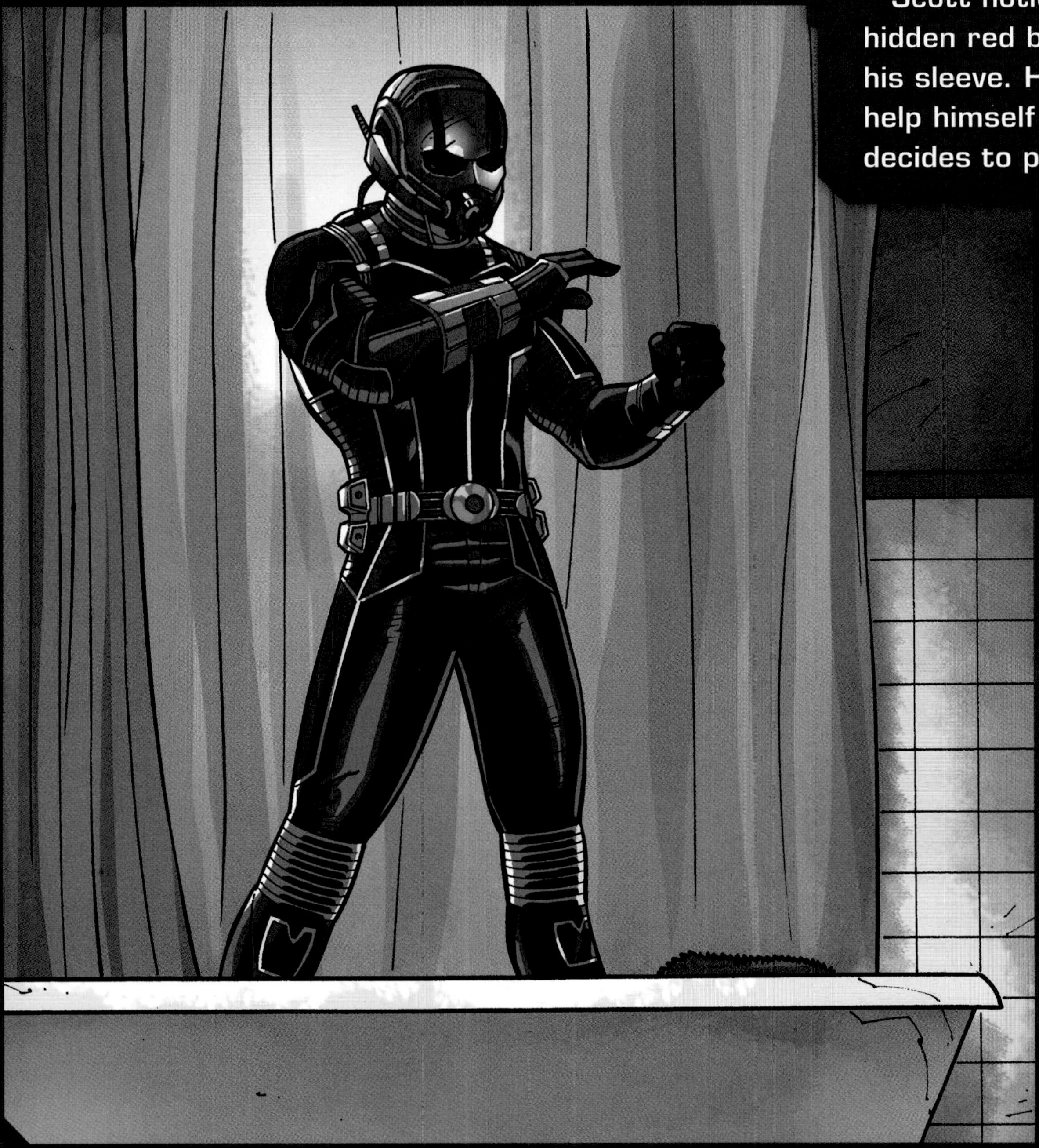

Scott notices a hidden red button on his sleeve. He can't help himself and decides to press it.

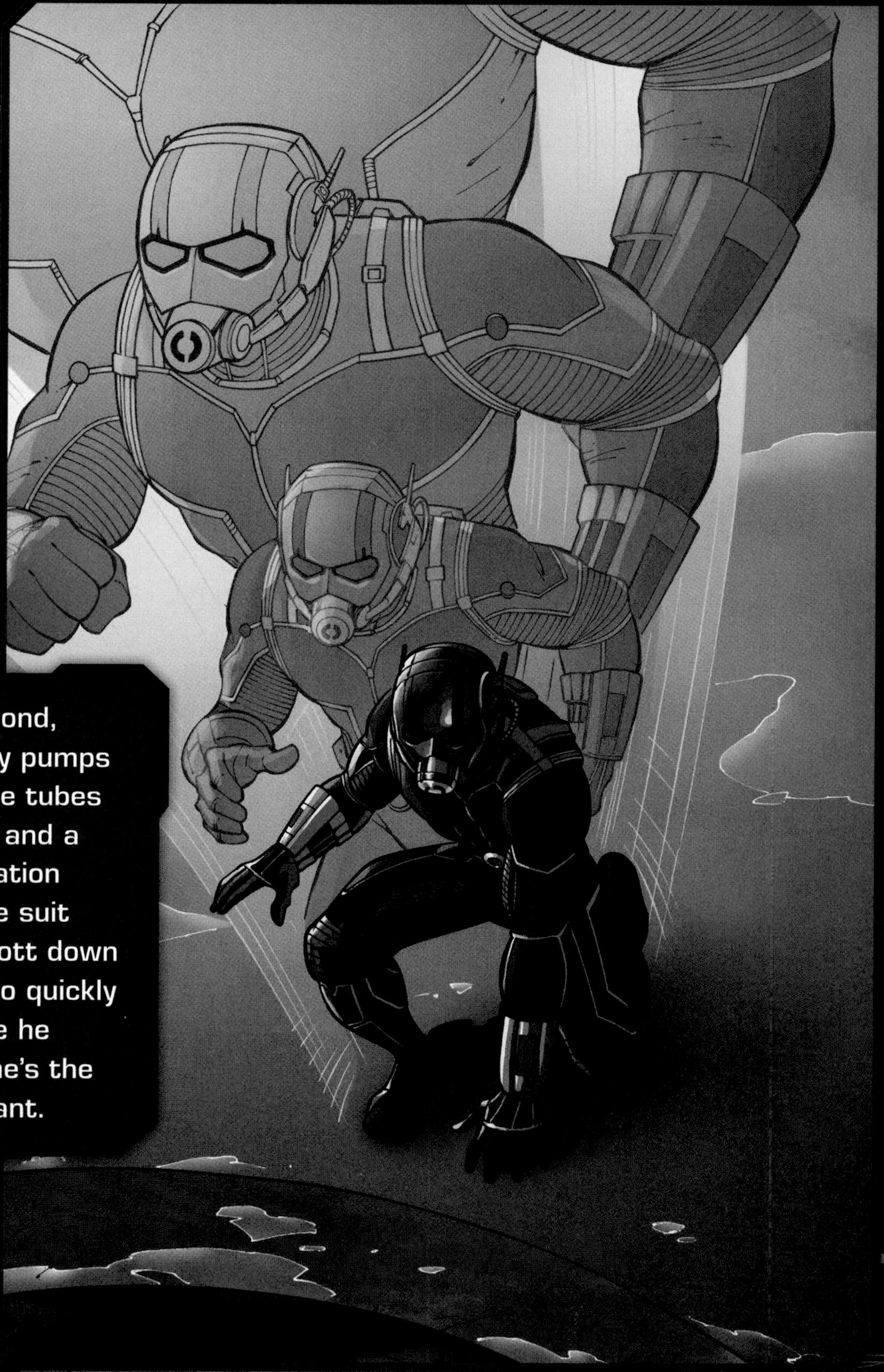

That second, fluid quickly pumps through the tubes of the suit and a transformation begins! The suit shrinks Scott down so small, so quickly that before he knows it, he's the size of an ant.

Looking up, he sees the walls of the bathtub are tall, like a mountain canyon. Scott's roommate comes into the bathroom, but he can't see his miniature friend at the bottom of the tub.

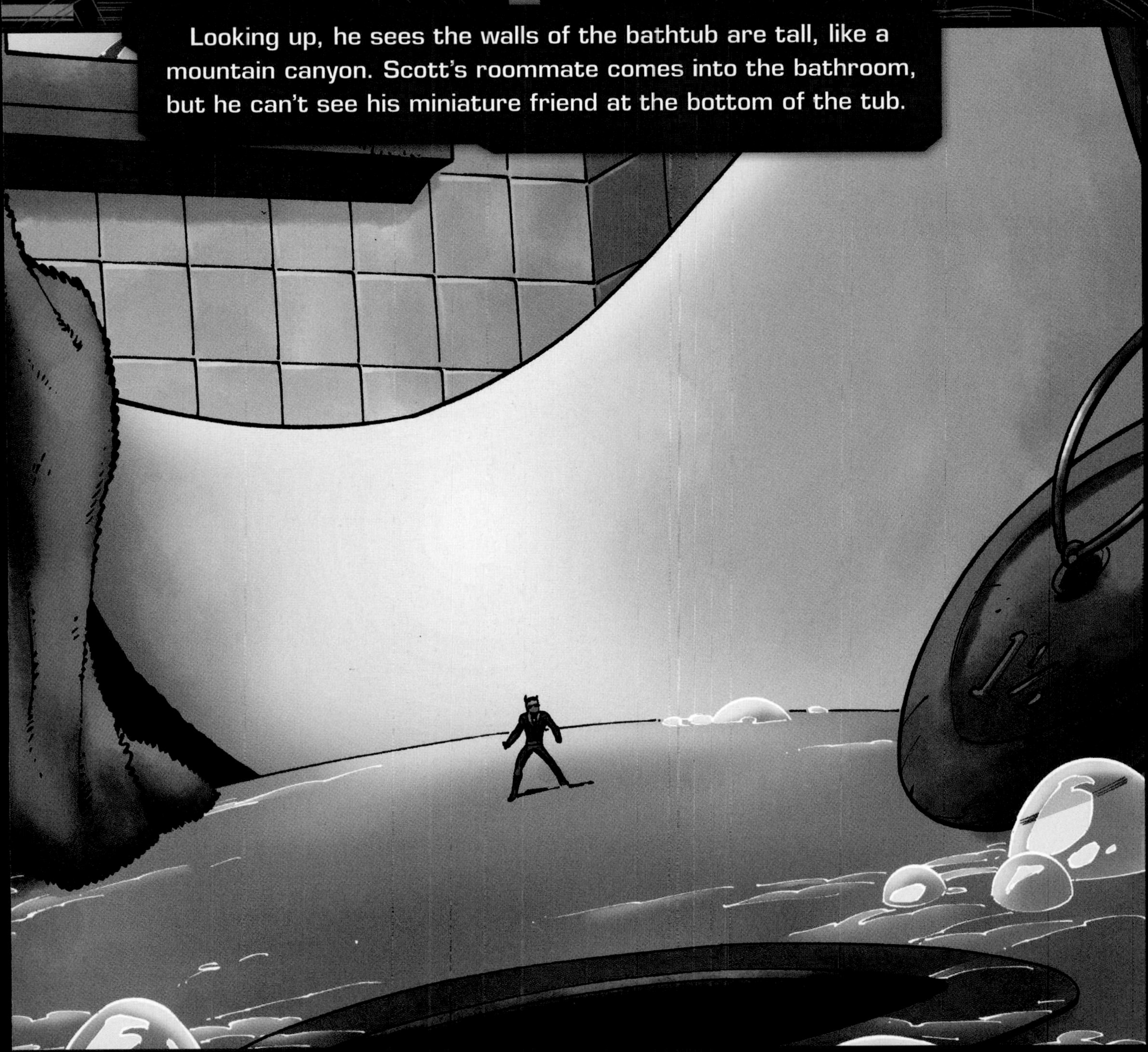

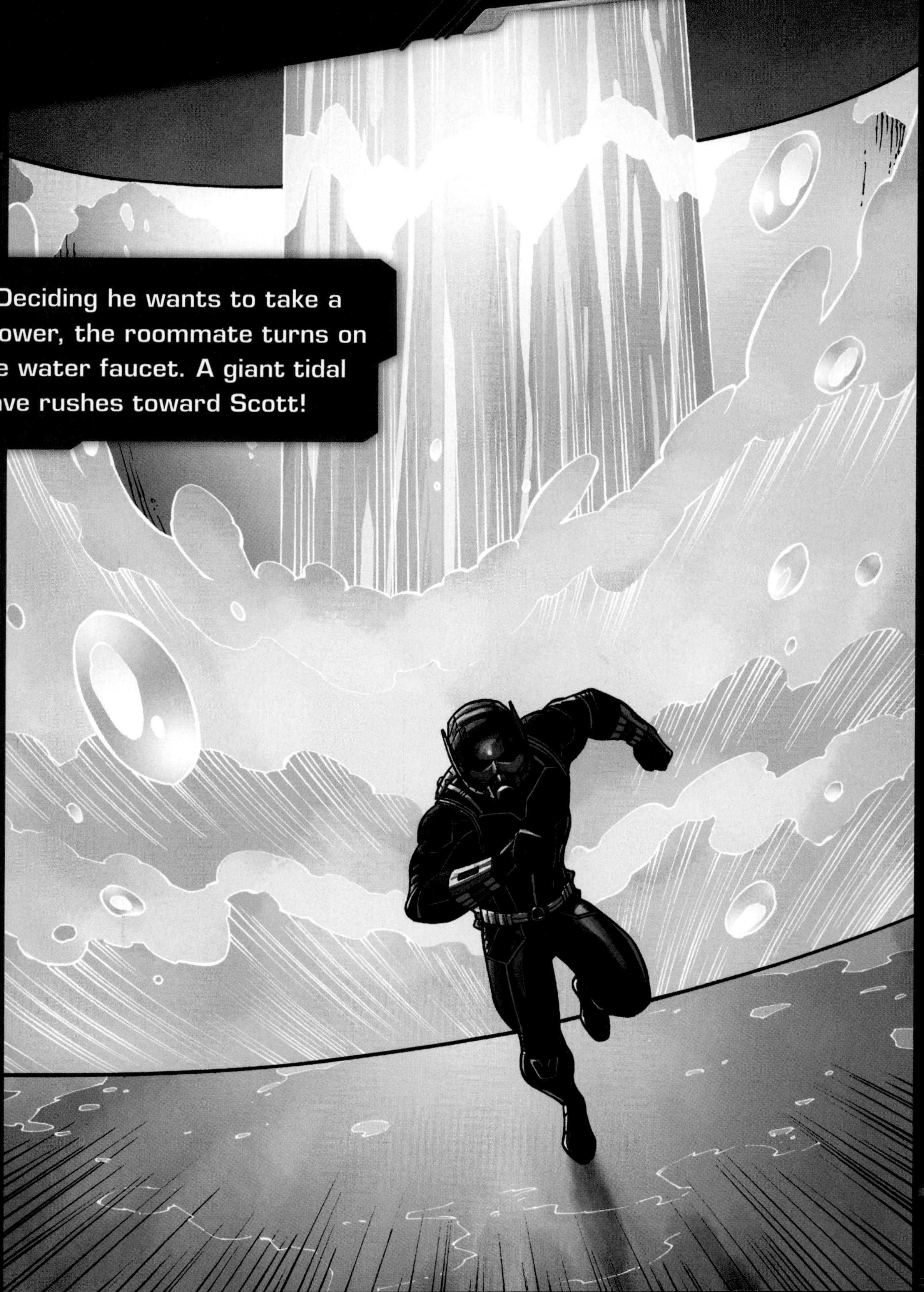

Deciding he wants to take a shower, the roommate turns on the water faucet. A giant tidal wave rushes toward Scott!

With a tiny leap, Scott springs high up into the air. He's out of the tub, shooting past his roommate and toward the floor!

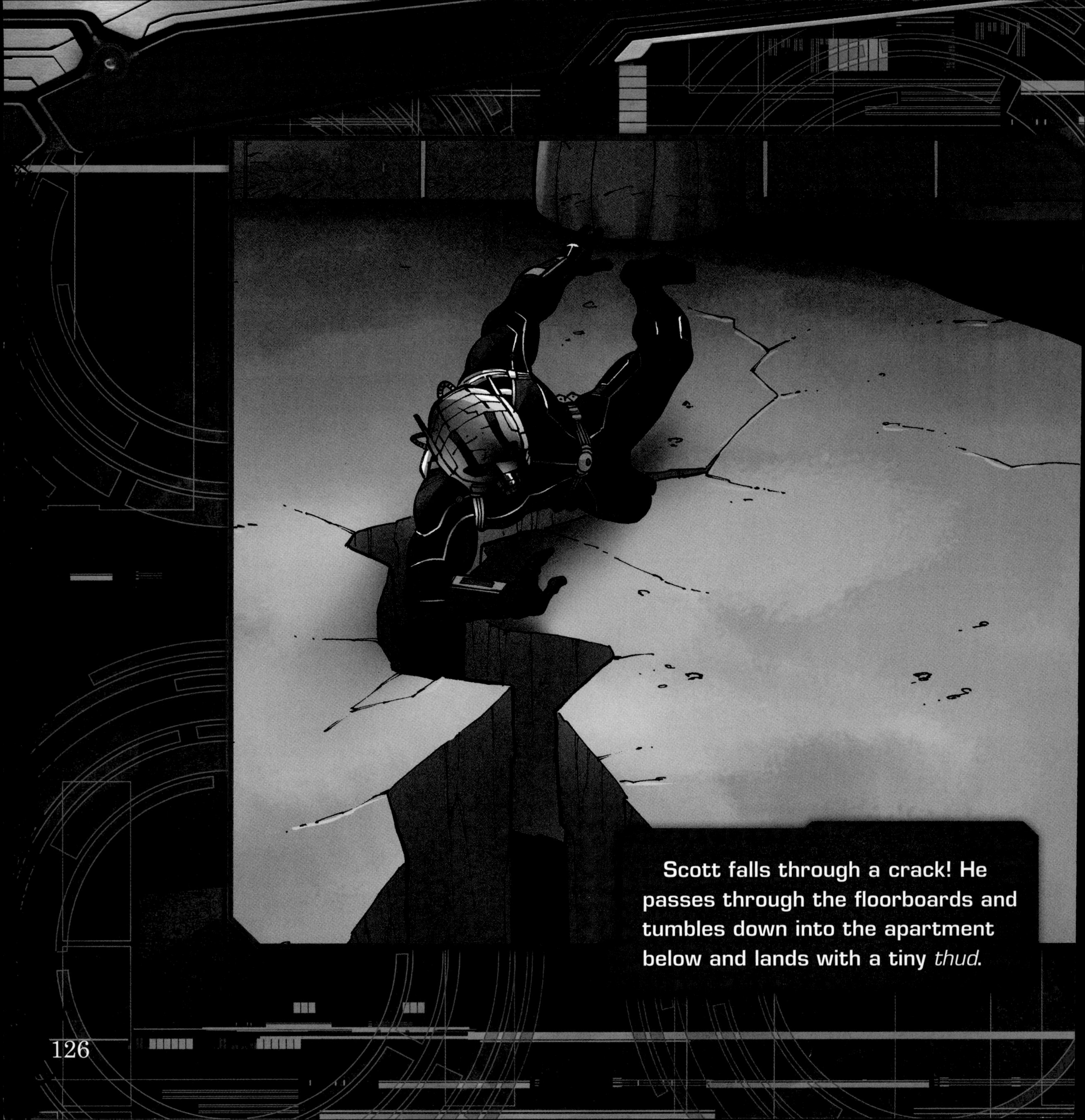

Scott falls through a crack! He passes through the floorboards and tumbles down into the apartment below and lands with a tiny *thud*.

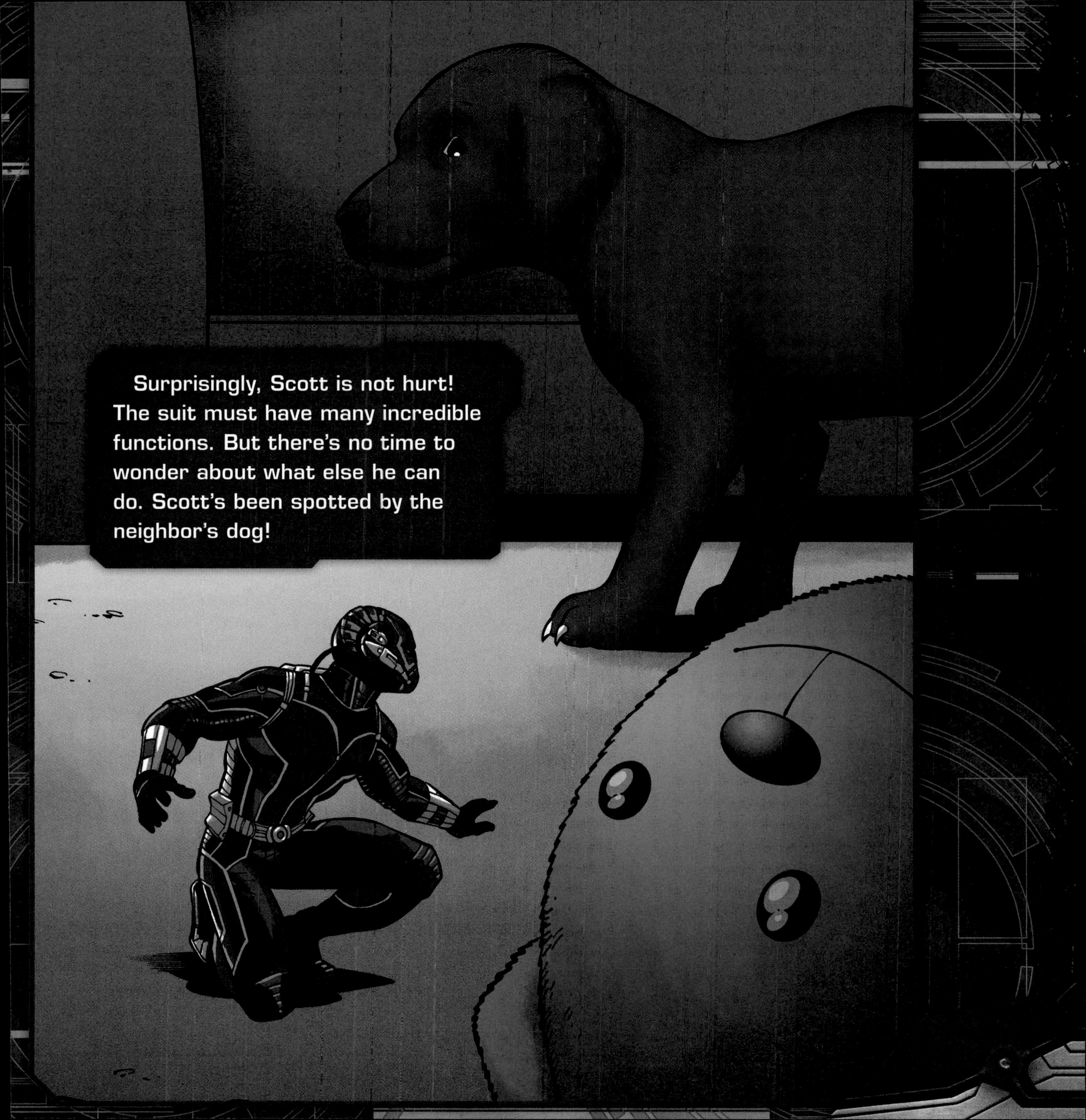

Surprisingly, Scott is not hurt! The suit must have many incredible functions. But there's no time to wonder about what else he can do. Scott's been spotted by the neighbor's dog!

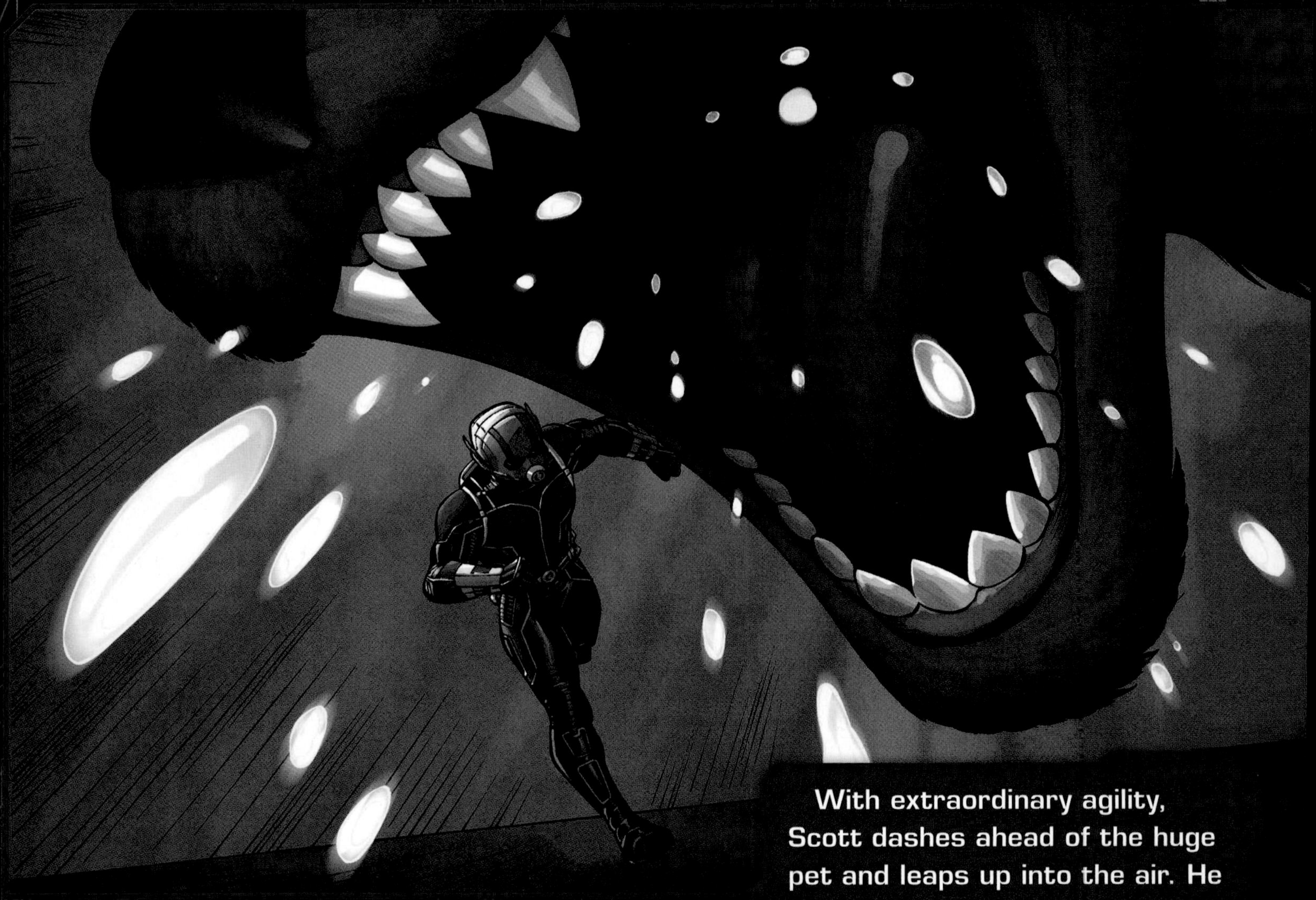

With extraordinary agility, Scott dashes ahead of the huge pet and leaps up into the air. He zips around a bed, chairs, and tables. The dog can't chase him like this for long.

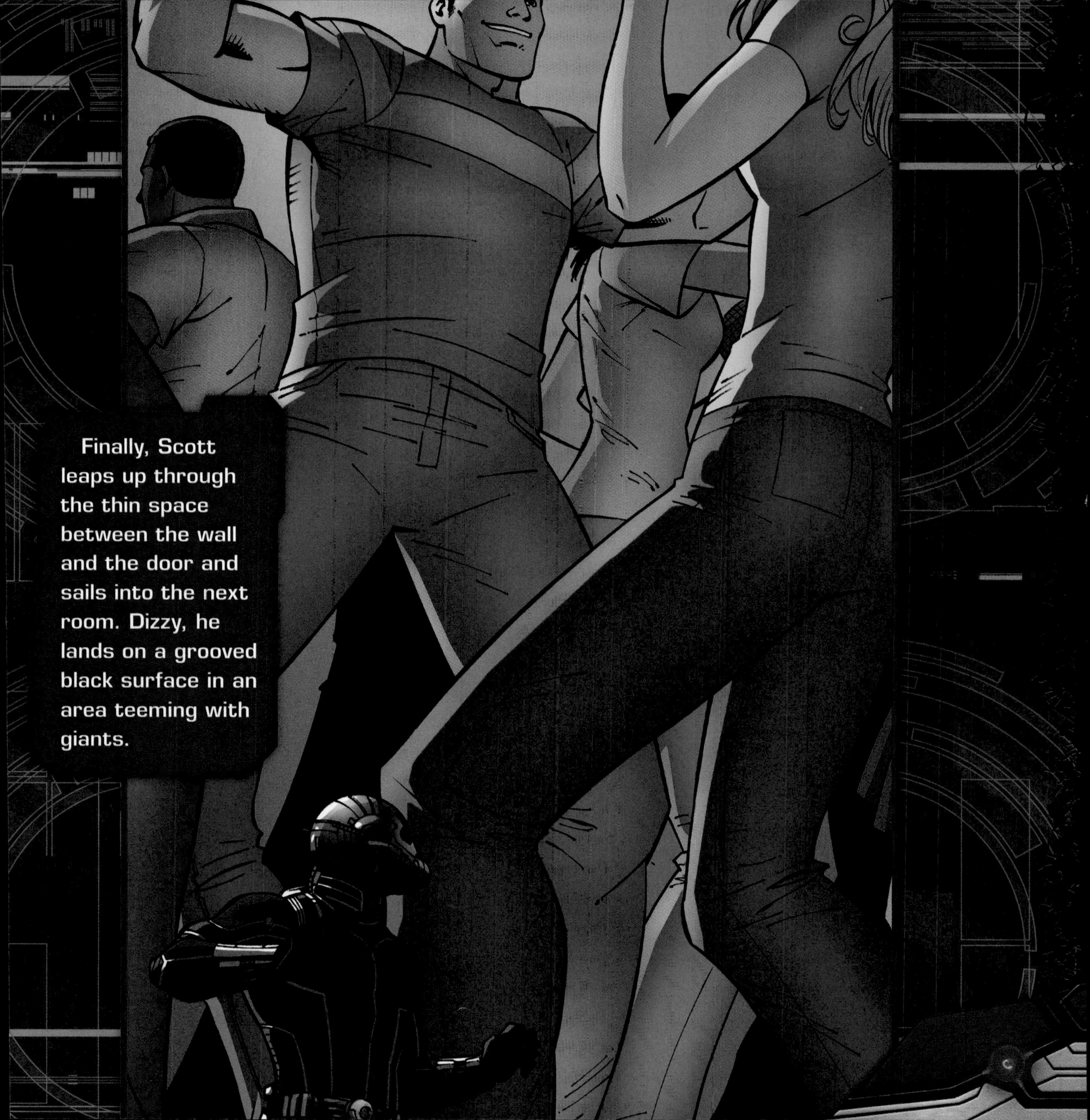

Finally, Scott leaps up through the thin space between the wall and the door and sails into the next room. Dizzy, he lands on a grooved black surface in an area teeming with giants.

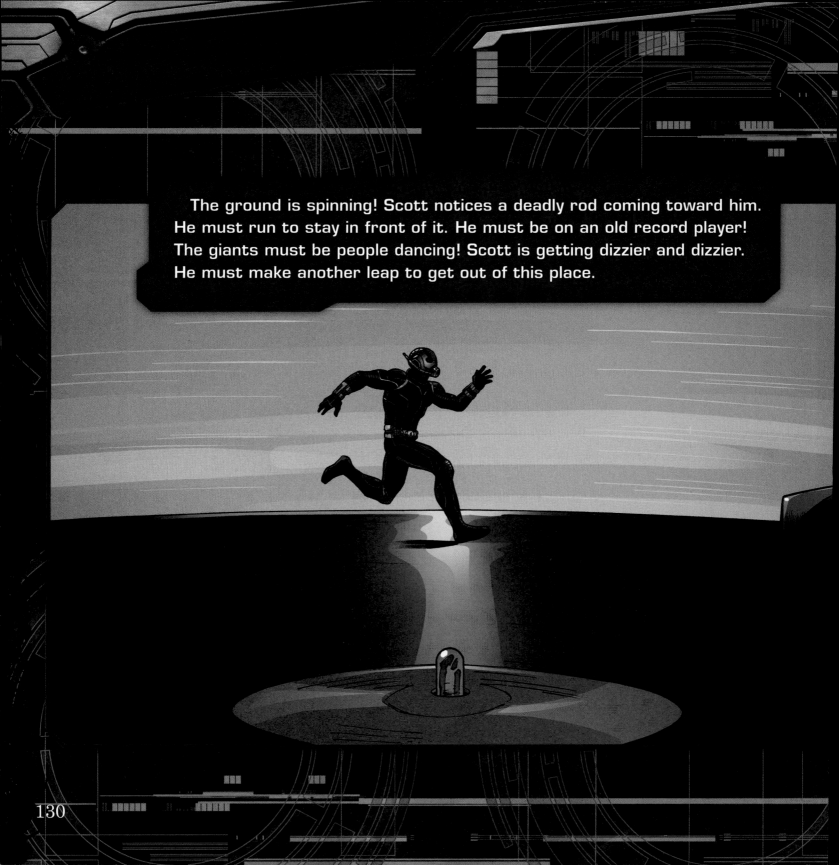

The ground is spinning! Scott notices a deadly rod coming toward him. He must run to stay in front of it. He must be on an old record player! The giants must be people dancing! Scott is getting dizzier and dizzier. He must make another leap to get out of this place.

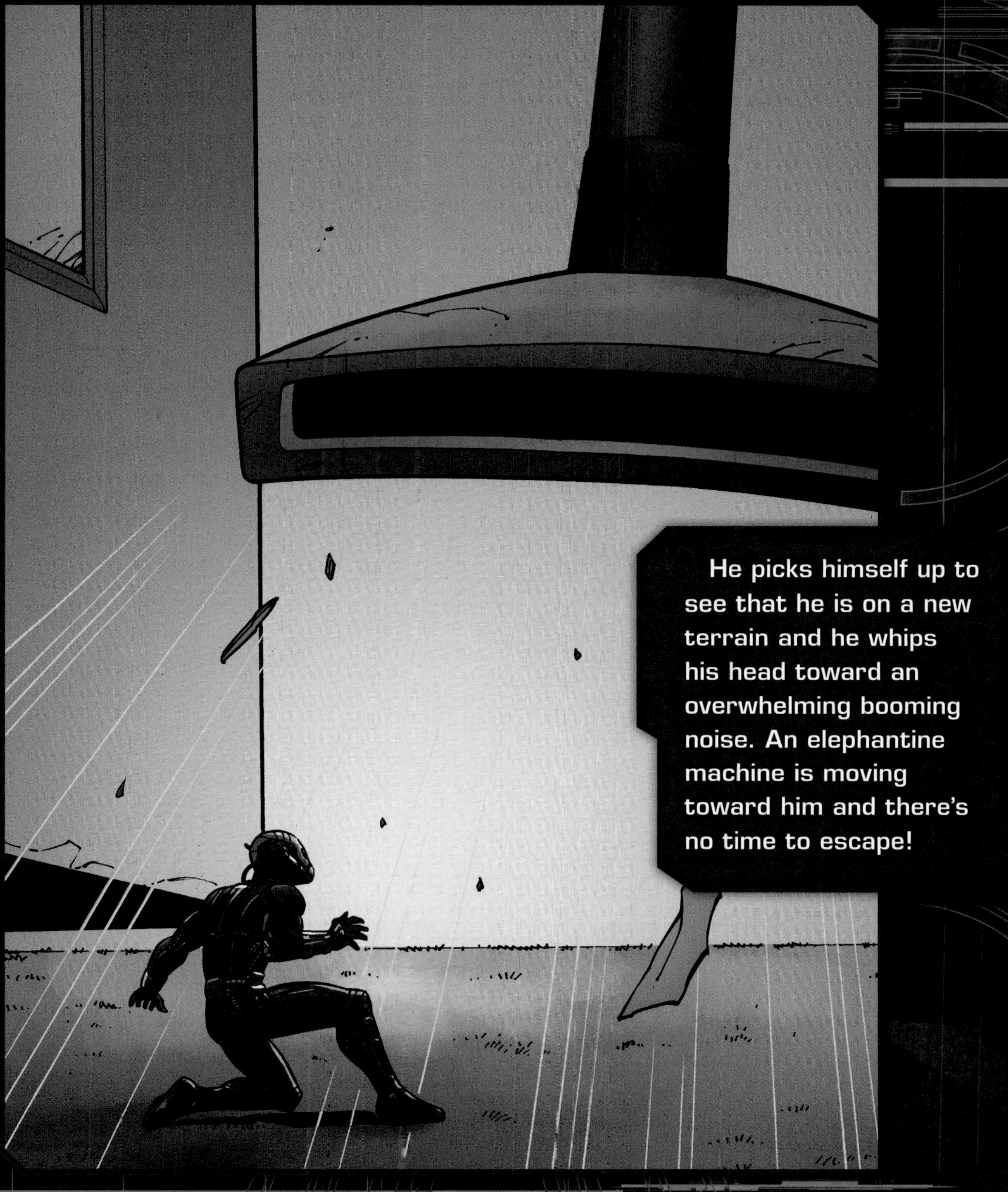
He picks himself up to see that he is on a new terrain and he whips his head toward an overwhelming booming noise. An elephantine machine is moving toward him and there's no time to escape!

Like a dust bunny, Scott is sucked up into a vacuum! The air currents spin him around with tornado force! Thankfully, Scott's helmet keeps him safe, and he is deposited deep into the canister with all the other small debris. He finds himself resting on a giant fluffy pillow of lint.

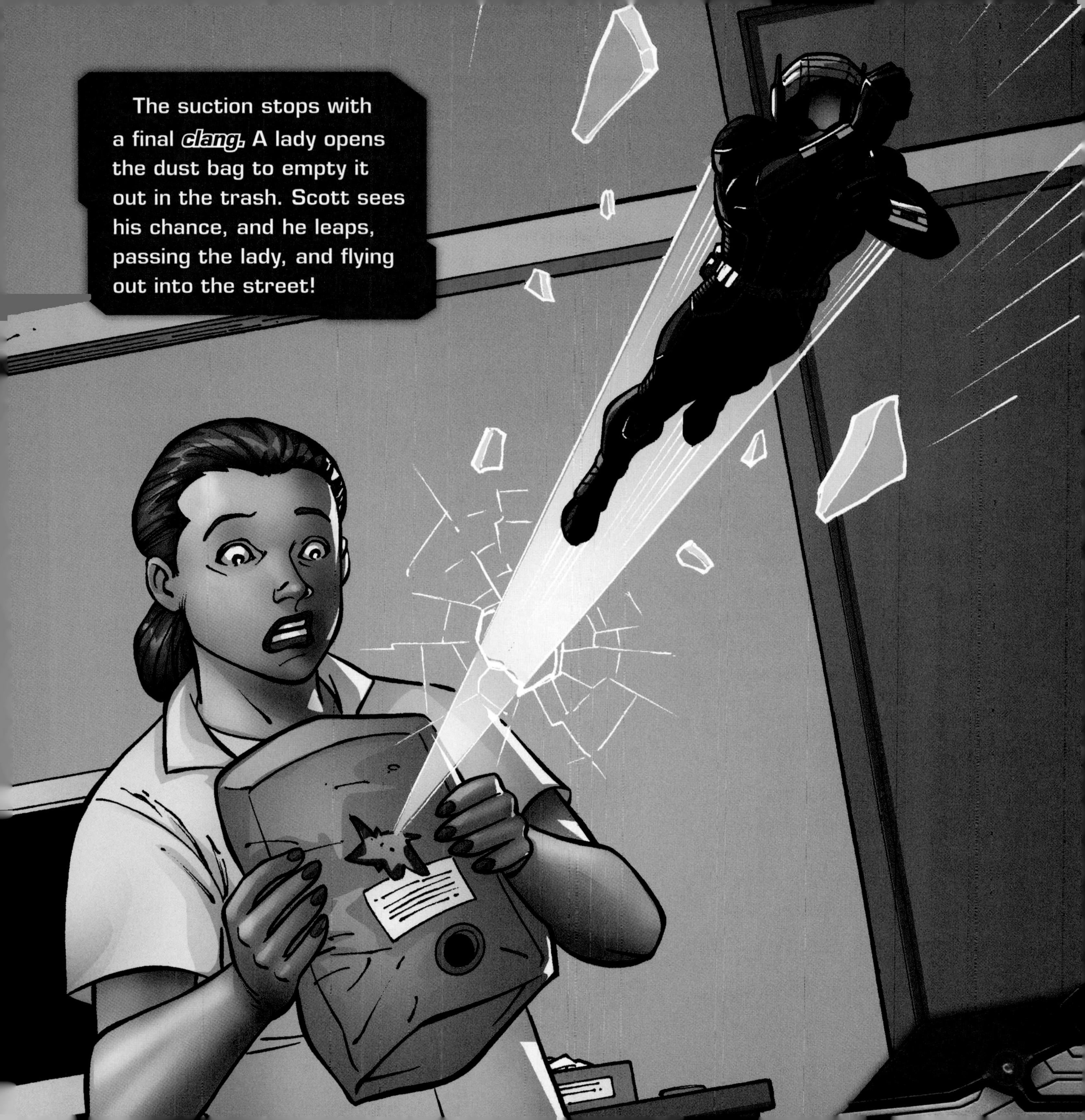
The suction stops with a final clang. A lady opens the dust bag to empty it out in the trash. Scott sees his chance, and he leaps, passing the lady, and flying out into the street!

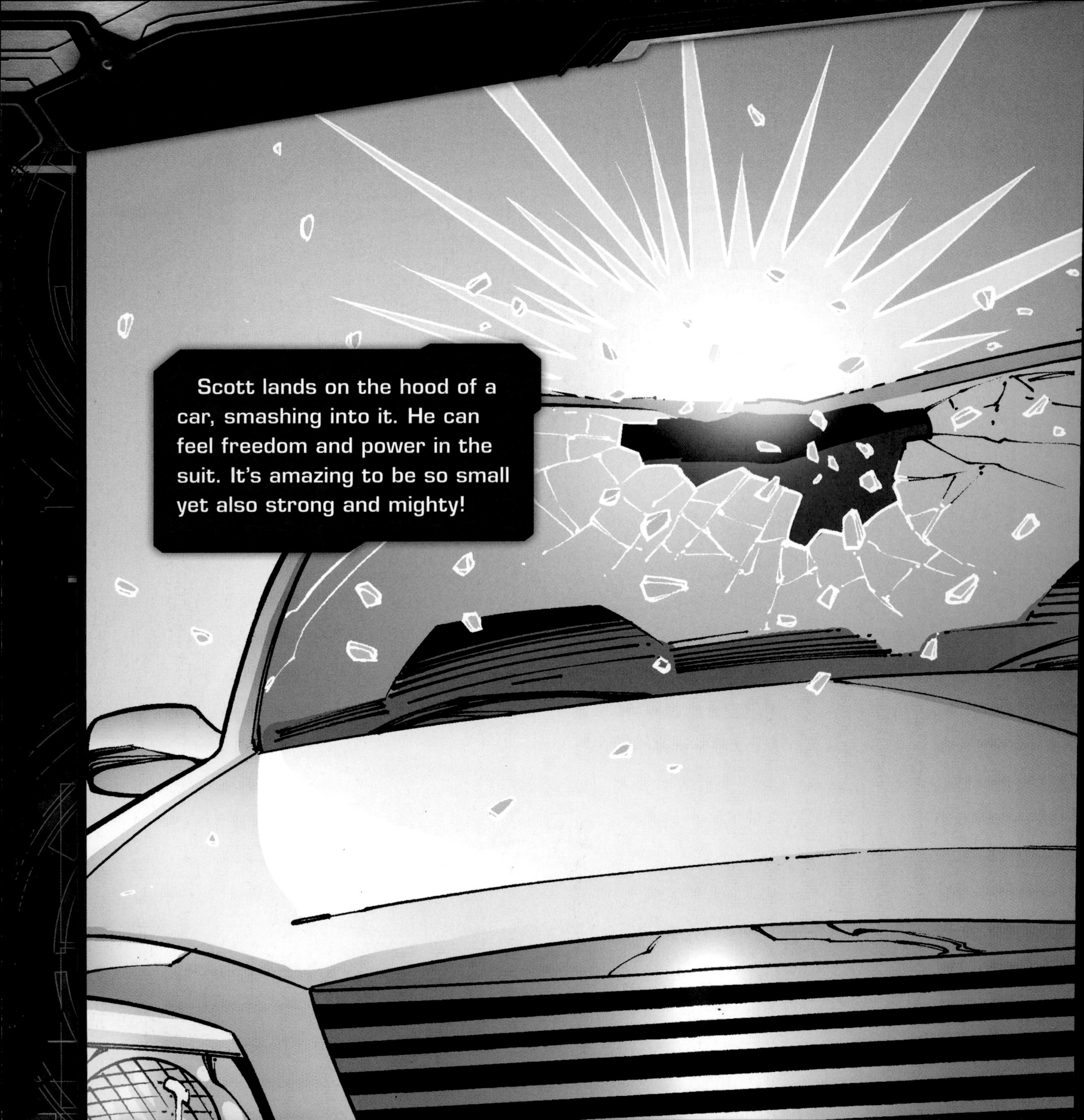
Scott lands on the hood of a car, smashing into it. He can feel freedom and power in the suit. It's amazing to be so small yet also strong and mighty!

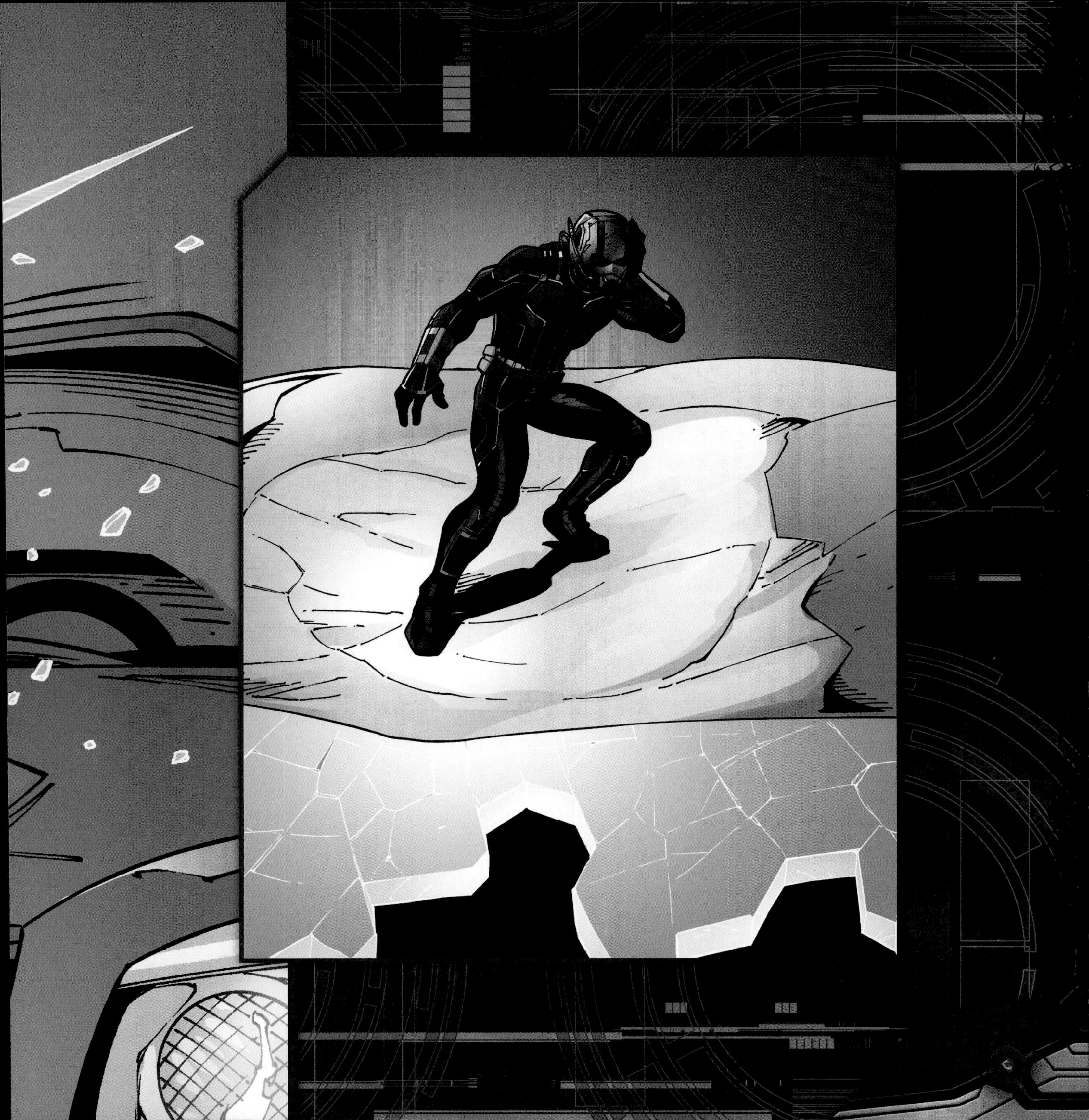

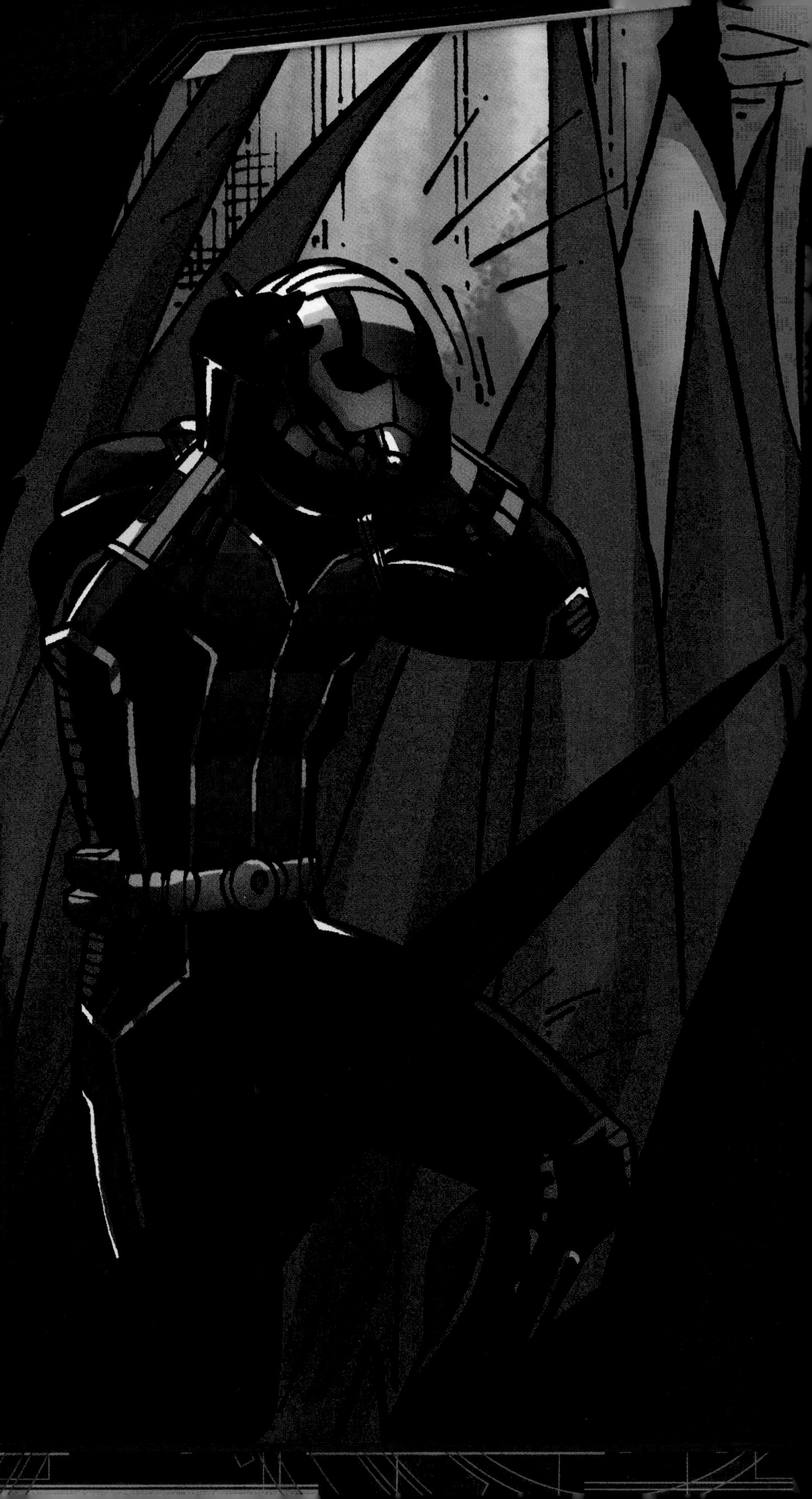

Being micro-size in this suit, Scott knows that he will be in great danger from average-size people and objects. But there are still powers that he can use to keep himself safe. Perhaps these powers can be used for more than just protecting himself.

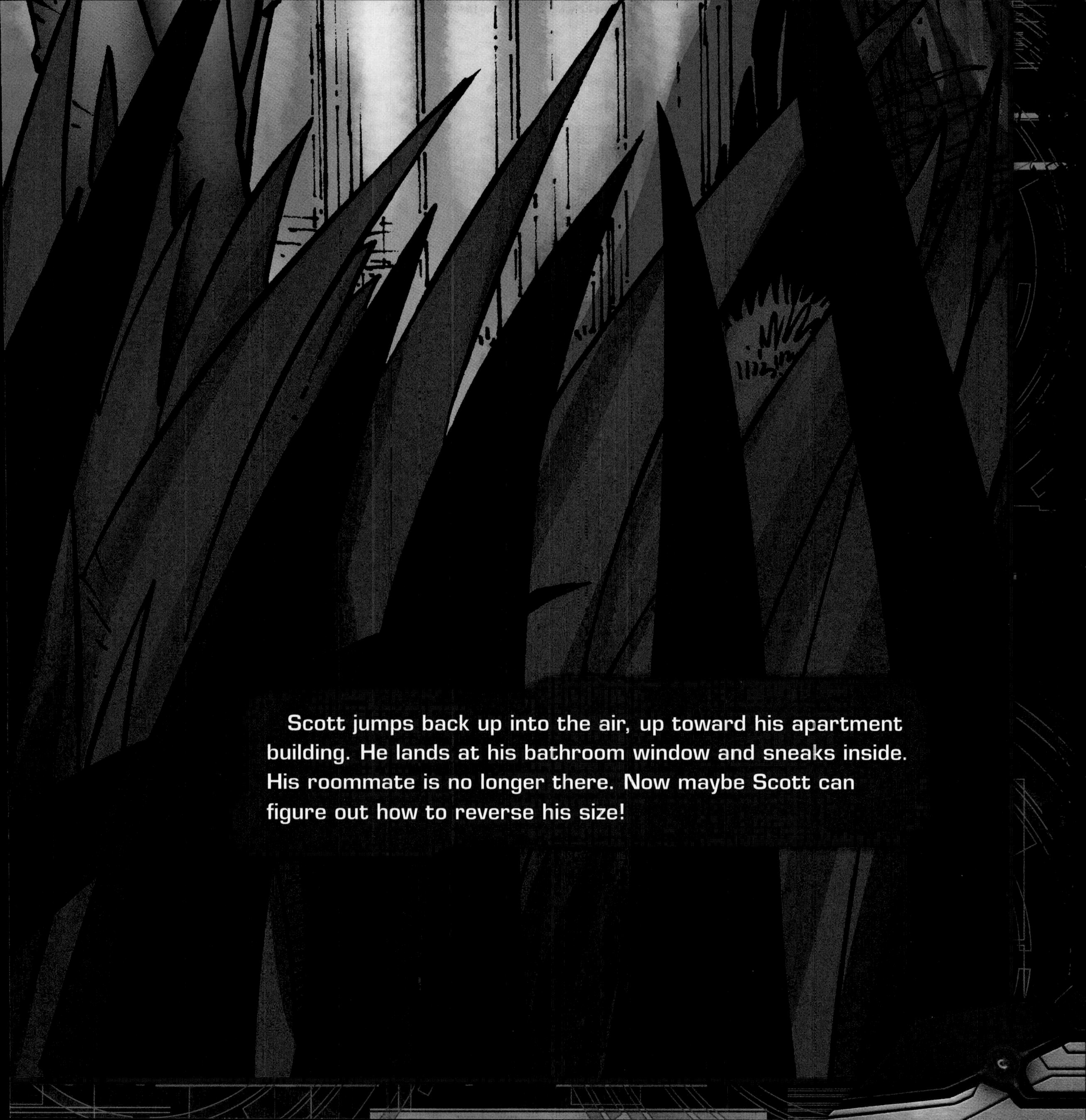

Scott jumps back up into the air, up toward his apartment building. He lands at his bathroom window and sneaks inside. His roommate is no longer there. Now maybe Scott can figure out how to reverse his size!

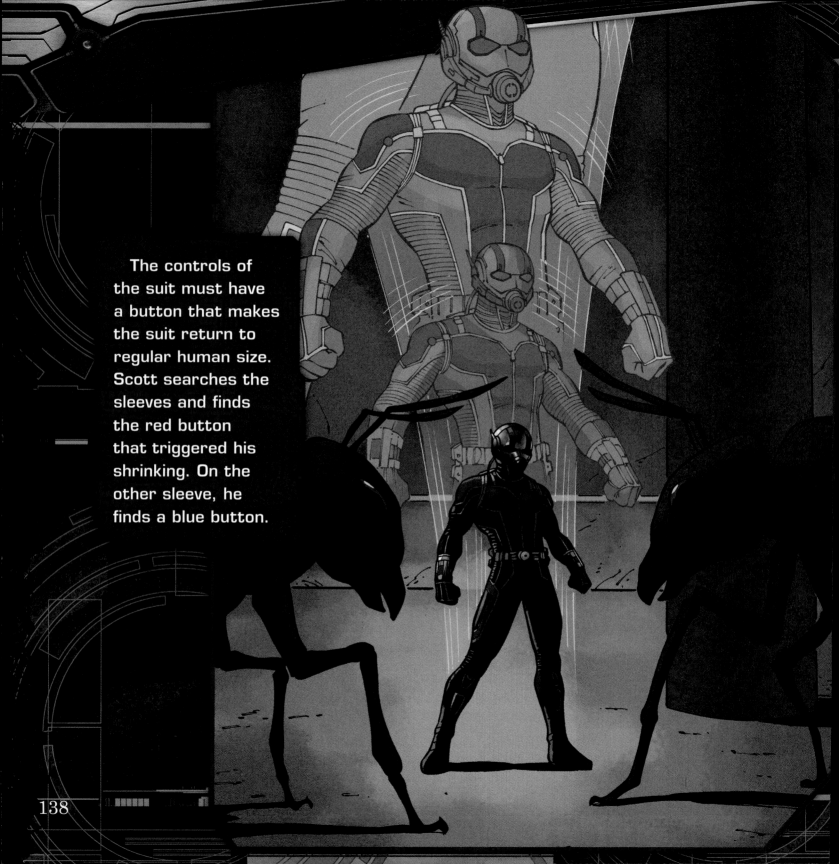

The controls of the suit must have a button that makes the suit return to regular human size. Scott searches the sleeves and finds the red button that triggered his shrinking. On the other sleeve, he finds a blue button.

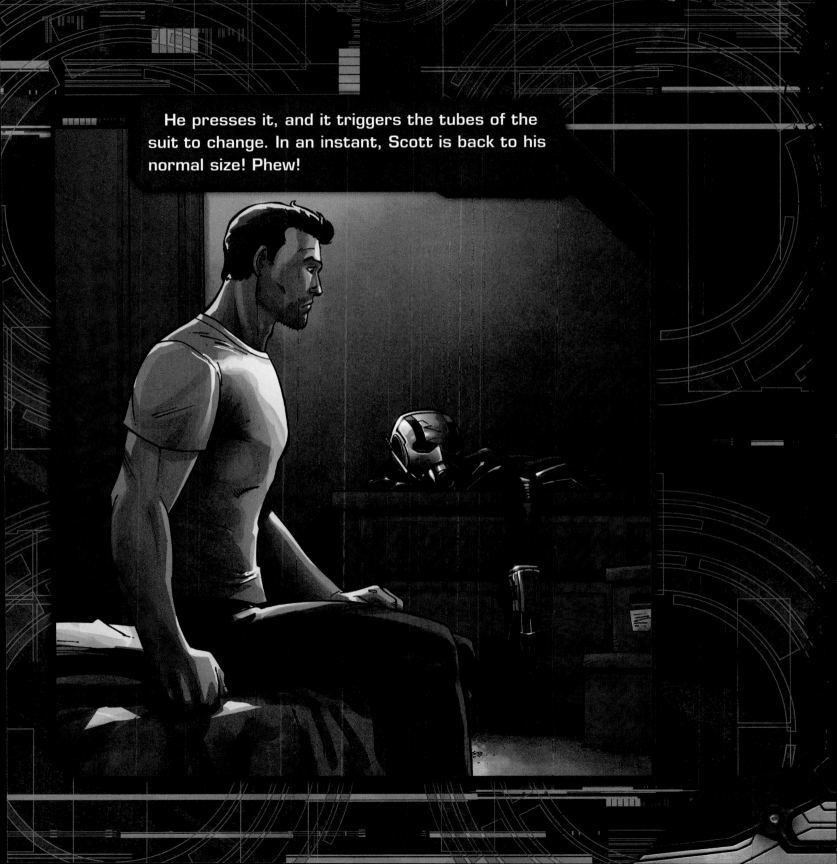

He presses it, and it triggers the tubes of the suit to change. In an instant, Scott is back to his normal size! Phew!

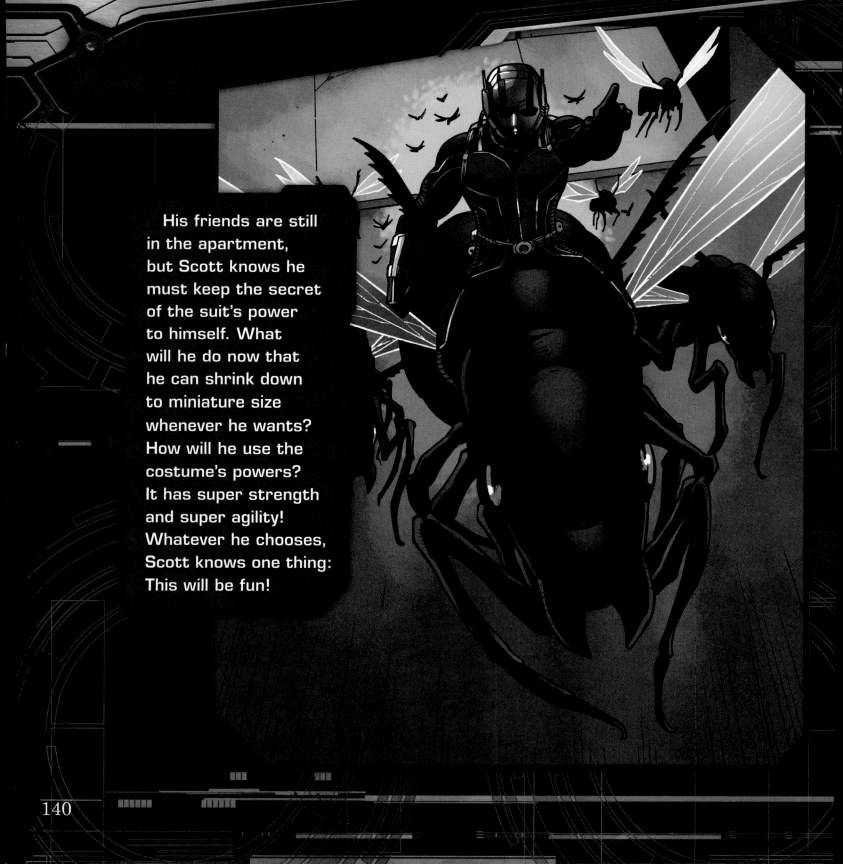

His friends are still in the apartment, but Scott knows he must keep the secret of the suit's power to himself. What will he do now that he can shrink down to miniature size whenever he wants? How will he use the costume's powers? It has super strength and super agility! Whatever he chooses, Scott knows one thing: This will be fun!

MARVEL
GUARDIANS OF THE GALAXY

ROCKET AND GROOT FIGHT BACK

Adapted by Adam Davis
Illustrated by Ron Lim, Drew Geraci, and Lee Duhig
Based on the Screenplay by James Gunn
Story by Nicole Perlman and James Gunn
Produced by Kevin Feige, p.g.a.
Directed by James Gunn

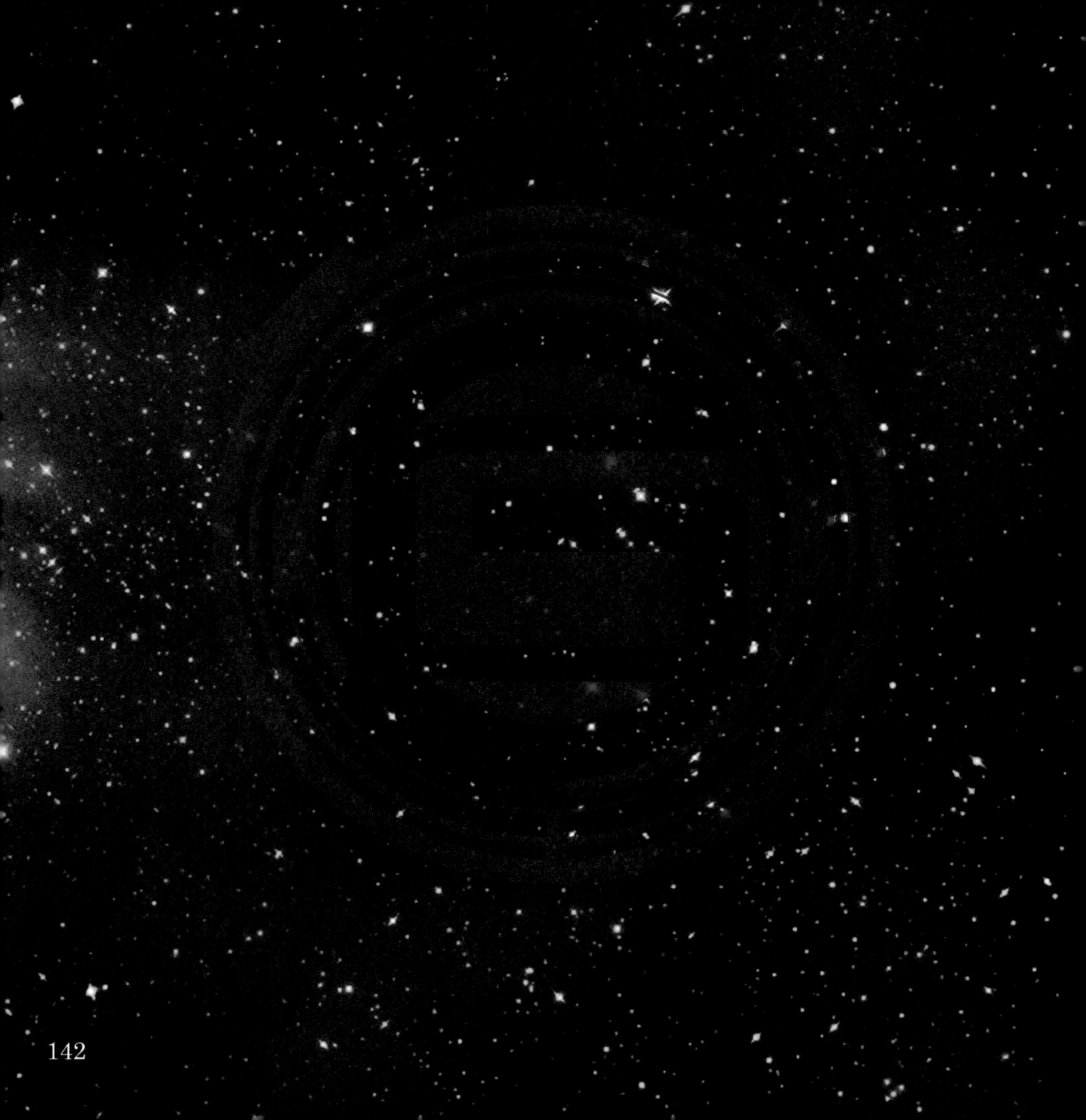

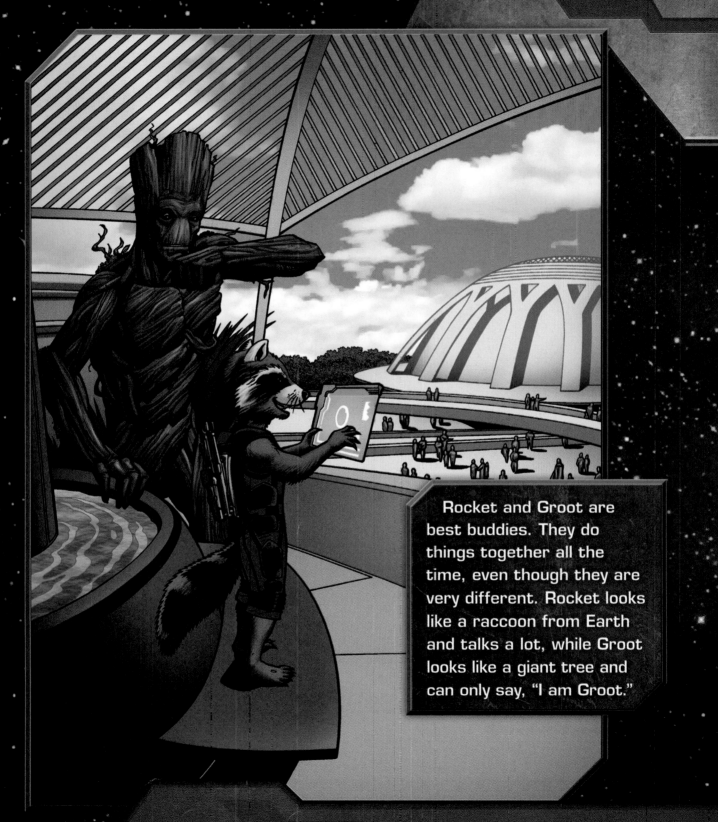

Rocket and Groot are best buddies. They do things together all the time, even though they are very different. Rocket looks like a raccoon from Earth and talks a lot, while Groot looks like a giant tree and can only say, "I am Groot."

One day, while hanging out at the mall, the friends see a green-skinned woman get into a fight with a man. Suddenly, the woman takes a shiny ball from him and runs!

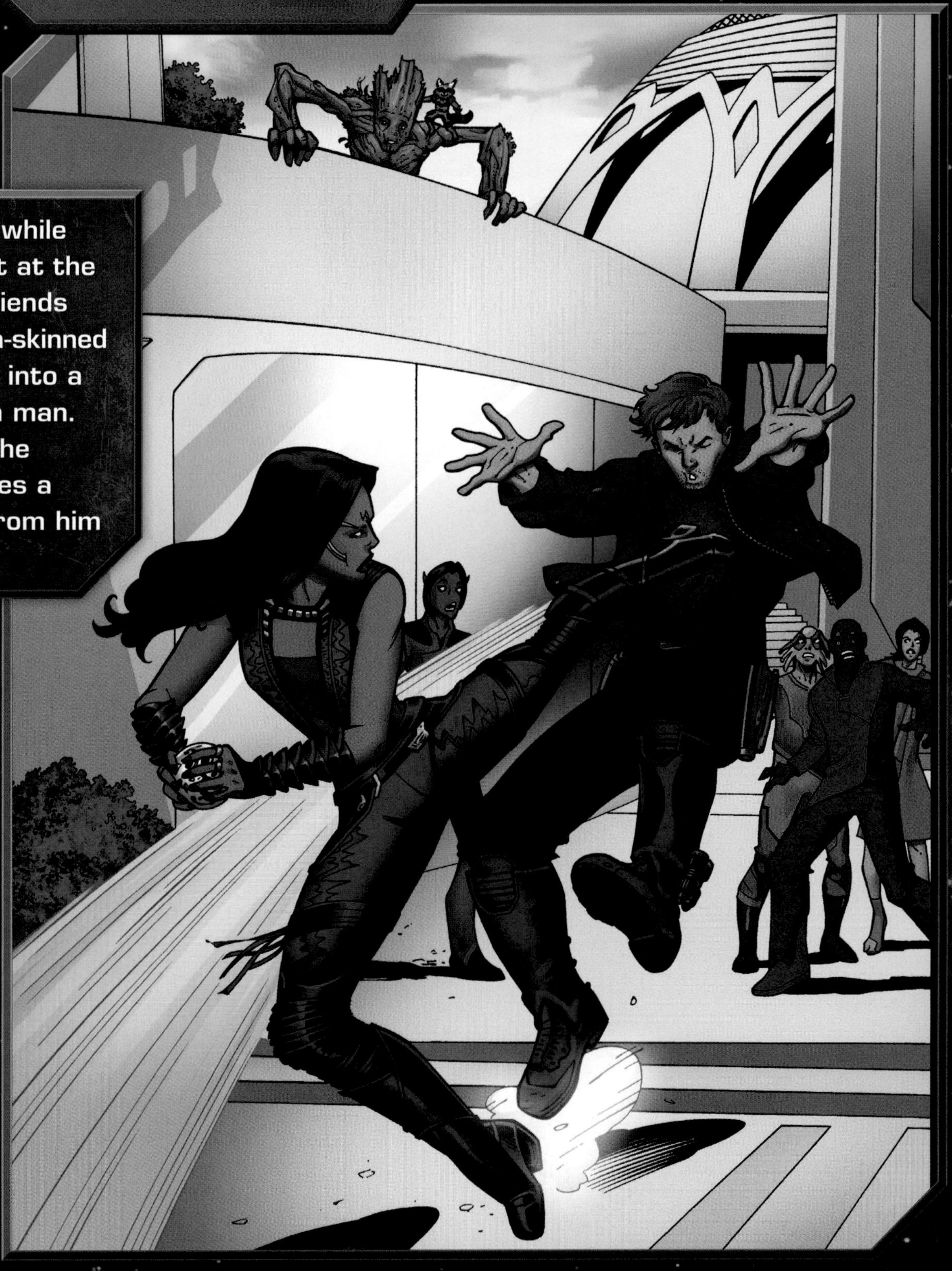

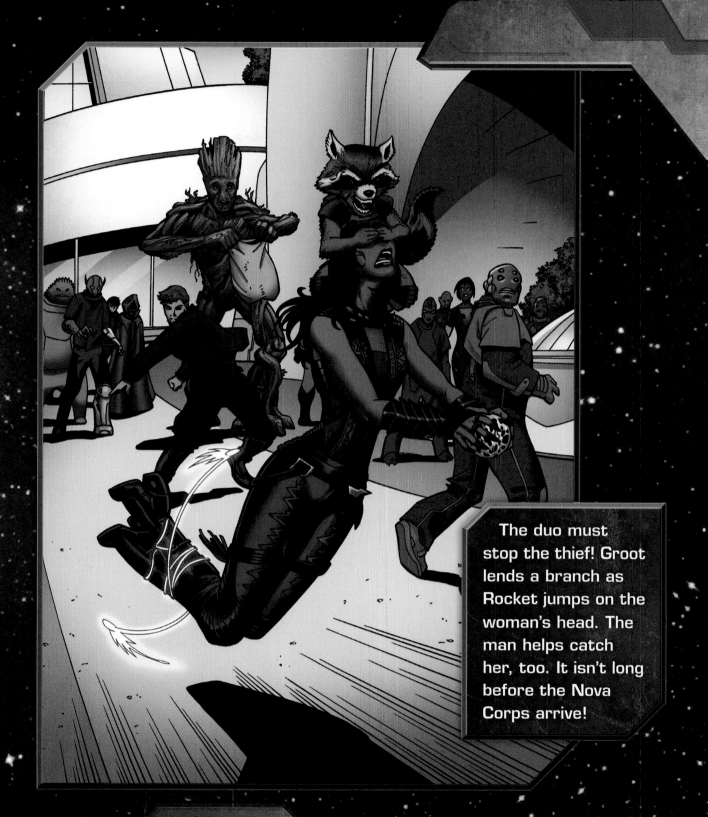

The duo must stop the thief! Groot lends a branch as Rocket jumps on the woman's head. The man helps catch her, too. It isn't long before the Nova Corps arrive!

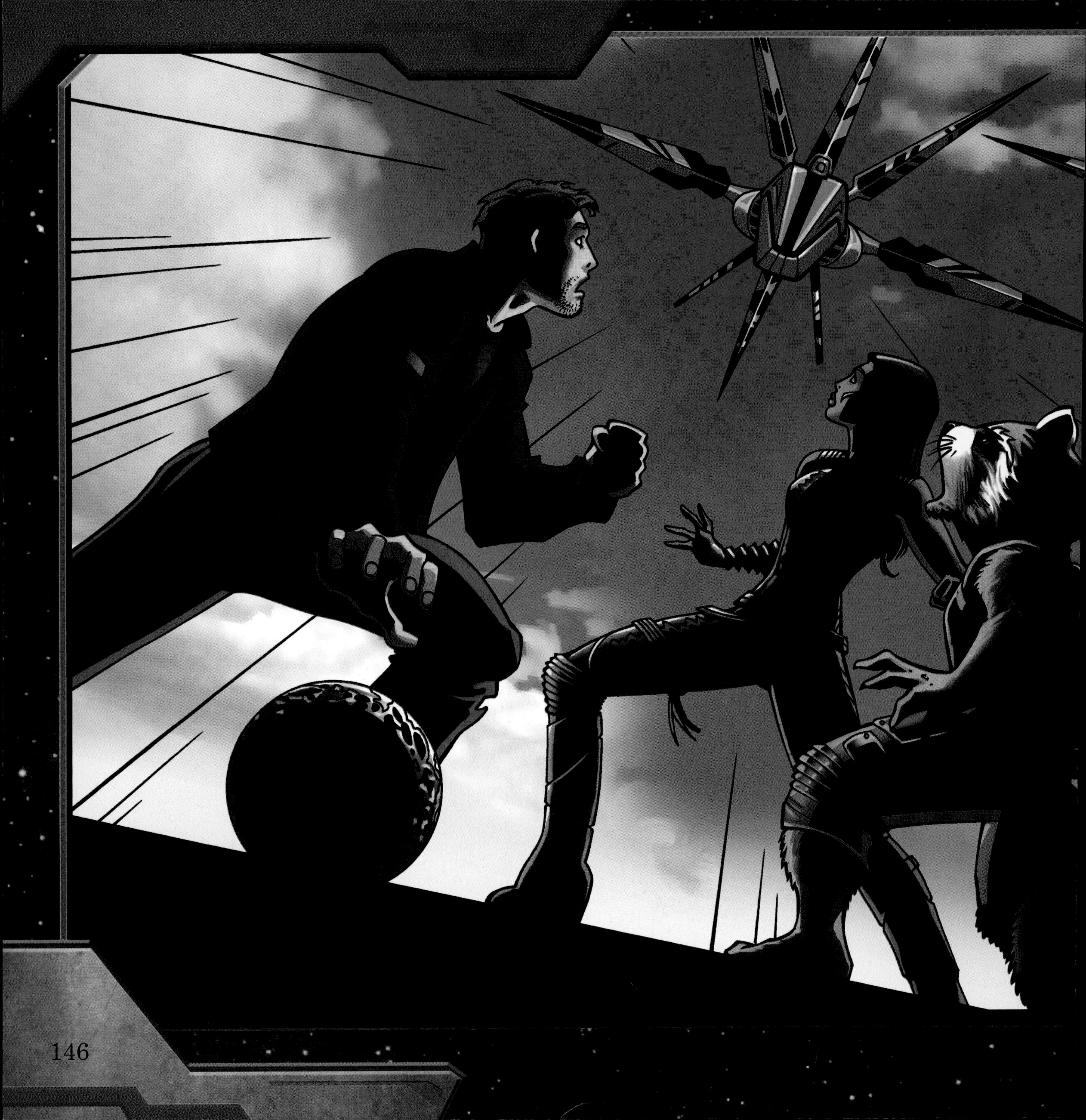

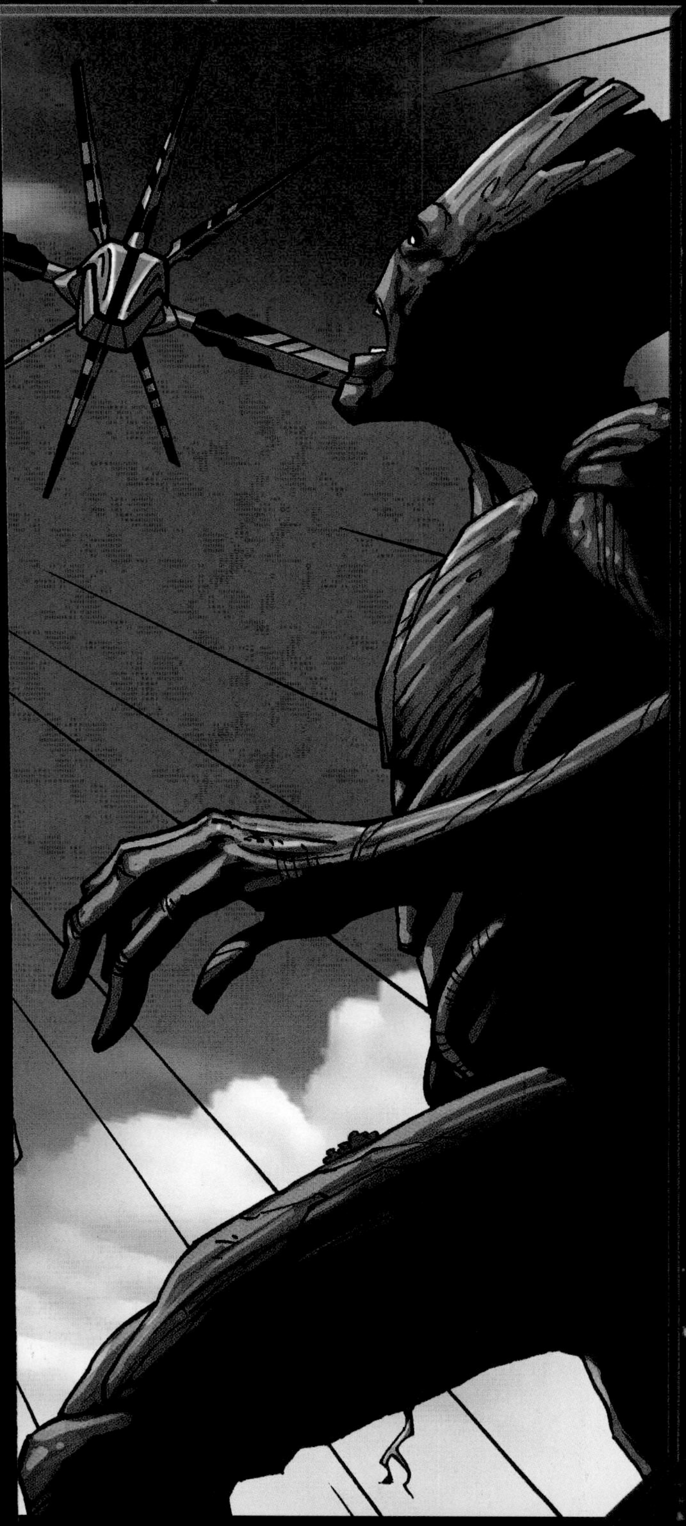

The space police stop the fight and take the group away. The friends learn that the woman's name is Gamora and the man's is Peter. Peter's ball is actually a very powerful Orb, and a lot of people want it—especially a villain named Ronan!

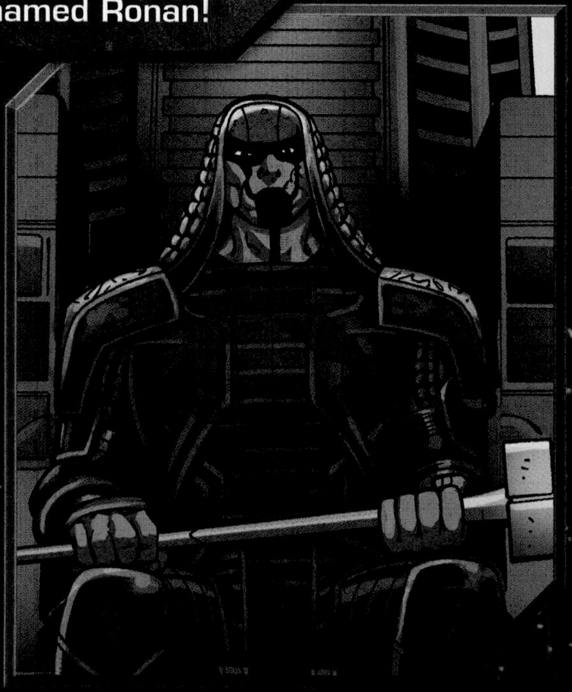

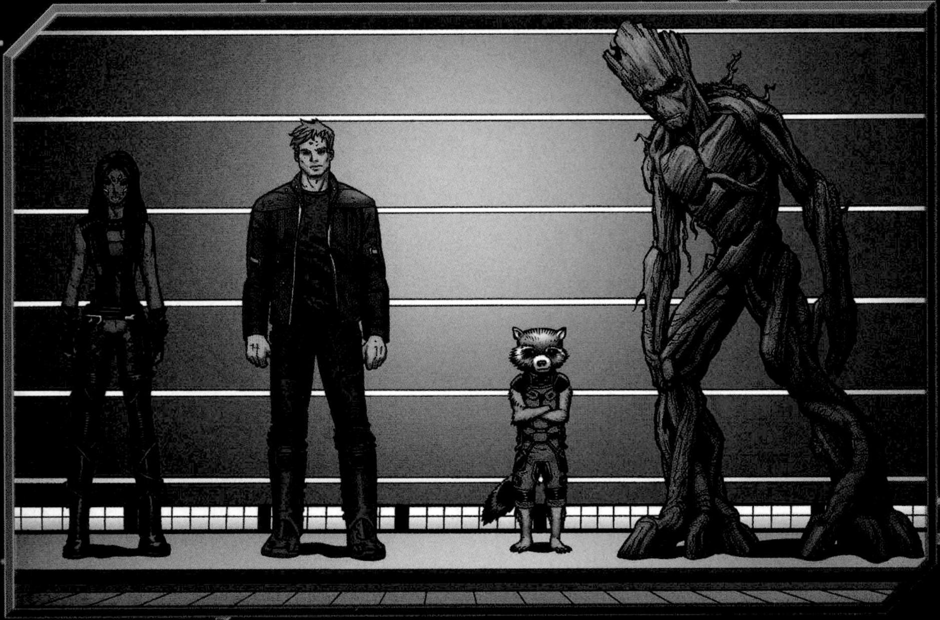

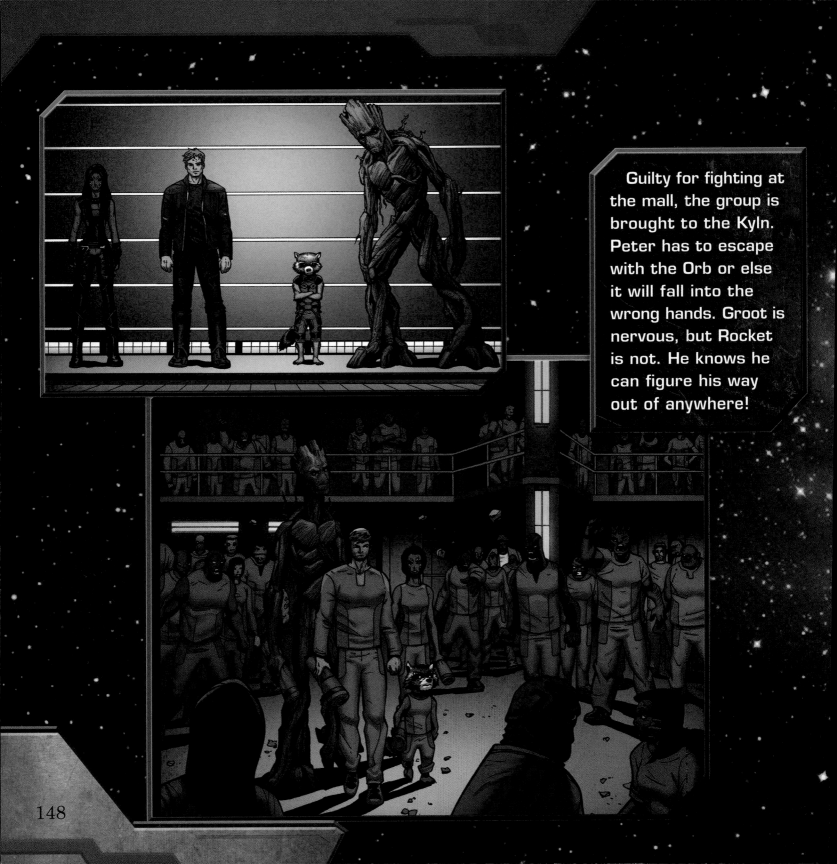

Guilty for fighting at the mall, the group is brought to the Kyln. Peter has to escape with the Orb or else it will fall into the wrong hands. Groot is nervous, but Rocket is not. He knows he can figure his way out of anywhere!

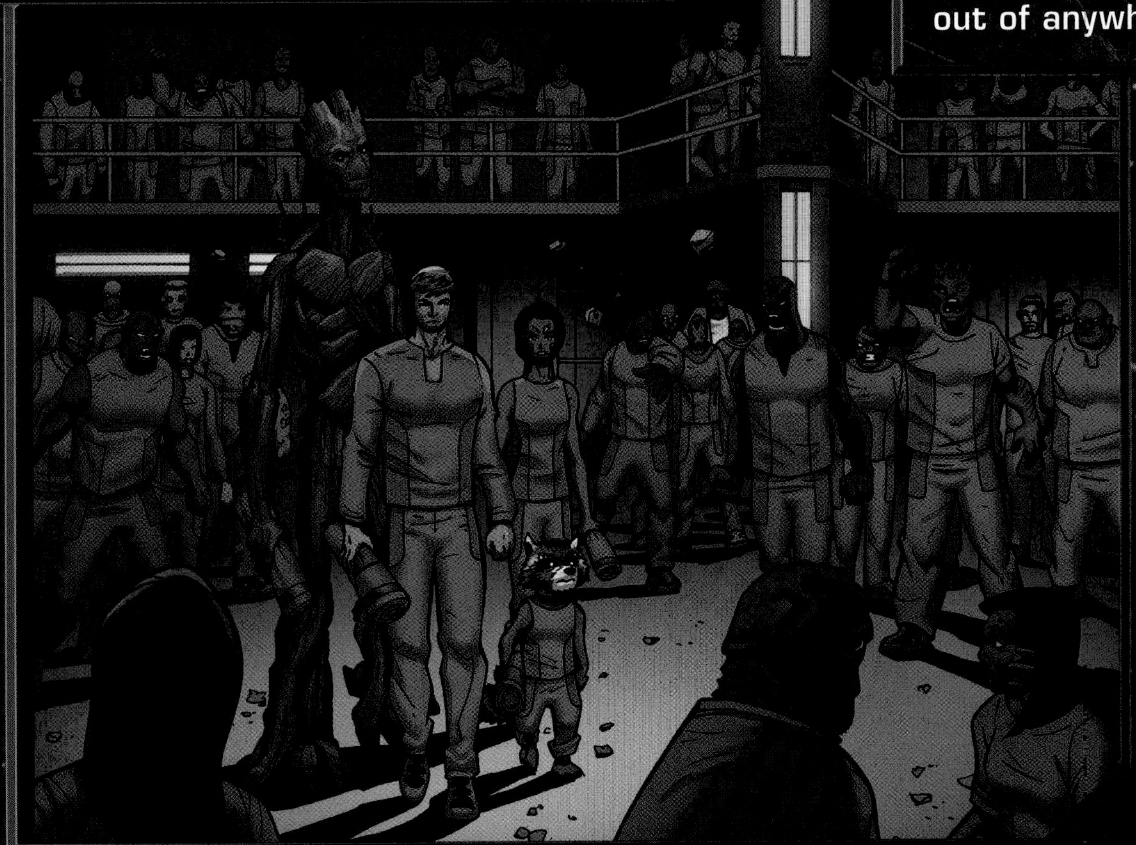

Rocket and Groot convince Peter and Gamora to be friends so the four of them can work together. A muscular prisoner named Drax overhears them talking and offers to help with the plan, too. He wants to escape as much as they do!

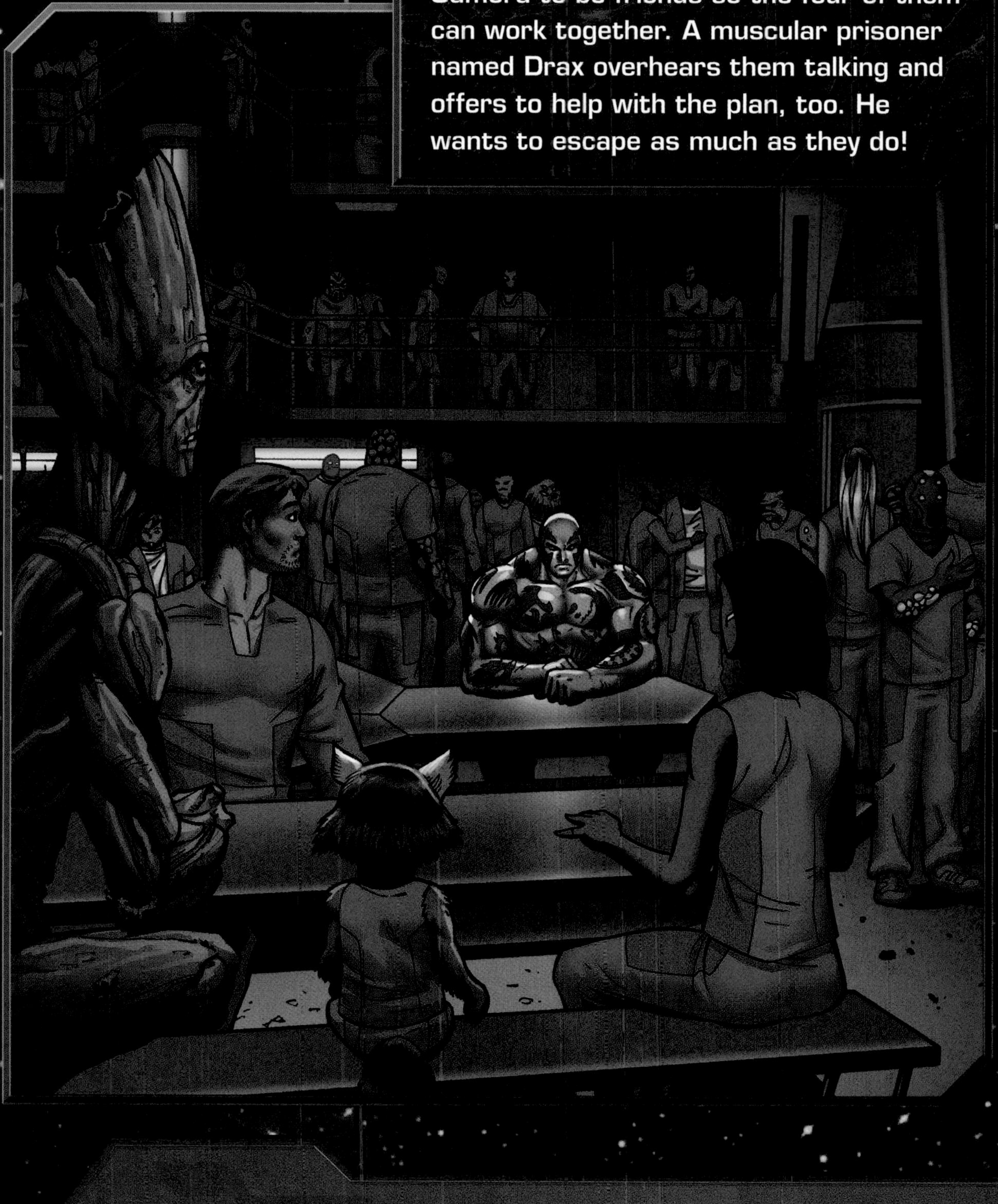

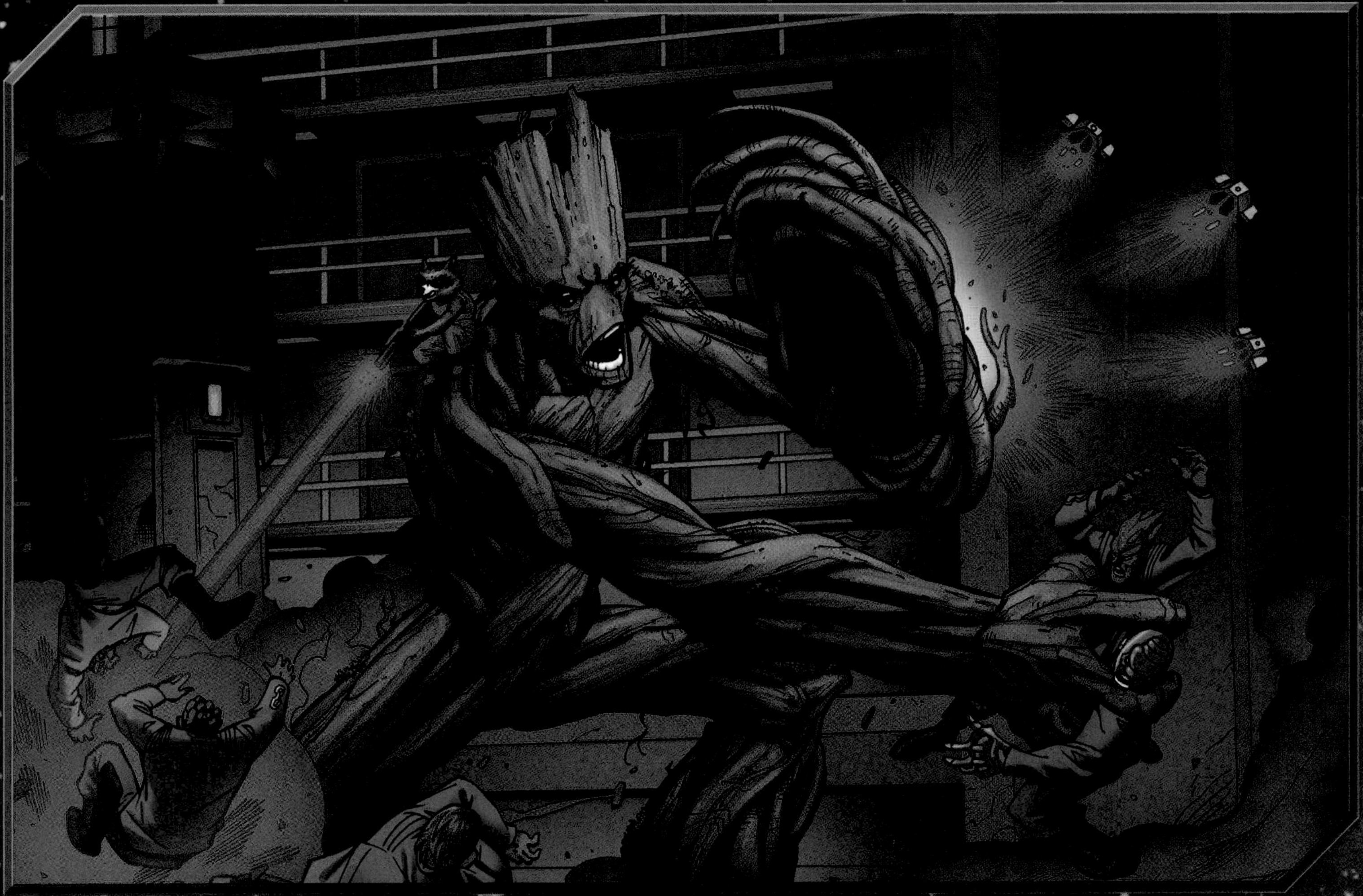

Soon Rocket has a plan! He tells Groot to grow to twice his size and smash the flying robot guards. Rocket rides on his shoulder, keeping other foes away.

Peter, Gamora, and Drax fight bravely, as well. They throw powerful kicks and punches!

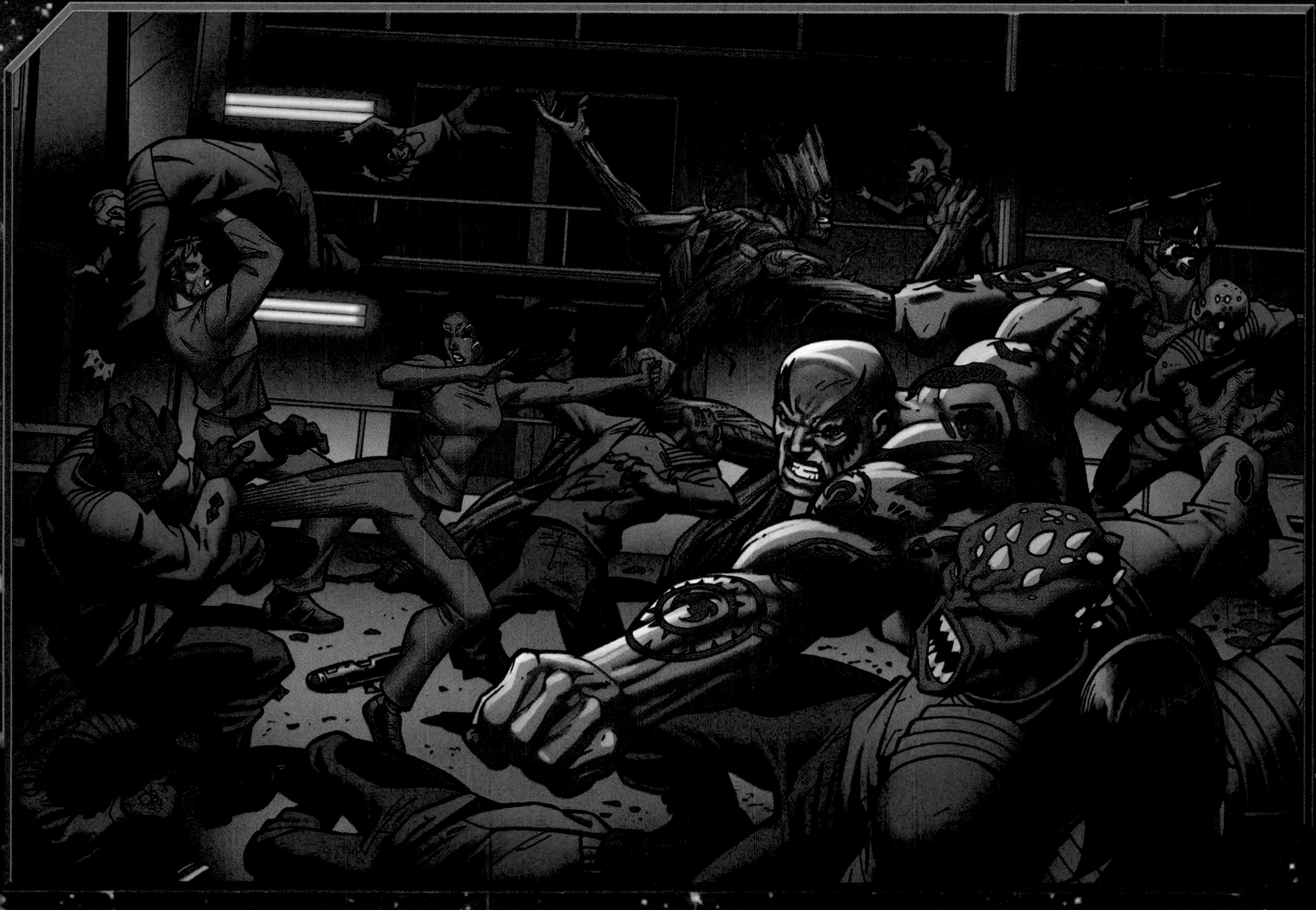

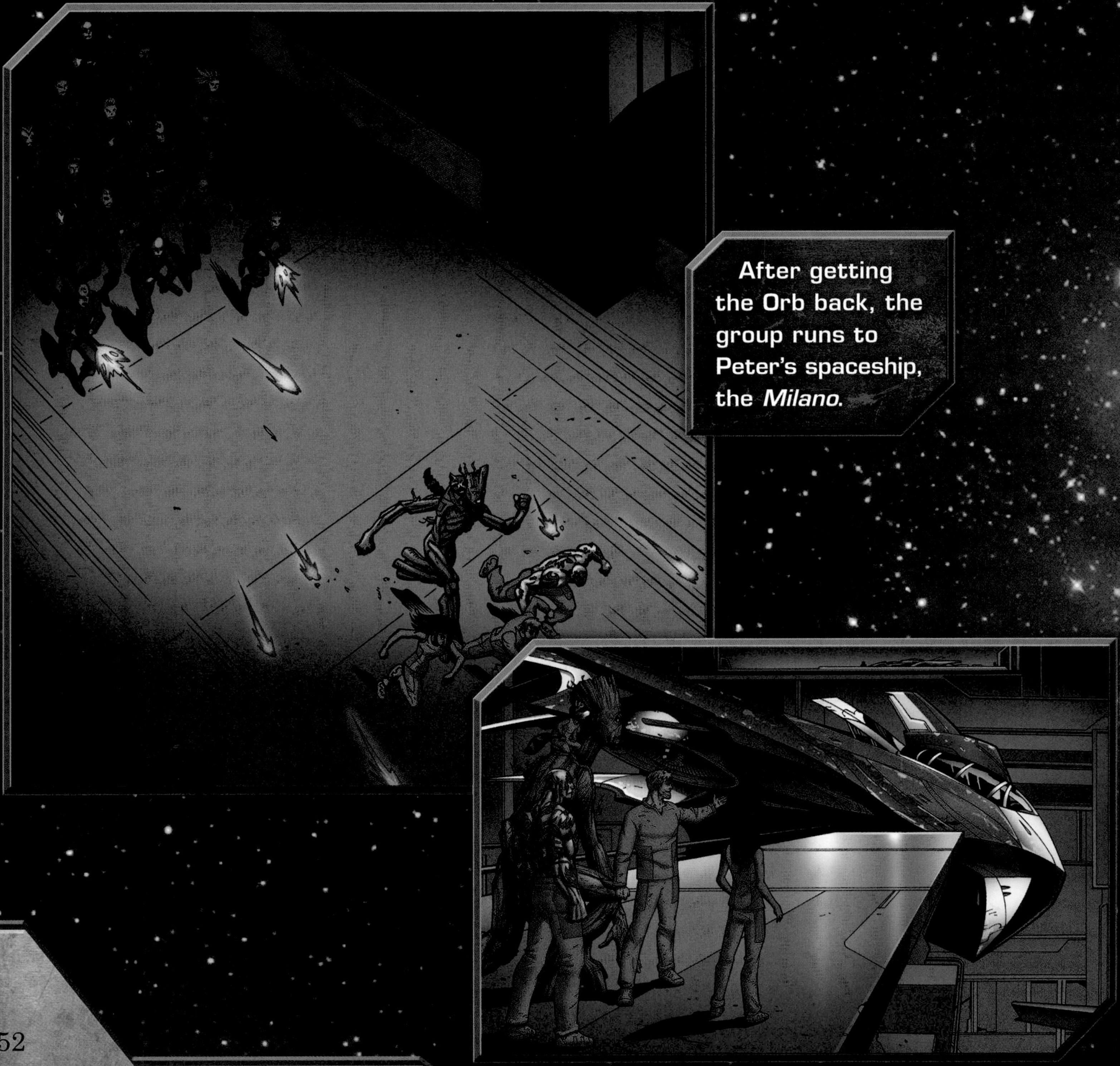
After getting the Orb back, the group runs to Peter's spaceship, the *Milano*.

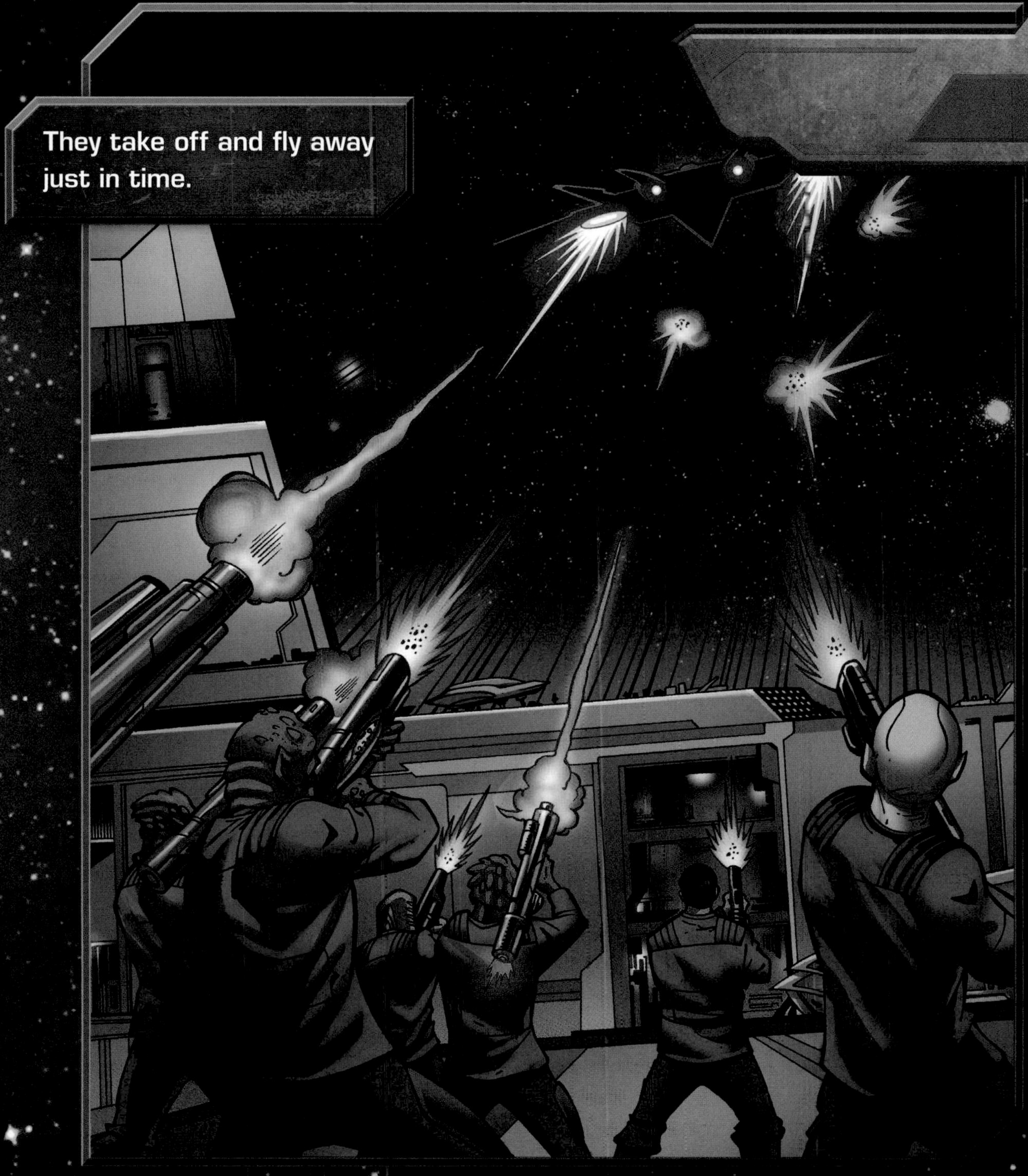
They take off and fly away just in time.

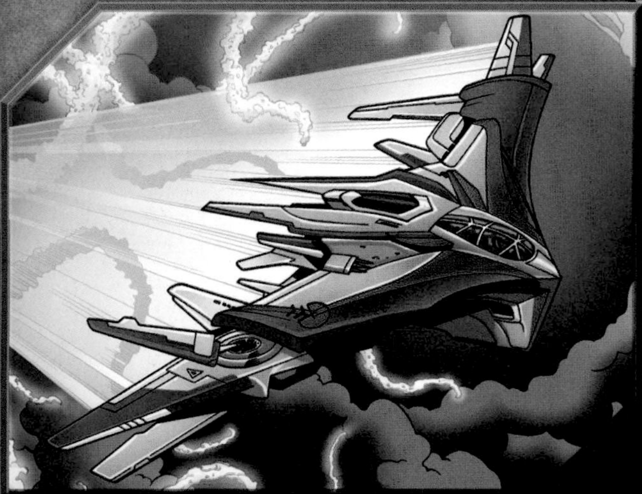

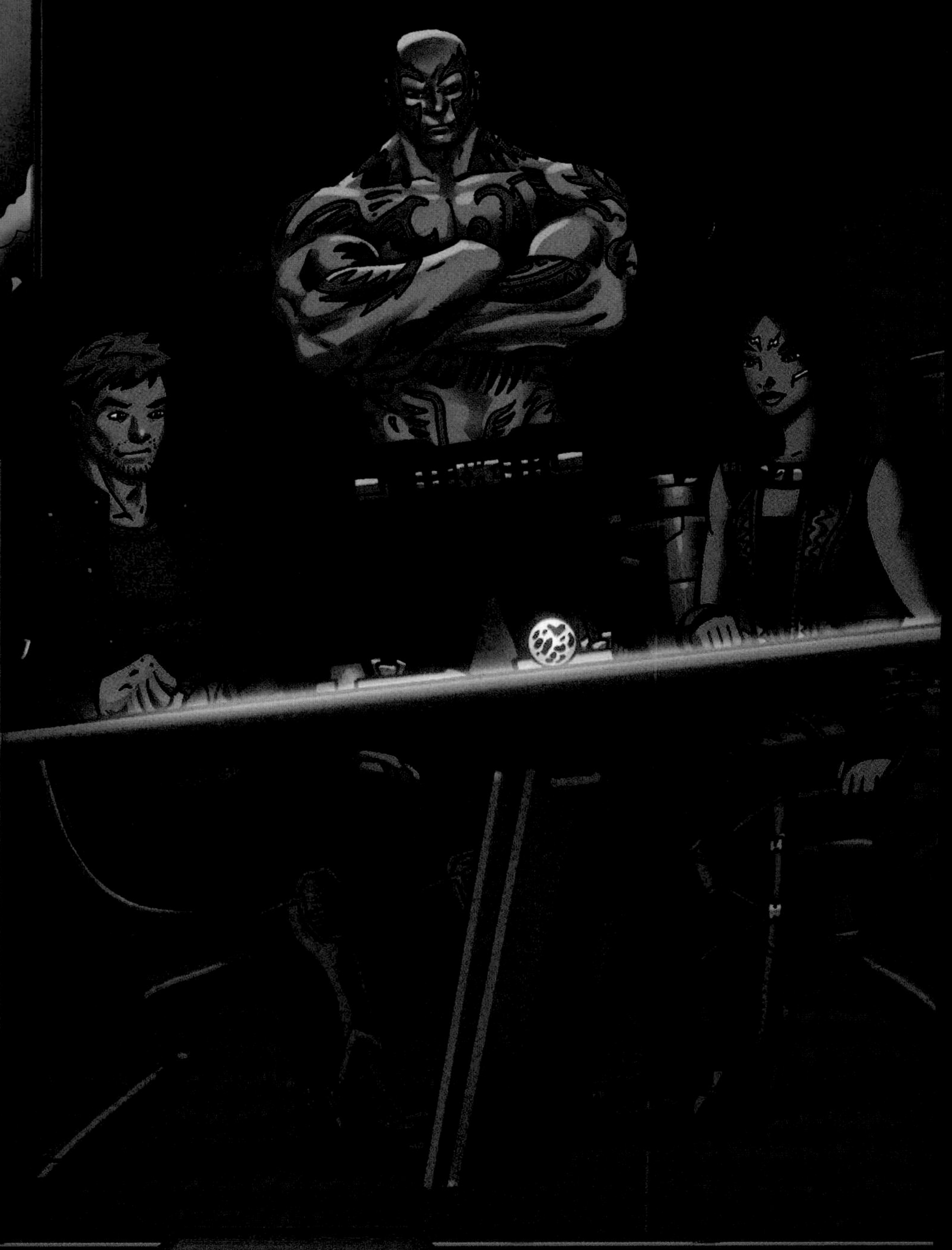

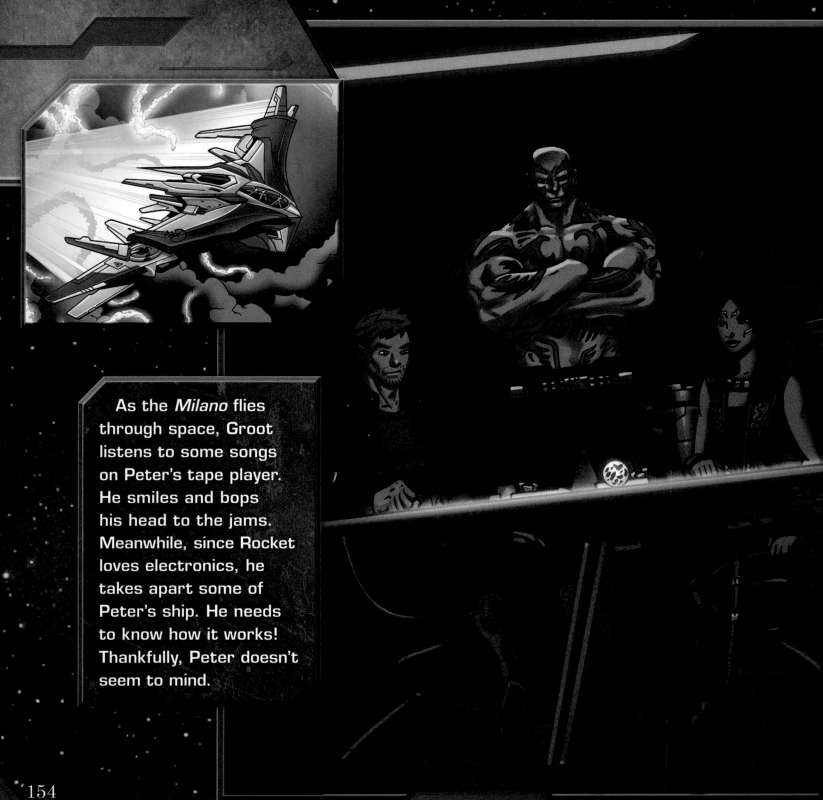

As the *Milano* flies through space, Groot listens to some songs on Peter's tape player. He smiles and bops his head to the jams. Meanwhile, since Rocket loves electronics, he takes apart some of Peter's ship. He needs to know how it works! Thankfully, Peter doesn't seem to mind.

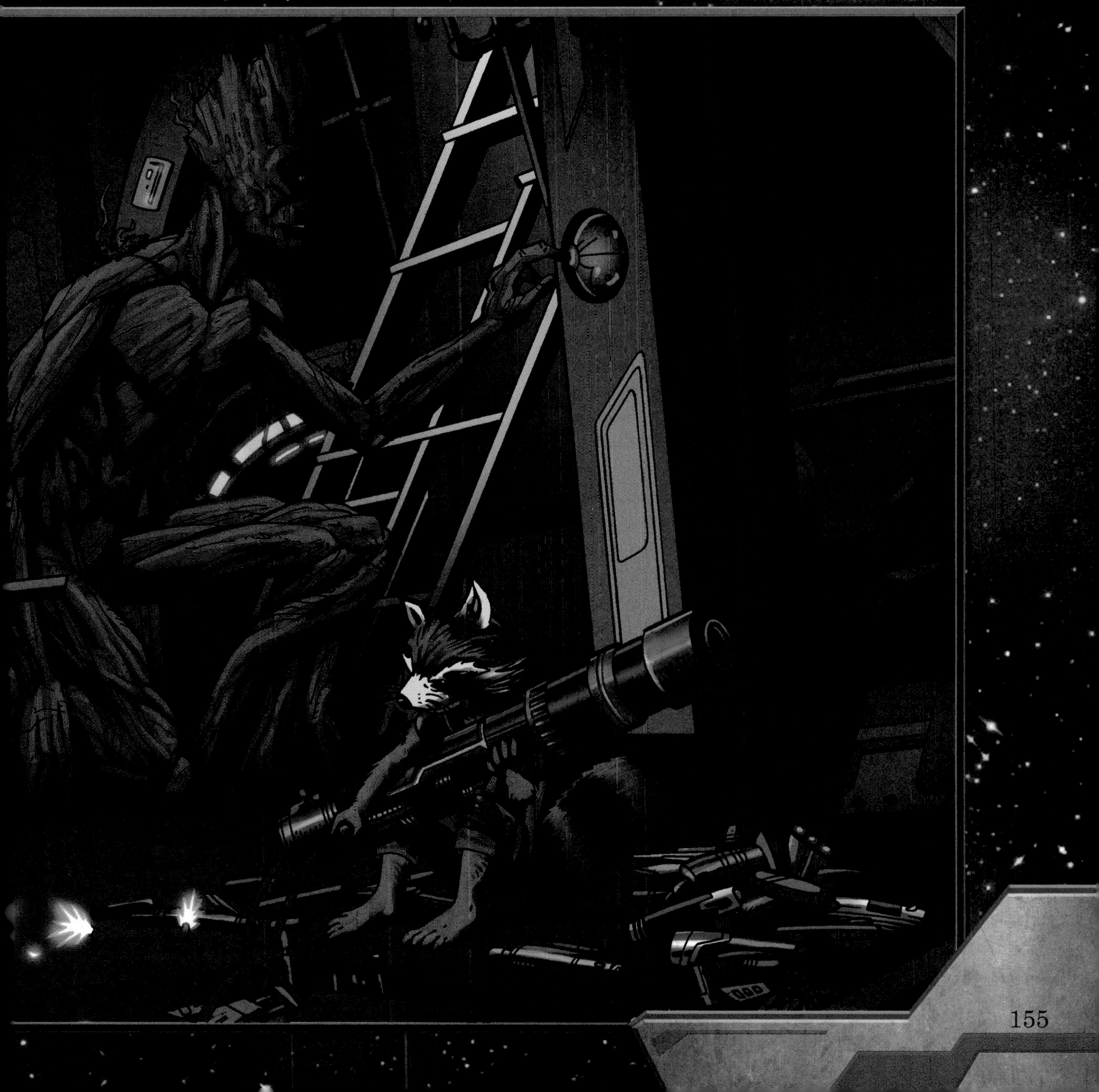

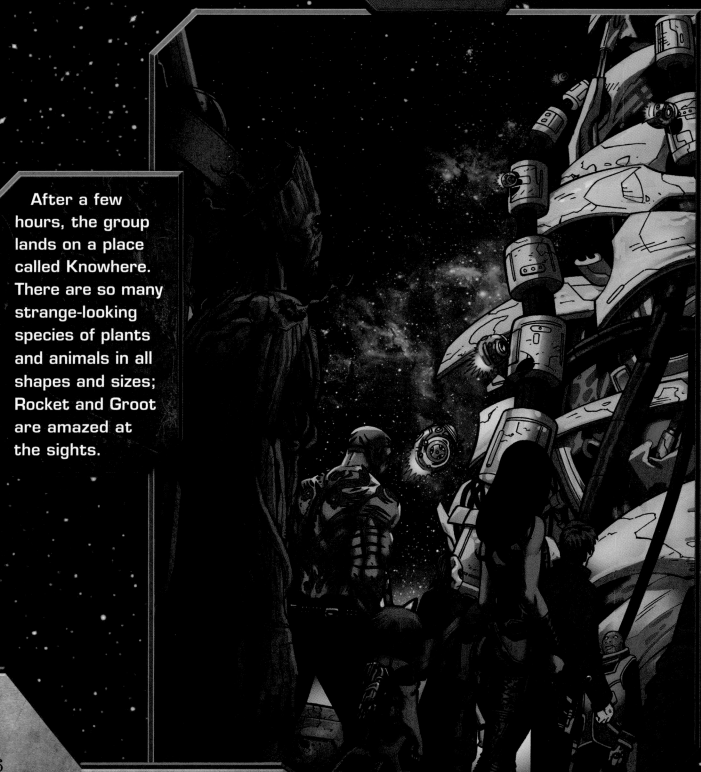

After a few hours, the group lands on a place called Knowhere. There are so many strange-looking species of plants and animals in all shapes and sizes; Rocket and Groot are amazed at the sights.

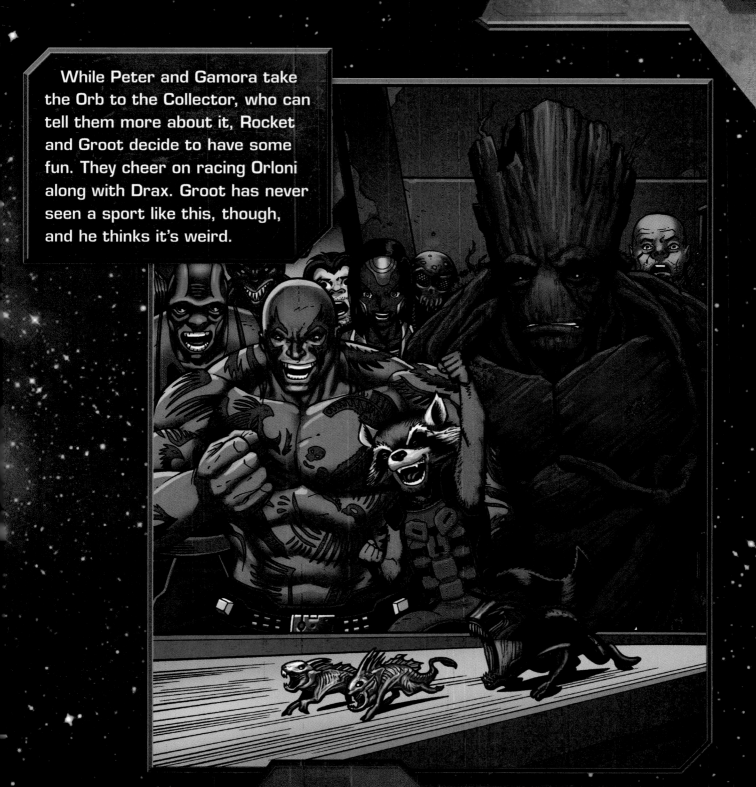

While Peter and Gamora take the Orb to the Collector, who can tell them more about it, Rocket and Groot decide to have some fun. They cheer on racing Orloni along with Drax. Groot has never seen a sport like this, though, and he thinks it's weird.

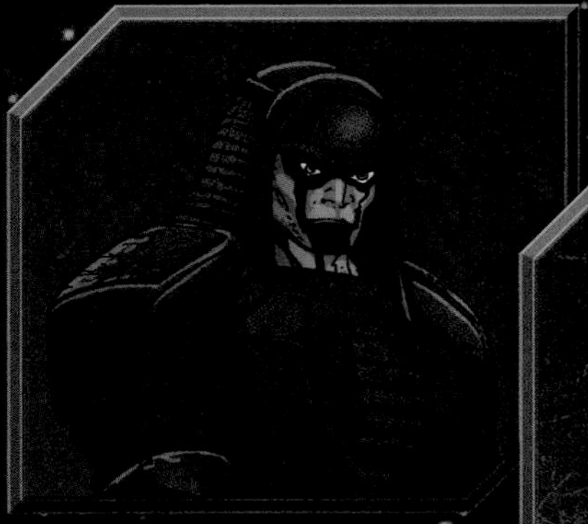

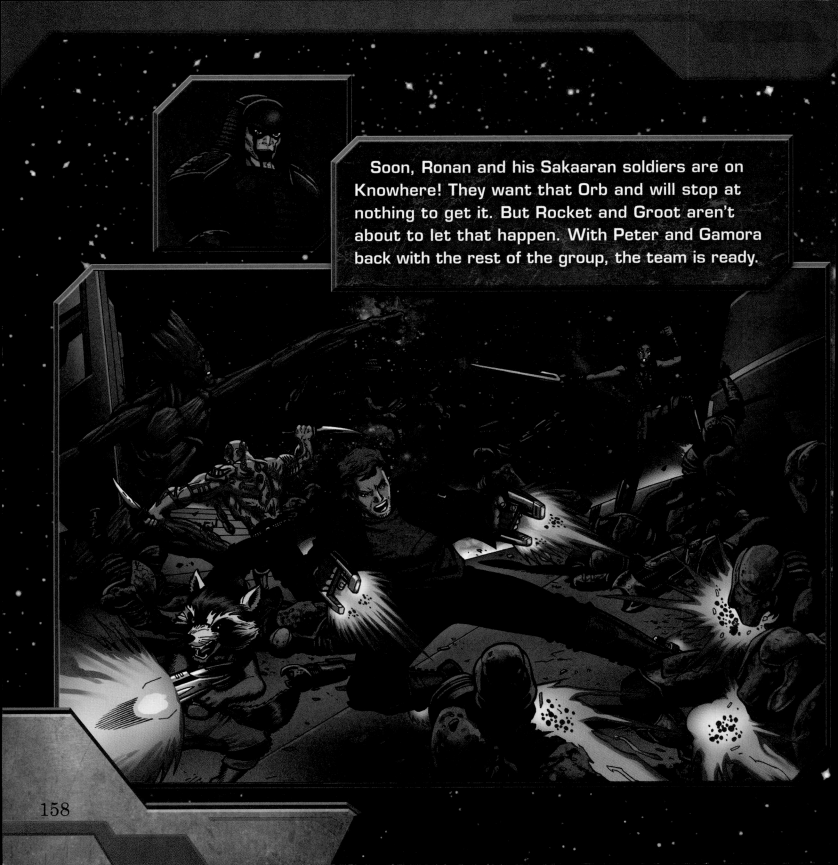

Soon, Ronan and his Sakaaran soldiers are on Knowhere! They want that Orb and will stop at nothing to get it. But Rocket and Groot aren't about to let that happen. With Peter and Gamora back with the rest of the group, the team is ready.

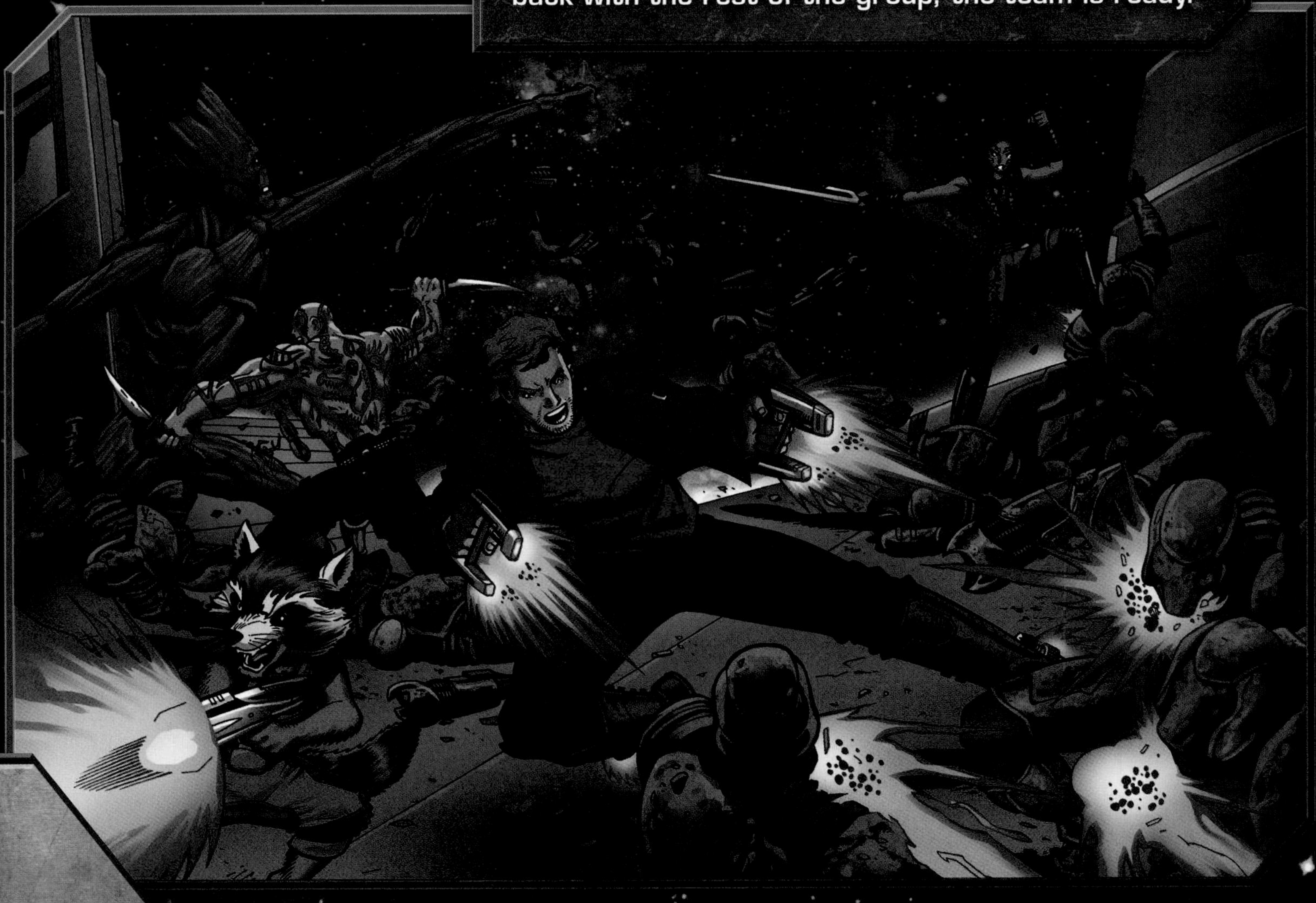

Rocket and Groot take on the troops alongside their new friends.

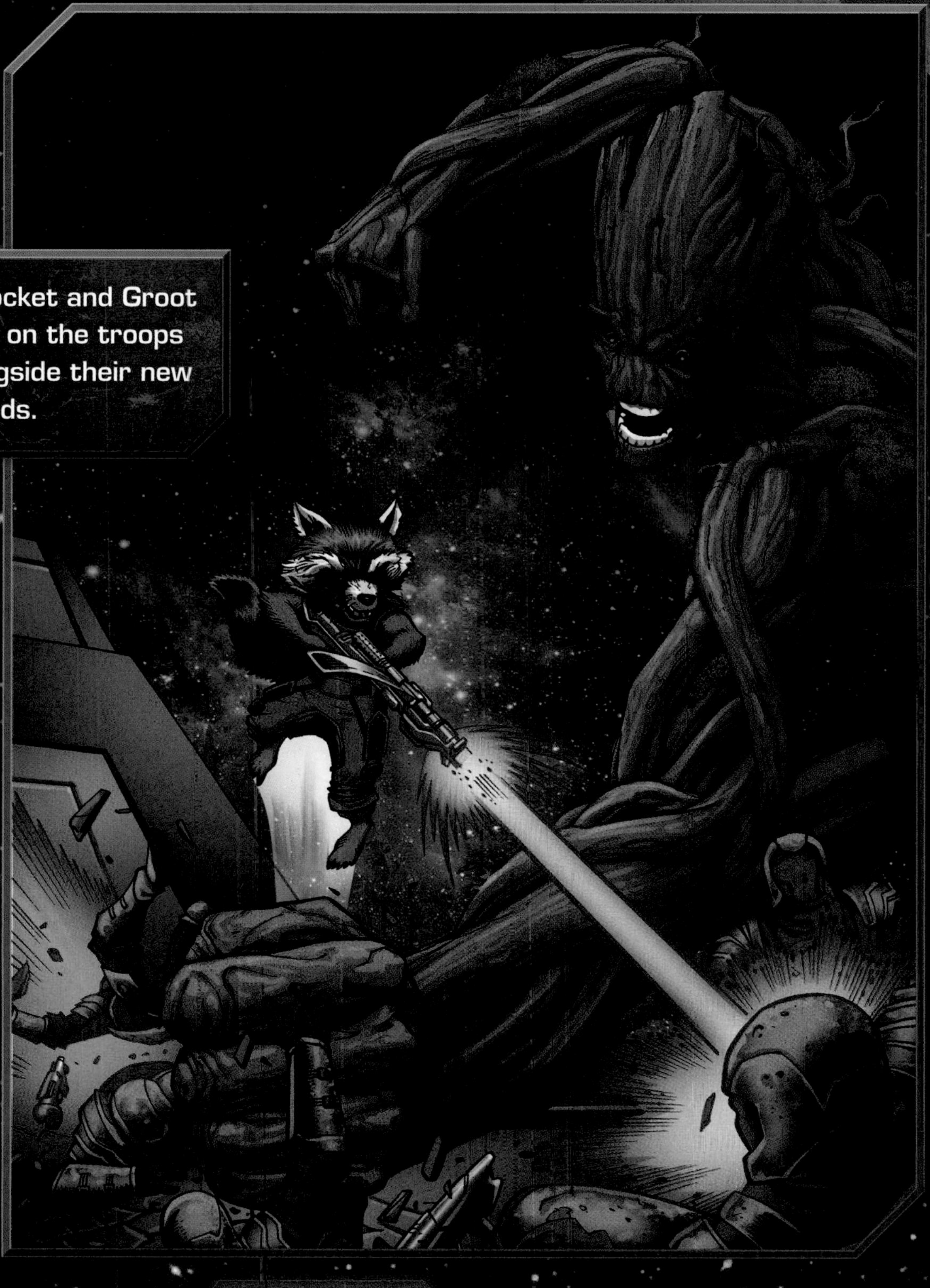

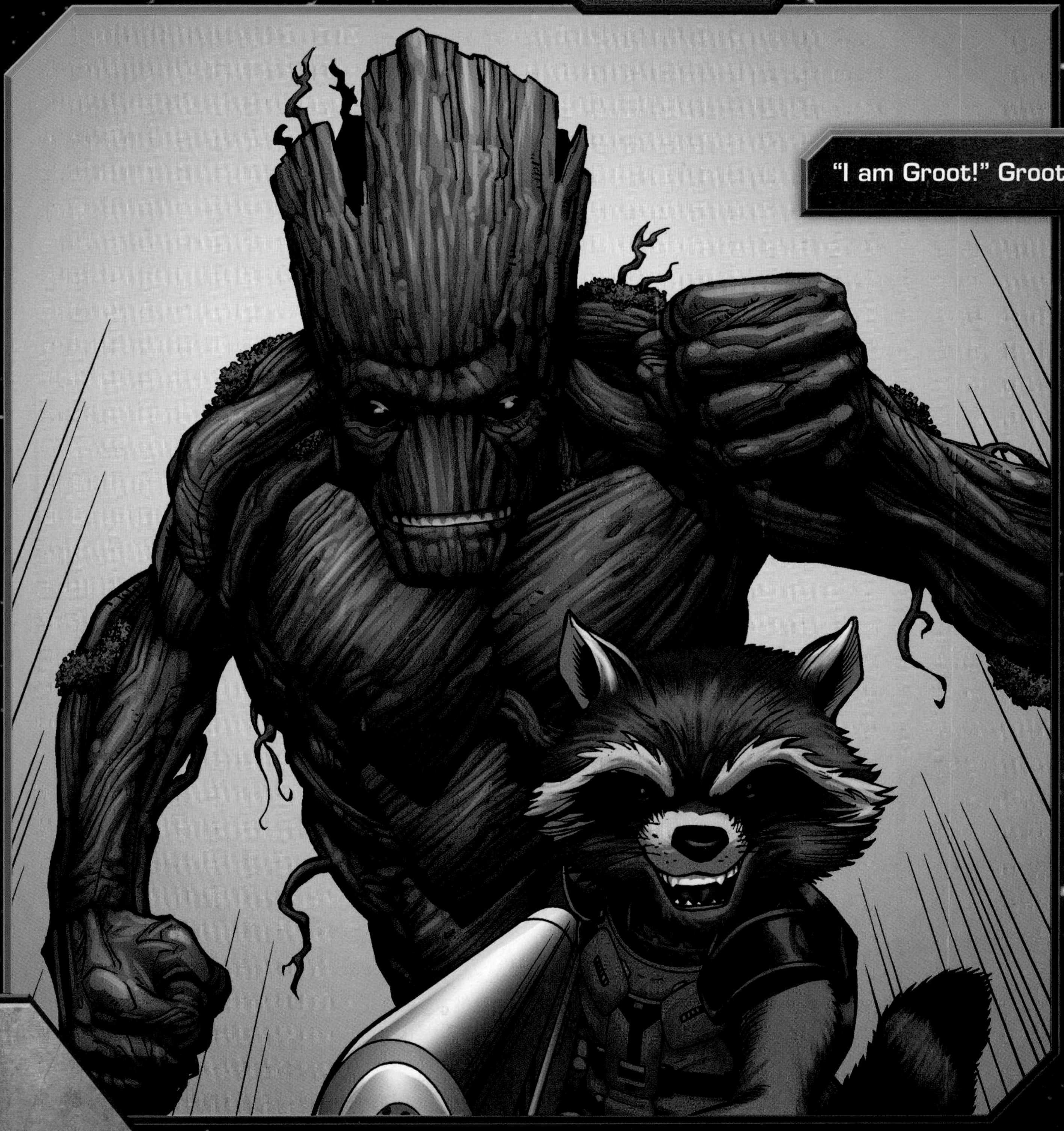

"I am Groot!" Groot yells.

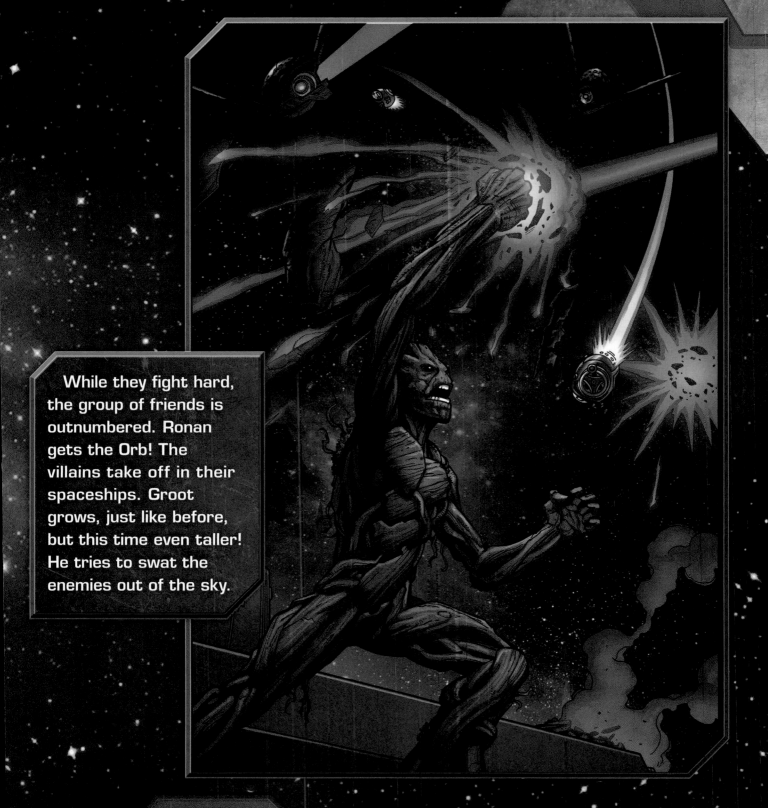

While they fight hard, the group of friends is outnumbered. Ronan gets the Orb! The villains take off in their spaceships. Groot grows, just like before, but this time even taller! He tries to swat the enemies out of the sky.

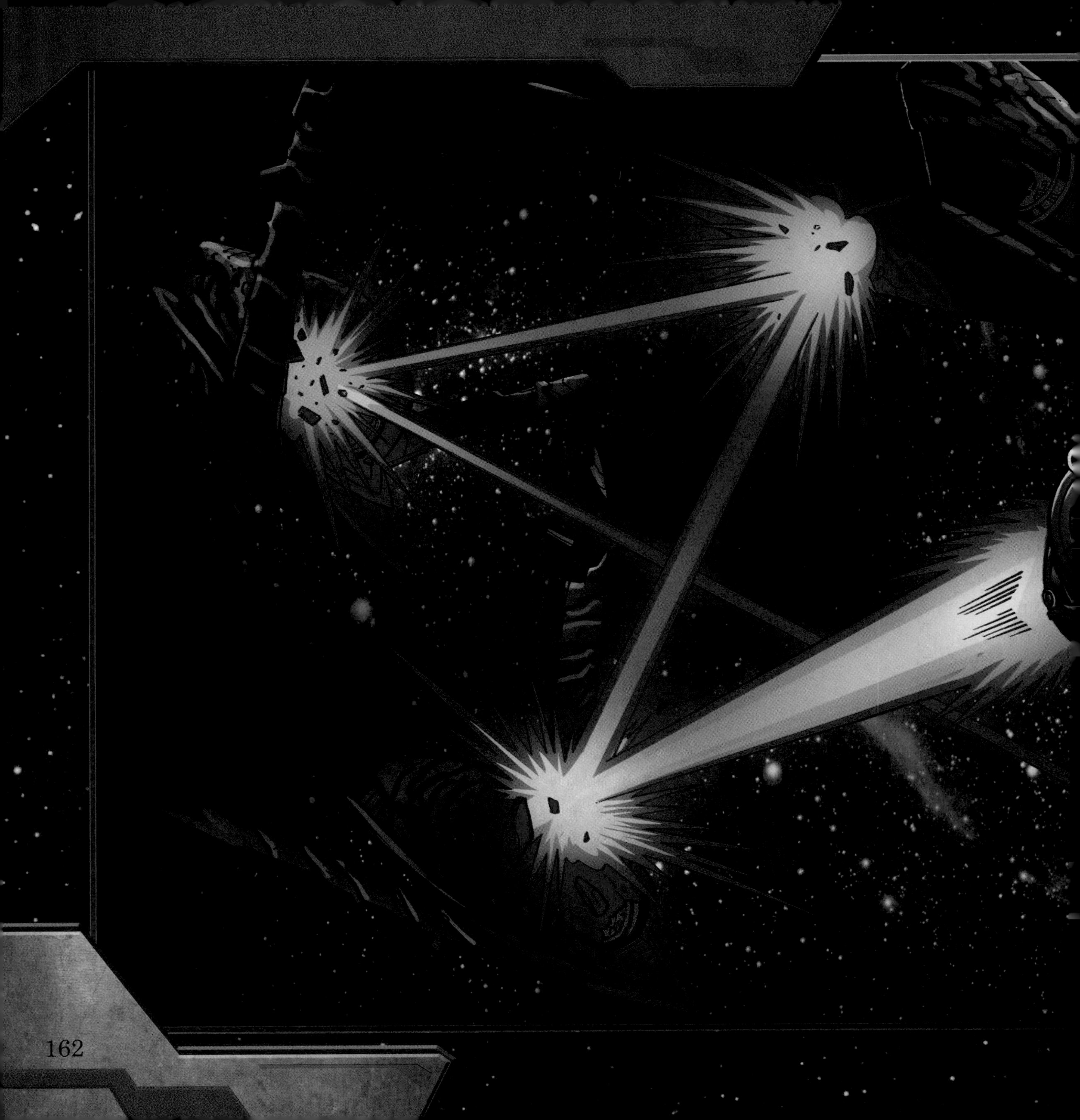

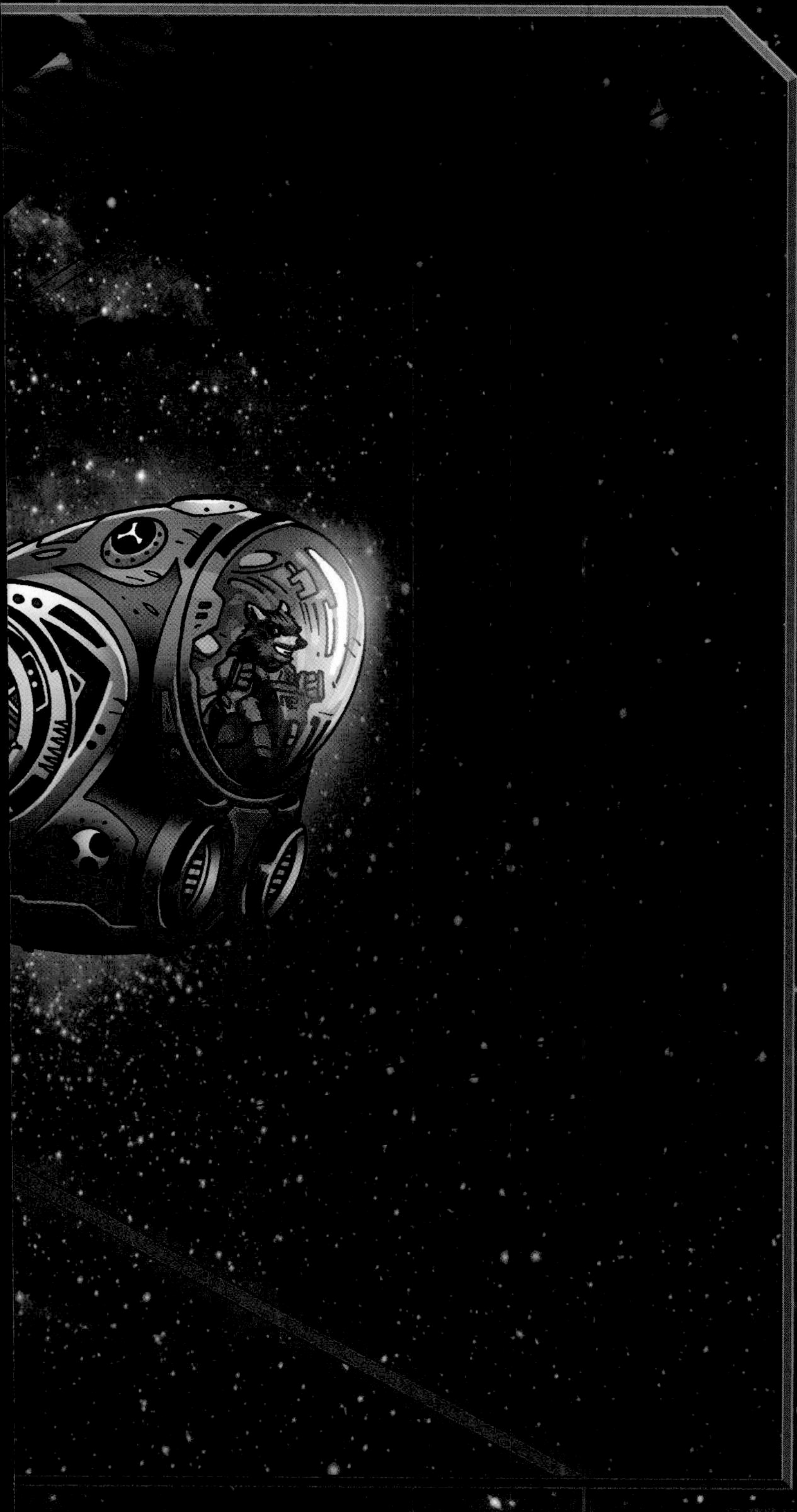

Rocket hops into an empty spaceship and takes off after Ronan. After smashing through two Sakaaran ships, he's close to reclaiming the Orb! But just then he's outmaneuvered by another ship, and Ronan gets away!

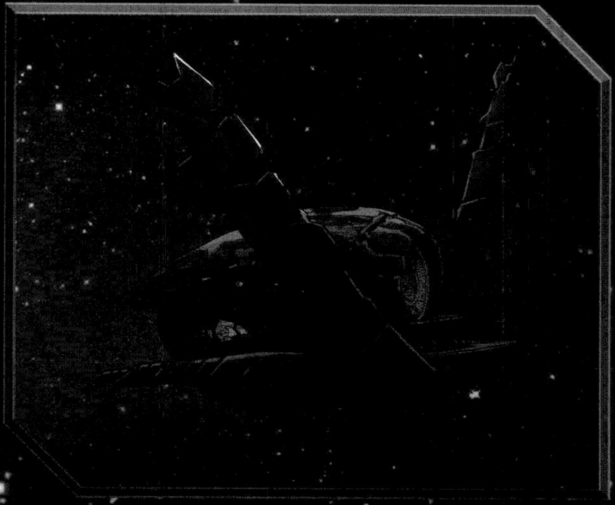

Back on the ground, Rocket and Groot are disappointed. But then they look over at Peter, Gamora, and Drax. Even though they lost the Orb to Ronan, they made new friends. More important, they're ready to keep fighting—as the Guardians of the Galaxy!

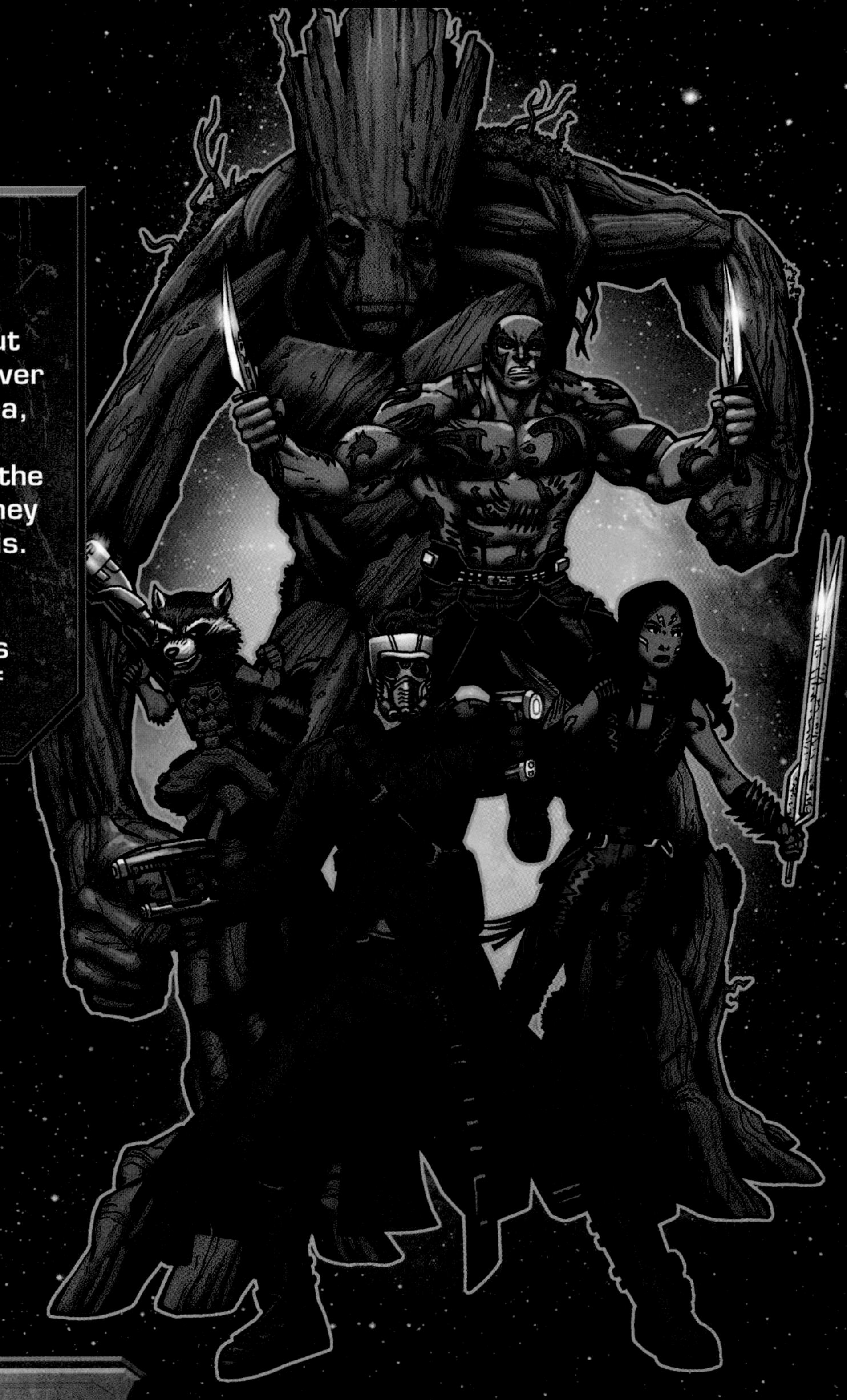

MARVEL

GUARDIANS OF THE GALAXY

BATTLE OF KNOWHERE

Adapted by Adam Davis
Illustrated by Ron Lim, Drew Geraci, and Lee Duhig
Based on the Screenplay by James Gunn
Story by Nicole Perlman and James Gunn
Produced by Kevin Feige, p.g.a.
Directed by James Gunn

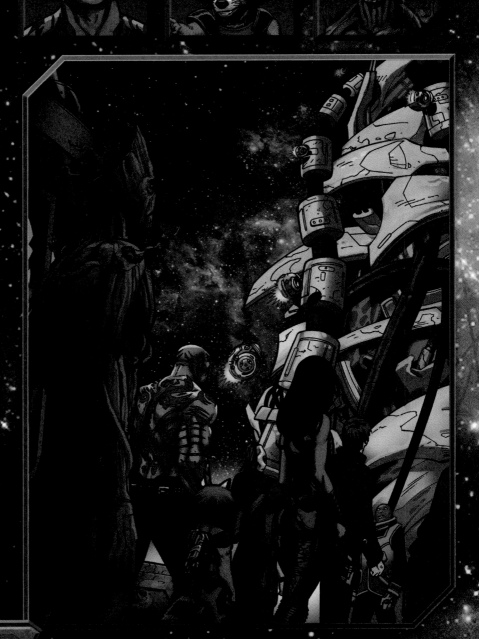

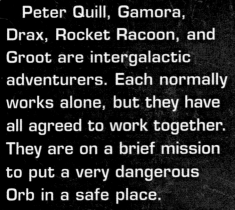

Peter Quill, Gamora, Drax, Rocket Racoon, and Groot are intergalactic adventurers. Each normally works alone, but they have all agreed to work together. They are on a brief mission to put a very dangerous Orb in a safe place.

As they walk through the streets of Knowhere, Peter suddenly ducks behind a building. He motions for everyone to hide.

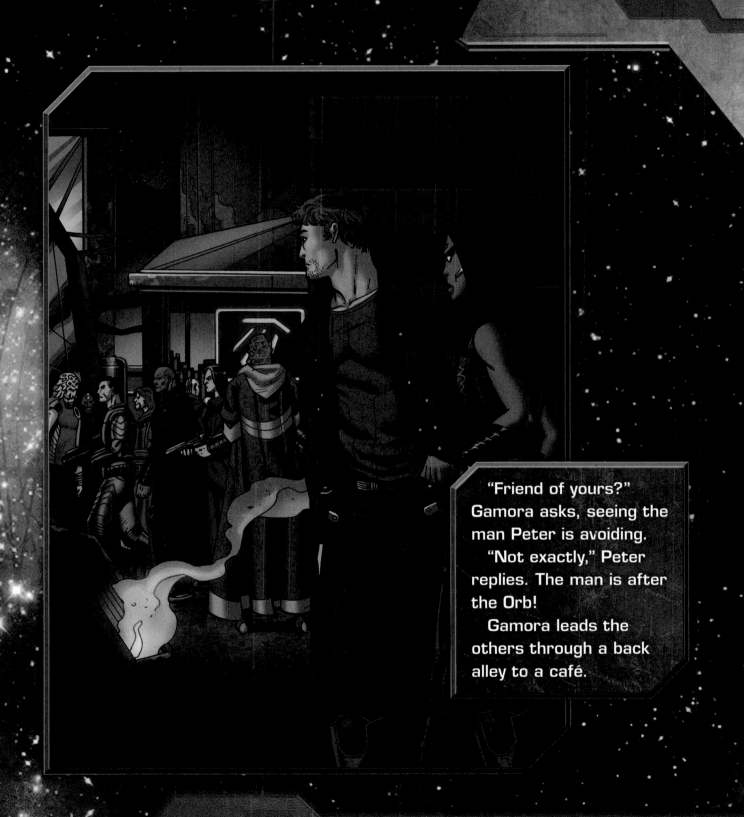

"Friend of yours?"
Gamora asks, seeing the
man Peter is avoiding.
   "Not exactly," Peter
replies. The man is after
the Orb!
   Gamora leads the
others through a back
alley to a café.

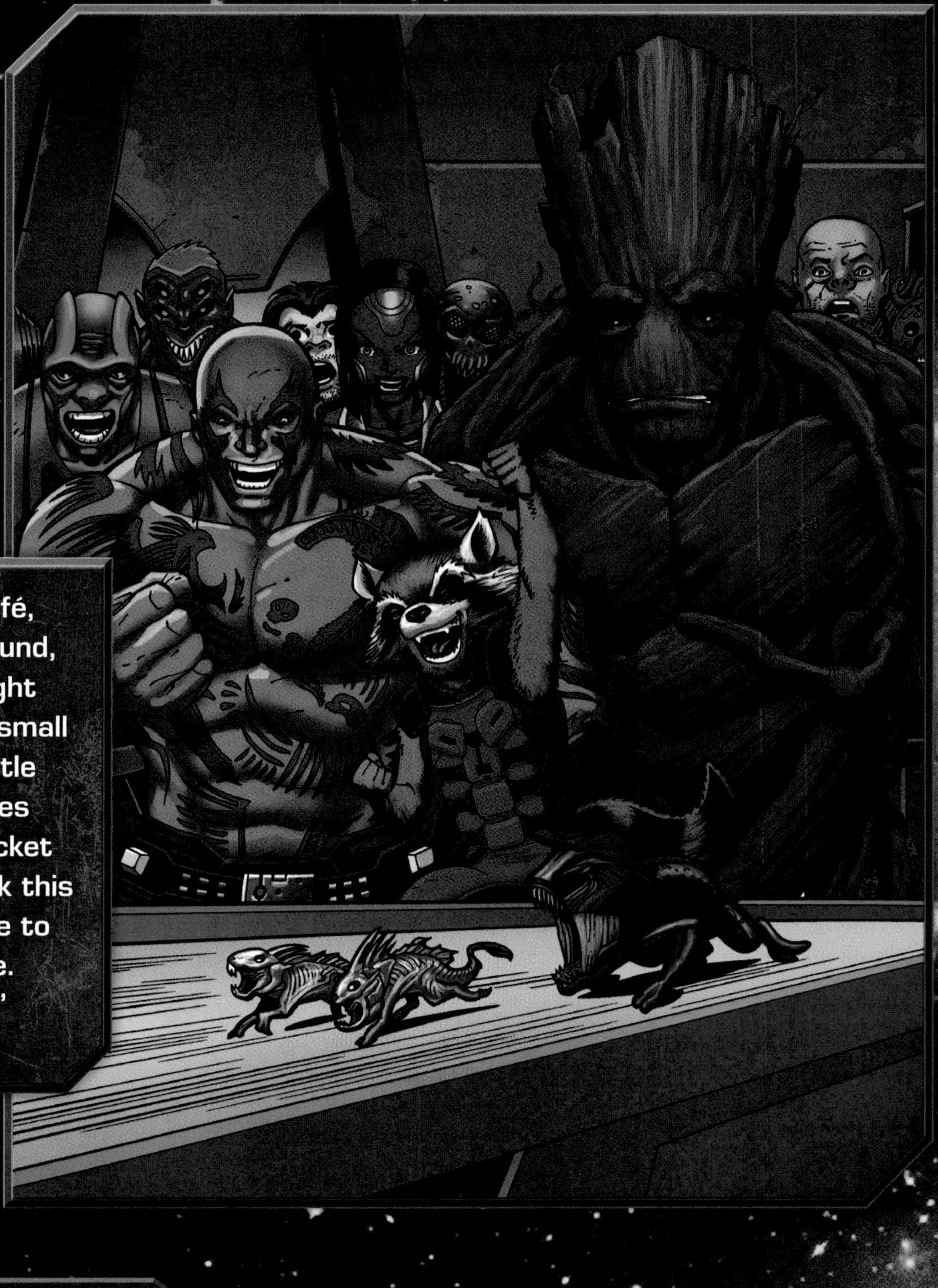

Inside the café, Drax looks around, and his eyes light up. There is a small track where little ratlike creatures are racing. Rocket and Groot think this is a great place to hide for a while.

"I am Groot!" Groot says.

As Drax, Rocket, and Groot watch the races, Peter and Gamora listen to music from Peter's home planet, Earth.

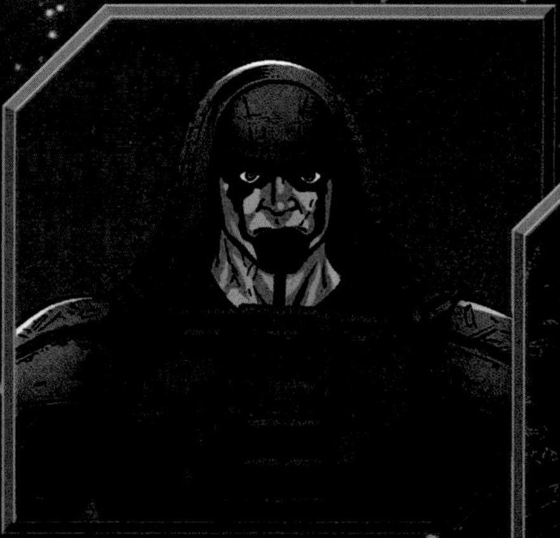

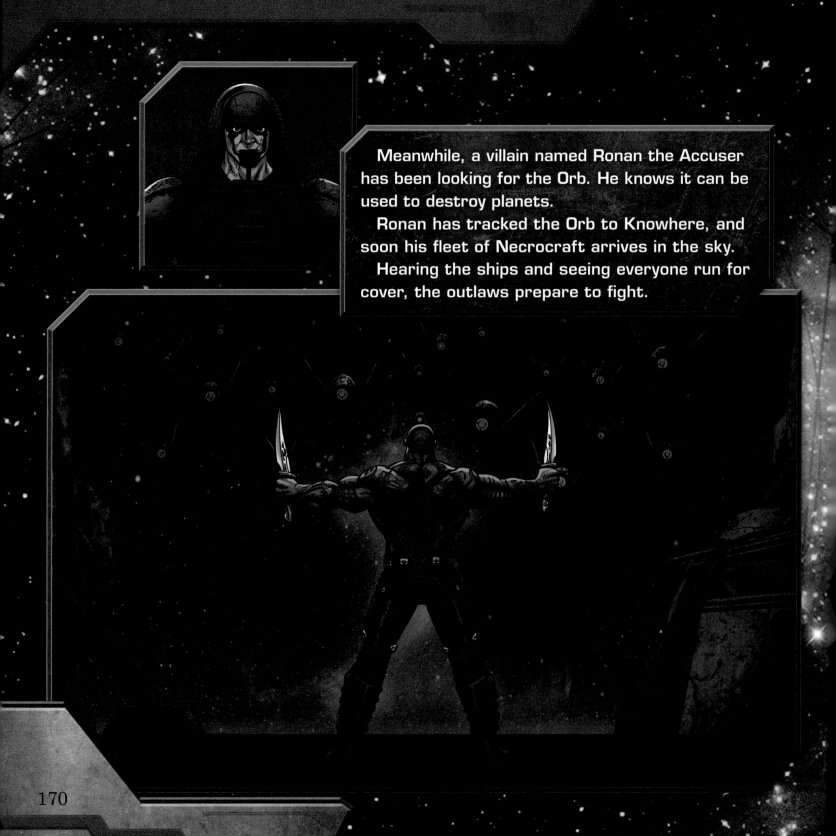

Meanwhile, a villain named Ronan the Accuser has been looking for the Orb. He knows it can be used to destroy planets.

Ronan has tracked the Orb to Knowhere, and soon his fleet of Necrocraft arrives in the sky.

Hearing the ships and seeing everyone run for cover, the outlaws prepare to fight.

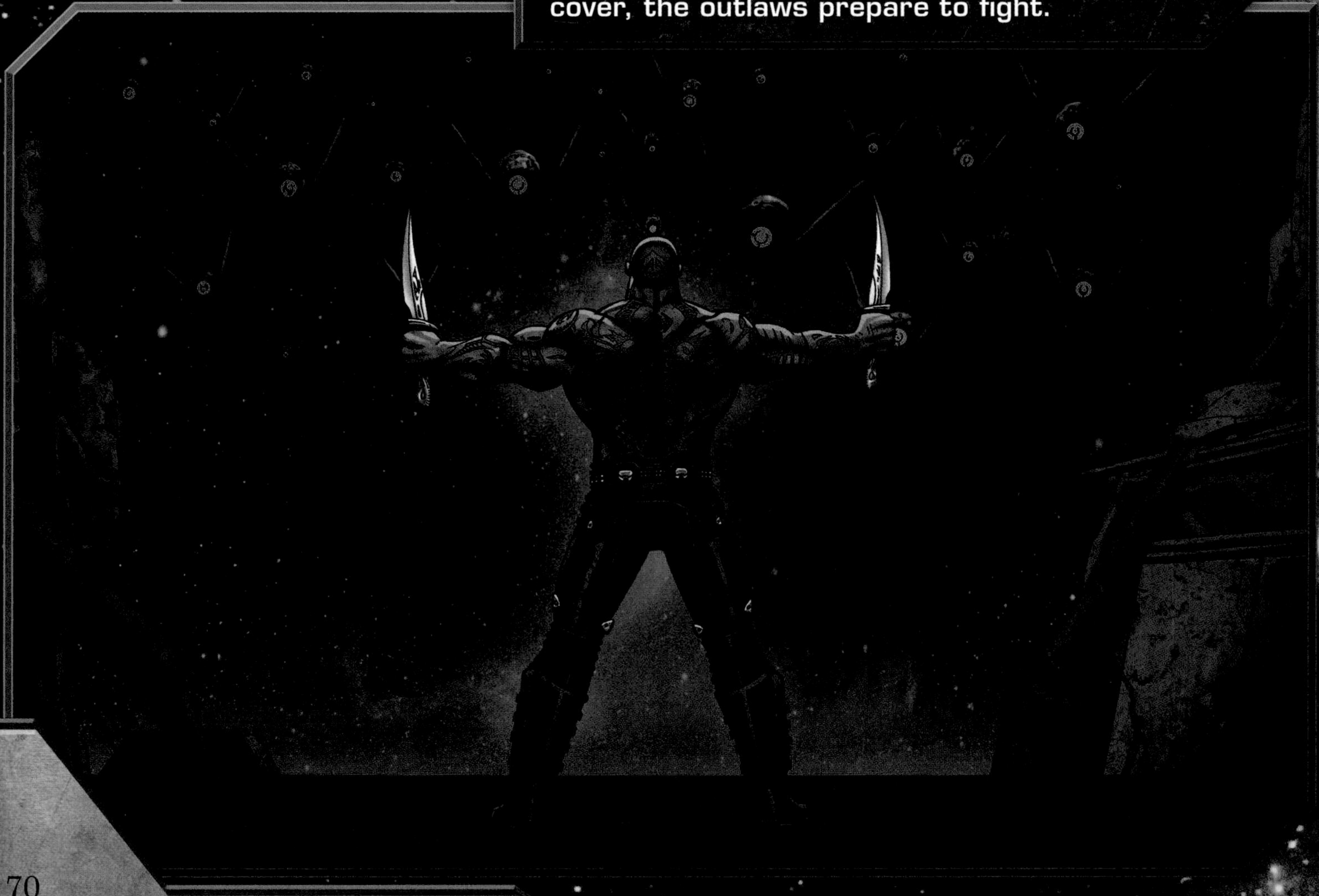

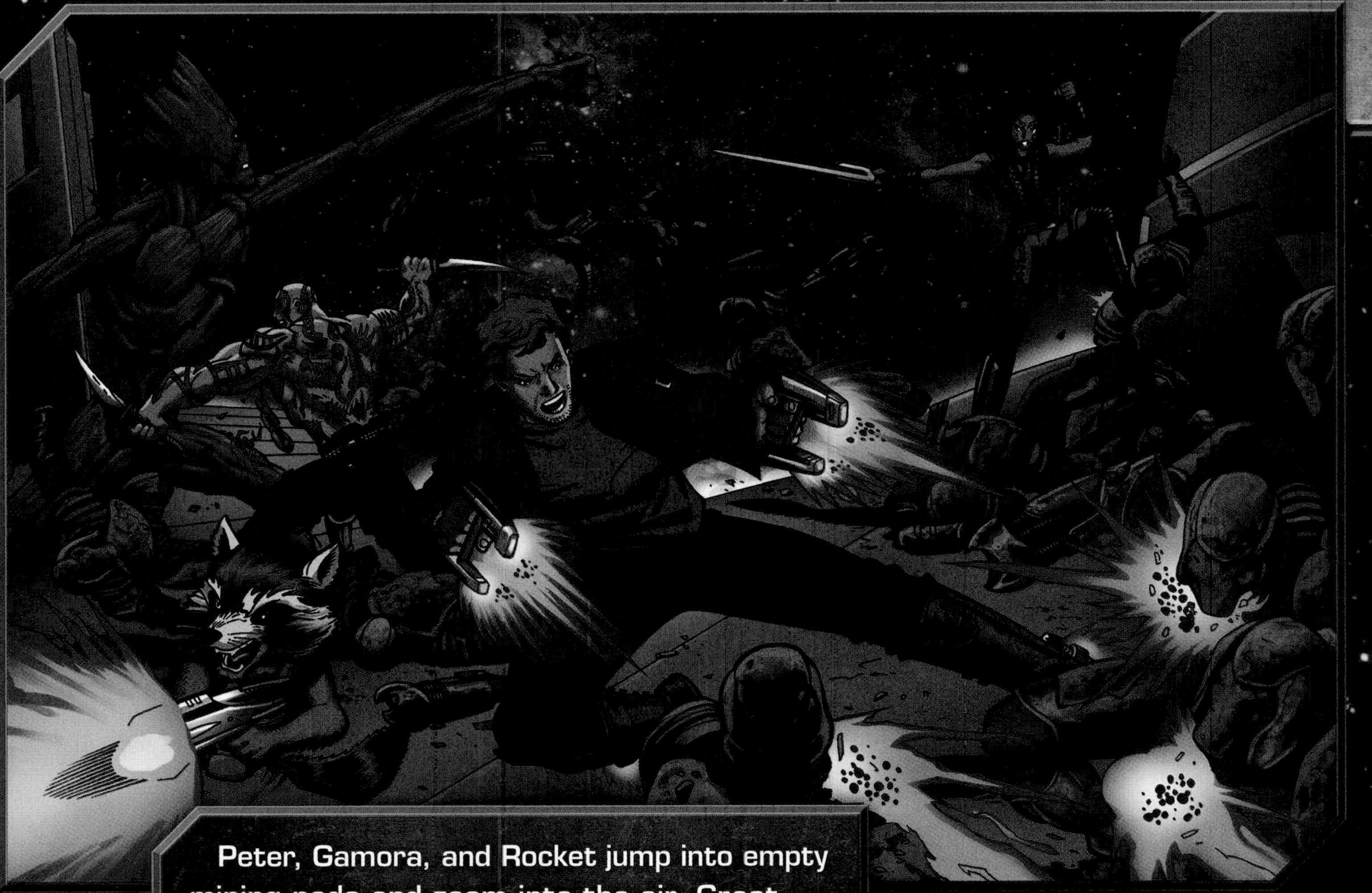

Peter, Gamora, and Rocket jump into empty mining pods and zoom into the air. Groot moans with sadness. He is too big to fit!

"Wait here. I'll be back!" Rocket cries out to him.

Groot and Drax face down the troops coming out of the Necrocraft ships that are beginning to land.

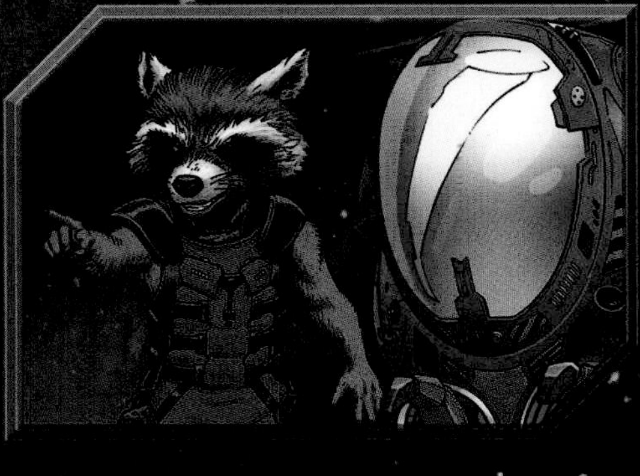

Ronan steps off one of the ships. Drax lets out a battle cry and charges Ronan, but the villain laughs at the futile attempts to hurt him. With enormous strength, Ronan grabs Drax and throws him.

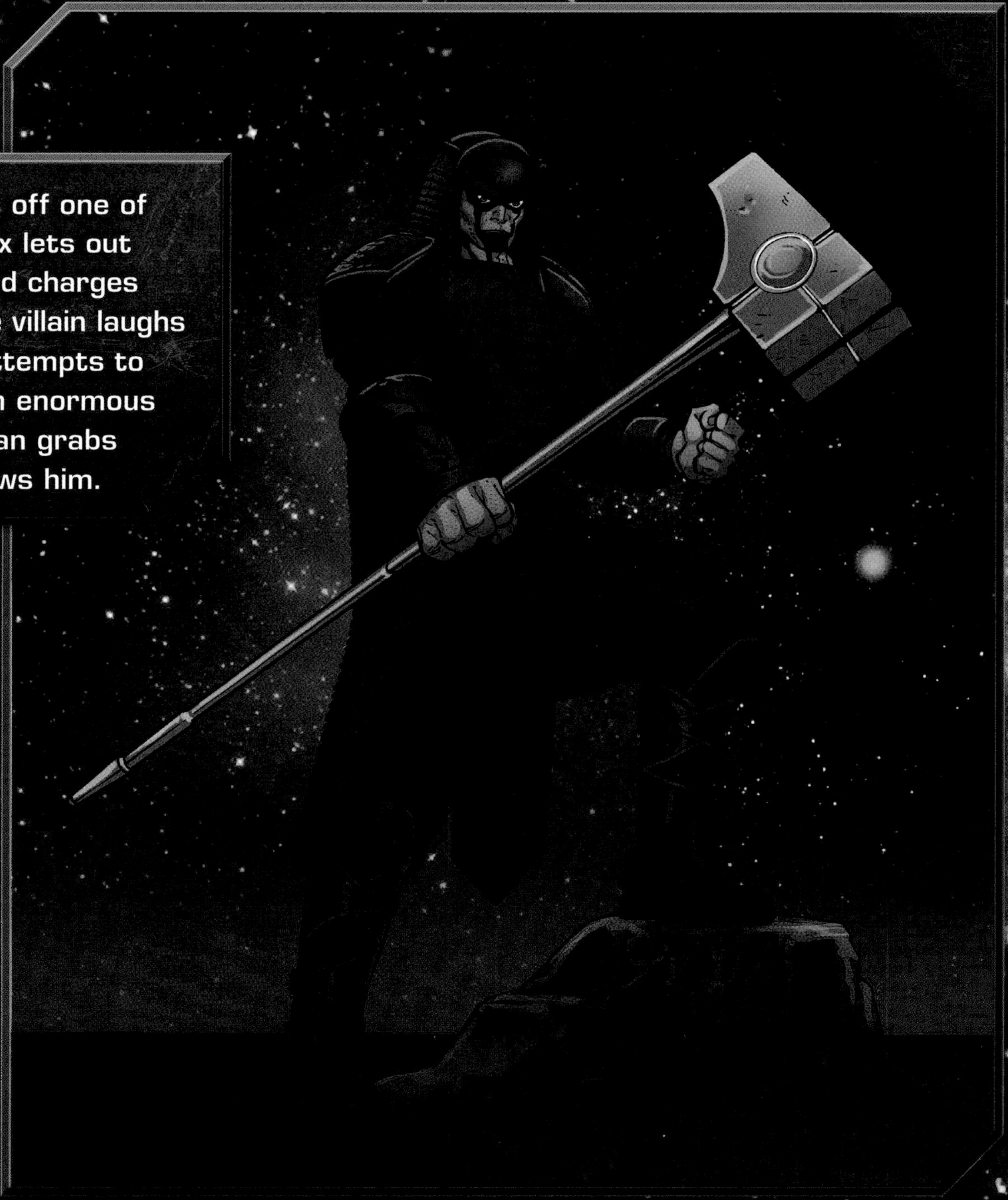

But this only angers Drax more. He gets back on his feet and swings at Ronan with his powerful fists.

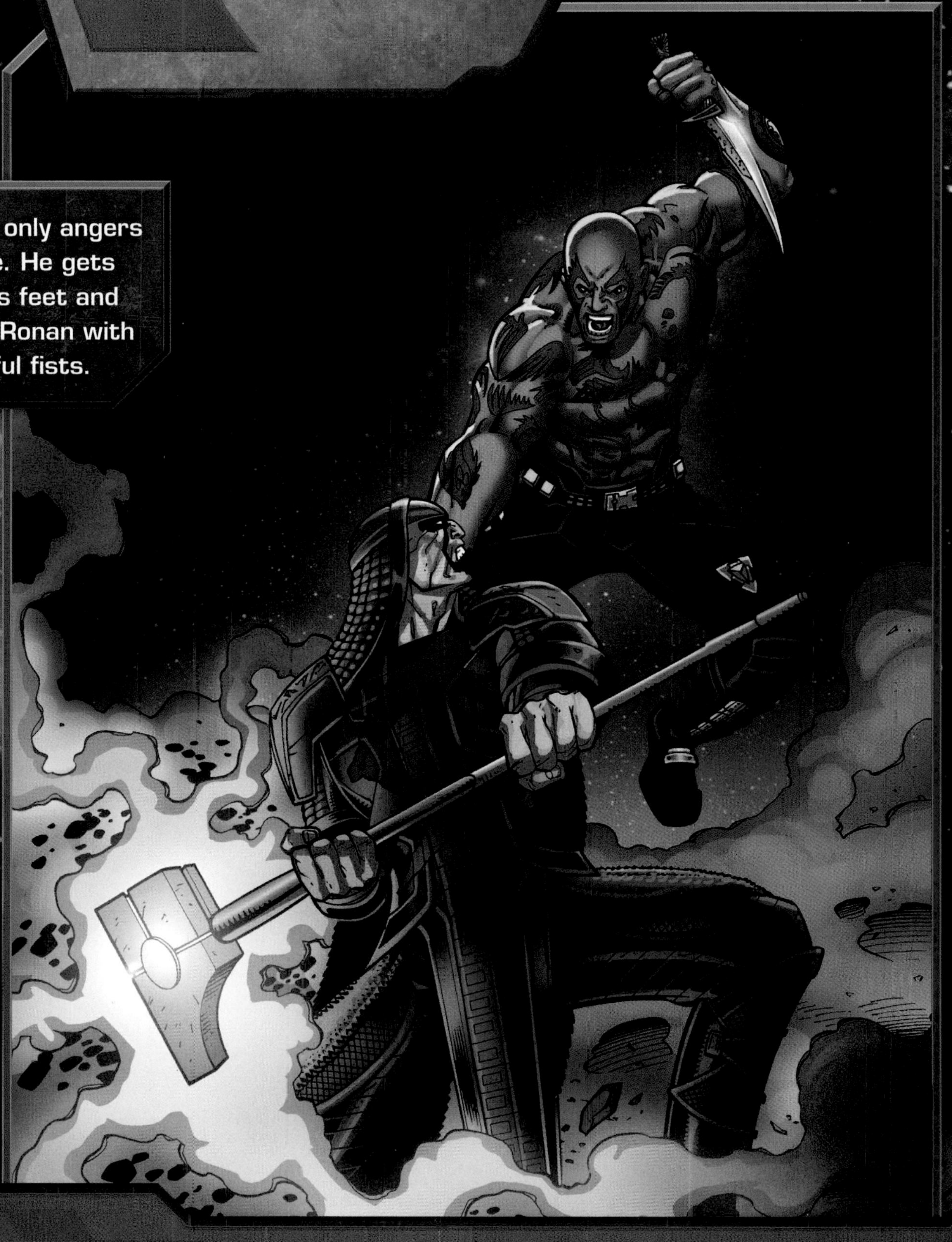

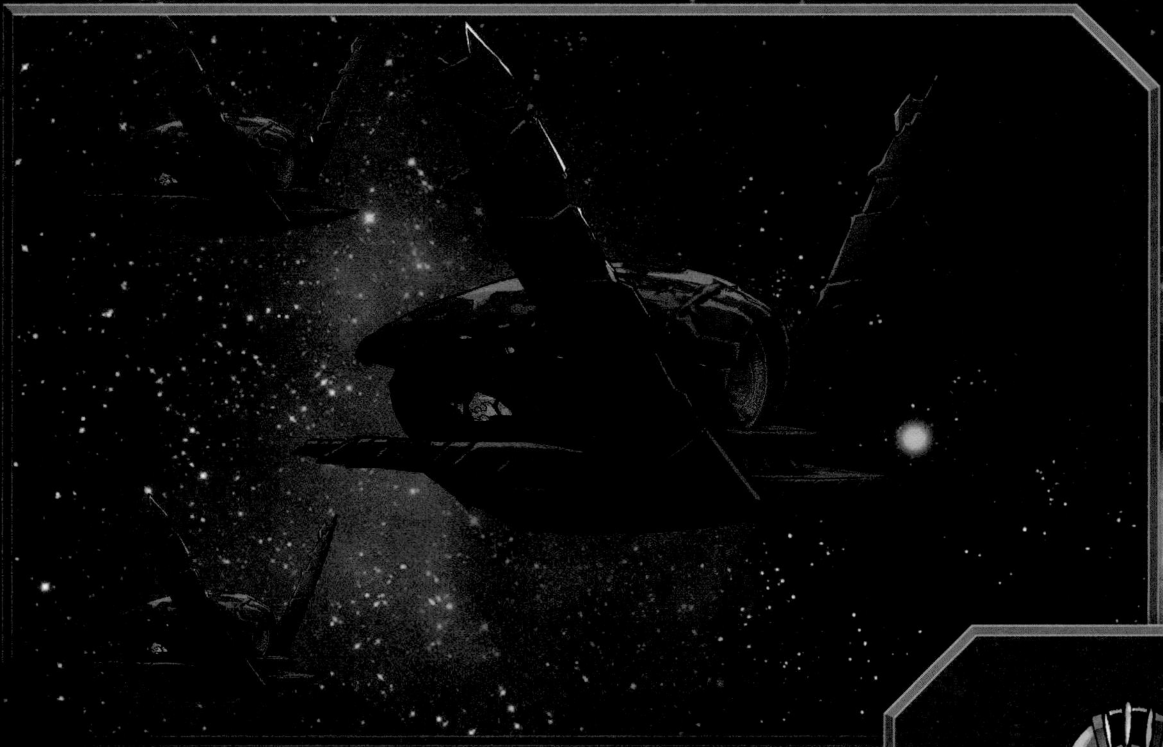

While Drax and Ronan are fighting on the ground, several Necrocraft lift off again to chase Peter, Gamora, and Rocket.

Ronan's lieutenant, Nebula, commands the squadron to find the Orb. She orders them to target Gamora's pod.

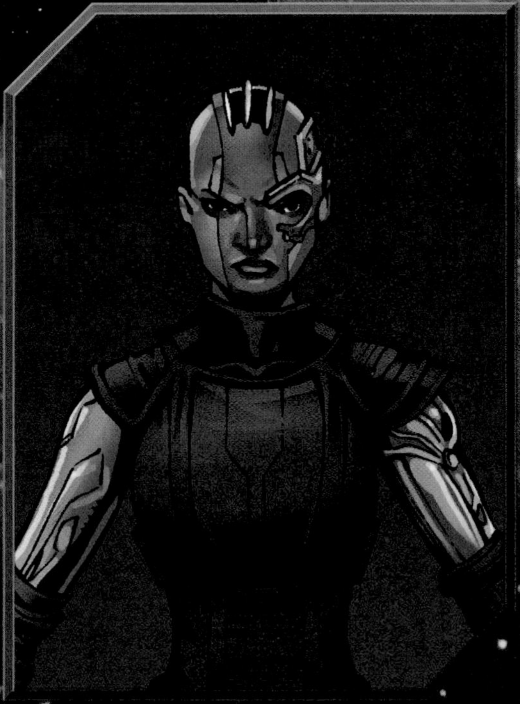

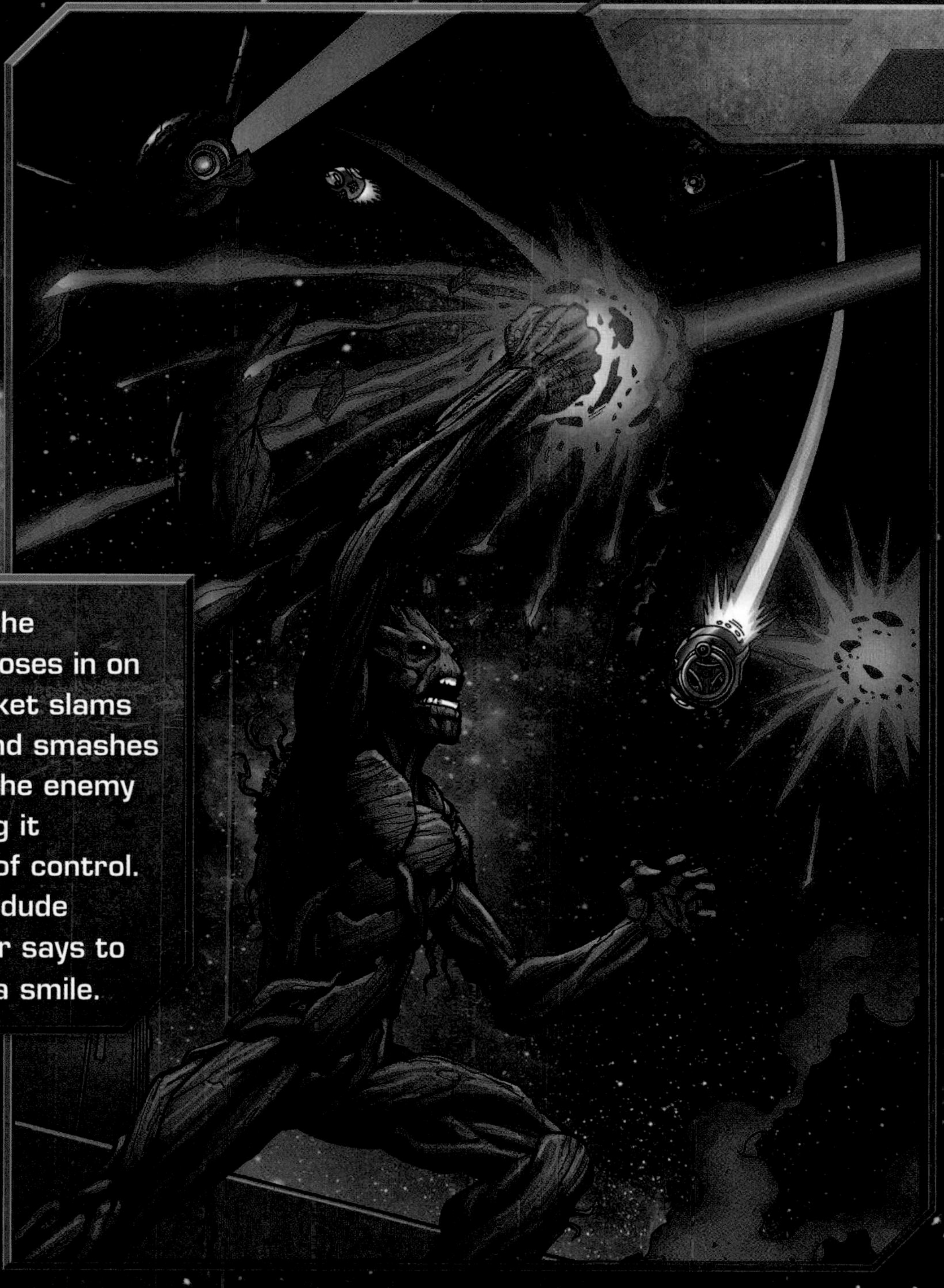

As one of the Necrocraft closes in on Gamora, Rocket slams on the gas and smashes his pod into the enemy craft, sending it spinning out of control.

"That little dude can fly," Peter says to himself with a smile.

Rocket navigates his pod like a pro. One by one, he blasts his way through the enemies.

But his mining pod can't take the hits! His pod is ruined, and Rocket is forced to jump ship. He looks around at all the fallen Necrocraft. He grins and runs back toward Drax and Groot.

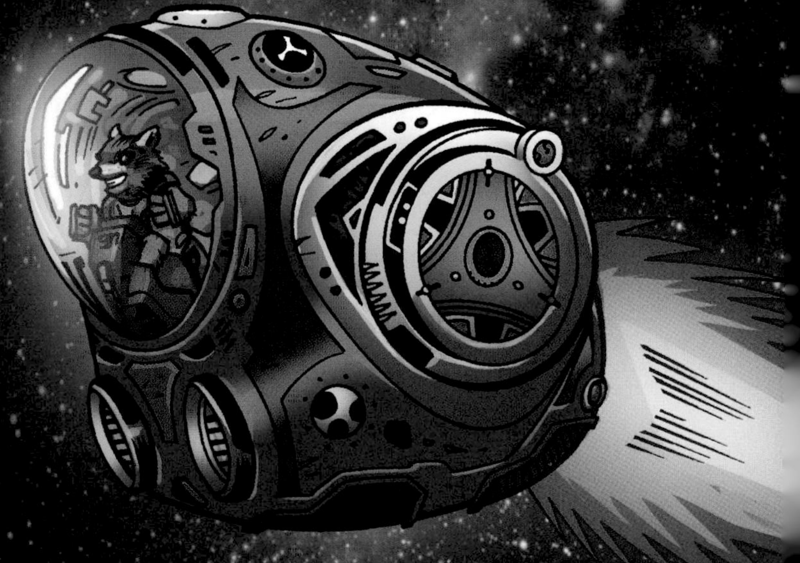

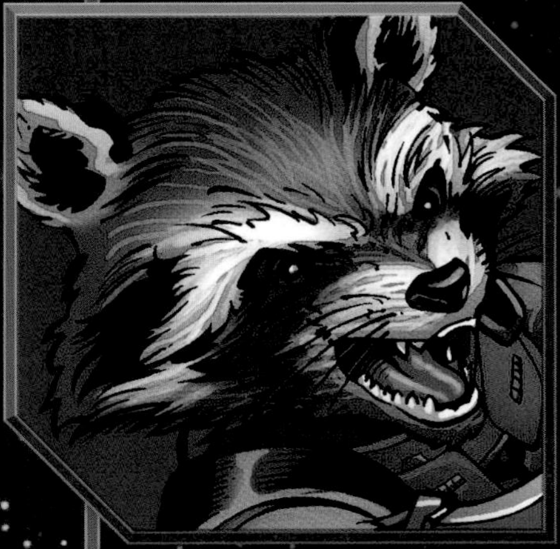

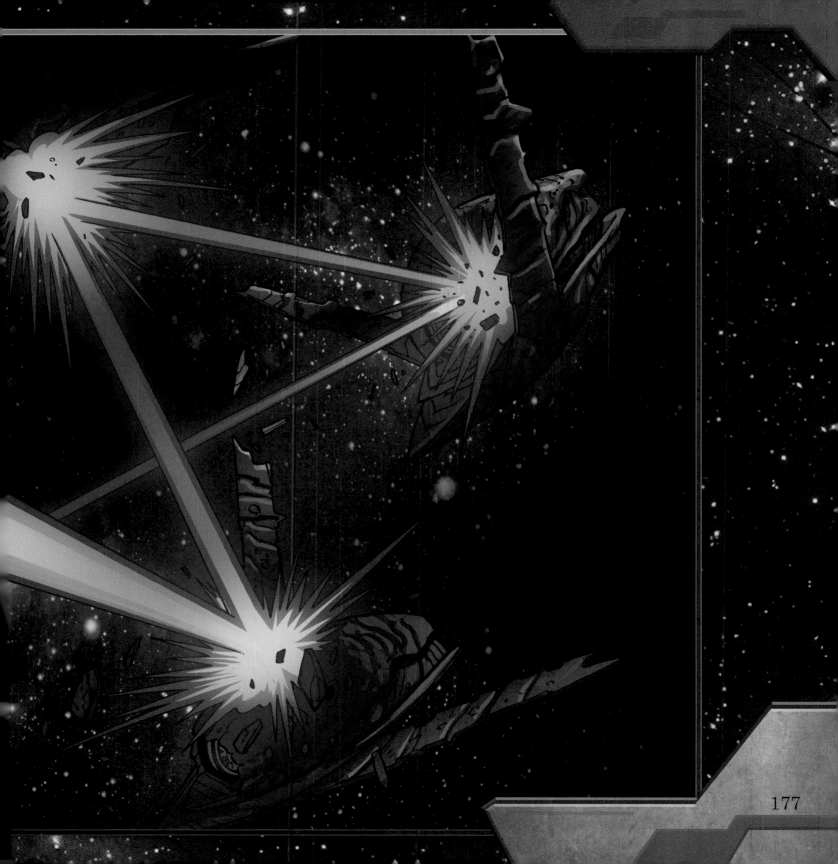

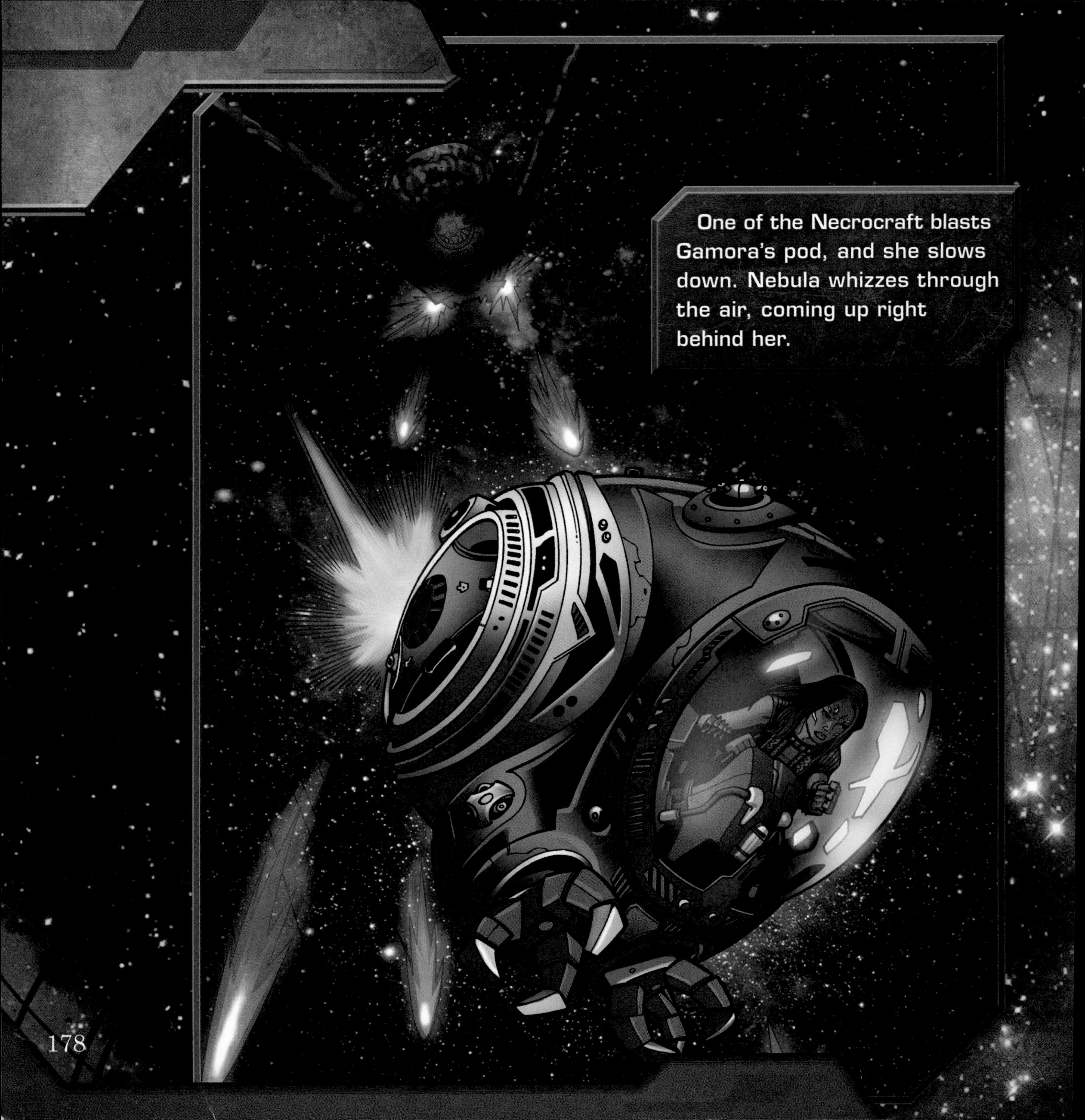

One of the Necrocraft blasts Gamora's pod, and she slows down. Nebula whizzes through the air, coming up right behind her.

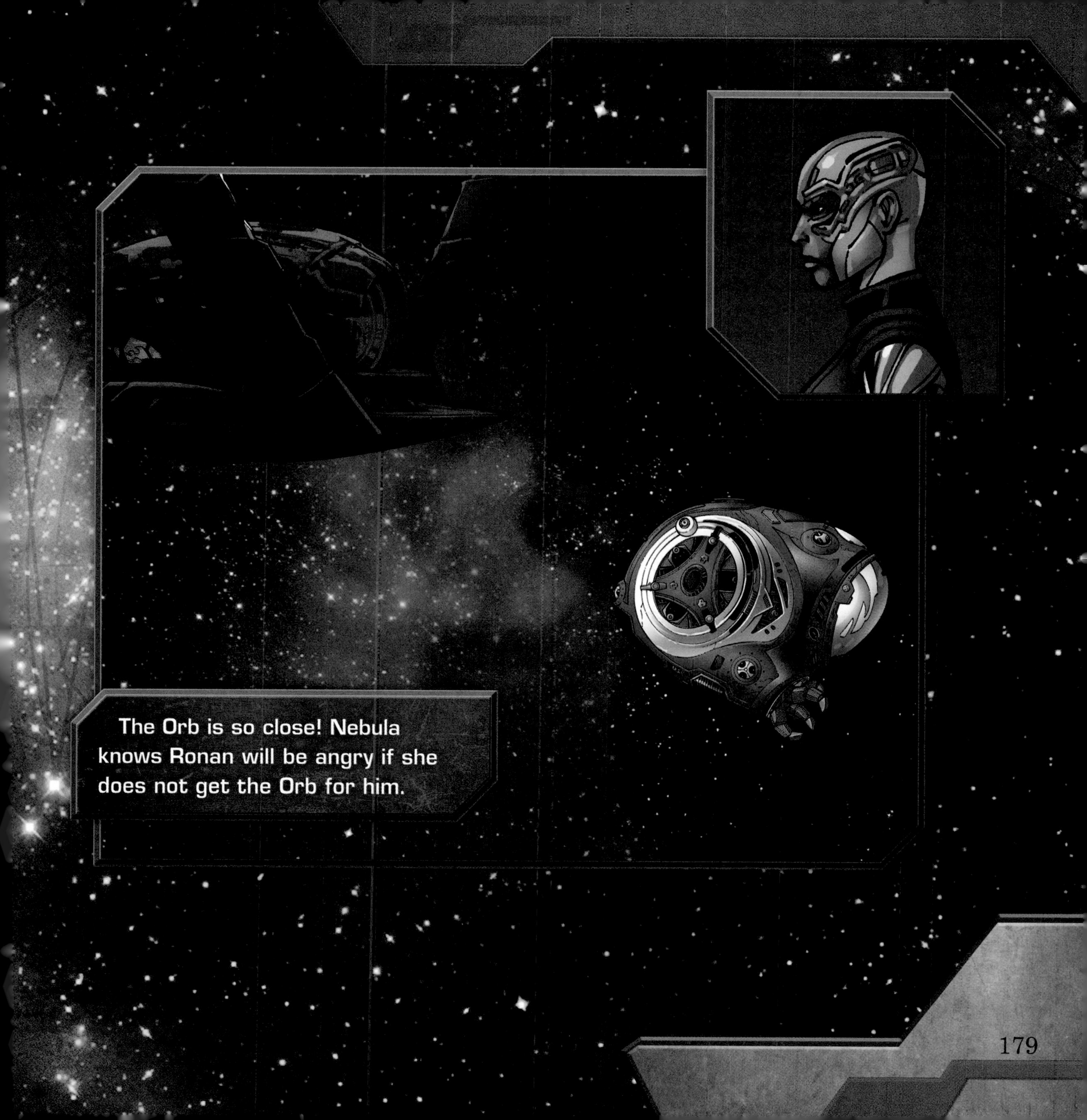
The Orb is so close! Nebula knows Ronan will be angry if she does not get the Orb for him.

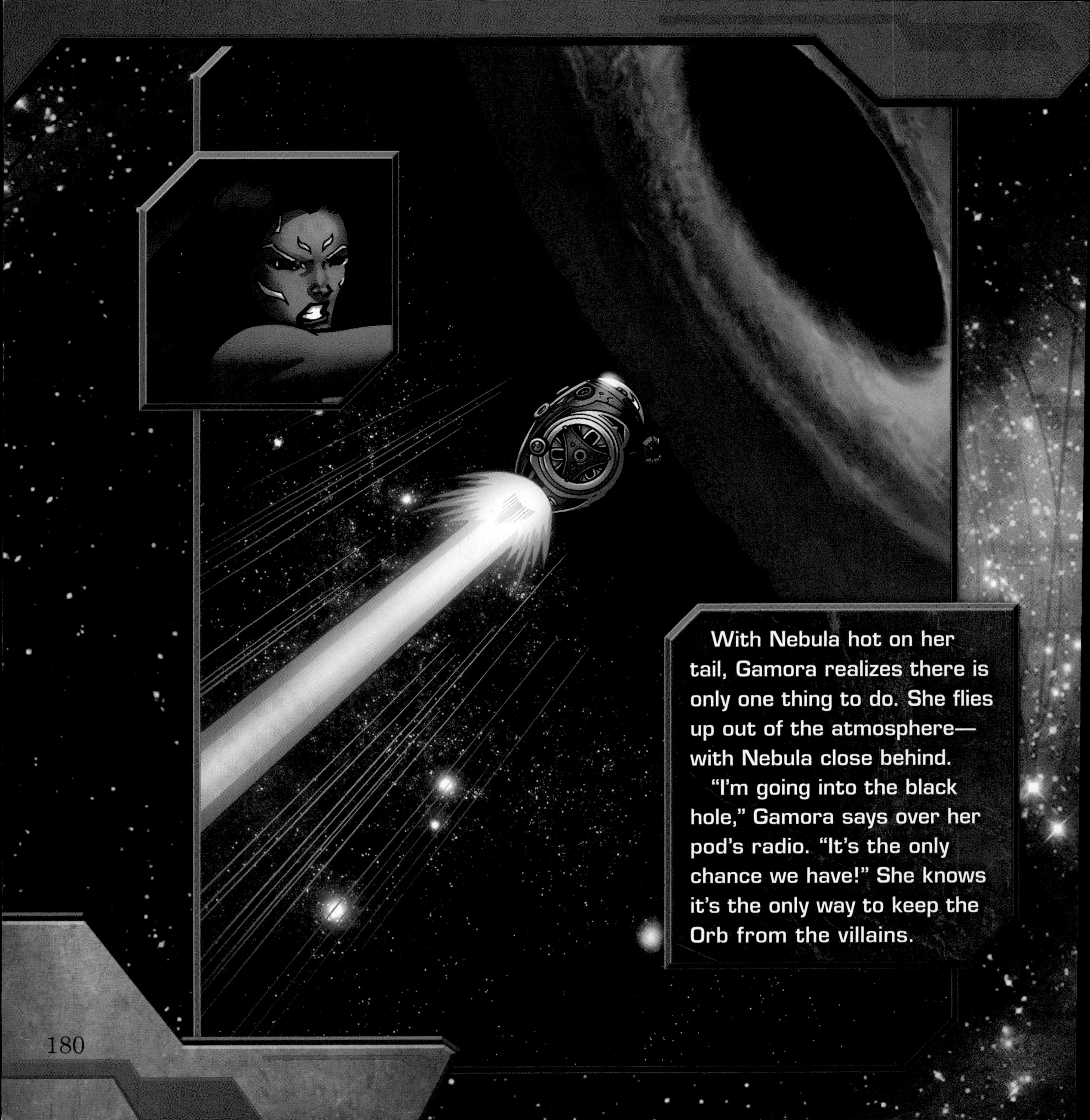

With Nebula hot on her tail, Gamora realizes there is only one thing to do. She flies up out of the atmosphere—with Nebula close behind.

"I'm going into the black hole," Gamora says over her pod's radio. "It's the only chance we have!" She knows it's the only way to keep the Orb from the villains.

"Gamora, wait!" Peter yells.
Nebula fires a direct shot at
Gamora's pod, breaking it apart!
Gamora falls out of the sky!

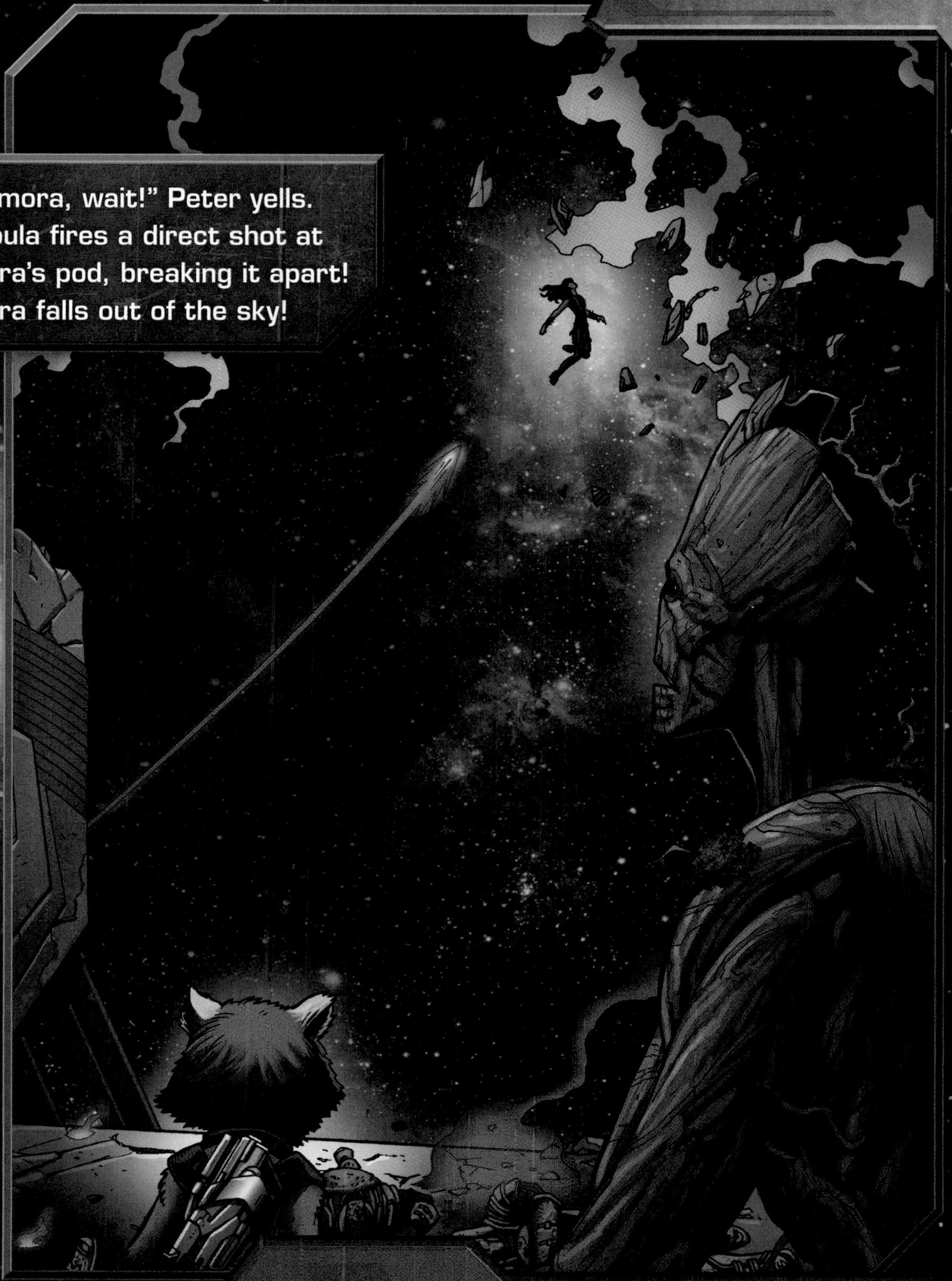

Peter puts on his mask and jumps out of his pod, activating his ankle thrusters. As Star-Lord, he can save Gamora. He can save the universe. He can do anything.

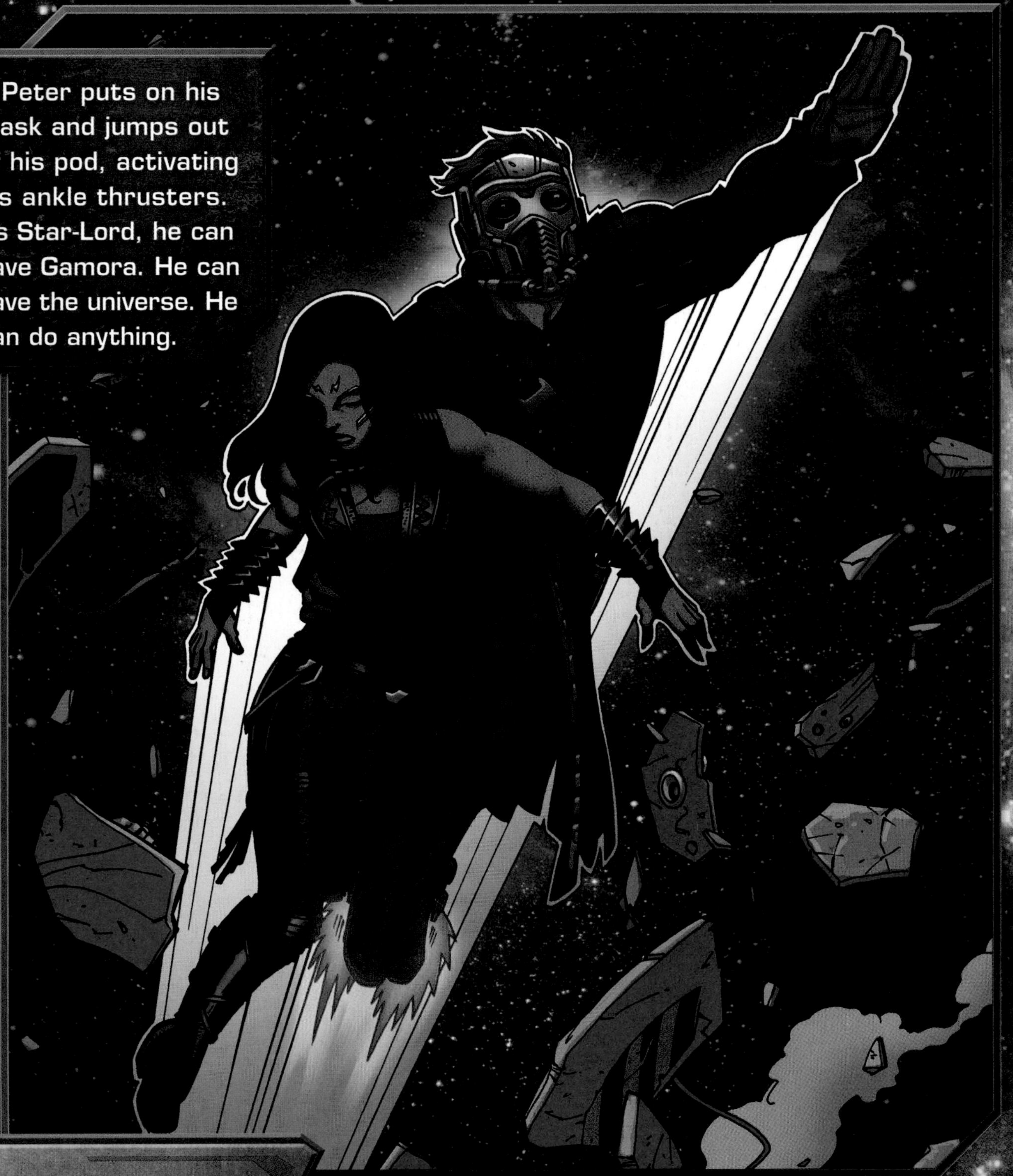

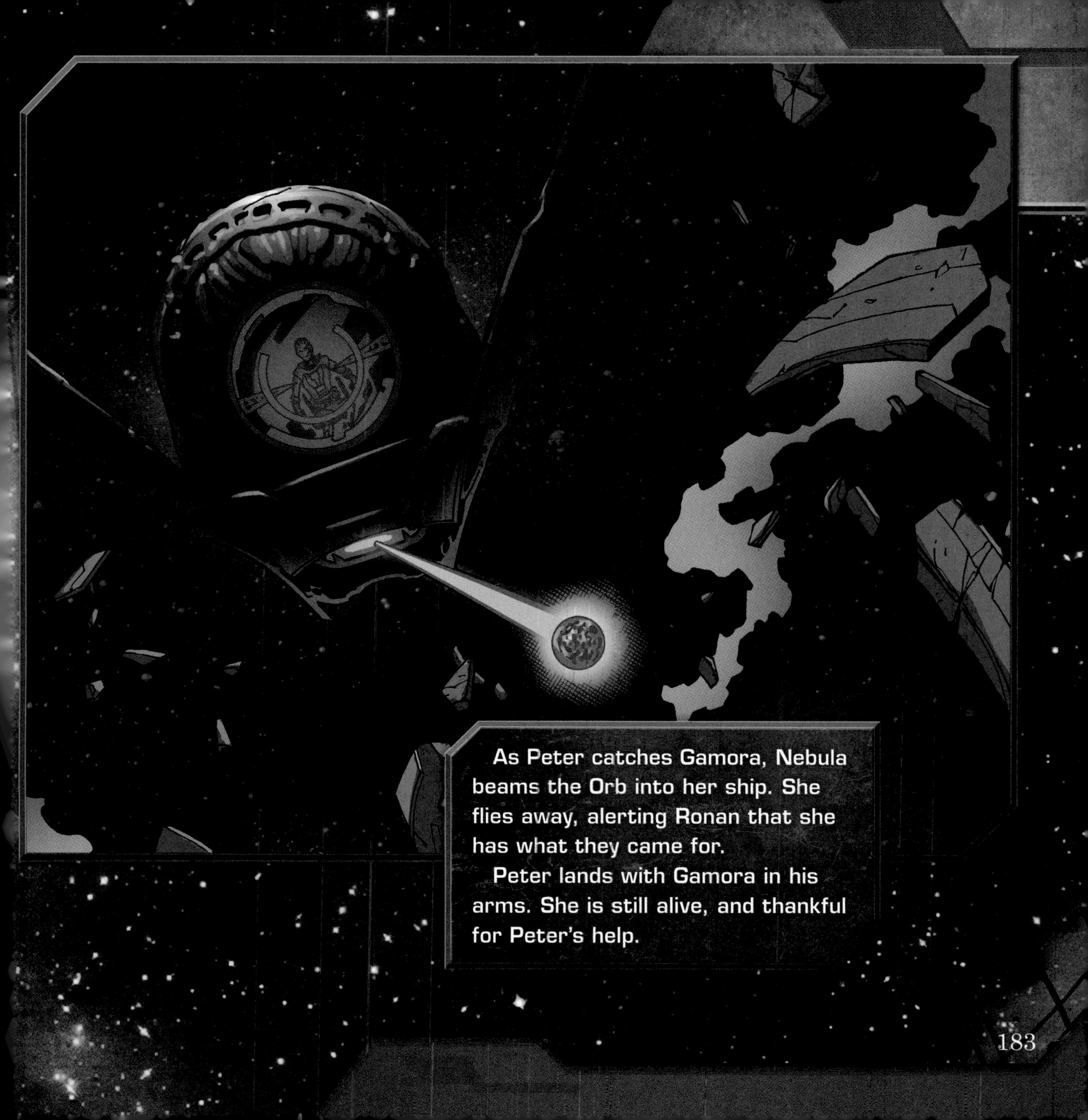

As Peter catches Gamora, Nebula beams the Orb into her ship. She flies away, alerting Ronan that she has what they came for.

Peter lands with Gamora in his arms. She is still alive, and thankful for Peter's help.

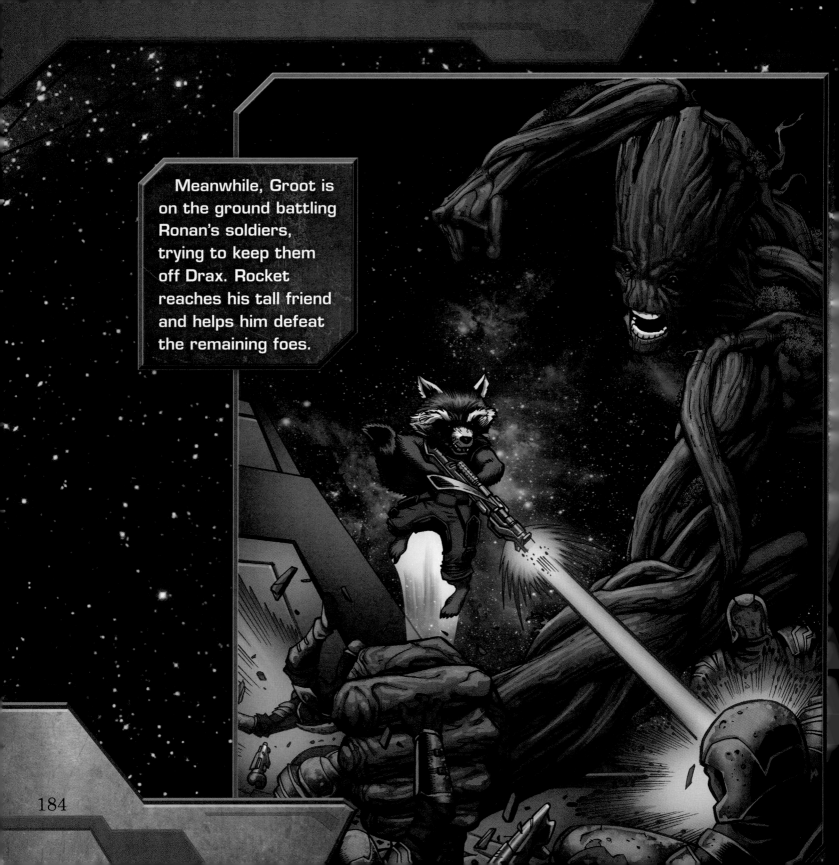

Meanwhile, Groot is on the ground battling Ronan's soldiers, trying to keep them off Drax. Rocket reaches his tall friend and helps him defeat the remaining foes.

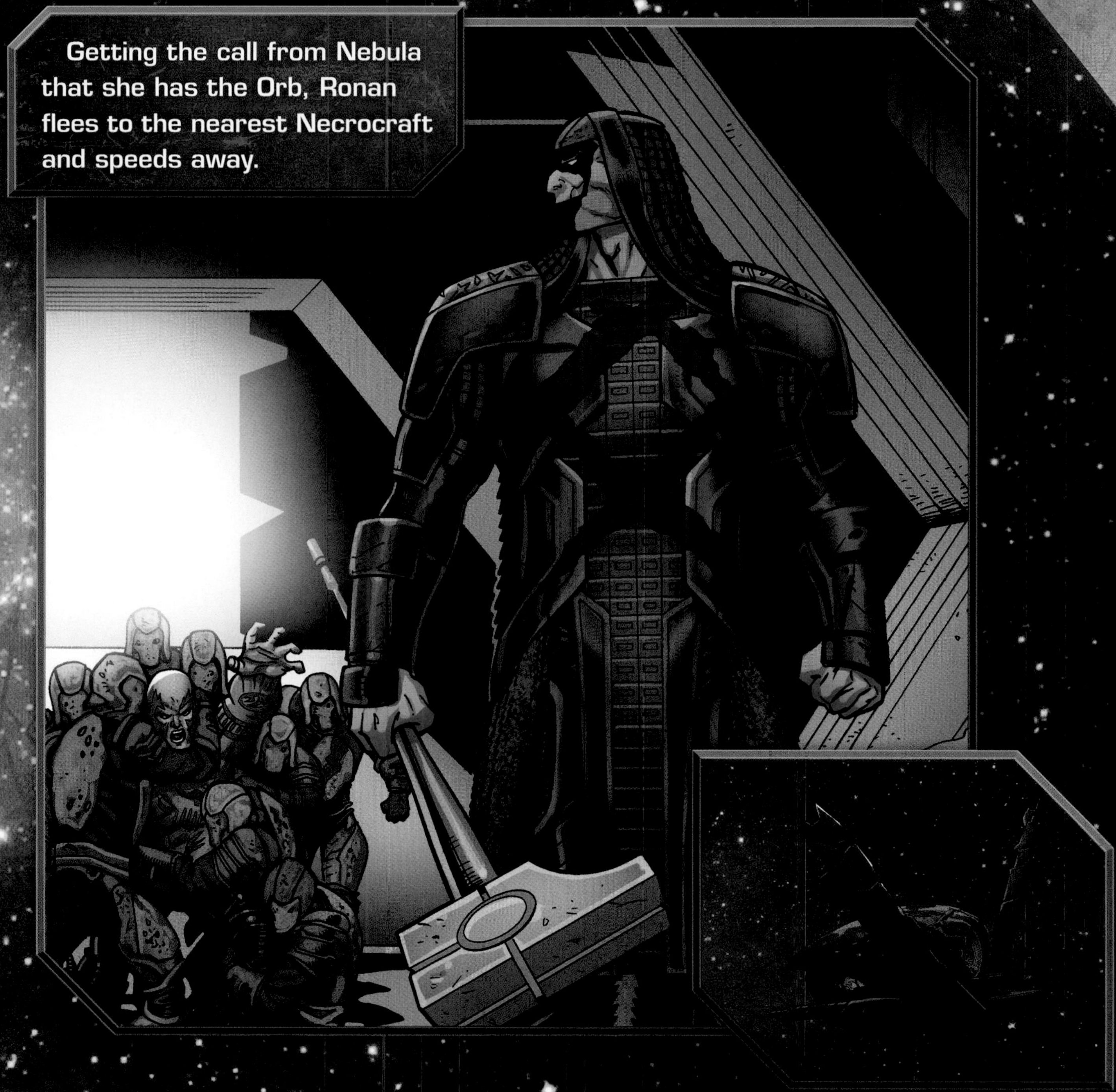
Getting the call from Nebula that she has the Orb, Ronan flees to the nearest Necrocraft and speeds away.

Together again, the group watches the last of the villains take off after their leader.

"I, for one, can't stand by and watch Ronan destroy the galaxy," Peter says. "We're the only ones who can be the guardians of it."

Peter smiles. The five heroes will now fight together—as the Guardians of the Galaxy!

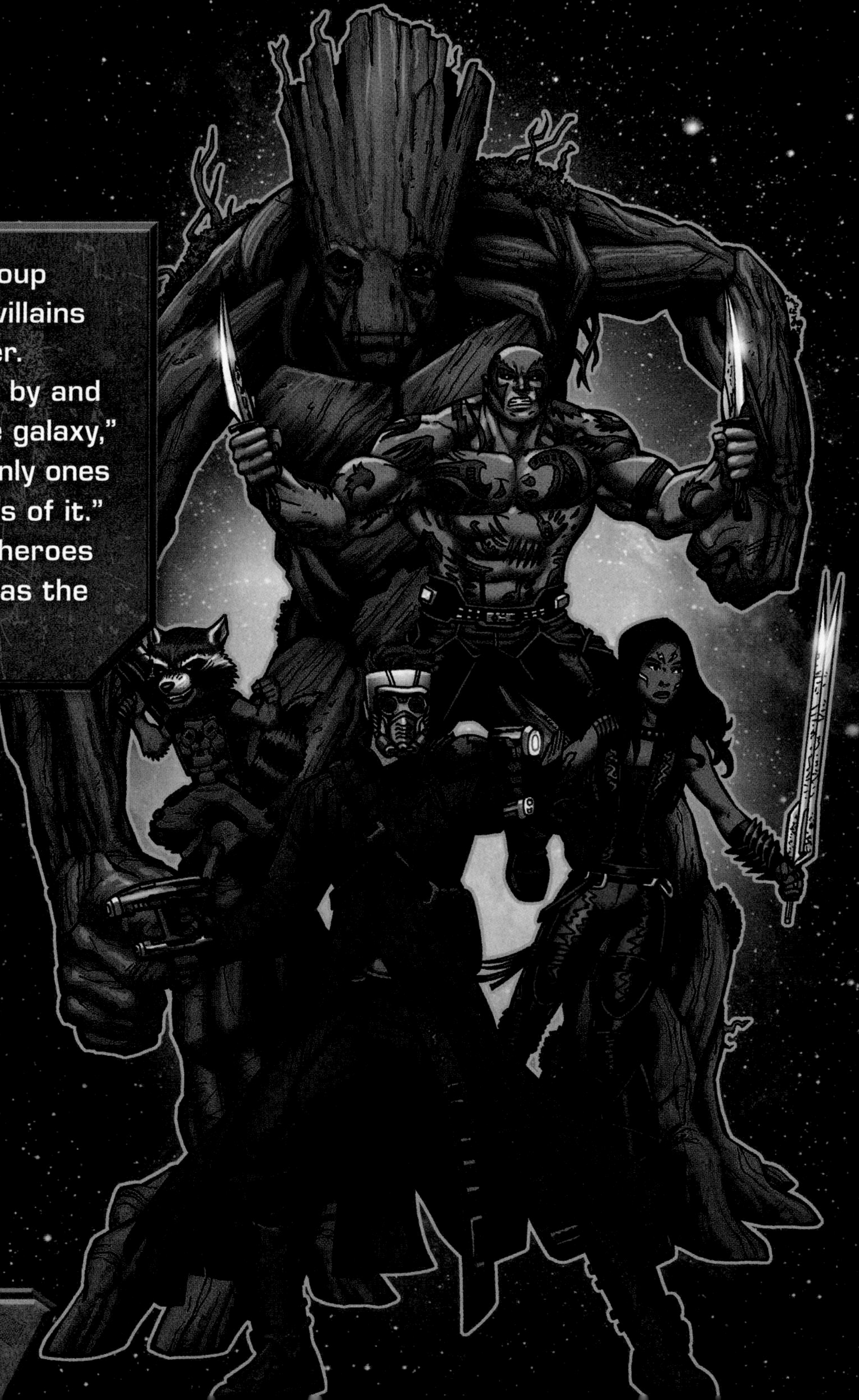

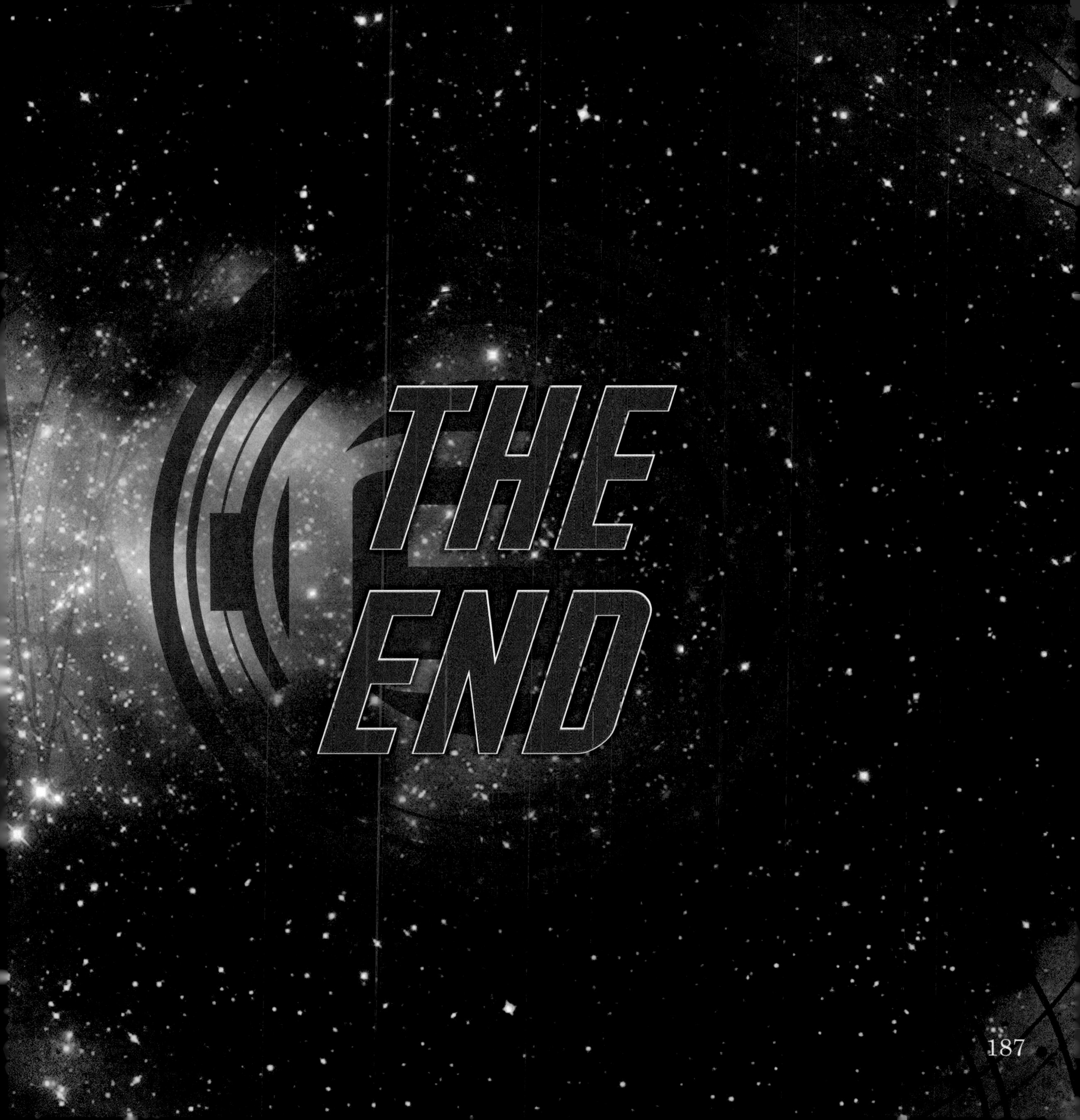
THE
END

READ MORE SUPER HERO STORIES!

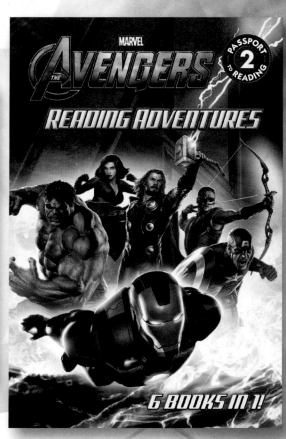